YA
YOUNG
ADULT

Pollock, Tom.

The city's son

DATE DUE   SEP 0 1 2012

THE
CITY'S SON

THE
CITY'S SON

THE SKYSCRAPER THRONE
BOOK ONE

TOM POLLOCK

Woodbury, Minnesota

First U.S. Edition
First Printing, 2012

Book design by Bob Gaul
Cover illustration © Chris Nurse/Début Art Ltd.

Flux, an imprint of Llewellyn Worldwide Ltd.

Library of Congress Cataloging-in-Publication Data
Pollock, Tom.
  The city's son/Tom Pollock—1st U.S. ed.
    p. cm.—(The skyscraper throne ; bk. 1)
  Summary: Expelled from school, betrayed by her best friend, and virtually ignored by her widowed father, Beth Bradley is introduced to the magic and wonder of a hidden London by Filius Viae, then helps him protect it from Reach, a malign god of demolition who wants to claim the skyscraper throne for himself.
  ISBN 978-0-7387-3430-9
  [1. Supernatural—Fiction. 2. Magic—Fiction. 3. Family problems—Fiction. 4. London (Eng.)—Fiction. 5. England—Fiction.] I. Title.
  PZ7.P76813Cit 2012
  [Fic]—dc23
                                                        2012010589

Flux
Llewellyn Worldwide Ltd.
2143 Wooddale Drive
Woodbury, MN 55125-2989
www.fluxnow.com

For Lizzie, for everything.

Acknowledgments

I am hugely grateful to the teams at Quercus, Flux, and DMLA who have let me put my name to their hard work. To my brilliant editors Jo Fletcher and Brian Farrey-Latz, and to Nicola Budd, Lucy Ramsey, Marissa Pederson, Steven Pomije, Sandy Sullivan, Don Maass, Susan Smith, and Meg Davis, thank you for your insight, skill, and patience.

Massive thanks also to Helen Callaghan, Sumit Paul-Choudhury and everyone at the T-Party, Akshay Mehta, Emily Richards, Lou Morgan, and Charlie Van Wijk for your invaluable support and advice.

Huge love and gratitude to my family: Sarah Pollock, David Pollock, Barbara Pollock, and Lizzie Barrett, now and always.

Finally, to Amy Boggs, agent and accomplice, my heartfelt thanks.

I'm indebted to countless writers, but the works of Alan Garner, David Almond, Neil Gaiman, China Miéville, and Patrick Ness were especially important to me while I wrote this book.

I

THE BOY
WITH THE CITY
IN HIS SKIN

ONE

I'm hunting. The sun sits low over Battersea, its rays streaking the brickwork like war paint as I pad through the railway tunnels. My prey can't be far ahead now: there's a bitter, burned stench in the air, and every few yards I find another charred bundle that used to be a rat.

I pick up the pace, racing eagerly over the tracks on my bare feet. Sweeping my spear in a low arc, I feel for the electricity in her trail—divining for the monster.

Around me, the city is oblivious. Under the brick arches, people are walking in and out of the newsagent's and the off-licence; a couple of schoolkids are chatting, swapping tall stories about some girl they fancy. And then, over their laughter, the moan of evening traffic, the bass from distant music, and all the other sounds of the city, I hear her wild, shrieking brake cry.

My heart clenches. They have no idea of the danger they're in, none of them, not now she's loose—now she's awake.

In Mater Viae's name, *she's awake.*

I'd picked up her trail at King's Cross, in the nest of interwoven steel north of the station. She'd left her train, a big freight engine, paralyzed without her spirit to animate it. The driver had just sat there stupefied, no clue what was wrong with his machine. Other trains tailed back from the obstruction in strings of brightly lit windows, their passengers grumbling, playing with their phones, and wondering what the hell the hold-up was.

I've pursued her doggedly since then: the relentless hunter.

Well…*almost* relentless.

Once, I let her go—I *had* to. Her trail led through the St. Paul's construction sites, past the cathedral, right under the clawlike shadows of Reach's cranes.

Reach—the Crane King. Even I can't trespass on his territory. I swear I could feel his metal-strutted fingers stretching out to claim me even as I turned to run.

I found the trail again easily enough. The dead boy made it hard to miss.

He lay tangled across the tracks under a burnt-out signal box. Judging by his size, he'd been about fifteen, maybe only a few months younger than me, but the damage to his face made it hard to be sure: the dried-out skin was cracked and blackened, and empty sockets gaped where the eyeballs had boiled away. Only the metal spray can in his right hand had survived the voltage intact.

It wasn't the body that made me hesitate—sad to say, I've seen uglier corpses. It was the bloody wheelprint bisecting the boy's chest, at a *right angle* to the rails, running *across* the tracks. For a moment I struggled to make sense of it. Then I saw the hole smashed through the bricks in the viaduct wall and a prickle of disbelief ran up the back of my neck.

She'd escaped the railway. She'd got out.

How in Thames' name—?

It was then that I started to doubt: if she was that powerful, would I really be able to bring her down?

Out across the city the streetlights were starting to shine as the Sodiumite dancers woke, stretching and warming their limbs to a glow inside their glass bulbs. I slid my fingers into the cracks in the brickwork and pushed myself over the edge of the viaduct, easing myself down to the pavement below. Then, nimble in the gathering gloom, I slipped into the streets.

Now I'm waiting in a dead-end alley, listening to the steady drip of water from a rusting pipe. I calm myself, letting the tap of the water become the rhythm of my heartbeat. My stance is open, my spear ready.

This is where her trail ends.

Thrum-clatter-clatter, thrum-clatter-clatter…

I can feel her vibration through the ground. A fox squirms out from behind a couple of steel bins and runs for the road, trailing stink. I let my breath stream out in a slow hiss.

Thrum-clatter-clatter...

The concrete shale on the ground starts to shift and a breeze picks up, spattering rain against my cheek. The burnt smell is emanating from the wall at the end of the alley, breathing out of the pores in the brick itself.

A high-pitched wail fills the air: steel shrieking on steel like screaming horses. The clatter grows louder and the bins clang as they are shaken to the ground.

I hear the ghost of a steam-whistle, her mournful, obsolete battle cry, and I hunker down low. Light starts to bleed through the mortar ahead of me, outlining two glaring, full-beam eyes. I hear the clash of her wheels, stampeding towards me on a path of lighting. The scream rises out of my throat to greet her, cursing her by all of her names: Loco Motive, Bahngeist, *Railwraith*—

—and as she roars out at me, I leap sideways and strike—

TWO

"Beth, *come on*," Pencil whispered. "We need to go."

Beth studied the picture she'd sprayed on the tarmac of the playground. She flipped her aerosol over a couple of times in her hand.

"*Beth ...* "

"It's not finished yet, Pen," Beth said. In the dim backwash from the lights nearby she could just make out the Pakistani girl's fingers worrying at her headscarf. "Don't be chicken."

Pencil paced fretfully back and forth. "Chicken? What are we, like ten? Have you been sniffing your own paints? I'm not kidding, B. If someone comes, this will get us *expelled.*"

Beth started shaking the spray can up. "Pen," she said, "it's four a.m. School's locked up. Even the rats have given up and gone home. We hid our faces from the cameras when we jumped the wall, but there's sod-all light there anyway. We can't be ID'd so what exactly are you worried about?" Beth kept her voice calm, but there was a taut knot of excitement in her chest. She swept her torch over the picture at her feet. Her portrait of Dr. Julian Salt, Frostfield High's Head of Maths, was coming out well, better than she'd expected, especially for a rush job in the dark. She'd got his frowning eyebrows down perfectly, and the hollow cheeks and the opaque, threatening glasses. The weeds bursting through the tarmac added to the effect, looking like unkempt nasal hair.

In fairness, Beth had also given him necrotic peeling skin and a twelve-foot-long forked tongue, so she was obviously using *some* artistic licence, but still...

It's unmistakably you, you shit.

"Beth, look!" Pen hissed, making Beth jump.

"What?"

"Up there—" Pen pointed. "A light..."

Beth glanced up. One of the windows in the estate overlooking the school was glowing a soft, menacing orange. She exhaled irritably. "It's probably just some old biddy going for a midnight wizz."

"We can be seen from there," Pen insisted.

"Why would anyone even care?" Beth muttered. She turned back to the picture. Everyone in Year 12 at Frostfield knew she and Salt were enemies, but that was just the usual teacher-versus-student aggro, and it wasn't why she was here. It was the way Salt treated Pen that demanded this retribution.

She didn't know why, but he seemed to derive this vicious delight from humiliating her best friend. Salt had put Pen in maybe half the number of detentions he'd sentenced Beth to, but she was always like on the verge of tears when she came out of them. And in Monday's maths lesson, when Pen had asked to go to the loo, Salt had point-blank refused. He'd gone on talking about quadratic equations, but he hadn't taken his eyes from Pen. There'd been this smile on his face as though he was daring her to defy him—as though he *knew* that she couldn't. Pen had kept her hand raised, but after a while her arm had started to shake. When she'd doubled-over with the pain of holding it in, Beth had dragged her bodily her from her chair and bundled her out of the room. As they ran down the corridor, they'd heard the laughter start.

Afterwards, standing behind the science block, Beth had asked, "Why didn't you just leave? He couldn't have stopped you. Why not just walk out?"

Pen's face was fixed in the clown-smile that meant she was panicking inside. "I just ... " She'd half swallowed the words and kept her eyes fixed on her shoes. "I just thought every second that went by, if I could hold on just one more second, one more, it would be okay. And I wouldn't have to ... you know."

Cross him. Beth had filled in the end of the sentence.

She'd hugged her friend close. Beth knew there was strength in Pen—she saw it every day—but it was a strength that withstood without ever resisting. Pen could soak up the blows, but she never hit back.

It was then that Beth had decided that something needed to be done. And this—this was *something*.

She trained the beam of her torch onto the painting and the tension in her chest was replaced by a warm glow of satisfaction. *A nightmare in neon,* she thought. *Ugly suits you, Doc.*

"Beth Bradley," Pen whispered. She still sounded scared, but this time she also sounded a little reverential. "You are a proper grade-A nutcase."

"Yeah, I know," Beth said, a smile creeping onto her face. "But I am *really* good—"

A high-pitched whine cut through the night: police sirens, fast approaching. Instinctively, Beth dropped to a crouch and yanked her hood up over her short, messy hair.

"*Bloody hell,*" Pen whispered, her voice panicky, "I told you they'd seen us! They must have called it in—they probably think we're here to steal something."

"Like what?" Beth muttered back. "The canteen's secret recipe for mouse-turd pie? It's not like the school's got anything worth nicking."

Pen tugged Beth's sleeve. "Whatever—we need to get out of here."

Beth yanked her sleeve away and dropped to both knees, frantically adding extra shading to the jawline. This had to be just right.

"B, we need to go!" Pen was hopping from foot to foot in agitation.

"Then go," Beth hissed.

"I'm not going without you." Pen sounded offended.

Beth didn't look up. "Pen, if you don't get running, and I mean *right now*, I'll tell Leon Butler it was you who Tipp-Exed that poem on his desk."

There was a moment's shocked silence, then, "*Bitch*," Pen breathed.

"'Leon, my lion, I would be all your pride. And not merely in it…'" Beth quoted in a sing-song whisper. She couldn't help grinning as Pen took off, swearing under her breath.

Beth got her feet up under her, ready to run even while she drew. The sirens were really close now. *Waaaoooh*—the whine soared once more, then cut off in mid-cycle. She heard car doors open and then slam. There was a rattling on the gates behind her. The school was locked up and the cops were climbing in just like she and Pen had. Beth sprayed color into a fat cluster of warts under one eye.

"Oi!"

The shout sent a jolt of fear down her spine. *Gross enough*, she thought. She stuffed her stencils and paints back into her rucksack, snapped off the torch, and ran. Heavy boots thudded on the tarmac behind her, but she didn't look back; there was no point in showing them her face. She sprinted with her head down, the wind rushing in her ears, praying that the police behind would be laden down with stab vests and truncheons, praying she'd be faster.

She looked up and panic clutched at her gut. The cops

were chasing her into a dead end. The highest wall in the school reared in front of her. It backed onto the dense tangle of scrub and trees around the train tracks: ten smooth, unclimbable feet of it. She drove her legs harder, trying desperately to build momentum, and jumped.

Her fingers scrabbled at concrete, inches short of the top, and she fell back.

Shit.

Again she threw herself at it; again she came up short. Breathlessness and despair made her chest ache.

"B." A whispered syllable. Beth whirled around. Pen was running along the base of the wall towards her, her headscarf pulled bandit-style over her mouth.

"*I told you to go,*" Beth hissed, both furious and relieved.

"As if. The minute I saw this I knew you were too short for it." She dropped to one knee and cupped her hands.

Beth flashed her a quick grin and stepped into the boost; a moment later she dragged Pen up after her.

"Split," Beth whispered as she hit the ground on the other side. She winced as pain spread over her hands; she'd landed them in a bed of nettles. "I'll catch you up at the usual."

They could hear their pursuers huffing and swearing on the other side of the wall.

One of the men panted, "Give us a boost!"

Pen veered to the right and Beth ran left, zigzagging between the trees. Her breath wheezed in and out, staccato in her ears. Twigs and discarded bottles crunched under her feet. A fence blocked her way, but she saw a ragged hole at the base and she dived for it, wriggling through into a looming concrete estate. She ducked down behind a rusting old car with broken windows, gasping for breath. A train rushed over a nearby bridge, angled slabs of light rocketing though the darkness. She tried to listen past its dying clatter and her own slamming heartbeat, but she could hear no sounds of pursuit.

She rooted in her backpack for a crumpled leather jacket, then slipped off her hoodie and shoved it in, on top of the paint cans. Adrenaline made her legs wobble so much she staggered and nearly fell.

Nice, Beth, she thought sarkily, *very cool. Now if you can just stop walking like a concussed turkey you might actually get halfway down the street before the Filth pick you up.*

Pulling her jacket closed, she walked on, casual as she could.

Pen was waiting at the corner of Withersham and Shakespeare Roads, where redbrick terraces with fussy front gardens stretched away on both sides. As she always did when she was nervous, Pen was checking and rechecking her reflection in her compact mirror, studying for the tiniest flaw.

Beth smiled despite herself; only Pen Khan would apply mascara for a night of criminal vandalism.

The postbox Pen was standing next to was probably the most graffitied piece of square footage in all of London: a rainbow-riot of obscenities, slogans, cartoon animals, and grotesque monsters. It was local graffiti tradition to make a contribution to the Withersham box, so last year Pen and Beth had painted themselves on in "Wanted" posters, pulling stupid faces. Those mug shots had long since been buried beneath the work of the neighborhood's other artists.

Beth flipped a lazy salute as she approached. Pen just stared back. "One of these days, Elizabeth Bradley," she said slowly, "you're going to get me expelled. My parents will bloody disown me."

Beth grinned at her. "Oh well, I'll have done you a favor then. You could come tagging without having to sneak around."

"Thanks. When I'm a homeless, starving disgrace to my family, *that's* the thought that will keep me warm, I'm sure."

Beth scuffed her trainer along the tarmac and smirked at Pen's sarcasm. "So come live with me," she offered. "At least you could marry whoever you like."

Pen's lips thinned and tension crept into her voice. "And your grand total of two boyfriends makes you the world's wedding guru how, exactly?"

"Two more than you," Beth muttered, but Pen ignored the interruption.

"My folks will help me find the right person," she said. "It's about experience, that's all. They know marriage, they know *me*, they—"

Beth interrupted. "Pen, they don't even know you're here."

Pen flushed and looked away.

Suddenly ashamed, Beth stepped forward and hugged

her best friend close. "Ignore me, okay?" she murmured quietly into Pen's headscarf. "I'm being a cow, I know I am. I'm just scared your folks will hitch you to some accountant with a beige suit and beige underwear and a beige bleeding *soul* and I'll have to redecorate the walls of East London all by myself."

"Never happen," Pen whispered back, and Beth knew it was true. Pen would never walk away from her. She looked over Pen's shoulder. The sky was just beginning to grow light. Telephone poles stretched down the street, their cables like reins drawing in the sunrise. When day broke, this day and every day after it, Beth knew it would break over the two of them, side by side.

"You okay?" she asked.

Pen gave a fragile little laugh. "Yeah. Only—that was all a bit bloody hairy, you know?"

"I know," said Beth. "That was backbone, hardcore—proud of you, Pencil Khan." She hugged her tighter for a second, then let go. "We won't get much sleep with what's left of tonight, though." Her neck muscles were taut and her eyes wanted to close, but still she felt restless. "I don't suppose I could persuade you to skip the first couple of classes with me in the morning?"

Pen nibbled her lower lip carefully, not smudging her lip-gloss. "You don't think that'd make us a *leetle* bit conspicuous?"

Obvious when you thought about it, Beth conceded, but as always, it took Pen to see it. She was like a small animal, always finding exactly the right spot for camouflage: she had an instinct for anything that wouldn't blend in.

"How's about we tag 'til school starts, then?" Beth countered. "Push on through—I'm feeling inspired."

Pen had told her mum she was staying at Beth's tonight. Beth hadn't needed to clear anything with anyone, of course. Out here in the streets it was easy to forget that she belonged anywhere else.

Pen shook her head at her own foolishness, but she unzipped her hoodie and pulled out her spray can. "Sure," she said. "I think I've got some game tonight."

They ran west into the heart of the city, ahead of the dawn, dodging between brick walls with peeling posters and boarded-up shop windows.

Beth crouched beside a pile of broken concrete next to some roadworks and sprayed a few black lines. To most people they'd look like tar or shadows; you had to be in exactly the right spot to see the rhino, formed by paint and the edges of the concrete itself, charging out at you. Beth smiled to herself. *The city's a dangerous place if you don't pay attention.*

She'd left pieces of her mind like this all over London, and no one else knew where. *No one, except maybe Pen.*

She glanced over at the taller girl. When the two of them swapped secrets it wasn't like the hostage-exchange Beth sometimes saw with other girls. Pen genuinely cared, and that meant Beth could risk enough to care, too. Pen was like a bottomless well: you could drop any number of little fears into her, knowing they would never come back to haunt you.

It started to rain: a thin, constant, soaking drizzle.

Pen wrote her poems on curbs and inside phone boxes, romantic counterpoints to the pink-and-black business cards with their adverts for bargain-basement sex, carnal specialties listed after their names like academic degrees:

CALL KARA FOR A WICKED TIME: D/s, T/V, NO S, P OR B

…you might be the puzzle piece of me,
I've never seen.

"That's gorgeous, Pen," Beth murmured, reading over her shoulder.

"Think so?" Pen eyed the verse worriedly.

"Yeah." Beth knew eight-tenths of sod-all about poetry, but Pen's calligraphy was beautiful.

The sun slowly bleached the buildings from the color of smoke to the color of old bone. More and more cars passed them by.

"We should head," Pen said at last, tapping her watch. She frowned, considering something, then added, "Maybe we should catch separate buses. We don't normally arrive at school together—it might attract attention."

Beth laughed. "Isn't that a little paranoid?"

Pen gave her a shy, almost proud smile. "You know me, B. Paranoid's where I excel." She led the way out of the narrow alley and they slipped into the hustling crowd.

Pen took the first bus.

Beth felt like a spy or a superhero, sliding back into her secret identity as she waited for the next.

THREE

Maybe it was one of his worms who found me, nosing through the thick sludge at the edge of the river, or perhaps a pigeon, wheeling overhead, from one of the flocks that nest on top of the towers. All I know is that when I wake, Gutterglass is crouched over me.

"My, my, you're quite the mess, aren't you?" the old monster says gravely. "Good morning, Highness."

He—Glas is a "he" this time—looks down at me with his broken eggshell eyes. Old chow mein cakes his chin in a slimy beard. His rubbish-sack coat bulges as the rats beneath it scramble about.

"Morn—" I begin to say, then the pain of the burns washes over me, choking off the words. I inhale sharply and wave him back. I need air. He's nabbed a tire from somewhere and his waist dissolves into a single wheel instead of his usual legs. Lithe brown rodents race around the inside, rolling him backwards.

I grit my teeth until I reach a manageable plateau of agony, then, groggily, I take in my surroundings. I'm on a silt strand under a bridge on the south side of the river —Vauxhall, judging by the bronze statues lining the sides. The sun shimmers high in the sky.

"How long?" My throat feels as tight as a rusted lock.

"Too long, frankly," Glas replies. "Even the foxes came in before you did. Do I need to remind you that you are my responsibility? Assuming, of course, that 'responsibility' is a word that your grubby little Highness comprehends? If anything happens to you, *I'm* the one who'll have to answer to Mater Viae."

I shut my eyes against the harsh light, biting back the obvious retort. Mater Viae—Our Lady of the Streets, my mother—left more than a decade and a half ago. I hate how Gutterglass still bloody nearly genuflects whenever he says her name.

"If she ever comes back," I say, "do you really think she'll care which particular pile of London crap I sleep on?"

"*When* she comes back," Glas corrects me gently.

I don't argue with him, because it's not nice to call a man's faith ridiculous.

Most mornings you can find him (or her, if that's the body Glas makes that day) at the edge of the dump, looking towards the sunrise over Mile End, waiting for the day when stray cats march in procession down the pavements and the street signs rearrange themselves to spell Mater Viae's true name: the day their goddess returns.

Air sighs out of his tire and he sinks down beside me. He opens the black plastic of his coat and chooses one of the syringes strapped there. He's been raiding hospital bins again. He slides the tip into my arm, depresses the plunger, and almost immediately the pain ebbs.

"What a mess," he mutters again. "Sit up. Let's take a look at the damage."

I creak gradually into a sort of shell-shaped hunch, which is the best I can manage. Neat cross-stitches lace my cuts together; the needle that made them has been thrust back in Glas' arm and the left-over thread is waving gently in the wind.

"Wow," I croak, fingering the stitches. "I really must have been out cold to not feel those."

"Dead to the world," Gutterglass agrees. "Not *literally*, though, thanks in no small part to yours truly, and in no part at all to you."

I have to use my spear as a lever to stand up. I can still feel the electric buzz in the iron where I stabbed the wraith. Glas dusts me down, wiping at my cheek with split, pen-lid fingers. Glas is oddly fastidious—I guess having to make himself a new body out of the city's rubbish every day means he knows where it's all been.

"I was hunting—" I start to tell him about last night, but he isn't listening.

"Look at you, you're *filthy*—"

"Glas, this Railwraith—"

"Doing these stitches has *destroyed* my fingers," he moans. "Have you no heart at all for a poor old rubbish-spi—"

"Glas!" I snap, a little harder than I mean to, and he recoils and shuts up, staring at me reproachfully. I exhale hard and then just say it. "The wraith got loose from the tracks. She got free."

For a long moment the only sound is the patter of the breeze on the surface of the river. When Glas finally speaks, his voice is flat. "That's not possible."

"Glas, I'm telling you—"

"It's not," he insists. "Railwraiths *are* electricity: its memory, its dreams. The rails are their conductor. They can't survive away from them for more than a few minutes."

"Well, take it from the son of a goddess whose bony arse it kicked around the block, three miles from the nearest stretch of track: *this one can!*" My shout echoes off the bridge's foundations. I squat down, trying to work the tension out of my temples with my fingertips.

"Glas, it was so strong," I say quietly. The memory of the fierce white voltage of its teeth is seared into my skin. I shiver. "I wounded it, but—it must have left me for dead. I've never met a wraith like it. It didn't even try to run, just came right at me..."

"...as though it was *it* that was hunting *you*?" Glas asks, and I look up sharply.

Because that's exactly what it was like.

Gutterglass' voice is very quiet. All of the rats and worms and ants that animate him go still and for a moment he looks dead. "Filius," he says softly. And he doesn't sound confused any more. He sounds very, very frightened. "Did anyone see you hunting that wraith?"

"What? No. Why?"

"Filius—"

"No one *saw* me, Glas, I was just hunting. I was—" Then I falter, because that isn't quite true: somebody did see. A sick feeling swells in my stomach as I realize what he's asking.

"It went through St. Paul's," I whisper.

"The Railwraith entered Reach's domain," Glas says.

I nod as I feel the cold seep through me, like my bones are blistering with ice.

"And emerged on the other side," he continues, his voice grim, "loose from the rails, more angry and more powerful than it had any right to be. And coming after *you*." I can hear the strain of forced calm on his borrowed vocal cords. "Filius," Glas says, "there's an ugly possibility here you need to face up to." He sinks down until his shells are level with my eyes. "What if that wraith didn't 'get loose'"? What if it was set free—?"

The question hangs in the air unfinished. I complete it in my head: *What if it was set free by Reach?*

Across the river, the boom and clang of construction drifts from the St. Paul's sites. Reach's cranes grasp at the cathedral like it's an orb of office.

Reach: the Crane King. My mother's greatest enemy. His claws have been part of my nightmares for as long as I've been dreaming.

He could do it. It dawns on me now, as it must have dawned on Glas, that Reach is an electric expert. His cranes and diggers, his pneumatic weaponry, they're all powered by it—so he could have found a way to channel that power into a wraith, to set it, frenzied and burning, on my tail: an opportunistic attack.

"What if it's finally happening, Filius?" Gutterglass whispers, half to himself. "What if Reach is coming for you?"

I grip my spear so tightly it feels like the skin on my knuckles could split

"We have to get you home—*now*," Glas says. He's wheeling himself round and round in circles, suddenly all urgency. "I need you back at the landfill, where it's safe, until I can find out what's going on. If this is Reach, he won't stop with a Railwraith.

"Soon there will be wolves and—Lady save us," he murmurs fervently, "*wire*." He begins rolling towards the edge of the bridge, yanking me by the arm, and I have to drag my feet in the sand to wrench myself free.

What if Reach is coming for you?

… Reach is coming…

The mantra goes around and around in my head, dizzying me, but it makes no sense: why *now*? I've been here for sixteen years without my mother's protection. What's he been waiting for?

But the longer I think about it, the more horribly easy it gets to believe. Reach has been the monster in every fairy tale I've ever been told. My mother hated him, and Glas hates him, and I hate him too. I can feel that hatred clotting around my heart.

Reach is coming… and deep down, I always knew he would.

"Filius?" Glas beckons impatiently. "We need to move."

I straighten up, wincing at a fresh wave of pain from my burns, and shake my head.

Glas arches a dust-drawn eyebrow. "This is no time to be stubborn, Filius. In case you've forgotten, that wraith is still out there. It almost killed you last night."

"So imagine what it'll do to the rest of the city," I say slowly. In my mind's eye I'm seeing the blackened corpse of the boy from last night, multiplied: one for every gutter. That impossibly powerful wraith is wild and indiscriminate and *free*.

What if Reach is coming for you?

The thought is too big; I can't grasp it. But if I let fear freeze me, then tonight it'll be me lying charred by the roadside. Reach is still a "what-if"; the wraith's a certainty, the immediate threat. I seize on it, almost gratefully. I can focus on *that*.

"I have to finish the hunt."

FOUR

At the front of the class, Mr. Krafte was rambling on about the Lady of Shalott, but Beth wasn't listening. As she doodled, a punked-up warrior princess emerged from under her pencil, blowing a mirror into fragments with her bazooka. Out of the window, she could see the tarpaulin the staff had draped over last night's work. The portrait had still been uncovered when she and Pen had arrived; other students had been crowded around it, whooping with laughter and snapping it with their phones.

Beth had felt a hot rush of victory and squeezed Pen's hand. Pen had squeezed back nervously.

"It's okay," Beth had said. "There's no proof it was us." They'd even buried their backpacks and paint-stained hoodies under a tree near the railway, in case of a locker search.

"We're safe. I'll find you at the end of the day," she'd promised before letting Pen go.

"Miss Bradley!" Mr. Krafte's voice jarred her out her reverie and her pencil snapped.

"Yes, boss?" She looked up warily.

The old English teacher eyed her with mild perturbation as he folded a piece of paper between his fingers. His face was as dark and wrinkled as the skin on old gravy. "Go to Mrs. Gorecastle's office, please. She'd like a word."

A muttered "ooooh" went round the classroom and Beth's throat tightened, but she shrugged, trying to look unflustered. She spent a few seconds folding the warrior princess drawing into a paper airplane, and sent it on a kamikaze nose-dive into the bin before she got up.

Okay, Beth: here goes. Time to put on your innocent face. She glanced at her reflection in the window and sighed. If she'd been holding up a board with a date and time of arrest on it she couldn't have looked guiltier. She grimaced and swung out into the hall.

The door to the headmistress' office had a little round window in it and Beth glanced through it as she approached—

—and stopped cold.

She could see four figures behind the wired glass: the headmistress; Gorecastle herself, gaunt and dressed all in black; Dr. Salt, who, frankly, looked better flat on the tarmac, rotting flesh and all . . .

. . . and a tall, slim girl standing in the corner, worrying at her headscarf.

Fury boiled up through Beth, along with an urge to get in there, to stand between Pen and the teachers, to shield her.

Pen's disciplinary record's spotless—what the hell? she thought. But then she saw the mud-splotched backpack on Gorecastle's desk and the dented spray cans arranged next to it and her indignation withered inside her. Beth suddenly felt very vulnerable, and very cold.

The headmistress opened the door and pursed her thin lips. "Ah, Miss Bradley. Do join us."

Beth pushed past her to the desk, grabbed the backpack and swung it onto her shoulder. She glowered at the headmistress, her face burning. There was nothing to do now but own it.

"So," the headmistress said. "Do you have anything to say for yourself?"

Beth stayed silent, but inside her head a stunned voice was repeating one impossible phrase: *Pen gave you up. Pen gave you up.*

Pen...

"This is very serious, Elizabeth," the headmistress was saying. "You will be suspended while we investigate this matter, and that may well lead to expulsion. It is only Dr. Salt's personal request that stops me involving the police further. You should be very grateful to him, frankly. Do you have anything to say?"

Beth kept her mouth shut and stared dead ahead. She'd show the traitor in the corner how it was done.

"Very well, then," Gorecastle said. "I have some telephone calls to make. Julian, a word?"

Dr. Salt escorted her from the room.

Beth couldn't make herself look at Pen. Maybe if she didn't look, it would somehow become someone else who'd betrayed her. She felt intensely, painfully weary and she dropped herself into Gorecastle's office chair. A sudden wave of anger went through her and she kicked the desk so hard is screeched back over the floorboards.

Pen looked at her incredulously. "B, you're mental—"

"How much more trouble do you think I can get in, *Parva?*" Beth snapped. She chewed out the syllables of Pen's real name, the first time she'd called her that in three years of friendship.

Pen gulped, and something glittered on her cheek: a tear.

Pen's crying. Instinctively Beth reached up to hug her, and then dropped her arms. They felt so useless by her sides.

"Beth, I'm—"

"*Don't* say it," Beth snarled. "If you tell me you're sorry, Parva Khan, I swear I will kill you dead. Just … just—" There was only one question, branded on her mind. "*Why?*"

"He said he'd—" Pen's voice went scratchy. She tried again. "He said he'd—"

"What!" Beth demanded. "What did he say?"

But Pen didn't finish; instead she huddled into herself and pulled her scarf around her.

"You made it worse, B," she said miserably. "You made everything worse."

Beth gazed into her best friend's face and for the first time in years she couldn't make sense of it. Pen's eyes were like slammed doors. A spidery feeling of wrongness crept into Beth's throat. "Pen," she whispered, "Pen, what does that even *mean*? What happened? Pen?"

Pen hugged herself in silence, and Beth realized that for the first time in years, she couldn't read her. It was a shattering thought. *I don't understand, Pen.*

And if she didn't understand Pen, she didn't understand anything at all.

Gorecastle returned a few moments later. "Parva," she said, "thank you for your help. You can go back to class."

As Pen bundled herself from the office, the headmistress eyed Beth. "Get up," she ordered coldly, and as Beth rose slowly from the chair behind the desk, never breaking eye contact, she sighed. "Children like you, Elizabeth," she said wearily, "*children* like you—perhaps I should just have just let the police have you." She picked up a form. "I have left a message for your father; you will wait here for him to pick you up. I shall take the opportunity to discuss this matter with him. "

Beth's heart, which had been hammering at a million beats a second, suddenly slowed and a sick feeling welled up in her. She started to stuff her spray paints back into her backpack. "We'll be waiting a while then," she muttered.

FIVE

They finally let Beth out at three o'clock. Her dad hadn't called. She walked to the park and spent hours pacing and chewing at the cuticle on her right thumb and squinting at the sky until the last of the color drained from it. She knew she'd have to face him eventually, but that didn't make it any easier.

At last, trying to ignore the clenching in her stomach, she forced herself to head for home.

The hallway was dark and she kicked over a mountain of junk mail on her way towards the sitting room door. Her hand was trembling a little when she set it on the doorknob; she hadn't been inside that room for weeks now. She fought down the urge to run back out into the street.

"Just try," she hissed to herself as she turned the handle.

The sitting room was buried in photographs; they were

tacked over every inch of wall space and strewn loose over the carpet like wreckage from a plane crash. Every chair but one was covered in more piles.

A thickset, balding man occupied the remaining chair. He was reading a paperback book; Beth could just make out the title, *The Iron Condor Mystery*, on the faded spine. He didn't look up as Beth approached.

Beth's lungs felt suddenly airless. She'd run this conversation over and over on her way home, trying to make it sound like something they could talk about rationally, but now—?

She looked down at the bald spot on top of her dad's head, the crumbs scattered on his shirt like an invitation to the birds. All her preparations felt useless. In the end she just blurted out, "I've been kicked out."

He turned a page; his eyes narrowed slightly as they followed the print.

The squeezing in the pit of Beth's stomach grew tighter. "Dad, are you listening? Dad, please. I really need you to focus. Social Services could come around, and the police, maybe. Look, I—Dad, I fucked up, seriously. Dad I need hel—"

She broke off as he looked up at her.

One night, three years and some change before, it had been Beth's mum reading the *Iron Condor Mystery*. She'd loved old Cold War spy novels, the safely sinister world of Fedoras and secret codes and briefcase bombs. That night she'd set down the dog-eared paperback with a little regretful sigh, having not quite reached the bit she'd been looking forward to, but happy in the knowledge that it would be waiting for her tomorrow. She kissed her husband gently, turned over, and hemorrhaged while she slept.

Beth's dad had woken with his arm curled around his wife. She'd been waxy and cold and her limbs were too heavy when he'd tried to move them.

It had been the morning of Beth's thirteenth birthday.

Ever since that night he'd slept in his chair—Beth knew he was afraid of the bedroom, though she doubted he would ever admit that. Ever since that night he'd read and reread that same book with an almost frantic intensity, until it was all but disintegrating in his hands.

And ever since that night, he'd looked at her like this, with the same desolate, pleading exhaustion in his face.

"It's fine," Beth stuttered, furious with herself for caving in so easily. "I'll—I'll find some way to—I'll sort it."

He didn't respond. She realized she couldn't remember when he had last spoken to her, *real* words …

She stumbled on her way out, accidentally stepping on the photographs of her mum's smiling face. Her dad uttered a protective cry and for a moment her anger spilled over, just a little, just enough for her to snap at him, her tone nasty. "I left money on the hall stand."

She felt a shameful little satisfaction when he flinched.

It's not his fault, she reminded herself forcefully as she grabbed her backpack and plunged back through the hall out into the night. *He broke. It's what people do.*

But people also heal, a harsher voice in her piped up; hearts thickened with scar tissue, but they kept beating.

Beth's dad had fallen, that she could understand, but every day he sat in that same bloody chair with that same bloody book was another day he wasn't getting up. Beth felt her heart plunge every time she looked at him, because even though she didn't want to admit it, she was teetering on the edge of that same dark hole.

She looked down in surprise at her hand. It was holding her mobile. Her thumb was poised to dial Pen's number, displayed on the screen; pure muscle memory. She recoiled and hurled the phone away. It clattered onto the pavement. Beth ran down the street as though an army of ghosts marched in her wake.

It had been raining, and the streetlights bled over the pavements like molten copper. Tears blurred her vision and she navigated the streets on instinct.

The chain-link fence alongside the old railway sidings reared up in front of her and she threw herself at it and clambered over, ignoring the rust and the loose wires that snagged her hands. The tracks she dropped onto were disused and inert, part of an old extension no longer served. She stumbled along them, kicking at the crisp packets and rain-melted newspaper that littered the ground. A tunnel entrance opened up in front of her and she ran in.

It was only after Beth had snapped on one of the three powerful torches she kept in the underpass that she finally felt able to be still. She stared around at the walls.

Lithe Chinese dragons chased tiny biplanes across the brickwork, jesters and skeletons waltzing together in their wake. A massive hand chose from a fruit bowl full of planets. Octopuses coiled around anchors and wolves reared and snakes fought and cities soared from the strata of dense clouds. This little burrow under the Mile End Road was Beth's sanctuary; five years of her imagination was sprayed and stencilled onto these walls.

She spread her hands across them, and their texture was like grazed skin. "What'm I gonna do, guys?" Her voice echoed in the tunnel, and she burst out in a strained laugh. She only talked to her paintings when things got bad; it had to be death-of-the-firstborn-bad for her to do it *out loud*.

Normally she used stencil and aerosol to reshape the city, carving a safe place for herself amid the concrete, room to breathe. Not tonight. Not without Pen to share it with. Tonight she felt shut out of her town.

Pen.

The anger went though her like a spark lighting a gunpowder fuse, leaving her cold in its wake. *I fought for you. When did that stop being enough? If you'd only kept quiet, we'd've been safe.* When had Pen stopped trusting Beth to protect her?

One picture caught her eye, a simple chalk sketch repeated over and over amongst the more outlandish images: a woman, long-haired, her back turned, glancing over her shoulder as if in invitation.

"What'm I gonna do?" Beth asked again, but her mum didn't answer. She only lived in two places now: in Beth's mind and on Beth's bricks, and she wasn't talking back from either.

Beth pressed her cheek to the cool, rough wall. She stood like that for a moment, and then pressed harder and harder until hot pain spread from the grazes on her face and hands, as though by sheer force of muscle she could burrow under the city's skin.

A low sound cut the night, snapping Beth out of her reverie. The sound came again, urgent and familiar. She sniffed her tears back. She was miles from anywhere where she ought to be able to hear that sound.

It came again, echoing off the bricks: the low moan of a train.

Beth felt a sudden heat on her back. She turned and found herself gaping at what she saw.

Two blazing white lights rushed at her from the dark of the tunnel, litter and leaves fluttering alongside them. A bulky shape formed out of the black, all jagged edges and momentum. Blue lightning arced and spat, illuminating clattering wheels. The sound of it crashed in on her ears like close thunder.

Thrum-clatter-clatter—

Her clothes snapped in a sudden gust of air. She tensed her legs to jump, but it was too late. She screwed her eyes shut.

Thrum-clatter—

The screech of metal on metal made her shudder. Every muscle in her body locked, but there was no pulverizing impact, no shattering of bones…

Barely daring to breathe, Beth opened her eyes.

Headlights, barely inches from her face, blinded her instantly.

She stumbled back in the glare and lost her footing, then crumpled and sat on the ground. Her heart was thumping like a pneumatic drill. Slowly her vision dissolved back through the glare. *What is it*, she thought, *a train?*

No—not a train, not quite. It was train-*like*, but more *animal*, somehow. Its whistle was a howl, it was draped in a pelt of tangled cables, and its chassis was scabbed with rust and graffiti. Cataracts of smashed glass covered its windows. Great rents had been torn from its hull as though by massive claws.

The train-thing emitted a hydraulic snort and impatiently shifted its wheels.

Beth wriggled back on her bum, still staring at it, until she felt the wall behind her. She pulled herself up—and then froze.

The headlights were tracking her like the eyes of a suspicious beast. It sounded again, more quietly this time, and turned up at the end like a question, like it was *curious.*

What are you? Beth squinted through the glare and stumbled forwards. On an impulse she reached hesitantly up past its wheels and patted its side. A whickering sound emerged from the train-thing, a sound of pleasure.

What am I supposed to do? she thought incredulously. *Scratch you behind the ears? Where the hell are your ears, and how am I supposed to scratch 'em?* She wondered if this was what a total psychotic break felt like. *You've snapped,* she told herself. *This can't be real.*

A sinuous curve of blue electricity danced over the surface of the train-beast and Beth jumped back. For an instant it looked new, its chassis gleaming pristine and bright—but only for an instant, and then the pitted metal skin washed back.

"What are you?" Beth said softly to it. "What do you want?"

The train-thing lowed again, as if in answer, and the doors of the front carriage hissed open.

Beth steeled herself and thrust a hand inside. She half expected it to burst into blue flame. It didn't. She felt like she was in a trance, adrift on a tide of total unreality. She placed her hands palm-down on the floor of the carriage, ready to push herself on board.

A cold thought jarred her: *What if I can't get back?*

She remembered Gorecastle looking down at her, and her dad staring up, and Pen, most of all Pen, huddled in her wounded fury.

Beth looked over her shoulder. From the wall, her mum looked back. She pulled herself inside.

SIX

The doors beeped and slid quietly shut. Beth rolled to her feet and looked around. She wasn't alone. Dozens of figures crowded together on the seats: men and women dressed in business suits, teens ignoring everything but their flickering phones, a pensioner half-buried under plastic bags.

"Er—er, excuse me," Beth started, forcing a way down the aisle between them. "Excuse me, but what is this? Where are we?"

No one answered; no one reacted to Beth at all. She approached one girl who looked about the same age as her. She was wearing a posh school uniform and blowing bubblegum like a manga fantasy. "Hey," said Beth, "what's going on?"

The girl didn't look at her but just kept blowing her bubbles, popping them and starting over: blow out, pop, suck back, chew; blow out, pop, suck back, chew.

As Beth watched she realized every bubble was *identical*, and each one was popping exactly the same distance past the girl's heavily glossed lips.

Beth stared. A thrill of understanding ran through her. *They're all the same bubble,* she thought.

She looked around her, and now she could see all of the carriage's other occupants were also doing one thing, over and over: scratching a nose, crossing their legs, tapping a mobile phone, turning a page. She hadn't seen it at first in the dim, flickering light, but looking closely, she could see the fraction of a second's discrepancy as each person reset. As Beth stared, the girl in front of her wavered, faded, until Beth could see the stained fabric of her seat back through her stomach. Then she was back again, blowing her single perfect bubble.

"You're not real, are you?" Beth said quietly, her whole body thrumming with the strangeness of it. She said it louder: "You aren't real—"

Are you ghosts? she wondered with a shudder. *Were you trapped here?*

But they didn't seem like ghosts to her. They were more like *memories*—memories of passengers, a few seconds of their lives, snatched out of time and imprinted within the train, repeating over and over like a scratched CD.

Beth rolled her gaze around the train carriage with its faded fabric seats and peeling panels. She remembered the questioning sound it had made. This was the inner architecture of a living thing. Was she inside its mind? *Are they your memories?* she thought, in a kind of dazed amazement. *Is it you remembering them?*

Brakes squealed and hydraulics hissed. The carriage began to sway. Beth felt her stomach plunge. The train was moving.

She ran to the door and hammered the button, but nothing happened. Panic clawed at her and she pressed her face to the window. Through the cracked glass she could see the crosshatched bricks of the tunnel whipping past, faster and faster. She was locked in—and they were speeding up. She reeled away from the door and threw herself at the entrance to the driver's cab; maybe she could stop it from there? Blue sparks flickered on the teeth of the ghostly passengers, who swayed with the train, unflinching.

The door to the cab was locked, and though Beth wrenched frantically on the handle, it wouldn't budge.

"Christ on a bike!" she yelled, drawing her fist back and slamming it against the door in frustration—

—and it went straight through the door.

Beth shivered and pulled her arm back. This time she pushed it forward more slowly; it passed through the metal as if it were vapor.

The door, like the bubble-blowing girl, was as insubstantial as a thought.

Beth hesitated, then pushed herself through.

The train exploded from the tunnel.

Beth stared wide-eyed around the cab. There was no driver. Air pummeled her face as though the front of the train wasn't there. She felt her fear level out, and as she swallowed down her panic, something else, a hot, raw excitement, rose in its place. She reached out and petted the thing's controls. The engine purred to her. Blue electricity danced around her hand but it didn't touch her.

The driver's window seemed to waver. Beth took a deep breath. She leaned forward and the windowpane parted around her like cold mist. She gripped the sides of the control panel and hung out over the train's insubstantial prow like a figurehead. Regiments of ties shot by under her. She tasted the diesel on the wind. She found herself laughing hysterically, and the wind snatched the sound. She uttered a wordless shout of elation and the train's whistle sounded joyously in response.

A bulky mass squatted low in the distance as they surged onto the vast, rail-matted viaduct leading to Waterloo Station. On each side, houses and billboards and glimmering towers boiled together into a continuous river of darkness and streaks of yellow light. Railway signals burned red through the autumn mist, suspended from a bridge as black and dark as hangman's scaffold.

Beth wasn't just riding the train, she was riding the entire *city*. The rush of it filled her and she crowed—but the yell of affirmation died in her throat: another pair of lights was coming towards them.

There was another train.

Beth stared. Each second brought the lights closer, and each second made her more and more certain. Excitement turned to horror. She gaped in disbelief, but it was true...

The other train was on *their* tracks.

"Stop!" she yelled to the creature that carried her. "Stop, we're going to hit it!" But the wind snatched her voice away and her train did not slow, even as the other engine, their lethal mirror-image, came on inexorably towards them. She could make out its shape now: a massive freight train, striped yellow and black like a wasp and armored in heavy steel. But *it* wasn't a natural train either: electricity whirled around it in a constant storm. Its fenders were hooked around like mandibles. The braying of its harsh steam-whistle shivered along her neck like a war cry.

The air felt suddenly thick with electricity. It tasted burnt. Beth turned and ran, plunging back through the driver's door. She lurching up the gangway between the fidgeting memories—

Move, Beth, move—

"Too slow," she cried out loud, "too slow!"

Christ, Beth, you're too slo—

Screeeeeeech!

There was a piercing scream of metal and the shudder of impact. The train slammed to a halt, hurling Beth backwards. Her stomach flipped over as she hit the floor hard. The chill mist of the train-thing's wraithlike front wall coated for a second and she rolled out onto the tracks.

No air! Her lungs clawed at the vacuum for a moment, and then she erupted into a hacking cough. Her arms were scraped raw and hot blood was smeared over her brow. She pushed herself up on her elbow—

—and gazed up at the impossible.

There was no wreckage, no twisted, smoking, white-hot

steel. The trains were *above* her: she was lying on the tracks and they were forty feet above her. Their front carriages were rearing up off the rails like snakes and...

And they were fighting.

They butted and grappled with each other, their fenders interlocked like horns. They emitted hisses and screeches of sheer machine effort. But the freight train was bigger and heavier. Its carriages bunched together like muscle as it hurled her train to the earth. The ground quaked, and Beth quaked with it as the freight train lashed down, cobra-nimble, chewing at the undercarriage of its enemy with its wheels.

Sparks and something like oily blood gushed from Beth's engine, and it screamed.

"*Stop it!*" Beth yelled, stumbling forward, waving her hands as if she was trying to ward off a wild animal. She was coughing, half-mad with impact and smoke, but she clambered over the ruined body of her train, hollering like an idiot. "*Get off it!*" she screamed again, smoke scratching at her throat until it was fit to bleed. "Get *away!*"

The vast freight train arched backwards, cocooned in blue lightning, ready to strike. It flickered, and blurred, leaving strange after-images: a steam engine, a squat underground train, a trail of memories as though it couldn't remember what it was. Its steam-whistle brayed like a tormented thing.

The cold white beam of its eye fixed on Beth. It snorted steam-breath. She felt its weight over her like a promise.

"For Thames' sake—*get the crap out of the way!*"

She staggered as something shoved her aside. Out of the corner of her eye she glimpsed a figure: a skinny boy wearing only a pair of filthy ripped jeans. His skin was as gray as concrete and his face was taut with fear.

And then the freight train crashed down, its fender-jaws tearing at the tracks. The shock of it wrenched the world out of focus. The figure vanished. Beth shook her head, trying to clear it, bewildered by the din. Had she imagined—?

No, there he was, on top of the monster, somehow. His ribs pressed through his chest with each heaved breath. He gripped what looked like an iron railing in one hand and as Beth watched he stabbed it down, again and again, into the train-beast's metal skin. The makeshift weapon punctured the steel like tinfoil, and every time it went in the beast *shrieked*.

Wheels whirred into motion, squealing against the tracks, and Beth rolled sharply out of their path. Her ears popped as the freight train clattered past her, the gray boy still clinging to its roof. The carriages it dragged behind it faded into insubstantial nothingness as it gathered speed.

Beth shook herself like a dog, trying to get some feeling back into her stunned limbs, some sense into her head. She pushed herself up and ran to *her* train's side.

It mewled pitifully at her with its whistle.

"Hey," she whispered. "Hey, you okay?" She patted and stroked it, though the metal around its wounds was almost searing to the touch. It stirred, and sounded again. She could feel the fear and pain coming off it, making the hairs on her arms stand up. Through its windows she could see the people-memories, repeating their actions, but now their faces wore terrified expressions.

The train groaned and rolled painfully up onto its wheels.

"Good boy," she whispered. "Good boy. Listen, there's a boy—that freight train's got him. He … he pushed me, got me safe—we have to help him … can you—?"

Maybe it didn't understand her—why should it? Or perhaps it was simply too scared. But no, after a moment it jolted itself into forward motion, all the while lowing in animal panic. Axles churning, it roared off towards the station.

Beth stood lonely and tiny in its wake, sucking in great gulps of air. "Wait … " she started, but her voice faltered as she stared after it.

A thunderous drumming grew loud on the tracks behind her: the freight train was clattering back, howling victoriously. The concrete-skinned boy had been shaken almost loose and now he dangled from its side, his body snapping in the wind like a pennant.

Beth watched in horror as the beast charged straight at the viaduct wall, but then, a second before impact, the train-beast wrenched itself sideways and a hideous sound filled the air as it scraped itself lengthwise along the bricks, a horrible, teeth-clenching metal sound—a sound pierced through by a human scream.

As its hind carriages passed she saw him, the concrete-colored boy, sprawled face-down on the tracks. Every atom of her body was screaming at her to run—she shouldn't be here; she should never have got on the train. But the memory of the boy's elbow in her side stopped her.

He'd saved her life.

And now she *was* running, but running towards him, cursing her reluctant legs, her battered arms pumping.

In the shadow of the station the freight train was already checking its momentum, like a bull, turning for a final charge to finish its enemy. It swept around, and she could see its mad, staring headlights.

She skidded onto her knees in the gravel. The boy wasn't moving. His ankle was pinned down by heavy chunks of rubble. His back was cruelly torn open where he'd been dragged over the bricks. The blood that glistened there was dark as oil.

"Wake up!" Beth slapped his face. "Wake up!" She shook him hard. She knew by the shudder of the rails that the freight train was close.

Thrum-clatter-clatter—

"Wake up!" she screamed.

At last he stirred, but sluggishly. He mumbled something, but she couldn't make out what it was. "Wake *up!*" She hooked her arms under his and tried to pull him away, but it was no good: his ankle was trapped fast.

The onrushing freight train stormed in her ears.

One of the boy's eyelids flickered. He mumbled again, and this time she could just about make him out as he breathed, "*Spear—*"

Thrum-clatter—

"Spear? What spear? Where—?" She looked around.

The iron railing lay across the track, shuddering with the monster's approach. Beth seized it in clammy hands and wedged it under the rubble. She threw her weight down on it and the smallest rock lifted, just a fraction.

The boy screamed as he exploded up from the ground. His shoulder caught Beth in the gut, driving her feet from the ground. The railing grazed her hand as he snatched it away.

Beth's head snapped backwards. Headlights washed over them and the freight train roared. The boy grunted and threw the railing. It pierced the front fender and skewered itself deep into the ground.

There was an eruption of blue light, an after-image of vast, blunt, churning teeth. And then darkness swallowed Beth whole.

———

The world returned slowly with a hiss of distant traffic. Beth's nose told her she was alive—as far as she knew, neither Heaven nor Hell smelled like a blocked Southwark drain. She didn't open her eyes. Footsteps crunched in the gravel near her head.

"Well, you look dead." The voice had a tinge of an East End accent. "But you don't smell dead, and if that's a heartbeat I'm hearing then you don't sound dead neither."

A hand slipped behind her shoulders, another cupped her head and she was hoisted onto her feet. "Up on yer pins, come on." The boy helped her to steady herself, then stood back. He frowned, leaning against his railing.

He looked about sixteen, but it was difficult to be sure because his eyes sat in deep pits and his cheeks were sharp to the point of looking starved. The skin stretched over his ribs was a mottled gray, as though he'd soaked up the soot and oil from the city and been permanently stained. He looked like a street urchin from one of those old books, but wilder, more feral, and halfway to being grown-up.

Beth stared at him, wide-eyed and confused. She looked around, but there was no sign of the train-beast. "Where'd it go?" she asked, breathless. It felt like a more urgent question than her planned follow-up: *Who the hell are you?*

"The Railwraith?" he said. "I earthed it, spread the charge out through the ground." He shrugged ruefully. "Should've thought of it sooner, I s'pose, but when something that big and angry comes rushin' out the dark at you, first instinct's to stick it with something sharp, know what I mean?"

He squinted at her critically as she started at him, then he laughed. "Second thought, maybe you don't. What in Thames' name d'you think you were doing, yelling at it like that? Trying to *reason* with it? You think Bahngeists can *talk*?"

Beth spread her hands helplessly.

Droplets of petrol-hued sweat stood out on the boy's bizarrely colored skin, etching paths around starkly defined muscle, tendon, and bone.

"You're *weird*," he said. He stared at her for a few more seconds like she was a particularly freakish museum exhibit, then he snorted and stomped past her towards the edge of the viaduct.

"Wait!" Beth called. "Wait, where are you going?" He ignored her and Beth had to run to catch him up. She became suddenly and painfully aware of the bruises covering her legs and back.

"You can't just *go*—hey, I'm talking to you!" She caught his arm. "I saved your life back there..." She stumbled as he suddenly spun round.

His teeth were bared like a hissing, feral cat. "Yeah?" he snapped. "Well, I saved yours first, and the way things are going I reckon my achievement's gonna last a lot longer than yours does."

Dawn was just beginning to seep in at the edge of the sky, and in the halflight Beth could see the tension around the boy's eyes. He scowled, trying to look fierce, and her fear faded: for the first time he wasn't some alien, cocksure street-creature but a teenager, frightened out of his wits.

"What's that supposed to mean?" she asked softly. "What are you so scared of?"

"I'm not scared."

Beth just kept looking at him.

"I don't see what business it is of yours," he said after a long pause, "but that Railwraith was *sent*—sent for me. Somebody's trying to kill me, somebody who—" He broke off and looked nervously at the horizon, where the dome of St. Paul's breached the skyline. Cranes clutched at it like cruel metal fingers.

"Trust me," he muttered. "If he wanted *you* dead, you'd be brickin' it too." He fell silent, squinting suspiciously at a pigeon flapping overhead.

"And?" Beth asked.

"And what?" He looked at her sullenly.

"Who's trying to kill you?"

"Why do you care?"

"Why do I *care*?" Beth was taken aback by the question. "I ... I just—"

He shoved his railing in between the tracks and folded his arms. The fear she'd seen vanished, hidden behind a veneer of bravado. "Yeah?"

"Look—" Beth gritted her teeth. He might have rescued her from being crushed, burned, and electrocuted, but his high-and-mighty attitude was pissing her off. "I just saved your bloody life, right?"

The boy made to protest, but she held up her hand. "*Don't* interrupt me. Admit it or not, *I* saved *your* life. Now, if you're going to turn around and get killed, I might as well not have bothered. Frankly, I resent the wasted bloody effort."

The boy's face deepened to an even filthier shade of gray. "I saved your life, too," he snapped.

"Yeah," Beth said, "twice. What's your point? Because you saved my life, I'm not supposed to give a crap that someone's trying to take yours?"

"What?" Now the boy looked confused.

"You *asked* why I should care." Beth pronounced the words with exaggerated patience. "Why *shouldn't* I bloody care? Why did you even tell me if you didn't expect me to care? Ooh, '*Someone's trying to kill me.*'" She slapped her cheeks in mock horror. "Am I supposed to be impressed by that?"

The boy blinked. His forehead wrinkled. "Well, aren't you?" he said in a small voice.

"YES!" Beth yelled. "I BLOODY AM! THAT'S WHY I'M ASKING!" She sat down hard on the gravel.

The boy, looking both sheepish and thoroughly confused, sat down beside her. "Thanks," he said. "Thanks for saving me."

Beth breathed out hard. "Back at you," she said, then stuck out a hand. "I'm Beth." He took it, but didn't say anything. "And your name is?"

He just shook his head.

"Fine, be mysterious." She sighed. "But if this was my school and you didn't give yourself a name they'd give you one of their own, know what I mean? And trust me, you wouldn't like it."

They'd probably just call you Urchin, she thought. *That's what I'd call you. That's what you look like: a five-years-later snapshot from a "Help a London Child" campaign.*

They sat a moment in silence. He rubbed at the inside of his wrist and for the first time, Beth noticed the mark there: a tattoo, slate-gray against his lighter skin. It looked like a semicircle of tower blocks, arranged to form the spokes of a crown.

"So who *is* trying to kill—?" she began, but he cut her off sharply.

"Don't," he said. "Don't ask questions—don't try. You saw monsters tonight." He gave a sickly grin. "And I'm probably the worst of the lot, so just forget me. You people can forget anything if you try hard enough."

"Come on," Beth protested, "whoever it is, he can't be that bad. The way you took on that train-thing—"

"He's worse," he said flatly.

"Yeah, but still—whoever he is, I bet we could take him." *We.* She didn't know why she'd said that.

Pavement-gray eyes met hers. He smiled, and she smiled back, but then he shook his head ruefully. "You don't know what you're talking about. Look, you're fun— in a bone-breaking kind of a way. Maybe, after this is all over, you can come find me." His smile was wan. It didn't look like he was holding out much hope that "after this was over" there'd be much left to find.

"Where would I look for you?" Beth asked.

He hesitated, and then said, "Your accent says Hackney…"

She nodded.

"All right, Hackney Girl, look for me at the dance where the light itself is the music, where the Railwraith's rush beats the drums." He eyed her appraisingly. "Look for me in the broken light, when this is all over, and maybe then we'll dance. But for now, go. It's gonna be bad enough *me* trying stand against what's coming. I can't be tripping over you too."

The dismissal felt like a fist clenching around Beth's guts. "Why not?" she whispered.

He gave her a lopsided smile. "Because *I* saved *your* life," he said, "and I don't want to resent the wasted effort."

"Look, mate—" Beth began, but in that same moment the gray-skinned boy sprang up and sprinted away along the tracks.

Beth swore and pushed herself after him. She had never run so fast; her battered muscles squealed in protest as the rails blurred under her. For a second they were side by side, but slowly, agonizingly slowly, he pulled away. Beth's breath seared her lungs, but he just ran faster and faster. His motion became strangely smooth, sinuous, like a street rat's. He almost didn't look human any more.

He jumped up onto the wall of the viaduct and was silhouetted against London. For an instant, the low tumble of the city's skyline was like an army, backing the scrawny boy. Then he dropped over the edge.

Beth arrived seconds later, wheezing and cursing. She craned her head over the wall. Early morning cars hooted up at her from the street below. But in between their fleeting shapes she saw nothing.

SEVEN

The Thames Barrier breaches the water, glinting like the knuckles of a giant gauntlet. It's a Saturday, and the industrial estates of North Greenwich are empty: little fenced-off wastelands. Gutterglass can manifest anywhere in London, but there are places where the spirit of rubbish is stronger, where it accretes in every brick and concrete pore.

I'm squatting in a car park, behind a car with two missing hubcaps and a cardboard for-sale sign in the window. Rats skitter past, but I ignore them. They'd get a message to Glas eventually, but I want it to travel faster than that.

I dig my hand into the ground. The soil crumbles between my fingers and tiny black ants teem over my palm. *That's better.* I pull a small bottle from my pocket, yank the cork out with my teeth, and allow the fumes to waft over an insect's antennae. It freezes for an instant, then vibrates ecstatically and races away over the back of my hand, down my leg and into the earth. You can't beat a hive mind for speed of transmission.

Now I wait.

I think of the girl from last night, her broad, flat cheekbones and messy hair. *We can take him,* she said; *we,* even though I'd only met her five minutes before and I could have smelled the terror in her sweat through the Oxford Circus crush on a Saturday afternoon. What kind of person *thinks* like that? *We.*

Because I'm alone, because it's a secret, I let myself smile at that.

Seagulls gyre overhead, cawing. As I watch, one of them drops out of its lazy circle and spirals fast towards the ground, flapping its wings rapidly to break its landing. The gull looks at me with one yellow eye. I can see a lump distending its throat. It jerks its head back and forth and gags.

With a slippery sound, a tangle of worms and woodlice spills from its beak onto the ground, spreading over the concrete. My little ant races away from the pack, its job done. It leaves a sticky trail of bird saliva behind it.

I watch as the bugs work, dragging empty foil tubes, crisp packets, and chunks of plywood to the center of the courtyard. Plastic bags are torn into strips by ferocious, gnashing weevils. Toes form first, and then legs and hips, and a higgledy-piggledy sculpture of rubbish rises uncertainly in front of me.

The eggshell eyes blink. They, and only they, are always the same. Glas is a woman this time, the rusting handlebars of a bike making up her hips, long strands of torn plastic her hair. The head of a worm wriggles unhappily at the end of one hand. I find an ice-lolly stick from the dirt near my feet and hand it to her. The worm coils itself around it and breaks it into knuckle-joints.

"Thank you," she says. Her eggshell-gaze catalogues the burns and black blood-bruises on my chest. Yesterday she'd have tutted or cooed in sympathy, but a lot's changed since then.

"Nothing beyond your ability to heal," she notes with satisfaction. "The wraith's dead, I take it?"

"Earthed behind Waterloo," I confirm. "I got off light. I reckon the extra power was too much for her; it broke her after a few hours. She was confused, already bleeding out. It was a mercy at the end."

"That's something, then." A little thing. Glas sighs like she has to be grateful for the little things now. She hesitates, and then says, "My pigeons have seen wolf-shapes stalking the building sites. And the Pylon Spiders report feeling a power surge through the grid at around midnight, night before last. Just when you said the wraith entered Reach's domain."

Sympathy edges into her voice. "I'm sorry, Filius, I really am, but Reach is gathering his strength. There's no doubt any more: it *is* him."

I feel like I'm trying to swallow a chunk of brick. I hadn't realized until now just how much I'd been hoping Glas was wrong. "I don't understand," I mutter. "Why *now?*"

She turns her head away. The breeze flaps the strands of her binbag hair against her face. "Filius," she says carefully, "there's something else you need to know. There have been rumors—if Reach is preparing for war, it can only be because he's been listening to them." She wets her lips with a tongue made from an old sponge.

Unease creeps through me. "What rumors?" I ask.

"That soon the street signs will rearrange themselves," she says very quietly, "and feral cats will walk with their tails high in procession through the streets."

For a long moment I do nothing but stand there, feeling, and no doubt looking, heroically stupid.

"She's . . . she's . . . coming *back?*" I'm not even sure I said that aloud.

Glas looks at me. "I'm sorry," she says, and I explode, all the tension in my chest multiplying as it unravels. I feel dizzy and scared and elated all at once.

"*Why didn't you tell me?*" I shout at her.

Glas shrugs wretchedly. "There was nothing firm. I didn't want to get your hopes up, and I didn't—" She hesitates. "I didn't want you to be scared."

"Scared of *what?*" I demand. "She's my *mother!*"

"She's also a goddess," Glas says, "and goddesses are not kind."

"What's that supposed to mean?"

"War's coming, Filius. The King of the Cranes and the

Lady of the Streets will not share the city. The gables and the gutters and manholes will bleed. Reach has been killing her kingdom for years, tearing it up and enslaving it to whatever he's building in St. Paul's, and you didn't stop him. You're her son, and you didn't stop him. That cathedral was her crown jewel, and you gave it up without a fight." Her tone is dreadfully gentle. She's trying not to make it sound like it's my fault.

"I *couldn't* have stopped it," I protest, bewildered and frightened now. "I was never strong enough—"

She shushes me, puts her arms around me. I can feel the warmth as her rubbish decays. "I understand," she whispers. "It was right to wait. It was safer. But if Reach is moving against us, we no longer have that luxury."

My thoughts are reeling.

Glas' voice turns low, urgent. "You need to act, Filius. You're right, I should have told you sooner. Reach has become strong—too strong—in your mother's absence. We need an army," she urges. "The Pavement Priests, the Mirrorstocracy—the old guard. We need to *move*, or by the time Mater Viae arrives, the Skyscraper Throne will be occupied, and not by you."

But I'm barely listening. All I can think is *she's coming back she's coming back she's coming back*—

"You should have told me!" I snap at Gutterglass. She tries to hold on to me, but I tear myself loose and run. I expect her to call after me, but when I look back she's just watching me with that desolate gaze. Gutterglass: the spirit

of the city's abandoned, the nursemaid who cared for me
in place of—
   She's coming back.
   I watch the body of garbage crumble like ash and fall.

EIGHT

Beth stood at the end of Wendover Road, watching Pen's familiar shape move behind a window across the street.

People hurried past, jostling her and tutting. The women were dressed in wildly contrasting styles: jeans and crop-tops, hijabs, the occasional full burkha. It was the end of the day and the cheap DVDs and plastic watches were being packed away on the market stalls. Men held intense conversations in glass-fronted restaurants over bowls of biryani, or watched hockey on the muted TV sets. The air was tinged with the smell of curry and spices and overripe fruit.

Everything screamed *Pen* loudly enough to make Beth gasp. She shifted her weight and changed her mind for the fourth time.

All she had to do was shout—one syllable would probably do it. Pen's window was cracked open; she'd hear. Just that one syllable and she'd come down and they'd sit with their backs against the bricks of the next-door alley and Pen would talk Beth out of this insane thing she was planning to do.

Beth came up on the balls of her feet; she felt that shout rise up inside her—

—but it stalled again, because there was a taste in her mouth, the same taste as there had been back in Gorecastle's office, and it made her want to spit; it made Beth not want Parva Khan anywhere near her.

Less than a day ago she would've thought Pen would believe her. She would have trusted Pen to *trust* her. That trust was broken now, and realizing that was like chewing tinfoil.

Besides, she didn't even know if Pen would talk to *her*.

B, you made everything worse.

The memory of Pen's stone-dead tone made Beth want to turn and run from the street.

But she couldn't leave without some sort of goodbye, no matter how much some blistered little part of her wanted to. She slipped her hand into her pocket and rubbed her thumb over the black crayon she kept there.

Dotted around Pen's doorframe were a series of pictograms: tiny trains with electric bolts under their wheels. Beth had drawn them in a little procession round the corner into the alley, like a trail of crumbs.

And there, on the bricks next to the metal bins, she'd drawn Pen's face, smiling, lovingly detailed: a parting gift.

Streetlamps flickered on as the daylight faded. Beth

struggled to focus on what the boy had said: *Look for me in broken light.* She'd been puzzling her way around that cryptic phrase all day.

The dance where light itself is the music, where the Rail-wraith's rush beats the drums.

She turned his words over in her mind, probing them for meaning. They sounded worryingly like the gibberings of a lunatic, which, she admitted to herself, it was entirely possible he was.

She remembered the shock of him shoving her, and she touched the bruise under her hoodie and winced. Her skin was apparently as determined to retain the memory as her mind was.

Think, Beth: what do you know about him? Well, he runs around London's railway tracks in the middle of the night without a shirt or shoes but with a bloody great iron railing, jabbering incomprehensible cryptic bollocks about light and music and monsters, and he risked getting flattened by five hundred tons of angry freight train just to save you. You've got to admit, these are not the characteristics of someone overburdened with sanity.

She slumped, but then a thought struck her: what if the directions weren't cryptic at all? He hadn't just looked like he slept in the streets, but like he *always* had done. It dawned on Beth that street names and house numbers might be a meaningless code to someone who'd never lived in one.

What if he'd told Beth where to find him as clearly and simply as he could?

Beth licked her lips. She wracked her memory for a place that fit. *Where the Railwraith's rush...* it had to be near a train line. He'd checked that she was from Hackney, so that narrowed it down. Beth's excitement mounted as she worked it through—but where was *the light itself music,* though?

A memory surfaced: a railway footbridge overgrown with brambles, the boards armored in chewing gum harder than concrete. It was a meeting place she'd shared with Pen, where they'd traded sweets and whispered secrets. When the trains shot past underneath, the sound of their wheels on the tracks was like drums.

There were four streetlamps in the cul-de-sac below. Their light had flickered as they lit up in what Pen described as a "fractured harmony." Beth had always thought that was kind of beautiful; there had been a definite rhythm to their flashes. And wasn't rhythm all you really needed to dance?

If nothing else, it was as good a place as any to start.

Beth looked back up at Pen's window and all her excitement drained away, replaced with queasy dread. Sure enough, when she turned away, there it was: a sharp white pain, hard up against her ribs. *It's like that phantom-limb thing you hear about,* she told herself sternly, *like soldiers get.* She tried to make herself believe that the hurt was coming from an empty space, a love already gone.

She made it all of three steps before she ducked back into the alley.

"You're a soft idiot, Bradley," she muttered as, despite

herself, she rough-sketched another figure on the bricks: a skinny boy holding a railing like a spear.

Gone hunting, she scribbled under the picture of her quarry. *Look for me in broken light.*

Her anger hissed at her spitefully from the back of her mind, but the secret was too big and too lonely to keep to herself, and, in spite of everything, Pen was still the only person she could imagine sharing it with.

Fractured harmony, remember? she scrawled finally, before shouldering her backpack and forcing herself, step by step, to walk away.

NINE

Night seeps in from the sky. The breath from the manholes starts to steam. The city shivers and draws darkness about it. This is when the Sodiumites dance.

I stand in a clearing between tower blocks, a pedestrianized island of asphalt beside a railway footbridge, away from the road. Streetlights puncture the pavement at the four compass points. A couple of kids stand on the bridge, smoking and studiously ignoring me as the warmth ebbs sluggishly from the air.

Slow, slow at first, a light begins inside the streetlamps; the first steps of the dancers behind the glass barely raise a glow, just a few tiny flashes where they plant their heels. A graceful hand twists and beckons inside one of the bulbs, sparks leaping from her fingers.

I crack my knuckles, stretch my back, breathe deep.

All four sisters are awake now, pressing themselves against the glass, blowing fiery kisses, feigning helplessness, coyly pretending to be caged. My heart begins to trip.

Now speed comes to the dance and bright lights flicker. My shadow dances, and I start to move with it, twisting my limbs to the rhythm of the light: visual music. The strobe is hypnotic; I feel drunk but perfectly balanced, high on light.

Thames! This feels good—

The girls on the bridge toss their cigarettes and one of them laughs as the other mutters something about the "junkie tramp."

They walk away and do not see the lamps, one by one, cut out.

Electra is the first, the boldest, as always. She slides her body smoothly down the length of the dimmed streetlamp until her feet scorch asphalt. Her glassy skin is perfectly clear. The fluorescent dust in her blood is blinding. Fiber-optic hair waves in a magnetic breeze I can only dream of feeling. I glance around; her sisters have all slipped their bulbs too now and they encircle me, swaying in time to the light, laughing soundlessly.

Electra starts clapping and the others pick up the rhythm, light flaring as palm hits palm in a complex, syncopated glow-and-dim. Once her sisters have it, Electra stops and stands tall, extending an arm to me in formal invitation.

I take her hand and we dance.

Each strobe is a flash of vision: a motion, a thud of blood in my head.

Flash. Flash. Flash.

She controls my pulse with her fingers. She owns my breath. I slide my hand close over her hip.

Flash flash flash—

She singes the hairs on my skin. Her neck arches back and her teeth flare as she grins. I can feel their heat by my ear. She dances, she shines, she is alive; I dance with her and so am I.

Eventually I have to stop, panting and laughing, and she slows, cooling enough to kiss my cheek. The heat of her lips is a shade below painful.

"Welcome, Son of the Streets."

The others keep playing. One plucks a spectritar, adding shades of color to the music while the remaining two sisters laugh and dance together, cheerfully mocking old-fashioned styles.

I sit and find the gravel chilly after her heat.

She turns and paces around me, and then stops and opens her mouth. *"What is it?"*

I read the word in semaphore from the pulsing light of her tonsils. "What's what?" I ask, exaggerating the words so she can read my lips.

"You are tense."

"Why do you say that?"

"I could drown a rat in toxic waste; it would make a better dancing partner."

My cheeks burn. "I didn't think it was that bad."

She shrugs disdainfully. *"You were stiff and slow, behind the beat even more than usual. Your mind was somewhere else—I hope so, at least, because it's either that or you have gone—*" She hesitates, groping for the word, and eventually strobes out the characters in her own language: something like "shines-not-brightly-in-contemplation."

"Retarded," I interpret, and snort. "Thanks."

She sits down beside me. For an instant she is still, and her light almost goes out, then she puts her arm around me and starts tapping my shoulder with scalding fingertips. She pulls me around to face her. "*You can talk to me, Filius.*"

I sigh. "I ran out on Gutterglass."

She's started some platitude, but this gives her pause. "*Tell me about it,*" she semaphores.

So I do, and she reads my lips in what passes for her as silence. Barely twitching enough to stay alight, she is almost invisible. She shakes her head when I finish. "*I heard a rumor recently, but I did not think there was anything to it. But if Glas believes…*" Her words are shaded with astonishment. "*So she really is coming back?*"

"And Gutterglass wants to prepare the way for her—wants me to go up against *Reach.*" I laugh exasperatedly. "She dropped the problem in front of me like a smiling foxcub with a bit of carrion it found behind bins."

Electra smiles.

"Glas wants an army raised," I say, "like in the old days before she left. She says if we wait for Mater Viae it could be too late."

Electra starts to answer, but she is distracted by a flare

of light, not the soft amber of her kind, but bright white, like a magnesium flare.

It's coming from her lamp.

Her face takes on an ugly cast. "*Whitey*," she snarls in a dim orange.

Her sisters have seen it too. They crowd around Electra's lamp. Another glass figure has climbed up the lamppost while we were talking. He emits a pallid white light as he casts fearful looks at them, clutching his limbs around himself as he tries to get inside.

The Sodium sisters flare bright yellow, displaying their colors. They spit like firecrackers, flashing in their own language, too fast for me to follow. I catch a few phrases, though, vile imprecations about parenthood and voltages. The Whitey squirms and shivers, his light uneven. He probably can't understand half the abuse being screamed at him.

It's Electra, always the boldest, who throws the first stone. Her fingers twist around it, weaving a magnetic field that lifts the rock up and it spins in the air, faster and faster, then shoots straight at the glass.

"Lec, *no!*" I shout, but she isn't looking so she's deaf to me. The others follow her lead and stones start to zip like bullets. The lamppost is dented, glass shatters. The Whitey twists frantically, trying to protect his filaments. I realize he can't help infuriating them: the faster he moves to avoid the rocks, the brighter he burns, the stronger his color, the angrier the Sodiumites become...

...and the faster the stones fly.

I gape: why is the Whitey taking this? Why doesn't he run? A look at the sky gives me my answer: heavy thunderclouds are swelling over the city's orange glow.

I make a decision.

Grabbing my spear, I jink between the sisters' bodies and scramble up the lamppost, waving my spear like a flagpole, trying to get their attention. "*Stop!* It's going to rain—*rain*, you get it? There's only one of him—he's not invading, he's only looking for cover."

They don't acknowledge me, but magnetic trajectories shift slightly and the missiles lose little momentum as they swerve around me to find their target. The whistle as they fly through the air can't quite drown out the terrified buzzing of the Whitey behind me.

Splinters of glass shower me. The tiny cuts heal fast.

Eventually I feel the heat behind me lessen as the Whitey slides down the back of the lamppost. He hunches for a second on the tarmac, his corona of white light shrinking as the Sodiumites advance on him. Then he shambles away, clutching himself, strobing off little mewls of pain.

There's a touch of moisture on the wind. My stomach twists. I know what will happen to him if he's caught out in a rainstorm...

... and so do they.

Electra's slap burns my cheek. She's climbed the lamppost as well. Her sisters stand around the courtyard, ostentatiously staring in the other direction.

"*What were you doing?*"

"It's going to rain!" I yell back at her, my skin stinging. "He just wanted *shelter.*"

"*He was trespassing. They have their own shelters.*"

"On a dozen streets in the center of the city, five miles away—he'll never make it in time!"

She stares at me. Her eyes glow a uniform clear amber from lid to lid.

"*Good,*" she strobes. "*If I ever trespassed on Whitey ground, a stoning is the least I would expect.*"

She looks down at her sisters. "*They wanted me to throw you out but I told them about Glas, and about Reach. They understand you are upset. They are not happy, not at all, but you can stay—as long as you never EVER get in our way like that again.*"

My stomach burns as fiercely as my face. How dare she apologize for me? I want to scream at her, but spots of rain are already kissing my forehead. Alarm flashes across Electra's face.

"*Rest. Recover,*" she murmurs hurriedly. She lays hot fingers on my chest. "*We will talk when the moon comes out.*" She vanishes into the filament of her lamp, which begins to glow after a second. There is a tinkling sound and the fragments of glass shattered by the stones begin to levitate, floating in her electromagnetic field, glittering as they catch her light. The glass closes around the filament. For an instant she burns hotter: a bright and unbearable white, almost the same shade as the Whitey she scorned. I turn my face away.

When I look back, the lamp glass has melted back together and inside, Electra's light is amber again.

I drop lightly to the ground. Electra's sisters have retreated into their own shelters. I shiver and thrust my hands in my pockets.

You can stay, she said. How river-pissing generous of her.

Am I in hiding then? That's what was in Electra's tone, the shade of her words. Can I really be *hiding*? The idea's absurd; *I* don't *hide*. No, I came here to dance, to relax, clear my mind and get ready for...

For what? I *am* hiding. I'm afraid. The realization weighs me down as though every blood vessel in my body is suddenly full of gravel. Reach is much, much too strong for me. All of the Wraiths I've fought, the Pylon Spiders, the city's petty monsters, none of them ever felt like this.

Out in the wilderness there is a faint glow that might be the Whitey.

The wind gusts and snaps at the hem of my jeans. I sit down cross-legged between the lampposts. And the rain comes down hard.

———

The Whitey danced for his life. He snaked and jerked, trying to dart between the raindrops. He could feel his magnesium bones tingling, stretching out to the water, almost like they *wanted* to react with it and burn. His frantic speed made him brilliant, and his light reflected off the concrete walls of the estate, leaving ghostly after-images.

The grass underfoot was wet and he throbbed off shrieks of pain as he ran, scrambling to find shelter.

The Whitey found a slick black tarpaulin crumpled into a corner by an outbuilding. He threw it over himself, but the rivulets of water that ran off it made him scream, so he stood and ran again, his light beaming out from the treacherous holes in the tarp. Curls of hydrogen twisted wherever the rain struck home.

Suddenly the wind changed and a puddle rippled, splashing a curl of water against the Whitey's leg. He *blazed* in pain and the metal in his ankle reacted: his foot vanished in a flare of light and gas and he fell awkwardly by a barbed-wire fence. He crawled in agony over the wet tarmac. The world around him was bright with lit windows, safe, *dry* lights, but there was no way in.

A jag of concrete snared the edge of the tarp and it was dragged from him. The Whitey lay there, unable to crawl further. He spasmed and his knee scraped over the concrete. A spark caught and he was bathed in flame as the hydrogen cloud around him ignited. The heat balmed him for all-too-brief a moment and then burned out.

It was only the needles of pain rippling over him that kept him conscious. He thought of his home, wondering how he had got so far from the bright gas-white globes on their posts over the Carnaby Street market. His brothers and sisters would be there now, with the rain ricocheting harmlessly off their bulbs. One orb would be dark, empty; where he ought to be.

Something moved above him, a thin, dark shadow, and

the Whitey looked up. A skein of barbed wire was coming off the fence towards him, twisting and coiling like a snake through the air. It shivered along its length and the barbs gave off a rattling hiss.

"*No*," he strobed. Even in his agony, a deeper fear gripped him. "*No, get back. I'm not yours. I can't sustain you.*"

But the eyeless thing kept coming and in the flickering light of his words he saw a tendril slither off the ground to caress his face. The moisture on it burned him.

"*Please*," he whispered, a dim flicker, "*please, not me. I can tell you things—there are threats, threats to your master. The Viae Child, he's raising an army against him, against Reach. I saw him—I hid and read his very lips—*"

But the thing kept coiling lovingly around him, tighter and tighter. Metal thorns clasped hungrily at his scalp, seeking a way in, as though they could plunder straight from his mind the information he was trying to bargain with.

Cracks started to spread through him and he shrieked brightly as the barbs pierced his glass skull and let the water in.

TEN

Beth sat on the bus to Bethnal Green. She looked around, but she couldn't see a wet dog so she was forced to conclude that the smell was coming from her. Strange blots were dancing at the edges of her eyes and it felt like a gnome in lead boots was tap-dancing in the back of her head.

She managed to doze off between ringing the bell and the bus hissing to a stop. Jerking awake, she leaped to her feet and shouldered her way through the closing door. A thunderclap echoed somewhere to the west and the rain redoubled, greeting her with soaking enthusiasm, plastering her hair flat against her skull.

Beth sighed and squelched onwards.

At first she thought he was a hallucination, just sitting there cross-legged, despondently getting drenched. The streetlamps were flickering on and off in some sort of sequence, making his shadow jump in a weird staccato dance.

"Hey!" she yelled. Relief and excitement fizzed through her. "Hey, you! Guy!" She didn't know what to call him. "Urchin!"

He looked up and his gray eyes widened as Beth came down the steps of the bridge three at a time. He scrambled to his feet. "What are you doing here?" he demanded.

Beth grinned. "You told me to look for you in the broken light."

She was buzzing: to have found him again, to have him be *real*. The tower blocks reared vastly against the sodium-soaked clouds and the way they dwarfed her was suddenly thrilling. "Is this your home?" she asked.

A grin to match hers sneaked onto his face. "Home? Well, part of it, I guess—I could bed down in any square inch of London town. Welcome to my parlor." He stretched his arms out as though to take in the entire city. "Make yourself comfy." He laughed, and then seemed to remember who he was talking to.

He folded his arms and looked at her suspiciously. "Who are you? Why are you following me?"

Beth crossed her arms too. Her stance was pugnacious, but she could feel herself trembling with the adrenaline racing through her. "Who are *you*?" she countered. "Why did you save *me*?"

"My name is Filius Viae," he said. "It means Son of the Streets. My mother is their goddess." He took a step towards her, his shadow slipping over her face. "She laid the foundations of the streets you walk on and the bones of the roads buried under them. She stoked the Steamwraiths' engines and gave the lamps their first sparks. She forged the chains that hold old Father Thames in place." He smirked at her. "And I saved you 'cause anyone mental enough to ride one Railwraith and stand in the way of another *shouting* needs all the help they can get."

"O-*kay*," Beth muttered. She drew a deep breath. "My name is Beth Bradley," she said. "It means—well, it means Beth Bradley. My dad's a journalist—a redundant one. I got kicked out of school and he didn't care. My best friend was the one who grassed me up. I suppose the reason I'm following you is because—" The truth of it dawned on her as she said it. "I like your answer better." She tried a smile and added, "'Cept for the name, obviously. I didn't realize you were called 'Phyllis.' I don't blame you for not telling me *that* before."

This time the boy laughed. "I wouldn't be so sure my answer's better; right now it mostly boils down to my arse being hunted all over the Smoke."

"Someone's trying to kill you," Beth said. "I remember."

"Oh, that's good of you," he said, sarcastically tugging a forelock. "Ta." He settled himself back down onto the wet tarmac.

Beth's jeans were drenched anyway, so she slumped down next to him. The wind sculpted half-seen bodies in the rain. "But if you're the son of this kick-arse goddess," she said, "what are you scared of? Surely she could take whoever's trying to mess with you?"

His smile never reached his eyes. "She's not here," he said. "I've never met her." Beth made to apologize but he waved it away. "I was raised by her seneschal, Gutterglass. I ran in the shells of her temples on the river and played with the fossilized entrails of the sacrifices the Green Witches made to her."

"There are actual *green witches* in Greenwich?" Beth was astonished.

"Nah, in Sutton—what, you think there's a sea of eggs and flour in Battersea?" His face was deadpan; she couldn't tell if he was joking. Then his voice took on a hard, brittle edge. "I learnt no ritual, no doctrine—*nothing* to prepare me, not for Reach." The fingers of his left hand crooked into a claw.

"*Reach.* Is that what's hunting you?"

He nodded unhappily.

"So what is it?"

"He's urban sickness," he said, "and greed, and cannibal hunger, and—and I don't know what else. I've never seen him up close, but I've seen the aftermath of him. He is the Crane King, and the cranes are his fingers and his weapons. He uses them to carve himself deep into the city, and when he does, everything around him dies." He snorted. "He's vain, too; he keeps building glass towers to look at himself in. My mother was his only rival; every generation he appeared, and she beat him back, over and over again … but then she disappeared, and ever since then he's been *growing* in that black pit of his under the cathedral."

He looked up at Beth. "But now she's coming back, to reclaim the Skyscraper Throne, and Reach can't wait any more. He wants to weaken her, wants anyone who could fight for her dead. Starting with me." He looked down and muttered, "She's nearly here, but I might never meet her."

He looked so lost that, on impulse, Beth reached out and pulled him close. After a second's hesitation, he yielded. It was frightening and thrilling to hold this hunted boy against her. As though the very act of it put her under the eye of a monster.

"Look, we'll sort him," she whispered—comforting, nonsensical bravado. The rain turned the dust in his hair to mortar that clung to her cheek. "He won't know what's hit him."

He pulled away from her, brushing rainwater off his face. "You're very free with that 'we,'" he said, "and that's kind and all, but what makes you so sure? I saw how you were with the Railwraith—I don't mean to be rude, but you were crappin' yourself."

"I was not! Beth protested. "I was—" But there was no point denying it. "Well, yeah, okay, I was. I was terrified. Happy? But you know what? I'd rather be that scared, every bloody day of my life, than go back to the way I felt before I met you."

A silence followed, long enough and deep enough for Beth to begin to truly appreciate the extent to which that statement made her sound like a stalker.

"But not in a creepy way or nothing," she added, far too late. He was staring at her like she was a different species.

Embarrassed, Beth looked away, and her eyes fell on the nearest streetlight. The rain had started to let up, and now individual drips were slowly becoming distinct. As she watched, the sodium light flared and guttered, then started flashing more violently.

"Oh, Thames, *here we go*," the boy muttered under his breath.

The light stretched and distorted in Beth's eyes like a captive yellow star, and then the burning rays reshaped themselves, the liquid light melting together into limbs and shoulders, a torso, a face—a young woman. She was naked, and Beth could see brightly burning filaments twisting like arteries under her transparent skin as she flowed down the lamppost to the ground. She walked towards them with a sensuously arrogant stride.

The urchin stood, apparently reluctant. "This should be fun," he muttered.

The glowing woman opened her mouth and a light flashed on and off in the back of her throat. She pointed to Beth.

"Just someone I met," he replied innocently.

The light-woman burned a deeply unimpressed orange. More glowing speech issued from her mouth.

"What did she say?" Beth asked.

"Yeah … I don't think you want to know," he murmured.

"Oh, I think I do."

He winced. "She called you the daughter of a forty-watt bulb."

"She what?"

"It—uh, it doesn't really translate."

The light-woman moved to stand in front of Beth, who could feel some kind of force pulling at the hairs on her skin. She curled her toes inside her trainers. Every molecule of her was thrumming with how strange this was.

The woman took another step forward. Beth smelled something she strongly suspected was her own eyelashes singeing. She smirked, quite deliberately, and the woman smirked too and strobed off a word.

"Lec!" The urchin sounded shocked.

The light-woman turned and blazed furiously at him for a moment before running off up the steps and over the bridge, the only sound the hissing of water evaporating away from her feet.

"We'll see who's ungrateful!" he shouted after her. "Remember who *got* you that treaty in the first place!"

"What was that all about?" asked Beth.

He rolled his eyes. "She's just being dramatic. But never mind her … " Using his iron railing like a shepherd's crook, he guided Beth back towards the footbridge. "I told you once, and I'm telling you again: go home."

Beth opened her mouth to protest, but he cut her off. "I'm not joking. Maybe I never acted like my mother's son before, but I can start now. Reach'll kill me, Beth Bradley." He spoke evenly, pragmatically. "And if you're with me, he'll kill you too. I'd hate to have to explain *that* to your redundant journalist dad."

"How're you going to explain anything when you're dead?" Beth asked before she could stop herself.

He glared at her. "Yeah, because being bloody *pedantic* is so going to change my mind," he snapped.

Beth said stubbornly, "Look, I know there's a risk. I know I might—"

"It's not a question of *might*." He sounded exasperated. "For me, maybe, it's a question of might: I *might* be able to run far enough and fast enough to keep ahead of him. But for you it's a question of *will*—I don't mean to be rude, but is there any way in which you wouldn't be a liability? Can you climb the outside of a skyscraper? Can you run the wire ahead of a Pylon Spider?"

Beth glared at him. "I don't even know what you're talking about now."

"Yeah, that's what I thought."

She gritted her teeth. "I did understand one thing you said though: *run*." She almost spat the word. "Is that your plan? Is that how you're going to live up to your mum's legacy? By running?"

"You have no idea what you're saying—"

"*Then teach me!* I'm smart, all right? I can learn—and maybe I can help. Or are you so damned arrogant that you think you're better off alone?"

He opened his mouth, but Beth cut him off. "What, you counting on your little streetlight girlfriend? Unless I very badly misread her bloody body language, you've got some chilly nights coming up.

"Lec's not my—"

"Yeah, whatever." Beth snorted. "Is there anyone else? Anyone else who's willing to stand up to this Crane King you're so scared of?"

As he stared at her she could feel the anger and embarrassment and loneliness coming off him like heat. "Well, I am," she said quietly. "Maybe I *don't* know, but I saved your life once, and you saved mine. I want to *help* you." She only realized quite how true the words were as she spoke them. "Let me help you do more than just run."

His gray eyes searched hers. "Why?"

"Because I'm alone, too." Beth said softly.

They fell silent then. The clouds had blown over and the night was clear and cold. Beth started to shiver.

"No, you're not," he said at last. "Hold out your arm." And without warning, he slashed the razor-sharp tip of his railing across her wrist.

Beth didn't know why, but she didn't jump back or yelp. She held herself completely still as he scratched her again and again, and she felt the blood welling up and dripping onto the wet ground.

She didn't take her eyes from his. "And that was?" She kept all but a tiny tremor from creeping into her voice.

He shrugged, almost shyly. "If you're going to be a soldier in the army, girl, you need to wear the mark."

She looked down at her wrist. Through the smeared

blood she could just make out the fine lines of the cuts: buildings, arranged into a crown.

A tight, exhilarated pride welled up in her.

"It's also a warning. The blood's the reminder: this is *real*, Beth. These things will hurt you, and there's no magic door you can run back through and slam shut to get away from them. You can never go home again, understand? Because they'll follow you—if you do this, if you draw Reach's eye, you give up safety. You give up home. Forever." His voice was as flat and cold as an open heath in a harsh wind.

Beth put her wrist to her cheek, then stared at the crown, immutably and irreversibly cut into her.

"Then I'm ready." Her heart was turning mad somersaults. "Son of the Streets."

II

URBOSYNTHESIS

ELEVEN

Beth looked at the spider. The spider gazed inscrutably back. Beth swallowed. It was as tall as a man, perched daintily on eight needle-pointed feet on the telephone cable that looped into the alley. Its carapace was as smooth as fiberglass, reflecting the light of the streetlamp below. A crackling noise came off it, like voices murmuring at a pitch just below audible.

"So." The pavement-skinned boy leaned against the wall, hands thrust into his pockets. "How do you like our ride?"

Beth gave him a flat stare. "Our ride? It's a giant spider."

He pursed his lips and shrugged in a "can't deny the obvious" kind of way.

"Is it dangerous?" Beth asked.

"Does it look dangerous?" he countered.

"Yeah: it *looks* like a giant spider."

"Wow, that's some impressive power of observation you got there…"

"I'm not finding this reassuring, Fil."

She'd taken to shortening "Filius" to "Fil"—as though being on single-syllable terms could tame this wild boy with the sharp bones and the soot-smeared skin. He'd led her into an ordinary, scratched-to-hell BT payphone on the High Street, picked up the handset, and hesitated. When she'd asked him if he needed change, he'd given her a half-smile, as if at her naïveté. "That's not how they'll want payin'," he'd said.

He had put the receiver to his mouth and then somehow he'd imitated the clicks and buzzes that you got on a line with really bad reception. He'd stopped and listened for a bit, then hung up, looking satisfied.

Then he'd led her around the corner into the alley and here she was, eyeball to eyeball with a spider the size of a small car.

"Remind me why we have to do this again?" she said. The thing's eyes were like glittering pits of ash.

"Communications." He didn't look away from the creature as he answered. "There's no point having an army if you can't talk to it." He edged closer towards it.

"O-*kay*," Beth said. There was a hesitancy in the way he was approaching the beast she really didn't like. An uncomfortable prickle ran up her neck. "And—sorry if this is a daft question—but why are we creeping towards it like we're scared it's going to eat us?"

The look he shot her said, *You really want me to answer that?*

He laid a hand on the spider's head. It went all fuzzy, like a TV picture with bad reception, then blurred back into solidity and crept down off its wire. Fil visibly relaxed. He beckoned Beth forward.

Proud that she was managing to keep the trembling to a minimum, she reached out to the thing. The spider's skin was cool and smooth. The voices coming from it grew louder and she could feel snatches of conversation pulse around her head.

"*Love you, honey,*" they were saying, and

"*Good luck today! I'm proud of you,*" and

"*Can't wait to see you tonight.*"

"*I love you.*"

"*I love you.*"

"*I love you.*"

Dozens of accents, male and female voices, all one on top of another, full of love and affection, thrummed around her skull. Beth felt her heart swell to them. Embarrassed warmth touched her ears and she realized she was smiling.

Dizziness washed over her and she felt like she would fall, but the spider extended a blade like limb to catch her. It pulled her closer into its abdomen—closer to the voices.

"*I love you,*" they whispered.

"Hey!" Fil rapped the spider sharply on its carapace with his railing. "None of that!"

The voices faded again to background noise and Beth's

head cleared. She shuddered. "What *was* that?" she breathed. The spider's leg sat cool as steel across her stomach. She pushed at it, but it didn't budge.

"Fil!" she protested.

"Overzealous little—" he muttered. He leaned right into the spider until their foreheads were touching. "Stow that, you little shite-picker. You get me?"

The thing buzzed static.

"Yeah, I'll *bet* you were just trying to relax her." He snorted. "Do that again and I'll 'relax' you: permanently. Onto the biggest bit of card I can lay my hands on."

The creature bent its forelegs, apparently in submission.

He looked up at Beth. "You okay?"

Beth met his gaze. Her heart was thundering and she felt like she was going to be sick, but all she could hear were his words, back at the bridge: *Is there any way you wouldn't be a liability?* She wouldn't show fear. "I'm fine."

Fil leaned close to the spider and whispered to it, and a forelimb coiled around him too. When he didn't struggle, Beth steadied herself. For an instant, she glimpsed her face, distorted in the curve of the spider's massive exoskeleton— and then the giant spider carried them away, scuttling up and over the phone lines at a speed that left her last breath stranded behind her in the air.

Houses, streets, factories, cars; all streaked past below them, distorted light and roaring, rushing noise. Filius, across from her, became grainy and faded away, and Beth felt her own body fizzing and saw her hand dissolve into pixels. She was breathless, but moment by moment she grew less afraid. The pulse of the spider soothed her.

All sense of motion dissipated. Time *changed*. The city lost definition, became dark and blurry. What was real, what was vivid, was the *web*: cables twisted between the shadowy buildings and ran underground, shining as they crisscrossed the urban darkness, alive with chattering voices.

A shape rose on the horizon: a slim steel tower, all blazing light and sound, rising from a hill in the south of the city. The strands of the web converged on it. It grew steadily, shining, blotting out the sky, burning her sight into nothingness. The murmur of a million conversations swelled to a roar—

—then there was blackness. The light was extinguished like a dowsed match; the voices were silenced. Beth lurched forward and caught herself on a metal banister. Chill air buffeted her and she groped around as her eyes adjusted to the gloom. She was up high.

Really high.

She was standing on a platform on a metal tower. It took her a second to recognize the interweaving metal struts of the Crystal Palace radio mast. The city, hundreds of feet below, glimmered like a firefly army in the darkness.

"I'm in Cryst—" She fought for breath and her skin tingled at the sheer lack of *anything* between her and the drop. "I'm in Crystal Palace Tower? That's—that's actually beautiful." Hysterical laughter bubbled out of her as she realized how far they'd come.

Spiders no bigger than you'd find in your house flickered in and out of existence all around her, crawling everywhere, fussing at bales of wire and satellite dishes with their sharp limbs. The spider that had carried them shivered and then splintered into hundreds of smaller eight-legged bodies, which quickly vanished into the teeming mass.

Beth shuddered at their skittering movements and the wagging of their tiny glassy heads. As her ears adjusted, the wind began to sound more and more like voices submerged in static: waves of crackling conversation.

Fil rubbed feeling back into his limbs. He peered upwards into the tower's upper reaches. "Stay here," he said. "She don't know you, and you won't wanna know her." He hesitated, his face pinched, worried-looking. "Be careful, right?" he said. "I got us an amnesty with the Motherweb for the chat, but the kids here"—he indicated the milling arachnids—"they can be a little *keen*. But they only eat voices, so keep your mouth shut and you should be fine."

He tested a strut with his bare foot, and then he began to scramble rapidly up the inside of the structure, as sure-footed as a spider himself, until he was lost to sight.

Beth hugged herself. A sense of freedom went through her like a chill. She thought of the people she knew in the city below, and she wondered if she'd ever see them again. *You were warned this could kill you, B,* she reminded herself. *You already said your goodbyes.*

She faltered. *B.* Why had she called herself that? Only one person ever addressed her with that kind of lazy familiarity. And then she was thinking of Pen, and there was an ache in her chest, a longing, a desperate desire to share this view, this sight that no one ever saw. She hurriedly shoved it down.

The height was making her queasy, so she turned to look inwards—and noticed the bundle. It was about five feet high and maybe three across: a bale of steel wires, hanging down from a strut above her like a fat metal wasp's nest. Something thin dangled from the bottom of it. She frowned and stepped in for a closer look.

It was a shoelace.

A tightness gripped Beth's chest and she became aware of the bundle's dimensions in a new and horrible way. She reached out and her fingertips brushed it, set it swinging in empty space.

The spiders chittered and ignored her.

Swearing softly, she grabbed the struts and began to climb towards the bundle. Her hand slipped on rainwater-slick steel and her stomach lurched, but she pulled herself tight to the metal again.

Easy, Beth, she admonished herself. *You've climbed worse than this to tag a bloody rooftop.*

As she drew level with the top of the bundle she saw a few strands of red hair poking between the wires, drifting like seaweed in the breeze. There were gaps between the metal threads and Beth made out a face: a girl, not much older than she was. The collar of her coat was street-stained. Cobwebs were matted over her eye sockets. A fat cable extruded from her mouth, and Beth almost gagged at the way her throat stretched around it.

Tinny voices bled into the air, as though leaking from the wires stuffed into the girl's ears:

We love you. Home, safe from harm. Safe. Never, never hurt you.

The red-headed girl's eyes were not quite shut and her eyelids flickered in time to their words.

They eat voices. Beth remembered Fil's words as the spider-calls swirled in the air. The cable in the girl's mouth flexed obscenely, as though milking the sound from her throat.

Beth reached out and grasped the cable. Everything became nightmare-slow as she pulled it free.

The girl's eyes snapped open. As the end of the cable left her mouth she screamed.

We love you we love you we love we love you we love you we love you we love we love you we love you...

The spiders turned instantly, order emerging from their chaotic motion. They swept over the metal in a glittering wave. Before Beth could even *think* they were crawling on her knuckles, through her hair, their needle-feet pricking her scalp and the skin over her breastbone. She lost control and shrieked, but a pair of pincer jaws pierced the skin of her throat and the sound dried up as though it had been siphoned off.

The spiders marched over her shoulders towards her ears. Beth could see them spinning out threads of wire from their abdomens. Their static voices swelled to fever-pitch.

We love you, we love you, we love you, we love you, we love you...

Their stolen words pulsed around her mind, suffocating her terror like morphine. Desperately, she tried to hold on to her fear, the true emotion, the only *sane* thing to feel, but she could feel it being drowned under the love of the spiders.

She waved her free arm desperately, slapping at them, crushing a handful, which vanished in a crackle of static.

We love you, the voices snapped viciously, *but you made everything worse.*

The thought pierced her like a lance. She sagged, dizzy and exhausted, against the metal. Her terror felt like a very distant thing now.

Something flickered in the air: a gray shape dropped through the tower's hollow core towards her. A bony arm took her hard in the gut and she plummeted, barely aware of herself, barely conscious of the fall.

Beth looked up in a daze to find Fil holding her. He was shouting at her, his face livid—

—but no sound came out of his mouth.

We love you, we love you, we love you, we love you: that was all she could hear. *Worse, worse, worse.*

He sprang from strut to strut, slowing their descent, Beth's body jolting at every impact until at last they tumbled into the wet grass at the tower's base.

He leaped to his feet and jabbed his finger at her angrily. At first there was no sound, then his voice began to crackle in his throat. "Thames and riverblood!" he swore. "When I said amnesty, I didn't mean you could go pulling the plug on their pissing *food supply!*"

Beth gaped at him. She rose, unsteadily, onto one knee. The spiders' voices were fading, giving way to nausea as the fright washed back. The red-headed girl's screaming face blotted out everything else in her mind. "There's someone," she gasped, "up there—"

"The ginger girl?" he said. "Yeah, I know. Thankfully, despite your clowning around, I think they've managed to reconnect her, so I've *probably* still got a deal with 'em."

"A *deal?*" Beth yelled at him, her terror sliding into fury. "How can you make *deals* with those things? We have to help her, she's a *prisoner!*"

"Is she?" His voice was a parody of shock. "Way I saw it, she didn't start screaming until you pulled her loose."

Beth was incredulous. She opened and closed her mouth a few times before she could find words. "You mean she wants to be there?"

"Why not? Her brain spends every minute sunk in love now, flooded with it. She used to be alone—they always are. That's how the Motherweb chooses 'em: finds 'em on the street, lost, lonely, cold, last bit of change in their hands to make their last phone calls to people who don't care. Their desperation's a kind of beacon to her: she homes in on it, and she offers them her choice."

"What happens if they change their mind?"

His face stiffened, but he didn't look away. "It's a one-off deal. The Pylon Spiders don't change *their* minds."

Suddenly Beth was seeing her dad, the teeming hive of his grief. She could imagine him weeping with gratitude as a team of spiders dragged a cable to his lips and stuffed his ears with their calming song.

"That's *crap*," she snapped. "It doesn't matter how bad it gets, how far down they are: people *heal*. You can't just let them bury themselves like that. You can't let those creatures offer them that choice. They're just taking bloody advantage! "

The Urchin Prince straightened slowly to his full height. His words burned with disdain. "Well," he said, "thanks be to Mater Viae that she sent us you to teach us the error of our ways."

He spat at the ground. "Why is it *you* who gets to decide how much people can take before they want out?" he asked. "Besides, even if you're right, what about the spiders? They're an entire species—you think they can't feel? And think? And bloody love? They can't eat nothing else, Beth; no matter how you or I might wish they could, they can't. They need a voice; they don't get it, they starve. That's not their fault, and it's not mine either, so you can stop looking at me like that." His voice was flat. "There's more lives at stake here than just the flesh-and-blood ones, the four-limbed ones, the ones that look *like you*. You'd better learn that, fast, or you'll kill our army before Reach even gets his cranes in gear."

Beth bit her lip and looked down. She could still hear the echoes of the spiders' sibilant stolen voices. *Everything worse.* Her mind felt dirty, scraped raw.

He stared at her with narrowed eyes. "What did they

say to you?" he said at last. "It wasn't just the usual love songs, was it? What else did they say?"

Beth bit her lip and refused to meet his gaze. She didn't answer. Dawn was breaking over the distant stubble of the city. He turned and stalked away from the tower without another word.

"Whose fault is it, then?" Beth called after him. "If it's not yours, and it's not theirs, whose fault is it that I'm those things' *prey*?" She leaned bitterly on the word.

He paused. "The one who made them that way," he said at last. "Mater Viae. My mother."

TWELVE

"I wondered if I might speak to Parva, please."

Pen glanced through her bedroom doorway. From her bed she could just make out the open front door downstairs, and a man with a Spam-pink bald spot standing on the top step.

"I am very sorry, sir," her mother said in her sing-song English. "She has been very ill. She has not been able to get out of bed."

Pen looked slowly around her room. She'd been stuck in here for three days now. It smelled like a hospital, and was starting to feel like one too. She'd taken to stashing the lamb samosas her mum had been bringing to her under the bed. "*Aap ki pasandeeda,*" Mum had said every time, "your favorite!" Pen's long-fought-for vegetarianism was dismissed in a stunning display of strategic amnesia now that she was trapped at home. She could smell the pastry and the fat in the meat congealing together into one artery-busting torpedo.

She hadn't read any poetry in days. (Her dad would smack her one if he ever found the copy of Donne stitched into her biology textbook. With typical awkwardness, he'd probably grasp just enough of the old-fashioned English to understand the dirty bits.) She was starting to feel genuinely ill.

"Could I ... could I possibly nip up and see her then? I wouldn't take ... " The man's voice tailed off. He sounded scared. Given the face that her mother was likely to be making to such a suggestion, Pen didn't blame him.

"Good*bye*." The door slammed hard.

Pen sat for a few moments, picking at the skin on her fingertips and on the palms of her hands. Her skin barely hurt anymore as it curled away like pencil sharpenings. The lower layer was shockingly pink against her normal tea color. Soon there would be no skin left that had touched anything the week before. Of course it would have rubbed off and become dust eventually anyway, but it made her feel a little better helping it along.

She heard the whine as the vacuum started up and above it, her mum singing contentedly to herself as she prosecuted her one-woman jihad against dirt. Pen's mum had wardrobes full of dresses still in their original plastic. "They are only new once, my sweetheart," she would cluck happily; "I am saving them for a special occasion."

That was exactly how Pen had felt when she'd come

home from school in the middle of the day claiming to feel sick, when her mother had welcomed her greedily, no questions asked, and tucked her up safe in bed: *Saved for a special occasion*. Sealed up like a dress in plastic, gathering dust.

Pen couldn't stop remembering Salt's office. There'd been a harsh disinfectant smell. Pen had sat there, rigid with terror. She'd expected him to shout, but of course he never did. Instead he'd read aloud from Beth's student file: the minor arrests for shoplifting and vandalism, the fights, the truancy. Her uniform was tatty, he said; he knew she sold paintings at Camden Market at the weekend; he suspected she sold cannabis at school every other day of the week.

Frostfield High had no record of Beth's father's occupation, he'd pointed out, and Mr. Bradley had never once been to a parents' evening.

"I can only conclude," he said with counterfeit regret, "that she's fending for herself. And then of course there's this little piece of vandalism you helped her perpetrate."

He'd brushed away Pen's protests with a wave of his hand. He *knew* it was Beth, of course he did, whether he could prove it or not. There was no one else it could have been.

"The Child Protection people will make their own assessment, of course," he said with grim satisfaction, "but I believe there's a solid case for rehoming your little friend."

It felt like he'd pulled a plug out of Pen's stomach. The midnight tagging, roaming around the streets, the access to the city, to the night: that *was* Beth. To shove her into some orphanage would end her.

Pen had thought: *She did this for you.*

"I don't want to do this, Parva," Salt had said, leaning forward so she could smell that morning's coffee on his breath, "but she's a terrible influence on you. It's your future she's wasting." He'd paused, as though the thought had just come to him, then said slowly, "I suppose if I saw genuine *commitment* from you to that future, a real willingness to change, I could put this away." He'd patted the folder.

Reluctantly, Pen met his eyes. They showed nothing but grave concern. He was taunting her, making her feel her powerlessness—showing her how *superb* at looking innocent he was.

"Twice a week, after school," he'd said softly. "This office. Extra maths. I'll help you out."

Pen had swallowed, her throat parched, and then again, until she finally found the strength to nod.

Salt's voice had hardened. "I want your little friend gone, Parva: that's non-negotiable. She can be gone from my school, or gone from her home. Those are your choices."

Then he'd smiled at her. "It'll be our secret," he'd said, and he'd leaned over the desk and kissed her on the lips.

Every muscle in her body clenched at the smell of the sweat in the folds of his neck, the scrape of his beard along her cheekbone. The hard points of his fingers had pushed down the small of her back and under the waistband of her underwear.

She didn't know if he wanted her because he fancied

her or because he knew how much it hurt her. She didn't know if there was any difference for someone like him.

Her heart shrank almost to nothingness at the thought of her mother finding out she wasn't *new* any more. What would become of the special occasion then?

Standing in the headmistress' office, Beth's wounded gaze burning a hole in her, Pen had wanted to shout, *Don't you dare hate me! I did this for you!*

But she couldn't. She'd just had to stand there and watch Beth turn away from her, her eyes full of betrayal. And now Beth did hate her, Pen knew she did, just when she needed her most.

She didn't want to need B. A tiny, spiteful, furious part of her heart hated her right back.

The breeze from the window tickled her neck. She went to shut it, and then stopped. The balding man was sitting in a battered car a few yards up the street. She stared out at him, but he made no move towards the ignition. He didn't look threatening. His shoulders were slumped, and he looked utterly defeated.

She bit her lip. "Mum," she called down in English, "I'm going to sleep for a bit. Could you ask Dad not to disturb me when he comes in?"

Her mum's assent floated back up the stairs. Parva shrugged off her dressing gown and pulled on her jeans and a T-shirt. She lifted her hijab from the faceless mannequin head by her mirror and wrapped it securely around her head.

What are you doing? a voice in her head asked. *He's a stranger, a strange MAN. It's not safe.*

Thoughts like that dogged her now, but she couldn't succumb to them. Beth wouldn't. Of course, *Beth* wouldn't have caved in to Salt. Pen despised that thought, but it was there, clinging to her mind like a leech: if only she could have been a little more like Beth, she would have been *safe.*

Pen arranged the pillows and the duvet, enough to fool a casual inspection, and switched off the light.

After days of staring at her bedroom ceiling, Pen found the day painfully bright, the sky strikingly blue. Her heart felt like a hummingbird caged behind her ribs. There weren't many people around, but still she flinched from those who walked too close. She tried to calm herself, and screwed up her courage, until at last she felt able to walk over and knock on the car window.

The man jumped and stared out at her and she immediately felt less afraid: there was no threat in his face. He had sagging cheeks. It looked like sleeplessness had sucked the weight off him.

The window whirred down. "Parva," he started uncertainly, and then, "Pen?"

Pen started at the name. She cocked her head sideways. "Who are you, mister?" she asked, although now she was sure she knew—he was only the second person to ever call her that.

"My name's Paul Bradley. I heard you were sick—thank you. Thank you for talking to me." He sounded pathetically grateful. And then he asked, "Have you seen my daughter?"

No; I haven't seen her, I'll probably never see her again—I don't care if I don't. I don't care if she drank her own spray paints, threw up a mural, and died, Pen thought, but what she said was, "What's happened to Beth?"

Mr. Bradley's forced smile fell away. "I was hoping *you* knew," he said. "Could we talk?"

"I can't go far," Pen said. "I told my parents I'm sick."

"Aren't you?" he sounded puzzled.

Pen considered it. "Yes," she replied, "but not in any way they can know about."

He pushed a button and the bolt on the passenger side of the car popped up. "We can talk in here if you like, since it's cold out."

Pen stopped dead, feeling herself freeze up. At the thought of getting into this man's car even her hair felt cold. She eyed the button he'd pushed, the locks on the doors, and gave a tight shake of her head.

"Okay," he said. "Where then?"

Pen pointed at a café across the street and crossed over before he had a chance to get out of the car.

Some indie band was playing over the café stereo. The espresso machine provided a whirring accompaniment. "Hey girl," the singer whined, "you got me in a whirl—"

And this'll be a hit, Pen thought, *even though it's sh—*

"No offence, Mr. Bradley, but Beth told me about your singing. She says your rubber duck's about the right audience for it."

"Oh, well—okay." He turned back to his car.

"Mr. B, wait!" She saw him stiffen, snared by the urgency in her voice. She was staring at her front door—or rather, the door*frame*. Tiny trains had been drawn around its edge, a trail that led away along the bottom of the wall like black breadcrumbs.

They followed it around the corner into a drab alleyway and peered closed at what had been painted onto the bricks.

"What's that supposed to—?" he started. "*Fractured harmony?* I don't—"

"I do," Pen said. She creased her stiff, sore hands into fists and then released them slowly. "I know what it means, Mr. Bradley. I've been there." She paused, and then found herself saying, "I'll show you."

"Who's that?" He pointed at the sketch of a skinny boy using a spear to pick his fingernails with a nonchalant air.

Pen shook her head. "Never seen anyone who looked anything like that," she admitted. "Tell you what though, if Beth's looking, she'll find him."

She dipped into her pocket, lifted out her phone, and snapped a photo of the boy. "And that means we need to find him too."

It was only on the way out of the alley that she saw her own face, daubed on the brick, and all the anger she'd been nursing towards her best friend changed into something else, something no less sharp, that caught in her throat.

"Gosh, is that you?" Mr. Bradley murmured. "It *is*—it *is* you. She did that from memory? Heavens, it looks just like you. I mean…" There was no mistaking the pride in his voice. Pen wondered if Beth had ever heard it.

"Yes, Mr. Bradley," she said, but it was hard to breathe. "She's very good."

THIRTEEN

It was morning: the daylamp's rays pouring into the bulb fell in rainbows, refracted by the glass. Voltaia shifted, the glow of her blood washed out by the surfeit of light. *Day.* Her eyes stung in the light. *Why am I awake?* The world outside was a seamless wall of glare. *Too early.* She shook herself and settled her head back onto her arms, feeling her consciousness ebb away.

The lamppost shook and her eyes snapped open again. It was too bright; she couldn't see anything, but she could *feel* vibrations coming through the metal. The filaments in her bones trembled. She started twitching and shifting, moving just enough to build up some magnetism, until she could stretch her fingers forward and push the field out, teasing the air.

Voltaia recoiled in horror; *something* was crawling up her lamppost. Her heart began to trip, faster and faster, until it was beating so quickly that even through the light of the daylamp she could see the yellow glow reflecting off the glass.

"*Lec!*" she strobed, but her elder sister had run away in disgust at the street boy's behavior and hadn't come back.

"*Galva! Faradi!*"

It was too bright, and she was blind. The daylamp was like a thousand furious Whities, battering on the glass. The lamppost jerked again, as though in the grip of a fit, and she flared off another distress call. *Useless*, she cursed herself; her sisters would be blind too. She could *feel* the tremors of the thing, whatever it was, dragging itself up the lamppost towards her. She shrank into the back of her shelter; wires pricked her skin.

A black shape smacked hard against the glass: a long, thin shadow studded with thorns. The whole bulb shuddered. The thing receded, moving nightmarishly slow, vanishing into the blur of light like ink being sucked out of water …

And smacked in again …

Voltaia tumbled backwards at the impact. The thin barbed shape vanished behind cracked glass and she braced herself, her lungs burning as she held her breath.

The thing struck again, and the lamp shattered.

Voltaia leapt from her home, falling for an instant, surrounded by a glittering rain of glass. Concrete drove the breath from her. She shoved herself to her feet, shaking off the impact and casting about. Everything was indistinct dark lines swamped by the glaring sun; *everything* looked like a monster, reaching for her. She fled to her left, towards Galvanica's lamp, probing through her fields, but she couldn't feel them. *She couldn't feel them.*

Calm down, she told herself, *calm down.* Her heart was beating so fast she was scared it might start to smoke.

"*Galv! Faradi!*" She knew they wouldn't see her cries in the light, but she couldn't stop herself calling for them. She reached into the space where Galvanica's post should have been and her fingertips groped empty air. She stumbled and fell onto something metal. Her hands trembled as she felt her way along it. It was twisted, pockmarked with dozens of tiny holes.

A cloud passed in front of the daylamp and suddenly she could *see*: she was holding Galvanica's post. It had been torn from the ground, leaving just a stump. The broken-off end was jagged and sharp. A glass girl was lying half-unfolded from the broken bulb, her light extinguished. Her nose and kneecaps were shattered and her skin was frosted with tinier cracks.

Voltaia stumbled towards her, barely noticing the pain as the shards of metal and broken bulb cut her feet. Her powdered blood spilled on the ground.

"*Galv—*"

As Voltaia approached, her sister's hair started to sway in the magnetic breeze she carried. It was a mean mockery of life.

Through her fields, she felt the metal of the thing behind her, and she turned. Its coils flew in fast, extinguishing the light.

FOURTEEN

I want to help you—I want to help you do more than just run.

Her words are like river silt, clogging up my ears. I look back at her arm, at the mark I gave her. City dirt has entered it; it will be a scar. It was meant to be a *scare,* but though she swore fancily at my clumsiness as I swabbed it with disinfectant and stitched it with a splinter of railway sleeper, she wears it patiently enough.

We weave through the crowds on Church Street. I'm ostentatiously invisible; people take pains not to look at me, I suppose because I look so much like the figures huddled in sleeping bags in doorways that they are also careful to ignore.

Is that how you're going to live up to your mother's legacy? Run?

It was an idiotic question, frankly. I can no more live up to my mother's legacy than I can wear her estuary-water skirts, or match her cruelty, or fill her Docklands throne with my bony arse. I'd be a laughingstock before I died.

Except now there are two of us laughingstocks: me and my idiotic, brave, scarred girl of a conscience. And that makes the odds against us half as bad. So here we are, entering the gates of a graveyard in Stoke Newington: a graveyard left to become a wilderness, and the last gathering ground for my mother's damned priesthood.

It was Beth's idea. "You're the son of a goddess, aren't you?" she said. "Doesn't your mum have a vicar or two to help us out?" It sounded so simple, so logical.

I'm going to have to talk very fast, and I'll try to sound confident, but the man I need to convince peddles bullshit by the steaming ton, so he knows it when he hears it. We plunge deep into the bracken, where the just-turning leaves filter the light gold. My tongue feels like a lead slug in my mouth. I'm desperately trying to work out what it is I'm going to *say*.

"A graveyard," Beth said flatly as Fil closed the gate behind them. Weeds had grown everywhere, making the railings more a hedge than anything. "Seriously? A graveyard?"

"What's wrong?" he said, tunnelling through the foliage. The growl of the traffic on the main road became muffled.

"Oh, nothing—having seen what you've got crawling around radio masts and lampposts, I can't bloody *wait* to see what you manage to pull out of a graveyard. If it's just ghosts and zombies I'm going to be sorely disappointed, Fil."

She was still in a temper after the spiders, and her feet were starting ache. They'd taken the long route from Crystal Palace to Stoke Newington to avoid the cranes that reared beside the main road in Dalston. Fil wouldn't go near them. Beth had never noticed them before and wondered idly when they'd appeared. They were sprouting like malign winter trees across the skyline.

She still hadn't seen Fil eat. In fact, she was starting to think he didn't. She'd ducked into a shop with a revolving sign and ordered food off a revolving spit—and now she was sheepishly readying herself for a revolving stomach. She'd offered to buy him a kebab too, but he'd politely declined. Last night, under the tower, his skin had been covered in oily sweat, but just walking barefoot over the tarmac seemed to revive him, as if he was drawing sustenance from the exhaust-heavy air. It suddenly struck Beth that the gray color on his skin wasn't dirt, it was *him*—and it was growing deeper the stronger he got. *He's feeding off the city*, she thought, *like a plant living off the sun*. She groped for a term and came up with "urbosynthesis."

The undergrowth gave way to a clearing filled with gravestones where life-sized statues stood sentinel. Granite monks stood side by side with scholars in stone togas. The Virgin Mary bent over her baby. Two marble angels wrapped their wings around one another as they kissed, and a statue of a blindfolded woman held a sword above a grave with the inscription, *John Archibald, justice. Hanged 1860.*

There were almost as many statues as headstones, arranged in a rough circle. A stone monk stood at the heart of the crowd, his heavy granite cowl shading his eyes. He held one finger in the air and his lips were carved slightly open, as though the sculptor had captured him telling a joke—a dirty one, judging by the lascivious twist to his mouth.

"Well." Fil gave a resigned sigh. "We're here."

"Where's here?" Beth asked. "Apart from the set for a bad vampire movie?"

"The garden of my mother's temple." A wry smile flickered across his lips. "Say hello, Beth."

"To who?"

"To your ghosts."

"What are you saying, Filius—that we're dead to you? I'm hurt."

Beth started. The voice was, well, *gravelly*—and it had come from the stone monk.

Fil bit his lip sheepishly and said, "Petris—I didn't recognize you." He looked at the statue. "Have you lost weight?"

"Indeed." The voice coming from the statue sounded parched. The monk's stone lips didn't move. "Off the face. Little vandals."

"Oh, a chisel job? I—I like it, very sleek. I makes you look ... " He tailed off, looking awkward.

"Yes?"

"Um ... "

The statue's sigh was like tumbling shale. "Clearly, *tact* wasn't one of the lessons I actually managed, by some Herculean effort, to hammer through your skull. Who's the young lady?"

The statue hadn't moved. Its stone eyes, behind their cataracts of moss, didn't twitch. But now Beth could feel it looking at her.

"Have you fallen foul of that lamp-lass' temper already, Filius?" the statue went on. "Or is the young prince sampling daytime delights as well now?" His tone was heavy with innuendo.

"She's just a friend, Petris," Fil said, "and I can't imagine how I failed to learn tact from someone as well-versed in sticking his nose in as you are."

"Alas, if only I still had a whole nose to stick in," Petris said mournfully.

"Yeah," said Fil, "you ugly bastard." He stepped forward and threw his skinny arms around the statue. Beth half expected the granite arms to enfold the boy, but they remained fixed in place as he hung around the stone monk's neck with his legs kicking in the air.

A grating laugh issued from the statue's mouth.

"Beth," Fil said, "this is Petris. He taught me nearly every dirty trick I know."

"Er ... pleasure." Beth looked quizzically at the statue. "I thought you said your teacher was called Gutter-something?"

"Gutterglass. Different teachers for different things. You get a lot of tutors when you're royalty. Glas was like an uncle to me, and an aunt, and she did a bang-up job. This filthy old priest here"—he jabbed a thumb over his shoulder at the statue—"was responsible for my—uh—*moral* education."

"I did my best to show you the difference between right and wrong," Petris said grandly.

"And 'wrong' you thought best shown by example."

The statue spluttered, and Beth could see little flecks of saliva wetting the stone around its mouth. "That's not fair, Filius."

"No? That garbage gin nearly killed me."

"You were a damn sight more interested in that than nineteenth-century gas-lamp theodicies," the stone monk said snippily. "I was merely doing what any good teacher would and linking the lesson to what you knew." His tone grew conspiratorial. "Can you honestly tell me you didn't have a religious experience with that magnetic massage I taught you? If you didn't, then your electric girlfriend certainly would have."

Fil laughed, but he blushed a little too. "Admit it, you were a terrible influence."

"Maybe, but a superb taker of confession. You never held anything back."

"There was no point! You were there with me while I was sinning!"

"I just teach the rules, Filius; I never claimed to be good at following them." A coughing sound came from the statue's immobile mouth and little clouds of powdery gray dust puffed out in front of his lips.

Fil winced, but said nothing.

"Anyway," Petris said when the coughing fit had subsided, "not that it isn't marvelous to see you, you little terror, but why in Thames' name are you here now? I haven't had word of you in months."

Behind his back, Fil had both hands on the haft of his railing. His grubby thumbs started to rub over one another. "I—" He glanced back over his shoulder at Beth. "*We* need your help."

Petris' laughter drained away. Any motion was far too small to see, but Beth was positive she felt all the statues in the clearing shift a tiny bit closer.

"Really?" Petris' tone was mild. "Do tell. What could a humble Pavement Priest do for the Son of the Streets?"

Fil looked straight at the statue's birdshit-speckled eyes. "Fight for his mother again."

Everything in the clearing froze. They weren't simply still—they'd been *still* before—but now every human-shaped hunk of stone seemed to emit a tangible chill.

"Well, what a request," Petris said slowly. His voice

was very quiet. "Filius, you know I'd need a heart of stone to refuse you anything, but—"

Beth snorted.

Fil looked up at her sharply and she felt Petris doing the same.

"Sorry," she said. "Don't mind me."

"Yes?" the statue said.

"Oh," she stumbled, "nothing, it's just it was funny. "Heart of stone." What with you being a—"

Alarm flashed across Fil's features and he shook his head curtly. She broke off, flustered by the sudden, intense quiet.

"Yes?" Petris said again, with the slightest edge to his voice.

"Nothing."

Another dry-shale sigh. "Come here, child."

Fil protested. "Petris, no—she didn't mean—"

"Keep your trousers on, Filius. I'm not going to hurt her. I merely think that she deserves to know which side she's picked."

Fil looked at the statue in chagrin for a moment, then hung his head. "Yeah, all right," he said quietly. He looked at Beth. "Go on."

Beth walked hesitantly towards Petris, gooseflesh rippling over her.

The Pavement Priest's brow and cowl had calcified together to a scabrous white. Beth could see what Fil had called *a chisel job*: a chunk of Petris' nose and right cheek had been sheared off. As she got closer, she could make out two tiny pinhead holes at the center of the glittering granite eyes.

"Closer." Beth stared into those holes; she thought she saw something blink. She found her heart hammering.

"Closer." His breath was stony dust.

She stopped an inch in front of his face. The statue's mouth was half an inch ajar, and inside it ...

Inside it she saw flesh lips, pink, parched, and peeling. They moved to shape the words as Petris whispered, "Did no one ever teach you that it's what's inside that counts?"

"How did you get in there?" she breathed.

"I was born here!" Petris announced grandly. "All the Pavement Priests are, for our sins: caged since squalling infancy in our punishment-skins."

Inside the granite eyes there was a flicker of motion towards Fil. "His mother is not as merciful as she might be."

Beth's brow furrowed. Her hackles had risen instinctively at the word *punishment*. "That doesn't make any sense. How can you be punished before you're born? What could you've done by then?"

"Petty crimes, I dare say, and dreadful ones too. Crimes to give a little girl nightmares," Petris said, a mica-like glint in his eye. "I didn't say this was the *first* time we'd been born, did I? We sinned in lives past, but Mater Viae felt that it would be *unsporting* to let us snuff it before our debt to her was paid. So she sold our deaths out from under us, right out of our still-warm corpses."

A grumble of assent went around the circle. Beth stared at them, imagining the pale bodies that had never seen sunlight, born entombed inside these stone figures. She wanted to ask how, but she knew she wouldn't understand. And, in the end, what did "how" matter anyway? Instead she asked, "Who'd buy a death?"

A hush fell on the clearing again, and Petris' lip curled. "In London? Only gentlemen of the most questionable tastes, I assure you. There are ... *collectors*."

"Conjurors," another voice put in, coming from inside a marble scholar.

"Con men."

"Cun—" Lady Justice began, but someone shushed her.

"The Chemical Synod, they call themselves. Our deaths are now ingredients in their stores." Petris' voice was bitter with contempt. "They are traders, bargainers, barterers."

"Bastards," Lady Justice spat, and this time no one stopped her. "Complete and utter *bastards*."

"They'll make anything a commodity," Petris growled. "Height, gravity, heartbreak—but *death*, oh, death they prize most highly, because with our deaths sitting ready in their larders, they can exchange each for another, and so *kill* any enemy they choose."

He sighed. "Of course, there is one small matter, a tragedy if you will, of afterthought. *Without* our deaths, we can't die. So we are reborn, into the stone, over and over again." Petris spoke with a self-deprecating dryness, but Beth could clearly hear the bitter note.

"You *want* to die?" she asked.

"Of course. Don't you?"

"Not that you'd know it from the fact I'm tailing his scrawny highness here around, but not really, no."

"I mean eventually," Petris said, as though this was obvious. "How old are you? Twenty? Thirty?"

"Sixteen."

"*Sixteen?*" He sounded surprised. "Great Thames, now I feel really ancient. Well, believe me when I say that you cannot imagine, with your sixteen birthdays, what it's like to be me, waking up again and again, morning after morning, when you've already done all you ever wanted to do, and seen all you ever wanted to see. My life had a beginning, but it has no end to give it shape. That's what our goddess took from us in payment for our sins: the outlines, the boundaries, the very *definition* of a life."

He took a deep breath, and then erupted into another coughing fit. "So," he said when he'd recovered, "when Filius here asks us to come and fight for her—and believe me, if there's anything this old priest does better than drink and fornicate, it's fight—well, there we have a little bit of a problem, because the infinity she has condemned us to is rather easier to tolerate without her actually around."

The other statues—no, not statues, *Pavement Priests*— were moving now. Stone ground against stone as, agonizingly, almost invisibly slowly, they drew closer around her. She felt her bones shiver and her muscles charged with the urge to run, but she held herself firm, even as their shadows crept over the sunlit grass. Wheezing breaths reached her ears over the churning rock. She marveled at the effort it must take to move that weight.

"Your scrawny friend here is asking us to be slaves again," Petris whispered darkly into her ear. "And while I love him, and I do sincerely love him, I don't love him that much."

She didn't know how he'd got so close. She shivered as his musty breath stroked her cheek.

"You're already slaves," Fil called.

Beth twisted around.

"You've sharp ears, boy," Petris grunted.

"Yeah, well, I'm a lot less drunk then I was the last time you saw me."

"So am I. Perhaps if you'd got me more so, I'd be more inclined to listen to your drivel. What did you just say?"

"I said, you're *already* slaves." He placed his spear-butt on Petris' chest. "'Cause while she's not here, you can't pay her back—the only way you'll get your freedom is in her service, and you know it. So here's the deal. Fight for me, and she'll free you when she returns."

The motion of the statues stopped.

Petris laughed. "Out of interest," he said, "it's hardly relevant, I know, but indulge an old man's curiosity. Have you ever commanded an army before, Filius?"

"Nope," he admitted cheerfully.

"Do you have even a basic grasp of strategy, tactics, supply chains, logistics?"

"Nope."

"And have you ever met your mother, the vengeful and—lest we forget—*jealous* goddess, on whose behalf you have elected to start making extravagant promises?"

"No."

"Well then, I can find no fault in your strategy." Petris' voice was as flat as slate. "That all sounds marvelous."

Fil hissed impatiently and rapped his knuckles on Petris' cowl. "Well, how's your current plan working? Shuffling around your old haunts in your stone pyjamas, hoping she doesn't come knocking on your mausoleum door? You're in limbo, Petris. I'm offering you an out."

He showed the inside of his wrist to the statue: the crown of tower blocks. He tapped his spear-head against the arm of Petris' robe and a fine filigree of cracks appeared. The stone flaked away, giving off a smell like damp caverns. A few inches of flesh were exposed, white as paper. A Tower Block Tattoo could be seen there, too.

"Please, old man," Fil said quietly. "I need your help."

A sound interrupted them, a high-pitched wail of distress. Beth wrenched her eyes away from them, looking for the source of the noise. It was the choking, snotty, unmistakable squeal of a baby. It was coming from the stone bundle cradled in the Virgin Mary's arms.

"Oh!" the Virgin said, sounding surprised. "Oh, hush now, shhhh shhhhh." There was a desperate note to her voice, almost as if she had been unaware of the child until it started crying. "Hush now, shhhhsh, shhhhhsh."

"A newborn," Petris murmured sadly, and his neck churned against itself as he turned his face away from Fil.

The baby's crying was joined by the dirge of stone on stone, cracks emerging and as quickly resealing as the other statues moved, planting their heavy feet with care.

Beth noticed that Petris' wrist had sealed over with fresh granite.

"There now…"

"It's all right, we'll take care of you."

"Are you thirsty?"

The statues clustered around the child, cooing in soothing granite tones. One of the angels crooked its wing, a tiny movement, allowing rainwater that had collected in the grooves of its feathers to trickle into the baby's mouth.

Beth looked at them. Though the blank stone figures hadn't turned towards them, she could feel the hostility emanating from them all: hostility to them, to their offer, and to the goddess they were there representing.

"Filius." Petris didn't turn away from the baby. "I'm sorry. We may have only a few inches of freedom inside the stone, but they're inches we need to protect. I don't trust her, and I don't trust you to speak for her. The answer's no."

Fil looked dejected. He turned to go, and as he walked past, he ran his fingertips over the baby's head. The limestone crumbled away and he bent down and kissed the exposed skin. His lips came up sticky with afterbirth.

The baby didn't stop crying, and as Beth followed him through the soaking bracken she heard the stone reforming over the child's head.

FIFTEEN

Beth followed Fil around the crumbling corners of East London, though he was half-dazed and there was no logic to their path that she could see. They weaved through narrow alleys and doubled back through dead-end mews. Every step carried Beth further from the city she knew.

The architecture grew darker, stranger: a heavily graffitied old cinema building, its neon sign long-dead and its doors shuttered; an electricity substation half-hidden behind a cloud of razor-wire; and everywhere, the cranes massed on the skyline like cruel sentinels.

By sunset they'd reached Limehouse. Beth slumped down inside a railway arch, exhausted, but her guide was still twitchy. He cocked his head as though listening for something, then he swore and leaped to his feet again. He dragged her away from the railway and finally let her settle in a narrow alleyway behind some bins.

She watched him for a while, resting her chin on her forearms. She was following him unquestioningly, she realized with a jolt; could she really trust him enough for that? This boy who consorted with giant spiders and served a goddess who entombed people alive for eternity: how could *this* be her side? And yet she was sticking as loyally by as Pen always had to her.

Pen. Beth sighed. She would have trusted Pen to know if this was the right side; Pen had always been her compass.

She curled up against the wall, suddenly realizing how much she wanted to see her friend again, to say sorry for whatever it was she'd done, to make it all right again.

She slept, and her dreams were full of tiny stone tombs.

———

When Beth awoke, Fil was gone. Anxiety stung her for a second, but she swallowed it down; she didn't believe he would have left her. For all his protests, all his strength and strangeness, she thought he wanted her there. She smiled briefly, surprised by how much she enjoyed that thought.

Graffiti tangled over the wall, but there was nothing interesting, only messy, graceless tags. Beth had no time for signatures like that. Bricks were a journal for her, not a megaphone; she didn't paint to shout about her impact on the city but to show the city's impact on her.

She dug some chalks out of her backpack.

Hazy yellows brought her sketched-in streetlamp girls alive, echoing their coronae of light. Beth smirked a little and added a bit more meat to the lippy one's backside.

She drew Petris on the opposite wall, installing him in a blurry shadow-garden of gravestones and weeds. Something snagged her attention: she'd drawn an emotion onto the stone face without even meaning to. Anger. The gaze that came back off the bricks was accusatory.

"You know," said a voice behind her, "I think he could look a little *more* pissed off, if you really worked at it. I mean, I know he wants to kill himself, but that's pretty much an occupational hazard for a Pavement Priest. He's properly cheerful when you get to know him." Fil stood at her shoulder, gazing intently at her picture. His approach had been soundless. "Otherwise, it's not bad. You should do me some time." He grinned and struck a pose with his railing, flexing his scrawny arms.

"I already did, once," Beth told him.

"Yeah? Where? How did I look?"

"Like you were cobbled together from old skin and pipe cleaners. It was pretty true-to-life."

He looked a little crestfallen. "Like you were with Electra?" He pointed at the painting of the streetlamp girls. "She'd dance a duel with you if she saw that."

"At least you can recognize her. This isn't as easy as it looks, you know. 'Sides…" Beth put a slight edge in her tone. "It's what's inside that counts."

Fil's grin vanished as he recognized the quote. He

slumped against a wall. "What is it, Beth?"he asked plaintively. "What it is you've been wanting to say?"

Beth sat beside him, feeling the bricks graze her spine. She opened her mouth three times before concluding there was no tactful way to put this. "Look, it's like this. You're all right—I mean, I like you. I owe you." She hesitated. "And I trust you, too. But this mum—this *goddess* of yours? Her, I'm not so sure about."

"What are you talking about?" he said. "Mater Viae's my blood; we're the same."

"Are you?" Beth asked. "Would you have made Pylon Spiders that had to prey on people? Would you have done *that*?" She pointed at her painting of Petris. "Really? You would've buried them alive?"

"They are guilty of the crimes they're being punished for—"

"That's not what I asked."

He was silent.

"There was a *kid* there, Filius!"

"Yeah, well, he'd lived other lives before this one—so has Petris. Neither of them are pure as the rainwashed marble, know what I mean? They know what they've done, even if you don't. *Look.*" He twisted to face her and his gaze was fierce. "Reach is a monster. Maybe my mother is too, but at least she kept him in check."

Beth was about to protest, but he just stared the words right back down her throat.

"What?" he demanded. "What is it you think you can say to me? You've met Mater Viae's priesthood one time and now you're some kind of expert? You wanna see the alternative? 'Cause Reach has a priestess too: the Wire Mistress, we call her. *The Demolition Clergy.*" He snorted. "She's a parasite: a barbed-wire fluke. She kidnaps whole families, for convenience, to use as hosts. She takes them one by one, the oldest first, always saving the ones with the most legs in 'em for later. And so the kids get to see their possessed mums and dads rip their own bodies to shreds." Anger tinted his cheeks basalt-black. "They're kids too, Beth. This is *war*, and there are kids everywhere."

The anger ran out of him and he slumped down. "*Do more than run.* That's what you told me. This is me trying, all right? So if you trust me like you say you do, if you believe in me, then believe in Mater Viae, like I—like I have to, 'cause for me it's not *faith*. It's *family*."

The car horns and train rattles and distant shouts that passed for silence outside in the city reigned for a moment.

Beth's heart clenched, but she had to say it. "I do believe in her, Fil, but I don't know if I like what I believe."

Fil stared at the ground. She couldn't tell if he was ashamed or angry. Then he stood up and seized his spear. "Come on."

Beth stuffed her chalks into her backpack. "Where are we going now?"

He was already at the mouth of the alley, silhouetted in pizza-shop neon. "To show you what we're up against."

———

The street was empty. Black spaces gaped in the terraced houses where windows should have been. A hundred yards back, traffic spilled light and noise down the Woolwich Road, but neither penetrated as far as these pavements. Beth read the sign: *Herringbone Way*. It felt like a street in exile, like London had forgotten about it.

Fil stalked in front of her. He'd led her on a perilous route, tiptoeing like a nighttime acrobat over brick viaducts. In his temper, he'd even crept right through the shadow of one of the cranes which frightened him so much.

He was acting up; it was obvious. *She* did it, for God's sake, so she recognized it in him. He was like a little kid sneaking towards a haunted house, everything about him screaming, *See? I'm not scared! I'm bloody not, and you can't prove I am!*

Of course, if he was posturing, then what was she doing, shinning awkwardly up rain-slicked drainpipes like the risk of shattering her bones into splinters hadn't even occurred to her.

"Oi!" His voice drifted down from above her. "Up here." He was squatting in a glassless first-floor window frame, black against slightly paler black. A fast blink earlier, he'd been on thc pavement.

"Coming?" he enquired. He gave his forelock a mock tug, took a step backwards, and dropped out of sight.

Beth couldn't help but smile. "Show off," she muttered.

Two grazed elbows and a lot of choice curses later, she

hit the ground on the other side. "Damn it, Phyllis, why can't you use a front door? Ow!"

She straightened slowly, taking it all in.

The terrace was a façade. The street-facing wall still stood, but it was a brick veil concealing the ugliness of the demolition site behind, where *everything* had been torn down. Dominating the space was a corkscrew drill rising fifty feet into the air, and collapsed at the drill's caterpillar-tracked base, rust-eaten and magnificent...

...was a crane.

An uncomfortable tension pricked under Beth's ribs as she walked towards it. The crane exuded a kind of dormant menace, like an unexploded bomb. Fil sat on a slab on the far side of the waste ground, watching her carefully.

"I don't get it," Beth said. She laid a hand on the crane's pitted metal. "These must have cost a fuck-load, but they look like they've been here for decades. Why didn't the owner take them back?"

Fil's voice echoed back off the derelict house-fronts. "The owner was in kind of a hurry to go. A crusading army whose one and only commandment is to rip your guts out will have that effect, know what I'm saying?"

"Not even remotely."

"You'll see," he promised her. His tone was oddly solemn. "Look, Beth. Look around you and you'll see."

Dutifully Beth looked, but in the darkness the heaps and valleys of rubble were just so much crenellated shadow. She frowned and rummaged in her bag for her torch.

"No!" His shout froze her. His eyes were pale in the

night. "We don't bring light here, Beth. Not ever. Out of respect."

Beth muttered imprecations under her breath but she dropped her torch back into the bag. She squatted and brushed the dirt off a jagged hunk of brickwork. She thought she could see some kind shape on it, but it was vague in the darkness, just a shadow of a shadow. She strained her eyes, trying to see it better until, bit by bit, it became more defined.

What are—? she wondered. And then she realized what she was looking at. And her shocked cry pierced the night.

Staring vacantly out at her was a face, rippling the surface of the masonry like a brickwork fossil. Through busted mortar teeth it screamed silently back.

Beth recoiled and turned away, but it was too late; her eyes had adjusted, and the bodies—

The bodies were everywhere.

They were withered like mummies, with stark ribs protruding from the surfaces of the broken brickwork. She could even see the outlines of blood vessels where limbs had been sheared away.

She cupped her hands over her mouth as if trying to catch the tiny noises of distress coming out of it. Her eye was drawn to one figure hunched over, hugging its knees. Eyes and mouth gaped wide between its legs. Its neck was utterly broken.

Beth reeled. She tripped and sprawled, her hands clutching dead things, and she yanked them away and curled them into fists. She shrank into a fetal ball and lay there amongst the brick corpses, gasping for breath.

And then he was there, hugging her, as she whispered, "*Who*—?" She could barely speak. The dust of the rubble sat in her lungs like blood. "Who are they?"

"Women in the Walls and Masonry Men," he said sadly. "They're just people, Beth: people who made their homes here."

Women in the walls. Beth couldn't help but imagine the huddled figure trying to flee, turning and turning and turning in panic as the wrecking balls crushed it and crushed it again, into an ever-smaller fragment of brick.

Slowly her body unclenched and she made herself look. A fat bore-hole blossomed from a boy's chest, the ribs splintered around the edges. She looked at the drill and knew it was the murder weapon.

"*What is this place?*"

When he answered, the shakiness in Fil's voice told Beth that he'd been here many times, and that it never got any easier. "We call them Demolition Fields. In the last war, this was the furthest Reach got from St Paul's. It's..." He hesitated. "It's also the smallest. There are others, closer to where we started, but...I brought you here because it's the easiest one to take."

Beth turned on him, her eyes gritty in her skull. "*Why?*"

"You needed to understand," he said sadly. "You needed to *get it*. He is murderous, Beth: he's the city's own greed, killing itself in its haste to grow. He's reborn, generation after generation, and every time he comes back stronger, like a cancer, and we get weaker. I needed you to realize that all those pretty little towers he builds out of glass and steel"—he spread his arms over the mass grave—"it's all built on that." His gaze was open, his voice pleading.

And then Beth understood why he kept coming back here: it reminded him of who he was. Despite his hunts and his streetlamp dances and his scrambling runs across the night-city, he knew this was what he'd have to face in the end.

And he needs your help to face it, Bradley, so get up off your arse.

Beth stood up unsteadily, shrugging off his attempts to help her. Horror made her giddy—she felt like a ghost drifting over the broken dead. There was nowhere to step that was not on them. Something cowardly in her wanted them to recede into the rubble, to disappear; she herself wanted to close her eyes and forget she'd ever seen this. She shoved the impulse angrily aside and instead forced herself to look at the bodies curled around their children, because inadequate though it was, it was both the least and all she could do.

"How did you do it before?" she demanded harshly. Her anger was mounting; there was a corrosive feeling in her gut. "How did you kill Reach before?"

He barked a short laugh. "*Kill* him? Mostly we try and make sure he kills *us* a little slower."

Beth glared at him and his forced humor fell away. "All right," he said. "So, once, my mother almost snuffed

Reach for good: she burned him with a fire hotter than—well, than *anything*. The Great Fire, we called it."

There was a moment while Beth took this in, then, "*The* Great Fire?" she asked incredulously. "Of London? That was your mother? That was—? Jesus Christ, that was a *weapon*?"

Fil's answer was a sing-song nursery rhyme: "London's burning, London's burning; pour on water, pour on water. Fire, fire; fire, fire: wash the blood of the streets from Pudding Lane." He smiled bleakly. "September, 1666: the baker's shop was her tinderbox, but the fuel was all hers. Yeah, Beth, it was a weapon—her greatest weapon; some'd say her greatest *power*, because sometimes it's the power to destroy that keeps all the other powers safe."

He raised his chin proudly. "The city burned for three days and nights, but not one hair on a human child was harmed. Remember that, next time you call my mother a monster. Gutterglass said that for the longest time they thought Reach had gone. But deep underground, some germ of him must've remained."

The anger was in Beth's mouth now, making her want to spit it, but where did it come from? She didn't know these people in the bricks; she hadn't even known there *were* people like this, so why was she trembling with an urge to avenge them?

The answer came to her fast, borne on a wave of fury: these were her streets; London was her place; and if it had a people, then they were *her* people. The city was alive, and she'd always known that, inside.

She hadn't run away from home. *This* was her home: her home, her people.

Her people, her fight.

She looked at Fil. His face reflected the same anger back to her.

"We should go," Beth said quietly. "We've got an army to rally."

He looked at her gratefully, then the gratitude on his face gave way to an expression Beth recognized, though it looked out of place on his cocky face. It was the same look Pen used to have before she followed Beth on some stupid stunt: an appeal for courage. *Please*, it said, *make me brave enough for this.*

Then he was off, scrambling hand over hand up the length of the dead drill until he was standing precariously on the hydraulics at its summit, a skinny shadow swaying against the clouds.

"Reach!" he yelled, wild and inarticulate. He shouted his defiance across the sleeping city, to the cranes on the dark horizon, repeating over and over, "Reach! *Reach!*"

At last he climbed down and staggered over to her, his eyes wide, and she folded him up in her arms and held him tight until he stopped shaking.

SIXTEEN

"So, where to now, guv?" Beth perched on a doorstep and ripped open the grease-proof paper on her bacon sandwich. The smell of bacon and hot melting butter drifted into the chilly air.

A few hours after leaving the Demolition Fields, Beth found that she could no longer remember exactly how it had felt to be there. In fact, she couldn't feel anything much at all: it was as though her emotions had blown a fuse and shut down, leaving just a basic awareness of her own body, the cold, the pressure in her bladder, the ache of tired muscles...

Beth took a big bite. Suddenly she was ravenously hungry. "You want a bit of this?" she mumbled around the mouthful of bread and bacon.

Fil declined with a smirk. "Don't need it."

Beth swallowed. "Oh yeah, your weird synthesis thing. Don't you ever just eat? You know, 'cause it tastes good?"

"Sure, a good bit of tarmac-cake or a few petrolberries, when I get time. Nothing like *that*." He eyed Beth's sandwich with a mix of curiosity and intense distrust. "Speakin' of which, what time is it?" he asked.

She glanced at her G-Shock. "It's 6:23 in the a.m."

"Then we can relax; the people we're going to see won't be up for a bit."

Darkness still covered the street behind Waterloo Station where they sat, but besuited office workers bustled to and fro. The news kiosks were manned and the headlines fresh. Cars and buses hissed over the asphalt.

"What I don't get," Beth said, "is why you think we're going to have trouble getting people on our side. I mean, Reach is blatantly dangerous, so why aren't your mum's worshipers queuing 'round the block to have him got rid of?"

He looked at her like she was a prize-winning idiot. "You're kidding, right? *Because* he's blatantly dangerous. We've never had to do anything like this before. Mater Viae always gathered the army, and she always led it herself, before Reach grew too strong to kill." He looked grim. "My mother's left us right in the lurch. With her around, people got scared, and so they acted. *Without* her, they get scared and pretend it's not their problem. They draw boundaries. 'Let Reach stay in the Square Mile,' they say, 'and we'll live and let live.' And when he breaks those borders, they give him new ones: north of the river, east of the park, stuff like that."

He picked dirt from under his fingernails and flicked it absentmindedly at a nearby pigeon. "And the longer they leave it, the stronger Reach gets, and the stronger he gets, the scareder *they* get, and so they leave it even longer. It's a vicious cycle. Stupid, but that's how it works."

Well, this is a carnival of bloody optimism, Beth thought. "But those people," she insisted, "those people, from last night—the men and women in the walls. Don't they have friends, families?"

"Sure they do," Fil sighed, "but for every man or woman demanding vengeance for their murdered brother, there're three more who'll curl up in a corner and beg you not to hurt them too."

He squirmed under Beth's appalled gaze. "Don't look at me like that," he said. "I don't know which way I'd go myself yet. And despite what you're thinking, I bet you don't either."

Beth wondered what had happened to the brash kid who'd declared, *I'm the most dangerous thing on the street.* He was sloughing off layers of bravado at a rate that frightened her.

When sunlight began to spear from behind the horizon's taller buildings, he stretched and slung his spear over his shoulder. "Come on, finish your munching. We need to get moving."

They threaded through the early morning crowds. A few people looked askance at the pavement-skinned teenager, shirtless in the cold, but only a few—after all, if you didn't inspect him too closely, there were dozens of weirder performers working London's streets.

They ducked off the main drag and hopped a fence with a diamond-shaped yellow sign warning *High Voltage: Danger of Death*. Fil climbed up a fire escape onto a roof and walked towards a pair of towering pipes that were belching out air-conditioning vapor. He leaned on the nearest pipe and paused, pursing his lips in thought. "Okay, Beth," he said, "the people we're about to meet are uppity, arrogant, and excruciatingly bloody irritating. I.e. they're nobility. I'm warning you in advance, because we have to be polite to 'em, and because—"

"Because I have a big mouth?"

He nodded emphatically.

"Okay," Beth said, "but I don't know what you're worried about. I *can* control myself, you know. Just now, when you said 'arrogant, uppity, and irritating,' I didn't say a word about pots, kettles, and being bla—"

He gave her a playful shove. "Walk. And take off your watch, I don't want the glass reflecting somebody's eyeball and causing a diplomatic incident."

Beth considered asking him what on earth he was talking about, but she was rapidly giving that particular question up as a waste of breath. She slipped the G-Shock into her pocket.

When they rounded the pipes they were confronted by a rectangular shape draped in black fabric, about the height and width of a shipping container. He yanked away the cloth to reveal a frameless slab of mirrored glass.

Beth studied her own reflection in the mirror. She'd lost weight in the two days she'd been on the streets. Her cheekbones jutted out now, and her skin was dirty. She looked rough, sleep-deprived.

"Did you put this here?"

"It had to be out of the way so they wouldn't hurt anybody."

"*Who* wouldn't?" Beth tried not to sound exasperated, but she did wish, just once, he'd give her a plain answer.

"You'll see." He stood a little straighter and tapped on the glass three times with the butt of his railing. "His Highness Filius Viae, Son of the Streets, Prince Ascendant of London, Heir and Protector to all her colonies," he intoned formally, "requests and requires an audience with the Seven Senators of the Most Noble Order of the Silvered Glass."

Beth leaned into him. "Nice title," she whispered.

"Yeah, the Mirrorstocracy love all that pomp and circumstance stuff."

"What, and you don't?"

They exchanged a long look, and he blushed.

"I believe that's what they call 'busted,' your Highness," Beth murmured.

"Hush."

They waited. Birds cawed overhead, but nothing else happened. Fil rapped on the mirror again. "His Highness, Filius—" he began again, but this time he was interrupted by a stuffy voice that sounded like its owner had spent about a century gargling dust.

"Very well, very well—no need to hurry. How very uncouth."

In the mirror Beth saw a stooped old man walk onto the roof. He appeared from the reflection's edge, as though he'd been lurking behind them, just out of sight. He approached until he stood right between mirror-Beth and mirror-Fil.

A shiver went up Beth's spine. A glance sideways confirmed what she already knew: there *was* no old man beside her. He existed only in the reflection.

"*Harrumph,*" said the old man. He was dressed in a purple uniform with gold piping and a beret and looked like a cross between a brigadier and an incredibly ancient bellboy.

He peered doubtfully out of the mirror at them. "You don't *look* much like a Prince Ascendant," he said. He plucked distastefully at the jeans of Fil's reflection and Beth was faintly appalled to see his *real* jeans ripple, just as if they'd been pinched by invisible fingers.

Fil cocked an eyebrow. "You don't look much like the Seven Senators of the Silvered Glass, so I reckon that makes us even."

"How very uncouth. I am the Senate's *agent-de-porte.* Anything you wish to say to them, you may say to me," the reflection of the old man declared haughtily. "I shall raise your petition with them at their earliest convenience."

"We need to see them now."

Wispy gray hairs jutted from the reflected man's chin as he stuck it out. "No," he said. And then he harrumphed again, and repeated, "How *very* uncouth."

While Fil hesitated, trying to think of some way to claw back the initiative, Beth stepped forward, mentally trying to calculate the consequences of pissing off the gnarled bellboy before deciding she didn't care anyway.

She cleared her throat noisily. "Right you are, Doorkeep," she said, in the most offensively chirpy tone she could manage. "Then when you've got a minute, you can tell the Senators that their goddess' son is outside—tell them he looks like he sleeps in a storm drain; they'll know it's him—and that he would very much appreciate it if they would get off their stuck-up, inbred backsides and come to the door so he can get on with the serious business of waging war against a maniac crane-toting god."

She waited until the reflected face of the *agent-de-porte* had gone milky pale before adding, "Do you think their earliest convenience might be *soon?*"

The Doorkeep hustled back out of the side of the reflection.

Fil let out his breath explosively. "*Beth!*"

"Fil."

"What happened to *polite?*"

Beth shrugged. "He was pissing me off. Besides, uppity bouncers are the same everywhere, Puffa jacket or tux, makes no odds. Give 'em a problem above their pay grade, they always kick it up the chain."

He stared at her, and she smirked. *All right,* she admitted to herself, *maybe I am showing off a bit.* "I can see you've never tried to blag your way into an over-21's night in Camden." She jerked her head at the mirror. "Who are they, anyway? He looked—well, I don't want to sound to crazy here, but he looked human."

"The Mirrorstocracy, lords-under-glass," he replied, still looking at her like she was utterly mad. "They're sometimes born when a person gets caught between two mirrors."

"You what now?"

"Two mirrors," he repeated testily. "You know all those infinitely receding reflections you get? Well, every reflection has a little bit of reality in it, and every now and then they add up to someone like Doorkeep there: a living, breathing copy on the other side of the glass. The Mirrorstocracy are really, *really* prickly—I can't believe you—"

"Shhh, they're coming back," Beth said, fixing on a smile. If this Mirrorstocracy were anything like the posh kids she occasionally sold paintings to, then you could bitch your heart out, as long as you pretended to be nice while you did it. She was going to enjoy this.

Seven figures—three men in gray suits, four women in gray skirts and white blouses—swept into view on the reflected rooftop. They walked like they had the deeds to the world in their back pockets. They stopped *exactly* level with Beth and Fil's reflections, not a fraction of an inch forward or back. They were marking their status.

One of the mirror-women directed a minute curtsey at

Fil. She had walnutty skin and a sour mouth. "Highness," she said.

Fil bowed his head at the Mirror.

"Excellency."

"Your friend gave our *agent-de-porte* quite a turn. What can we do for you, Son of the Streets?"

He smiled. "I'm here to invoke your vassalage. Load your glass guns and unwind your garrottes." He frowned, as though something was only just occurring to him. "Have a dig around for any welding torches that might have been caught in-mirror as well, will you? The scrap we're heading into, I think we'll be needing them."

If this bizarre request startled the woman, she didn't show it. "You're recruiting."

He nodded. "It's a man's life in the army, but don't let that put you off."

The lines on the woman's brown skin contorted as if she was struggling gamely for a smile, but not quite getting there. "And I assume the target of this expedition is Reach?"

He grinned.

"So the Urchin Prince is finally stepping into his mother's footprints. How do they feel, Highness?"

"A little on the large side," he admitted. "But I'll grow into them."

"I'm sure you will." The Senator pursed her lips, then said, "I'm afraid we can't help you, Filius Viae, as much as we would like to."

His smiled hardened. "Really? Why not?"

"If you consult Imago 73 of the Treaty of Palindromes, it specifies that only Mater Viae herself is empowered to enforce our vassalage. Well, it actually states: *egalassav s'ycarcotsrorriM eht ecrofne yam sseddoG eht ylno*, but it's polite to translate." The Senator's voice dripped with phony diplomatic regret. "Obviously, we would gladly release the legions to *her*, but as everyone knows, she has been missing this last decade, and in her absence, the treaty must remain in abeyance. Even in the face of such an august figure as yourself, our hands are tied."

You could have napped flint with Fil's smile now. "What's this about, Maggie?"

The Senator sighed, as if to say, *Well, if you're going to be so ill-mannered as to insist on me being honest…* "We suspected that such a request might soon be made. It doesn't take a mathematician to count the cranes on the horizon. The appropriate response to this delicate question was debated in Senate. I can assure your Highness that there were full-throated opinions on both sides—"

"I'm sure."

"—but, after due reflection, it was felt that given Reach's current proclivity for building glass towers, he might make a better ally than a foe."

Fil's jaw dropped so far you could have shoved a football down his throat. "*What?*"

"Well, the more reflective surfaces there are in *your* city, the more opportunity *we* have to redomicile conventional, singly reflected persons to *our* city, as Plebeians."

He said in disgust, "You mean slaves."

"Servants, technically." The Senator, like all politicians, was clearly sweet on semantics.

Fil stared at her in silence for a long moment. Then his expression changed from furious to thoughtful and he rocked back on his heels. He shoved his spare hand in his pocket and his smile returned. "Okay," he said, and he turned back towards the fire escape.

Beth started. "*Okay?* Fil, that's it?"

He spread his hands. "You heard Her Excellency. They've made up what passes for their minds; nothing we can do to change them now—" He paused. "Of course, there are three obvious reasons why that decision'll result in their republic collapsing into raging bloody anarchy. But I'm sure they'll have covered those in their 'full-throated debate.'" He shrugged, as though to say *some you win…*"

The Senator's clearing of the throat was delicately audible. "I am sure we will have discussed them, you are right, of course—but just to be certain, might I enquire, Highness, what reasons?"

He smiled like an adder and ticked them off on his fingers. "First, there's the fact that Reach is a psychotic monster, so only someone with a really cavernously empty skull would rely on him to do anything.

"Second, Mater Viae *is* coming back, stomping up the warpath like she does, and she'll be *bloodlettingly* unhappy that you didn't come when her favorite little boy called." He shrugged. "But if you're okay with that…"

The Senators in the mirror looked at each other in consternation as he put his foot on the fire-escape ladder.

"Um, Fil?" Beth started. Somehow she felt this was her cue. "You said three reasons?"

The gray boy folded his skinny arms on the top rung and set his chin on them. "So I did." His smile vanished, his cheeks darkened and for a second he looked furiously, frighteningly angry. "The other reason you should think again, your Excellencies, is this: if you don't, I'll stick up pairs of giant mirrors facing each other across Trafalgar Square, Bishopsgate, and Oxford bloody Circus."

Senator Maggie paled, but there were confused laughs from some of the others, and one old man said defiantly, "So what?"

He sucked his teeth. "So I reckon that's at least a couple of hundred thousand people being caught between them every day. Say only five percent of them cross over; that's ten *thousand* new Mirrorstocrats. *Daily*. I'll flood London-under-glass with sodding aristos until the mirrorsquitos can't suck a drop of blood that's not blue." He licked his lips as if savoring the prospect.

"I'll tip your bottom-heavy society right on its face." He waved at them. "Bye! Enjoy cleaning your own palaces and breaking your own backs on the sun farms, because you can kiss goodbye to your fat-arsed privilege when there's only one of your poor-bugger Plebeians to every hundred of you."

He hawked and then spat, very deliberately, on the roof. "Think about it," he said, and turned away.

Beth looked back at the faces of the Mirrorstocracy.

They were all white with impotent fury, except for Senator Maggie, who kept that sour smile on her face.

"Fat-arsed privilege?" she said mildly. "Spoken like a true prince."

———————

They hit the ground, jumped over the fence, and ran down the alley back towards the main road, laughing wildly. Beth felt immense euphoria surging in her, like when she and Pen pulled off some beautiful mural.

At that thought, Pen's brown eyes flashed into Beth's mind and she stopped short and swallowed, but the gray-skinned boy was still grinning at her and she felt her own smile burst back.

"Got 'em!" Fil shouted jubilantly. "*Now* I'm having fun."

"You're sure?"

"Definitely. There's no way they can face down a threat like that." He embraced her impulsively, squeezing the air from her, then let her go.

"What was that for?"

"For your big mouth. You were so river-bleeding rude to 'em, and they took it, so I figured I could take the high hand too."

His skin was shiny with city grease, and when Beth looked down she saw her hoodie was smeared with it. "Wow," she said, "that's pretty gross, you know that? Do you *sweat* motor oil or something?"

"Get used to it," he said with a grin. "Stay with me,

you'll get a good coat of it yourself in no time. It's handy—keeps out the chill."

"So sign me up—I'm freezing."

"Right you are." He reached around her and smeared her face and her clothes with it and she squealed and struggled and laughed and he laughed too as he wrestled her to the ground. They struggled in the dirt for a few seconds, struggling to fight, breathe, and giggle all at once, until Beth slid out from underneath him and got on top, bending his arm back and pinning it down.

For a fraction of a second her mouth hovered over his. He stopped laughing. Beth was suddenly, shockingly, aware of the strength of his thin arms, of the fact that he was *letting* her pin him. She felt the heat of his breath against her lips, and she panicked.

Heat flooded into her face, and to cover her embarrassment, she stuck her tongue out at him and jumped away. Then he cracked up again, and she felt hysterical laughter boil up out of her.

When the echoes of their laughter had finally faded, they were both lying on their backs, panting for breath. Hesitantly, she slid her hand over the asphalt and took his. Her sleeve had hitched up and their bare arms touched, their tower-crown tattoos resting side by side.

"Thank you," he whispered to her.

"What for?"

"For being here."

———

That night they drank to celebrate what Fil assured her was their first successful recruitment. He'd boiled up clear green liquor over a fire he'd set in a metal dustbin. Beth felt her head swim as the heat of it trickled through her, turning her limbs to warm mud. The skinny boy drank twice as much as she did, and sang stupid Latin songs horribly off-key. He would have fallen flat on his face if she hadn't caught him. They folded together into a comfortable heap and with her head resting on his shoulder and him already snoring, Beth, contented, drifted off to sleep.

––––––––––

She woke in the pale silver dawn, bleary-eyed and stiff, her cheek glued to the concrete by early morning frost. Fil sat opposite, winding fresh strips of torn poster around his burns. A train sounded in the distance. Its whistle was wrong somehow. Beth couldn't quite say why, but it sounded thin ... wounded.

He cocked his head, listening, then he noticed she was awake and gave her a tired smile. "Recognize that sound?" he asked her.

"The train?"

"Not just any train: that's your Railwraith, the one you were riding the night we met. He's been following us for two days now, keeping as close as he can on the tracks. Any idea what he wants?"

Beth shook her head. "I don't even know why it picked me up in the first place."

A broad smile split his face. "Seriously? You don't even

know that? But that's obvious—you were a passenger. You wanted to go somewhere—*anywhere*—and he sensed it. Wraiths *get* passengers: passengers are what they remember, what they do. Passengers make 'em happy."

He stretched and settled against the wall next to her. "Mind you, what he wants with you now you're with me is anyone's guess. Maybe he blames you for getting him mauled by that freight train; maybe he's looking for payback. Then again, p'raps he's lonely and just wants a friend. Railwraiths are pretty unstable at the best of times, and after what that one went through, he's bound to be a little barking."

Beth winced. The clash and churn of the immense ghost-engines was burned into the memory of her body. She huddle up and pulled her hoodie down over her knees.

"Cold?"

"No," Beth said flatly, "practicing for my future career as a contortionist."

He threw an arm around her. His bony hip jabbed her uncomfortably, but he gave off a surprising amount of heat. "S'all right. He can't survive away from the tracks for more than a few minutes. We stay off the rails, we'll be fine. Besides, you're with me now."

Beth snorted. "Given everything, I have a hard time believing that makes me safer, Fil. But thanks."

"Fair point, but tell you what: I'll do my best to make sure I get killed before you do. Can't say fairer than that, can I?"

A little shiver, at the thought of him dying, went

through Beth as he spoke. That'd been the first thing he'd told her about himself: *Someone's trying to kill me.*

"Nah," she said, forcing herself to smile. "Very kind."

SEVENTEEN

"You're sure this is the place?"

"Positive."

Mr. Bradley's fingers drummed on the small stack of photos they'd run off on his home printer. Pen knew them pretty well, as they'd been taken from her mobile. She wished she'd been surprised that he didn't have a recent shot of his daughter.

On the off-chance, she'd also printed a couple of copies of the sketch of the scrawny boy; it was just possible they'd find someone who might recognize him.

He hesitated and then said, "Parva, you're Beth's best friend. I want you to know that if she isn't—well, if we don't…" He muttered, "Well, then I'm sorry."

Pen flinched but didn't reply.

His words spilled on into the silence. "Beth was always

Marianne's little girl more than mine. When Marianne died, I ... I went inside myself. It was like I was trapped there." He swallowed. "I couldn't get out to Beth. I *tried*, inside I tried, to find a way to make myself, but I couldn't reach her."

She wouldn't let you, Pen thought. *If it had been me, I wouldn't have let you either.*

"I just," he went on, "I didn't know how to go about caring. There wasn't anything to *grip*. I don't do well with all that stuff, emotional stuff, I mean. It doesn't come naturally. What else was I supposed to do?"

Pen couldn't bring herself to deliver some platitude. She bit her lip and then said quietly, "Try harder." She let herself out of the car and stamped up the rickety wooden steps.

She heard Mr. Bradley's car door slam as he climbed out and followed her, wheezing, up the steps behind her.

"Come on, Mr. B," she said, trying to get past the awkwardness of the moment, "the workout's good for you. I bet she's ... " She tailed off.

"What?" he asked, but then he too saw and fell silent.

Ahead of them, the bridge gave way to nothingness. The stairs on other side of it had been ripped away and the ends of the planks protruded like split, dirty fingernails into the black.

And it *was* black. Every streetlight was out, and the concrete clearing behind the estates was invisible. On the other side, a light glowed weakly for an instant, barely disrupting the murk, and then it was gone.

Mr. Bradley looked bemused.

"How do we—?" he murmured, but Pen had already jumped down.

Glass crunched under her feet as she landed. On the ground she could make out the clearing a little better. Her breath stalled.

The place had been ripped *apart*.

The streetlamps had been uprooted like metal trees, wire roots sprawling from the concrete clods at their bases. The glass bulbs were smashed, the remains strewn across the ground.

She heard a *whoomph* of breath and a muttered swearword. Mr. Bradley came up behind her shoulder. "What happened here?" He sounded bewildered.

Pen tried to answer, but her throat constricted and she couldn't speak. She stared at the place where she'd thought her best friend would be waiting for her, where she'd found only the aftermath of violence.

The light on the far side of the yard flared again. Briefly illuminated, something glinted by Pen's foot. She uttered a little cry.

Mr. Bradley shouted, "What is it?"

Pen pointed downwards as the light pulsed again. A severed hand clutched at the pile of planks that had once been the steps of the bridge.

He collapsed to his knees and reached for it. "Oh God, oh God—" His voice faltered, and then relief flooded into it. "Parva, it's all right." He lifted the thing up. "Look, Parva it's not real, it's—ow! It's glass, it's made of glass!"

It was immaculate: the bones, the muscles, even the pores of the skin were all sculpted in smooth glass, and fine strands of dull gray metal twisted through it in place of veins and arteries.

The glow came again from the other side of the courtyard. Mr. Bradley stood marvelling at the glass hand, but Pen shouldered past him and walked towards the light source. A thin wheezing sound carried through the dark: stuttering little breaths, and Pen felt her heart flutter.

The glow came again and at last Pen saw the source clearly. She broke into a run, skidding to her knees beside it.

It was a glass woman, and she twisted her head, her eyes wide, as if she'd sensed Pen arriving but couldn't see her. Both of her legs and one arm ended in short, ragged stumps, surrounded by glittering dust as though the limbs had been crushed to powder. Pen could see her lungs through her transparent skin. Each time she breathed, the lungs compressed and her glass heart beat, and with each heartbeat, the wires that ran through her glowed.

"It's okay," Pen found herself whispering. It blatantly *wasn't* okay, but she didn't know what else to say. She cooed as if to a small child, gently lifting the shattered woman's head and grasping her one remaining hand. It was smooth and hard, and rapidly giving up its heat to the air. "We're here now," Pen said softly, "we'll help you." Although she had no clue how she could help at all.

Suddenly the woman sat up hard. She opened her mouth so wide Pen could see glass tonsils. Her eyes were screwed up as though she was screaming. She didn't make a sound, but flared off a brilliant flash.

Pen was blinded. The world vanished into coarse-grained darkness. She groped around for the woman and something snagged her finger. She felt blood. She heard the clink of the woman falling back, and her own breath was panicked.

Then Mr. Bradley cried out, "*Parva!*"

Pen stumbled through the darkness towards his voice, yelling, "Mr. B! Mr. B!" over and over. Her voice sounded thin and deranged.

"Parva!" He was close; she could hear his panting breaths through the night. "Parva, my leg—"

She was close enough to make out the shape of him now, lying face-down on the tarmac. He had something wrapped around his ankle, a tourniquet of barbed wire. A taut strand led away from the prone man and disappeared into the black mouth of a nearby storm drain. Pen crouched and pulled at it, but it was tight around his leg, and her fingers came back bloody.

Mr. Bradley lurched suddenly, and the wire started dragging him backwards over the pavement. He screamed in pain as he slid along the ground, twisting and flailing for purchase on the asphalt. Pen cast around for something she could use to cut him free. She clutched absurdly at her clothes, as if she carried pair of wire-cutters in her pockets.

"Hang on, M-Mr. B, just, just hang on; I'll—"

Orange light flared then, shattering the darkness like an instant dawn. Pen gaped at it as it stormed up over the broken bridge, coalescing into human shape as it came close. She scrambled out of the way as the figure jumped from the bridge and landed lightly on the concrete. It was another woman, like the first, but not identical—a sister, maybe—and she was burning with a far stronger inner fire. The woman extended one hand towards Mr. Bradley and flexed her glowing fingers in a peremptory motion.

With a sickening, adhesive sound, the wire's barbs began to come free, glinting in the woman's light. The wire strands wavered, as if they were fighting some invisible magnetism.

The glass woman crooked her fingers into claws and bent her back in effort. Tendrils of barbed wire snaked grudgingly out of the storm drain: yard after yard, the inch-long thorns gleaming. The wire-thing thrashed, apparently trapped by whatever force the glass woman was projecting.

Her head was bowed and her hand extended as though in prayer. She sagged, her glass knees shaking with the effort.

A single skein of the barbed-wire thing reached for the ground. It wound and snapped in frustration, laboring through the heavy air.

The shining woman dropped to one knee. The glass rang on the pavement like a bell.

The barbed wire touched earth—

Suddenly, the monster was free from the glass woman's power. It accelerated instantly, lashing out at her. Barbs bit into glass with a sickening crunch and she staggered back, her light flickering. The wire blurred and coiled in the air, like a metal cloud anchored to the earth. Tendrils curved like hooks and struck with venomous speed, not towards the glass woman, but towards *Pen*.

She had no time to get out of its way.

Metal whirled around her, whipping her hair. Pen gasped for breath, trapped in a vortex of wire. The whirling strands tightened around her, enclosing her in a spinning cocoon. The gaps closed up, extinguishing the light from the glass woman. Pen sucked in her stomach and screwed up her eyes, waiting for the barbs to touch her.

Silence. She heard nothing now, saw nothing, but she felt the needle-tips of the barbs on her eyelids. They were gentle, like a blind person learning a new face. They tickled her. Then pinpricks erupted all over her body, probing: under her arms, along the back of her neck, between her thighs, between her fingers. She felt the thorns sink in.

She wanted to scream, but she couldn't expand her chest.

A second passed. Then another. Pen still didn't dare open her eyes, but a spark of a thought filled her head: *I'm alive*. It was only now she realized she hadn't expected to be. Warmth trickled over her body—wet, sticky warmth. *I'm bleeding*, she told herself, trying to be clinical, *but there's not that much blood. I'm alive.* The wire thorns were in her, staunching the very wounds they'd made.

Pain rippled like fire over her skin, but it felt insignificant next to being alive.

Something like cold thin fingers prodded at her eyes, teasing her eyelashes; as a reflex, they opened.

Mr. Bradley was staring at her, his face slack with

horror. She could see him because the glass woman was still there, kneeling on the ground, glowing.

I'm—I'm okay. It hurts, but…

But she realized she wasn't speaking. Barbs held her throat tight and she could feel the fine metal thorns grip her lips when she tried to move them. There was a bead of blood under her nose; it tickled madly and she tried to brush it away, but she couldn't. Her hand wouldn't move either. She rolled her eyes as far as she could, trying to see her arm. It was wrapped in wire—her whole body was bound in a barbed-wire exoskeleton, and it was paralyzed.

She was paralyzed.

"Parva?" Mr. Bradley said uncertainly. "Parva, can you hear me?"

Pen couldn't speak or make any sort of sign, but before she could follow that thought she felt her arm rise, dragged upwards by the wire around it. Her finger extended into a point—

—and suddenly the wires around her lips yanked them open and something lashed into her mouth. Pain stabbed through her tongue as the wire seized it.

Droplets of blood hit the floor of her mouth.

"*Where is he?*" The voice that came from her throat was grotesque, twisted, as if it was being *squeezed* out of her chest.

Mr. Bradley looked ready to faint, but he straightened. "W-w-where's who?" he stammered.

"*Where is he?*" The wire jerked Pen's hand.

Mr. Bradley looked after the pointing finger, and so

did she. Lying on the concrete were the photos that'd spilled from Mr. Bradley's pocket. Pen was pointing straight at the picture of the skinny bare-chested boy Beth had sketched.

"I—I don't know where he is, Parva. You *know* I don't. We don't know *who* he is. We don't know where Beth—"

He was right: she *did* know that. It was the thing coiled around her that didn't. The tendrils lashed out of her mouth and resealed it, leaving her tongue swollen in their wake.

To Pen's utter terror, her feet began to move. The wires pulled and their barbs chided and her right foot stepped forward, and then her left. After a moment, her arms began to swing too, as though the creature that gripped her had needed a few steps to get the hang of it. The last thing she saw, before it turned her around, was Beth's dad, reaching out to her.

But she'd already gone. The wires were moving her legs far faster than she ever could. As she began to pant for breath they relaxed their grip on her lungs and finally, as she ran out on the path past the tower blocks, she could scream.

———

Paul Bradley ran after her, as fast as he could, but his leg was still bleeding and he couldn't keep up. He stumbled to a halt, hands on his knees, panting. *Too fat and too slow, old man*, he cursed himself.

Warmth touched his back for an instant, and then the

glass woman burst past him, her feet ringing off the tarmac as she pursued Pen. He glimpsed her face, fixed in a snarl of agony. She was holding shards of the shattered bodies in her hands.

"Wait!" he gasped. "Take me, help me—I have to—"

But she didn't look back. He crumpled onto the ground as he watched her, the only light, disappearing into the distance.

Another one. It was a chill, venomous needle of a thought, but it was true. *You lost another one.*

He scrambled around in the darkness, groping for the fallen photos. He strained his eyes to make out the shapes in the photos, tracing a finger around the sketch of the boy with the spear.

Then he staggered towards the lit-up estates in the distance. A new wilderness had unfolded around him. There was a new logic. He didn't know what was real, what was alive. He didn't know the rules.

Where is he? The rasp that the metal thing had forced from Parva's throat grated through his mind. *Where is he?*

Certainty crystallized in him. All the people out there driving cars, tossing burgers, having sex, watching late night TV: they all faded into irrelevance.

Beth was not in *that* city. She was with this boy's city. *With him.*

EIGHTEEN

Steel yourself, Petris. Or, given the circumstances, should that be stone yourself? No, definitely steel. Stoning would be completely different. And painful. And tough to accomplish single-handed.

Of course, Petris reflected, if any of his flock caught him at what he was about to do, there would be no shortage of volunteers to chuck the first rock.

He was standing in a children's playground in the middle of Victoria Park, a typically decayed seat of London infancy with heavily graffitied slides, a climbing frame, and four carved horses wobbling on rusty springs, grinning like they'd had too much ketamine.

He began to shiver, which, he told himself, was because the autumn chill had seeped into his punishment skin and *definitely* not because he was afraid.

After all, what did he have to be scared of? He was encased in granite armor two inches thick. His grip could tear steel plate. He'd led warrior priests against scaffolding monsters and crushed them with his bare hands. What did *he* have to fear?

Well, a treacherous inner voice supplied, *there're the two thousand other bronze and stone-clad soldiers who can also tear steel. Let's not dwell on what bits of you they might crush with their bare hands if they catch you, shall we?*

Petris swigged down a pint of sewerspirit, wincing as the fermenting fecal taste filled his mouth. It was vile, but it was the strongest drink he could brew, and the warmth of it was already drizzling into his muscles, its fug washing over his brain. He relaxed.

Cromwell had stumbled in on him as he'd been setting up the distilling apparatus. The bronze Roundhead had eyed the booze in the bell jar and asked, "What's the occasion, old man?"

Petris had given an unconvincing laugh. "Oh, I'm celebrating, you know. *Finally* telling that jumped-up street rat to swivel on his own railing."

Cromwell had laughed himself, and even made the effort to tip his bronze helm to his high priest. Behind his stone mask, Petris' eyes had tracked the tip of Cromwell's sword as he'd swept from the room.

What do I have to be afraid of?

As if in answer, one of the swings started to move back and forth. *Cr-eak, cr-eak.* It was difficult to see, but the space above the swing's seat looked more solid than it had a few seconds ago. A vague human shape had appeared on it, black against the darkness, and now it kicked its legs and rocked the swing like a child. Slim fingers gripped the chains and viscous liquid oozed from under the fingernails and down the metal. A strong acrid smell pierced Petris' nostrils.

Cr-eak, Cr-eak. Cr—The oil spread to the swing's hinges and they stopped squeaking.

The black figure continued to swish back and forth, the silence now broken only by the *drip-drip* of the oil off his bare feet.

His teeth wanted to chatter but Petris grimly swigged from his bell jar, swamping any circumstantial evidence of his fear in 76 percent alcohol.

The swing came to a stop. "Petrisss." The name came on a hiss of chemical breath. Viscous liquids were drawn into threads between the dark figure's lips as they parted.

"Johnny. Always a pleasure. "

"Iss that why you asssked my attendance?" The sibilants ghosted on the air. "*Pleassure?* You are notoriousss for itss purssuit—ssstrange, then, if our pressence iss ssuch a pleasure, how sseldom you sseek it out. One might ssuspect we of the Sssynod … unsettle you."

"Oh, you always unsettle me, Johnny." Petris' good humor was cinder-brittle.

"I ssee," the black figure sighed. "Sspecify the sservice you would ssolicit, stonesskin." Johnny Naptha inspected his black fingernails where they held the swing. "And hassten—I hate to hurry you, but my presscence here isn't helping the health of the herbsss, you undersstand." He pointed over Petris' shoulder, and even in the dark, the priest could see the nearest tree sagging as the poisons dripping from Johnny Naptha's feet leached into the soil.

Petris gazed at that richness of death like a parched man at water fountain. "Who said I was looking for service?" he croaked. He was hoarse with thirst.

"Why elsse would you be sstanding here, ssqueezing your sstone into that abssurd vissage, and trying not to sspit your intesstines out in fear?" Johnny Naptha's voice remained a quiet, courteous hiss. "*Of coursse* you need ssomething. Everyone needss ssomething, that'ss why they come to usss."

Petris tried for a smile. "Perceptive as ever, Johnny. Yes, I'd like to strike a deal, for a fair price."

"Alwayss fair, Petriss," Johnny Naptha chided him. "We are the Chemical Ssynod. Our equationss *alwayss* balance. Ssymmetry iss in our blood."

Petris drew a deep breath. "All right. There's someone I want you to protect. The little twerp's going to get in over his head with a nasty character and I think he'll need guarding."

Johnny sat back in his swing, considering the request. As he thought, he produced a cigarette lighter from the pocket of his oil-soaked jacket and began snapping the lid open and shut. "'There'ss ssomeone I want you to protect,'" the acid hiss echoed. "*I,* not *we.* Well, I ssuppose that answerss my firsst question: vizz, why the oh-sso-fearssome Pavement Priestss cannot protect their own people.

Leaving only my ssecond, vizz, what causse is sso critical you would rissk being caught by your compatriotss courting *me*? I am intrigued now, Petriss; who is this persson? Who is sso *contentiouss* that you cannot even command your own Priessthood to guard him?"

Petris swallowed, and felt his Adam's apple graze granite. "Filius Viae," he said.

"Filiuss Viae," Johnny Naptha echoed. "Ah. Sso I take it this 'nassty character' is Reach?"

There was a long silence, broken only by the click of the lighter. Petris couldn't take his eyes off it. *Just one spark... all that oil.* The very thought made him sweat into his armor.

"A '*little deal*,'" Johnny Naptha said eventually. "Hmmph. Your sskillss in undersstatement are unparallelled." He sighed and straightened his oil-soaked tie. "I'm ssorry, old sstonesskin, I ssincerely am, but to battle *Reach*? You ssimply couldn't afford our price."

Petris started to argue, but Johnny Naptha held up a hand. "The rissks in ssiding against the Crane King are conssiderable, as you are cognissant, and to be ssuccint, your ssuppliess of what interestss uss are already ssapped—"

"What *interests* you?" Petris interrupted desperately. "Johnny, you'll commodify *anything*. Surely—"

"Sssome ssecuritiess are more interessting than others." Johnny Naptha cut him off without raising his voice. "A deal on thiss ssubject could not ssimultaneoussly sserve both of our interessstss."

It was brisk, blunt, and brutal. The Chemical Synod were discreet to the point of deception, but they never lied. Their contracts were constructed so neatly that there was neither the need nor opportunity to cheat.

Petris stared at him in disgust, feeling exposed and humiliated. His stone felt a hundred times heavier as he turned and strode away, faster than he could really spare the energy for. His granite feet sank ankle-deep in the mud.

I'm sorry, Filius...

"Let me know if you need anything elsse a little lesss exspenssive," Johnny Naptha called brightly. "For the price of an eyeball, or a few happy memoriess, sssay... We have sservicess to ssuit all ssituationss."

And then there was silence, except for the snap of his lighter and the swish as he started to swing again.

NINETEEN

How many crazy tramp-god kids does it take to change a lightbulb? Beth mused as she watched Fil argue with the glowing man. She sighed. *More than one, I guess.*

The cobbled courtyard behind Carnaby Street was filled with glass men all pulsing with snowy-white inner light, the same hue as the posh, pure tungsten lamps that lit the richer streets in Central London.

Apparently they'd turned up in the middle of market-night. A shifting inkblot of shadows flooded the walls as the figures ambled about, bartering for lengths of wire and batteries, dabbing their wrists with bottled shades in semi-visible wavelengths as subtle as scents. One figure lay flat on a doorstep while another crouched over him, working his glazed-skin with a buzzing tattoo needle plugged into his own heart. Fine lines of red light followed the blade of the needle, like blood. The etched man's shoulder became frosted, opaque, outlining a shining dragon on the skin that remained clear. All around them, gossip was swapped in rapid semaphores.

After the past few days, it had been a relief for Beth to see something even half-familiar.

"Oh, right," she'd said as they'd rounded the corner, "it's more of your girlfriend's lot. Only paler."

His head had jerked in alarm and he'd muttered, "She's not my girlfriend. And don't mention Electra."

"Gotta say, though …" Beth was eyeing their glass forms critically. "They look a bit fragile to stand up in a fight against a bunch of cranes, not to mention—what was it you said? A barbed-wire monster?"

"Don't mention that either."

"Is there anything I *can* mention?" she'd asked testily.

"Good point." He'd patted her on the shoulder. "You'd probably better leave the talking to me."

"Why?" Beth had felt a twinge of wounded pride. "We made a good team with the Mirror-toffs."

"We did, yeah," he'd admitted, "but this lot won't listen to you."

"Why not?"

"Because they … um, they don't really think that much of girls." He'd had the good grace to wince.

Beth had looked back at the glass men. They were, she'd noticed then, all *men*—fat men, thin men, heavily muscled men: moving nude glass statues with white-hot metal veins.

"Well," she'd said flatly, "now I just want to hug them."

All commerce had ceased when they walked into the cobbled square. The glowing men were eyeing them suspiciously and Beth thought one, a bulky one, looked positively scared of her.

A tall, rangy man with tightly curled fiber-optic chest hair stood up.

"*Crap*," Fil hissed.

"What?"

"It's Lucien, one of the Blankleit Elders. He doesn't like me."

"Why not?"

"I locked him inside a bulb once." He caught Beth's startled look. "*What?* Didn't do him any harm. He was at the treaty talks with Glas a couple of years back—we weren't making any headway, and he wouldn't *shut up*."

Beth snorted as Fil cracked his knuckles and said grandly, "Leave the negotiation to me."

She didn't need to understand the semaphore language to realize that the "negotiation" had instantly become an argument, which had slowly dissolved into a row, and the row simmered into a fine stew of personal abuse and sarcasm, seasoned with a light dusting of gamesmanship.

Beth was able to follow the diplomatic disaster with the help of a bearded homeless man who'd apparently bedded down in the square. He'd come over, introduced himself as Victor, and appointed himself her translator. He huddled beside her, leaning against a shop wall wrapped in a worn sleeping bag. A faded woollen hat with a hammer and sickle logo covered about a tenth of his copious hair. He watched the glass man's semaphores carefully and then loudly called out the English, which turned out to be doubly helpful because the street prince, as it turned out, didn't speak the white-lamp people's language very well himself.

The Lampman drew himself up and flared off a sentence.

"We will not leave the purity of our districts," Victor croaked in his thick Black Sea accent, and Fil rolled his eyes.

Beth leaned over to Victor. He smelled of wet dog and pee. "Hey, Victor?" she started. "How's it you speak their language when even he doesn't?" She pointed to the skinny boy, who'd thrown his spear down on the cobbles like a pissed-off tennis player.

Eyes puddled in rheumy lids rolled upwards. "Blankleit lingo is simple. Anyone can learn." He produced a bottle of clear liquid from his sleeping bag and opened it. The fumes from it peeled the moisture off Beth's throat.

"I come here from St. Petersburg, you know? Had to learn English—you learn English, you learn *anything*," he tutted. "English is crazy language. Nothing make sense."

In the square, Fil was trying to be nice. He dropped a friendly arm on Lucien's shoulder, muttering rapidly, but the glass man gave a single emphatic flash and turned away with his arms crossed.

"You need I translate that, my friend?" Victor called out.

"I think I got that one, thanks." He sighed.

Victor nodded amiably and settled back into his sleeping

bag. He offered Beth his bottle and she peered at it, wondering what sort of motor engines it was designed to clean.

"Ta, but no," she said. "Victor, I don't mean to be rude or anything, but you're not … *special*, are you?"

Victor frowned. He flexed a brawny, tattooed forearm. "Da. In Leningrad I could deadlift two hundred kilo for Soviet Olympic team," he offered. "Is pretty special, no?"

"Yeah, well cool—*two hundred*, no kidding? But I mean, you're *human*, right? You're a regular bloke?"

He nodded and relief flooded through her. It was a little guarantee of her sanity. "So—don't you think this is *weird*? Mute, man-shaped walking glassware? I mean, haven't you ever been tempted to tell anyone?"

Victor shrugged. "Tell anyone what? Is none of this real: either I am drunk or crazy. My father died in insane asylum for protest against Kruschev. Do I want follow him? *Niet*, I do not, so me, I make sure I am drunk all of time. Drink enough of this, you can explain to see anything." He raised his bottle in a toast. "*Za tvojo zdorov'je.*"

"I'm real," Beth protested.

"You, maybe, but you see this also, so you drunk or crazy, too." He grinned and patted her on the shoulder. "Which no mean I not like you. I like you as much as I like much prettier sane girl."

In the middle of the square, Fil spun back towards Lucien and said triumphantly, "Don't forget, it was me who negotiated that treaty for you, me and Gutterglass. You *owe* me. If weren't for me, these streets would all be Amber by now."

The Blankleit Elder's face set into a sneer, visible even through the light coming off his glass brain. He folded his arms and flashed his reply.

"He say," Victor called out, "that deal you are talking about is oppressing to him and to his nation. Is affront to dignity of whitelight race. Traps them in crappy little ghetto in middle of town."

"Jesus *Christ!*" Beth was incredulous. "A minute ago this "crappy little ghetto" was the sanctum of his purity!"

"Apparently it can be both," muttered Fil. He shot her a look which said, *Good point. You're not helping. Please for the love of God shut up.*

"Ghetto is shameful to them," Victor announced as Lucien strobed on, "white lights who can trace their lineage from Holy Gaslamps themselves."

"*Blood in the river!* You're NOT gaslamps!" Fil shouted at Lucien. "There's not a bloody one of you has got an ounce of spirit-vapor in your blood. Just 'cause you're half a shade paler, you think you're *holy? Thames!* You're metal and glass and sparks, same as the Sodiumites..." He tailed off, eyes wide. He knew he'd said something stupid.

Lucien pounced, his expression haughtily offended. "How dare you compare us to Ambers, filthy bulbstealers!" Victor translated as he strobed furiously. "Of course, we all know how fond you are of *them*—how you fraternize with their little *princess.*"

"Just 'cause you never *fraternized* with anything but your own right hand," Beth said under her breath.

Everyone froze, and then looked right at her: a dozen

glowing faces, and Fil, his shocked eyes two pale islands in the filth of his face. That was when Beth realized the Lamppeople were deaf; even though Fil was shouting, they'd been reading the words off his lips. And everyone in the square could see her—and that meant they *all* knew what she'd just said.

Beth licked her cracked lips. Her throat was dry and she flushed with embarrassment. Lucien was looking sneeringly at her, and she felt dislike for the tedious glass bureaucrat coming off her like steam.

Lucien made some patronizing hand-gestures and Victor winced as he translated the flashes for her: "Come on then, little fleshgirl. If you have something to say—"

The look Fil gave her could have bored through brick, but Beth would drink her own paints before she let someone talk to her like that.

She stood up and straightened her hoodie. "All right then," she muttered and marched into the middle of the square. Blankleits shied away as she passed them. "Don't worry," she muttered, "I'm not gonna to get *girl* on you. I'm just gonna talk a bit."

She came to stand in the center of the courtyard. Fil was looking at her like she was a live cable. She put her hands on her hips. She had an idea of what she was going to say—it was a bit mental, but if they wouldn't listen to him because they thought he was partisan, maybe, just maybe, they'd listen to an outsider. Even if she was just a *little fleshgirl.*

"You lot can all understand me, right?" she called out. "You can all read my lips?"

A paparazzi-attack of flashes responded.

"They say *da*," Victor said unnecessarily, but taking his role seriously.

She fixed Lucien with a look. She focused on how satisfying it would be to introduce her kneecap to his glass testicles and her nerves subsided. She licked her dry lips and started. "You know, we got people like you where I come from. Old men—always *old*—you see 'em on the telly. All they ever do is shout about the "good old days" and how grand they used to be, and how they got screwed over, and now they reckon that means they're *owed*."

She smiled humorlessly. "But not one of them bickering, whining old bastards ever made a difference to the world."

She started walking into the Blankleit crowd and they parted, making way for her, until, once in their midst, she deliberately turned her back on Lucien, blinding him to her lips, cutting him out. It was about as blatant a gesture of disrespect she could think of on the fly. The glass men had stopped fidgeting now, and every glowing eye was fixed on her.

"The one we're fighting controls them." She pointed to the horizon and the cranes. "And he doesn't give a crap what you think you're entitled to. Reach is clearing the city, tearing it up block by block. You think your *pure sanctum*, your *crappy ghetto* or whatever you want to call it—

you think it can survive the Demolition God? You think you'll hold out any better than your yellow cousins?"

It was deliberate provocation. The Blankleits stirred angrily at the word "cousins" and one or two of them flashed something, but Victor shouted angrily, "*Niet!* Not for lady!" and the strobing died away.

Beth stared them down, and she could sense their shock in that. She knew she still had their attention. "You're proud of your history, I get that," she said, "but Reach won't care who your ancestors are, who you *used* to be. He's going to kill who you are *now*. And he won't hesitate. So if you want a future, boys," she said quietly, "you've gotta let go of the past."

That was it, her pitch. She fell silent, her heart pounding. The bright glow of the Lampmen felt a lot more threatening now it was spilling over her.

Fil stole up to her side. "That was *incredibly* stupid," he murmured, "but incredible."

She blushed.

"The way you talk about Reach—"

"He scares the crap out of me…"

"He does? Thank the river! I was starting to think you were too daft to be scared of anything."

Lucien was stalking around in circles, all lit up and waving his arms frantically. He looked like he was signalling an airplane in to land.

"He say you full of something I not translate for nice lady," Victor called.

Beth swallowed hard, but one of the other Blankleits,

a short man with a softly glowing belly, had pulled out of the crowd. After a shamefaced look back at the infuriated Elder he walked hesitantly towards Beth. When he reached her he semaphored, and even Victor sounded surprised as he translated, "He will follow. He says he will fight."

Beth gasped and her heart felt like a balloon, inflated to dangerous levels with euphoria. A sudden raw awareness hit her: everyone was watching her. They were still looking at her as an outsider, but no longer as an interloper. *God,* she thought dazedly, *they know what I'm saying is right.*

Under their bravado, their *denial,* the Blankleits were deeply afraid. What had Fil said? The stronger Reach got, the scareder people became…

I guess it's not hard to become a leader, she thought. *All you have to do is step forward while everyone else's looking for a place to run to.*

At this point, Beth thought wryly, they'd probably follow a sock-puppet if it offered them a way out—as long as it wasn't known for *fraternizing* with their Amberglow enemies.

One by one, other glowing men drifted from the crowd towards them. Lucien kept protesting, flashing brighter and brighter, but Beth saw the mistake he was making: by shouting, he was taking her seriously, and that gave the others permission to take her seriously too.

A tall, muscular Blankleit and a lanky, sharp-eyed one took each other's shoulders. They whispered to each other in soft flickers, then nodded and embraced. They walked over to the humans and each shook first Fil's and then Beth's hand. Apparently they came as a pair.

"So ... " Beth barely moved her lips as she whispered, "Can I do the talking next time?"

TWENTY

Tower blocks reared up around the St. Paul's Demolition Fields, black against the city's incomplete darkness. They formed a perimeter of sorts around Reach's stronghold, with a crooked crane looming over every alley or lane that led in.

Electra paced back and forth along the roof of a corner shop, blazing her heart out against the night. She felt trapped, like the entire city was her cage, and only the acre of land that surrounded the cathedral was freedom— the acre sitting tauntingly beyond her, in the palm of the Crane King's hand, where the Wire Mistress and her bleeding prey had slunk off to.

Reach's servant had led her on a harum-scarum chase across London. She'd hurled herself bodily after it with her hands and fields and feet, scrambling over rotten garden fences, leaving scorched footprints on neatly tended lawns.

They'd climbed to the rooftops under the moon. The Wire Mistress' barbs made it surer on the tiles, and it'd squeezed more and more speed from its host. The fleshgirl had wept and made shapeless moans with her punctured tongue, and obeyed.

Lec had chased it mile after mile, fuelled by a hundred thousand volts of hatred, and only when the cranes had appeared suddenly over the rooftops had she skidded to a stop. Now she raged and spat sparks. For one insane moment she thought she might leap from the roof and charge, cranes or no cranes, but even in her anger she knew exactly how that would end: with Reach's metal claw turning, the chain hissing over pulleys, the rusting hook swinging in fast, bringing pain and blood, and then nothing at all.

"*If the Crane King kills you,*" she glimmered to herself, phrasing the light as simply and carefully as though she were talking to an infant, "*the Wire Mistress escapes.*"

She felt the last warmth of her momentum leave her and, in its wake, a chill crept in that didn't belong to the night. Lec hunkered down on the tiles, staring into space with tear-scorched eyes. There was a sensation in her stomach of standing on a precipice, as if one step forward would bring an endless fall into darkness. She'd felt something like it before, she realized, although with her sisters dead, comparing it to anything felt like a betrayal.

The feeling dredged up a memory: standing outside the Stepney warehouse on the very last night of the Spectrum War, her hand flat against the wood of the door. She had been barely more than a kindling, but the Tel-Nox clan blooded its children early. She was just a scared little girl trying desperately to remember the steps of her barely practiced war-waltz, her gut heavy with the knowledge that if she stumbled, she was dead, and not just her, but the other girls behind her too.

But there'd been no marauding horde of Whities behind that door, just dim shapes that turned out to be glass bodies, stacked head-to-toe alongside the walls with horrible neatness. In death they shone no color, so it wasn't until Luma had recognized her cousin that they knew they were theirs. The Whities had retreated, but they'd killed their prisoners first. The young Sodiumites had looked down at their sisters and cousins and aunts, at the pucker-burn marks around the holes in their foreheads where their captors had dripped the water through. At that moment Lec really understood what her grandmother had meant when she told her you couldn't trust the Whities, or Blankleits, or whatever name they went by. They were pale, treacherous killers.

She thought of Filius, capering absurdly around her lamppost, trying to protect the Whitey that had trespassed there, and the flash of annoyance that swept over her surprised her so much she almost fell off the roof. Not that she wasn't used to being annoyed by Filius—wanting to wring his scrawny neck was one of the anchors of their friendship—but she felt so charred and used-up that she was a little shocked she had the energy to be irritated with him.

Still, if she was honest, the urge to smack the little guttersnipe god around the ear was comforting. He'd embarrassed her in front of her sisters, and many a streetlamp daughter less proud than her would've danced a lethal measure for that—or at least that's what she'd tell him.

But then he was always doing thoughtless things like that. When they were really tiny, it had rained and he'd run straight out into it and Lec's heart had almost sparked out. She'd thought the water would kill him, like it would her, and as she'd imagined it, it had felt like the fright would shatter her.

That same vein-darkening, skin-chilling fear entered her now; fear at the memory of the Wire Mistress flexing around the flesh of her new host, squeezing her skin obscenely through the gaps in the steel, and at the way she had uncurled the poor girl's finger and forced her to ask *Where is he?*

The creature had destroyed her family. Now it wanted to do the same to a thoughtless, hopelessly naïve boy with no sense of rhythm, always half a beat too late. A boy who was the only living thing left she cared about.

An empty streetlamp poked up above the roofscape a couple of houses away. The bulb was cramped and old-fashioned, but Electra squirmed inside anyway. She couldn't get comfortable, but she flexed her fingertips and then, gradually, she began to push her fields outwards. She stretched the magnetism further and further, groping with it over the textures of brick and concrete and window-glass, slipping it over the mouths of alleys and doorways and manhole covers until at last she'd covered every opening into the Demolition Fields she possibly could. Her muscles tingled. She knew she couldn't burn this bright for long. In time that tingle would become an ache, then the ache would start burning until she was in exhausted agony, but this was all she could think of to do.

The magnetic blanket she draped over Reach's kingdom was so thin that a wireworm could push through it and not even feel it, but Electra would perceive the ripple when the field was broken. She'd know when and where her prey had emerged.

She closed her eyes as exhaustion washed through her. Somewhere beyond the low rubble of London's horizon the daylamp was coming, but she wouldn't sleep, not while the glittering pieces of her family waited behind her eyelids. The creature that had shattered them would come hunting again, sooner or later, seeking the Son of the Streets.

It would be ready to kill.

And so would she.

TWENTY-ONE

Beth and Fil looked at their new recruits. A hundred walking lightbulbs, ragged and disorganized, looked back.

For a moment the street prince flinched under their gaze. Then he drew himself up and reached for his spear.

"Victor, will you hang around?" he asked. "Help us translate?"

"Da."

"We won't be taking you away from anything important?" Beth put in. She'd taken a liking to the old Russian.

He smirked under his beard, stepped out of his rumpled sleeping bag, and scuffed his shoe over the cobbles, sweeping a crisp packet out of the way. "I think housework can wait for few days."

Beth laughed, then a thought struck her. She rummaged in her backpack for her torch and offered it to Victor.

"Can you use this to talk to them?" she asked. "In their language I mean?"

Victor snapped the light on and off in a strange syncopated pattern a couple of times. The nearest Blankleit nodded and flashed a response. The tramp pursed his lips.

"Da," he said.

Fil gave Beth a quizzical look. "What made you do that?" he asked.

"I—I just thought it'd be nice, you know, for us to talk to 'em in their own lingo, you know, more respectful."

He gave her a small half-smile, and Beth could see he was trying to look amused. She thought she could see a hint of admiration there too.

Victor grinned broadly and slapped Beth on the back. "You are sweet girl, I come to make sure you not get too horribly killed."

Beth was jubilant. Lucien caught her eye and she did a small air-punch for his benefit, which he loftily ignored. It didn't matter that there were only a hundred of them.; what mattered was that *she'd* won them over. She was proving she belonged here in this strange city.

As Fil led them into the maze of alleyways, the glare of the Blankleits sprang back at them off the bricks, mingling with their shadows: soldiers of light and darkness on the march. Small sounds, London sounds—the growl of a night bus down a deserted road, drunken whoops, bass thumping—echoed distantly. They walked a fine tracery of reality inlaid in the streets. It was a groove worn by centuries of magic, a groove anyone might stumble into.

Anyone might, Beth thought, *but* I *did*.

Victor prattled as they walked. "I was colonel in KGB. No worry, I have this rabble kicked into shape in no time."

"KGB?" Beth said. "I thought you were in the army."

"Was in both, my little Tsarina, in Moscow—"

"You said St. Petersburg."

"Moskva first."

"You in the Russian Ballet and all?" Beth asked, suddenly skeptical.

"*Niet,* but had girlfriend once who was."

Beth laughed at the tramp in his musty greatcoat. "This girlfriend, was she a much prettier sane girl?" she asked.

"Prettier, *da*. Sane, *niet*, crazy as squid in vodka. All ballerinas are." He chuckled.

They turned onto a narrow road lined with small steel-shuttered windows and battered stairwell doors. Something about it nagged her, striking a dim spark of recognition off the inside of her head, something more than the sense of anonymous familiarity that she got from almost every London street. Then they passed a graffitied wall by a corner shop and all of sudden she knew why.

She stopped and stared. Nestled unassumingly in amongst the brighter, brasher graffiti was a patch of writing in black marker pen, so badly faded that only three letters were still legible:

… one.

"What'cha looking at?" Fil came strolling up behind. "One? One what?"

A little "oh" slipped from Beth's lips. She felt like someone had slid a fine blade into her chest. It didn't say "one," not really. She knew exactly what had been written there.

She'd watched Pen do it.

It had been one of those warm September afternoons that drags summer behind like a lame leg. The sun had pounded down from an infinite sky, and the street had smelled of trees and baking pavements. The two of them had sat on the wall, kicking their heels and watching traffic as they listened to the radio on Pen's phone, one set of earphones between both of them, alternately singing along and cracking up.

The tracks had switched; a ballad crackled through.

"'You saved me!'" Beth had crooned daftly into the empty air, recognizing the tune. "'Girl, your love saved my liiiife—'"

She'd sensed Pen's mood as it went, an instant before the slim Pakistani girl snorted and yanked the earphone free. "What a load of bollocks," she'd said.

Beth had sighed and snapped the ring-pull on a can of Coke. There was pretty much only one thing that could get Pen's mouth into the same postcode as a swearword, even one as mild as that. And if they were having this conversation again, Beth was going to need caffeine.

"Bollocks love songs with bollocks lyrics that mean *bollocks* all!" Pen snapped.

"Leon ignored you again, huh?"

"No." After a few seconds silence Pen had conceded,

"Well, okay, so maybe he did kind of blank me after assembly, but—"

"Pen, you could just ask him out—I mean, I know it'd lead to the eternal shaming of your ancestors, or whatever. But at least it would get it over with."

"This isn't about *Leon!*" Pen had protested hotly. "It's just—'you saved my life'—seriously? Who talks about being in love like that? Love isn't the NHS or the bloody Samaritans; it's not about saving lives. Love isn't about keeping people *whole*. It's … " She tailed off, flailing her hands in disgust.

Beth gestured for her to go on. She didn't often get a chance to hear Pen rant, and it was kind of entertaining.

But a thoughtful frown had crossed Pen's face and instead of speaking, she'd pulled a marker pen from her pocket. She'd jumped off the wall and scrawled on it:

The one you love is the one who breaks you
The one you owe, and the one you own
The one who shatters and remakes you
Sets you crooked as a broken bone.

"It's more like that," she'd said at last, lamely.

Beth read it and promptly burst out laughing. "That's cheery. Pen, if Leon's making you feel like—"

"It's *not* about *Leon*," Pen had insisted again, her voice hard. She'd blushed deeply, not meeting Beth's eye.

It was only now that Beth realized she should have stopped laughing then.

The image in her mind changed to the headmistress' office, to Pen hugging herself tight, like her arms were all that held her together. Like she'd been shattered and needed someone to remake her.

And Beth had been too full of fury to even try.

She shook her head hard, bringing herself back to now and the autumn night, their regiment of glowing glass soldiers. Their war.

She looked at Fil. "My best mate wrote it." She was a little surprised at the tears she was sniffing back. "It doesn't say 'one.' It's the end of this poem, it says—"

But he wasn't listening. He was looking past her, and so was everyone else.

A tall figure was coming up the middle of the deserted road towards them, past the empty restaurants and the window displays of gaudy, mile-high shoes. It lurched with a peculiar, rounded gait, as though one leg was a lot shorter than the other. It was dropping rubbish; scraps trailed behind it like it was shedding them. The figure was too far away to see it clearly, especially with the flaring of the Blankleits in her eyes, but the *smell*...

Beth looked at Fil. His nostrils twitched as an odor of rotting fruit and mildew gusted up the street. He didn't take his eyes off the man-figure as it stumped into the light. She swallowed hard; she'd never seen the figure before, but she knew who it was.

"Filius." The garbage-built man's voice was weak, squeezed from punctured football lungs. "I'm so proud of you."

Gutterglass tottered forward two more steps, then his lips slipped across each other, giving his jaw a dislocated look. An eggshell slipped from his eye socket. His body disintegrated from the head down, collapsing into a heap of rubbish on the tarmac.

TWENTY-TWO

Down the roads of roof-slate, over battlements of brick,
My lord wants you to come to him, quick! quick! quick!
Across the Demolition Fields, where dozers plough the dead,
Your fleshy body through the cracks, thread! thread! thread!
Scale the tower, kiss the glass,
Break the wood and burn the grass.
Gaze across the barren beauty,
Cranes construct and do their duty.

———

Pen's finger came away from the wall, the metal barb that surmounted it caked in dust. She stared at the verse she'd carved—but had *she* written that, or had *it*, the wire-thing that had enveloped her? She was terrified and exhausted, but she couldn't cry any more.

She was so tired that without the wire holding her up, she'd have fallen. The metal thorns had goaded her across rooftops and through backyards and down streets until the office blocks had reared up around her like the sides of a gorge. She'd barreled into pedestrians, sending them flying. One old woman had stared up in horror at her face, but the wire pushed her on so fast that she'd barely glimpsed herself in passing windows—torn nostrils, ripped cheeks, bloody teeth—before she went barreling on.

A wall had reared up in front of her and she'd ducked under a lintel and through doorways, clambering through tiny spaces into a labyrinth of tumbled-down concrete. The air stank of wet cement and she'd wriggled and wormed her way through in silence.

Once, the wire had gone suddenly still, freezing her in the dark, and Pen forgot herself and screamed. Her lips tore on the barbs and blood ran back down her throat. She mewled around her ripped tongue, afraid she was being kept here to die, but no, the wire twitched and shifted, piercing her skin in a new configuration, and resumed its sprint.

It was only when a police siren wailed far below that she realized how high she'd climbed.

She'd burst out onto the top floor of a half-built tower. The concrete was bare, and one wall was missing. All that separated her from the construction site below was a thin tarpaulin and five hundred feet of empty air. Wind whistled and the tarp snapped aside.

Neon lights mounted on cranes like eyes on stalks turned on her, bleaching her skin bone-white, whiter than a white girl. Her blood, where it caked the barbs in her arms, was black.

Pen could feel herself slipping away. She wanted to vanish into herself, to feel nothing, to be dead—it would be so much easier. She wanted to close her eyes, so much...

She started to let her eyelids drop, but a barb caressed the water on her eyeball, oh so lightly. She found new reserves of fear to keep them open.

The wire wanted her attention.

Machines raged in the building site, even in the depth of the night. Cranes whirred, metal screeched on metal, bulldozers roared, and there was the distant, dreadful note of hammers.

Why? She breathed the word up into her throat and felt her arm come up again. Pen was grateful—she didn't want to be grateful to it, but she felt the hot wave of relief wash through her anyway: relief because it didn't seize her tongue and squeeze her like an accordion to make her answer her own question. Instead it took her hand and scratched its answer in the dirt.

The crane's clear cry, glass and steel
In the shaking earth you feel
Hear him, Hear him
Love and fear him.
Blessed, abased in holy waste.

Pen didn't understand. Frustrated breaths wheezed out

of her nose. Was the wire mocking her with these stupid rhymes? How did it know about her poetry?

Are you in my mind? The idea twisted her into even tighter panic. It was easy to believe, as the wire bent her neck to stare at its nonsense verse, that it was leaching her thoughts through her scalp, that even her mind was within the barbs' reach.

Reach.

A scream of steel rent the air, a screech that echoed her own thoughts.

Reach.

The tower shook. A voice formed at the edges of all of the sounds carried on the tongue of the wind: bulldozers and jackhammers and the crackle of distant radios.

The barbed wire gripped Pen tighter and she gasped. The barbs let her lips open and teased along her tongue. The words she'd scrawled stood out starkly on the naked wall.

"Hear him," she whispered. "Hear him. Love and fear him."

She looked down at the building site, a hive of frenzied construction and destruction, and felt herself retch. Cranes turned and diggers chewed at the earth like hungry dogs. Echoes crashed back off half-born architecture. Even from here she could see none of the machines had a human controller, but it wasn't this that sickened her. It was the fact that things were *dying* down there.

Screams rang out in the shriek of steel on rubble. She blinked, and in an instant she perceived the foundations and exposed pipes as bodies and bones. She saw the digger's mouths opening wounds. These were *people*—maybe not flesh and blood, but people nonetheless, like the glass woman who'd tried to help her. People made of the city itself.

From up here she could see patches of black across London, hidden amongst the winking lights: building sites, demolition sites—dozens upon dozens of killing fields: a hidden holocaust.

Listen. She didn't know where the thought came from.

Needle-points squeezed into her chest and the breath rushed out of her. The wire exoskeleton bent into a ragged S-shape and she collapsed, coughing, onto her knees. Cold air stung her eyeballs. At the edge of her vision she could see her finger, scratching a word onto the floor.

"*I am Reach.*" The voice sang in the screech of the cranes.

The word was next to her eyeball.

Listen.

TWENTY-THREE

Fil ran forward, unnaturally fast, his hands darting into the rain of rubbish as it fell. He caught some—a chunk of plaster in the vague shape of a brain, a moldy carrot—and let the rest bounce off the cobbles. He crooked his ankle under the eggshells, braking their momentum so they tumbled whole onto the ground.

Beth raced over to help, but the rubbish and insects flooded out in a puddle under her feet. The stench of rotting things washed up at her and her stomach flipped over. Disgruntled flies batted her cheeks.

"Mind his eye!" Fil barked and she jerked her foot instinctively, just missing crushing the fallen eggshell. "What you trying to do, blind him?" he snapped, his gray skin pale. "Give it here."

She bent and passed it over. Rodents and beetles

scurried through the debris. One moment they looked like they were pulling the stuff back into some semblance of a body; the next, they had forgotten themselves and turned on each other, hissing. A body-like heat radiated out from the pile.

Fil began to rearrange the rubbish, helping the vermin. For a moment Beth watched, perplexed, then she got it. It was like a game of make-believe surgery, building Gutterglass from the rubbish, placing drinking straws that could be ribs over the bicycle-pump heart. She joined in. The droplets of sour-milk sweat on the patient made it feel real.

"Is wounded?" Victor stumped over. "Can help; was medic in the Spetsnaz ... " He tailed off when he saw what they were doing, and then he rummaged around in the scattered trash and yanked out a roll of discarded wrapping paper. "Here, is good for forearm."

Fil took it with a curt nod; they had a torso, a head, and one arm now, and the deflated-football lungs were stuttering, starting to breath again. Rubbish juice sprayed like saliva over them as Fil placed a hand atop the chest, counting under his breath. He swore.

"He needs energy. Victor, go through the bins, grab any food you can find—the rottener the better."

"The rottener the better?" Beth asked as the old man hurried off.

"Easier to break down," he muttered tersely. "He needs all the help he can get right now."

Victor returned with a double handful of slimy vegetables and a half jar of moldy mayonnaise. Fil fumbled in his

pocket and pulled out a small glass vial and sprinkled a few drops of liquid on each, then poured the food directly into the black-sack belly. Noses twitched, antennae wavered, and the vermin seethed in around it. Once they'd eaten, they returned with renewed purpose to the task of pulling the rubbish spirit back together. His shape emerged from the little pile of landfill as suddenly as a Magic Eye picture.

Gradually his breathing began to ease and some of the tension left Fil's face. He slipped a hand under his teacher's filthy hair and gently tilted his head up "Glas, what happened?" he murmured.

For a while it was all Gutterglass could do to breathe. His paper lips opened and shut on nothing. Finally he uttered one word in a dry whisper: "*Reach.*"

Fil's knuckles paled slightly where they gripped the old man's hair. "Reach?"

Gutterglass whispered, "He knows about—" With tremendous effort, he sat up and looked at the Blankleits, who were glowing back at him sullenly, uncertain.

"He knows what you're doing," Gutterglass concluded. Bugs shifted subtly under cardboard, and suddenly the pride shone out through the patchwork skin. "Filius, look what you're doing: you're finally growing up," he croaked happily. "I'm so proud of you."

Beth could have sworn Fil actually blushed. "Well," he mumbled, "they're only a start. I can really see us rocking up at the Demolition Fields with a hundred Whities and a few reflections. 'Oi, Crane Face, quake in the face of my

awesome army!' I just hope it doesn't rain." He shook his head ruefully. "They're not even trained yet, but—"

Gutterglass was staring up at him, an oil-like film stretching between his eggshells. He seemed to be looking past his shoulder. Or not looking at all.

Glas!" Fil yelled. Fear made him warble. "Glas, stay with us!"

Gutterglass' head snapped around, eggshell eyes stretched wide. "They'll have to do, child," he whispered. "They'll have to learn fast."

"Glas, what are you talking about?"

Beth felt the silence before Glas answered. "It followed me—it hid on the buildings, Filius." His tone was beseeching. Rich garbage air gusted from his mouth. "I *tried*," Glas said again, "I tried but it—it *mauled* me."

"Glas, what are you saying?"

The white inside of Glas' eggshell eyes glowed in the Blankleit glare. "*Scaffwolf*," he breathed.

A tiny tremor of shock ran through Fil; Beth was sure no one else had noticed it. Then the muscles in his shoulders and his arms relaxed, became visibly supple, and his grip on his spear tightened. His face took on the same cocky tension it had when Beth had first met him. Her heart tightened in her chest.

He was gearing up for a fight.

"Victor, mate?"

"Da."

"Be a champion and get our Christmas tree cousins ready for a scrap."

Victor flashed his torch imperiously. The Blankleits milled around, their faces uncertain. A couple flashed questions back.

"They want to know what comes."

As if in answer, a sound carried over the city: a clattering, ringing sound like an iron landslide.

"Tell them it's worse than an Amberglow scalping party."

The Blankleits fanned out with Fil at the center of their rough semi-circle, crouching over Gutterglass. Beth stood behind him, her knees sagging. She was sweating despite the chill of the night, alternately feeling very hot and very cold.

"Um, Fil?" she said. Her voice was shrill. "What should I, you know? What do you want me to ... ?" She tailed off as the sound of tumbling metal drew closer. It concentrated itself into a rhythm, focused knots of ringing. She caught sight of a flicker of motion above the slates to the right: something vast and fast and gray.

Fil lifted his spear from the ground and swept it around in a smooth arc, as if following the path of something hidden behind the buildings.

The hollow ringing was deafening now, enough to smash glass and burst eardrums. *How?* Beth wondered: *how could it be that loud and not be on them?* She twisted left and right, but she couldn't see it.

Suddenly, chillingly close, came a low metallic howl.

Scaffwolf.

Steel screamed around the corner. Beth hurled herself to the ground, feeling the wind of its passing. Metal pipes whirled over her at decapitation height, catching a Blankleit and shattering him into phosphorescent powder. A sooty man-shape burned on her retinas for an instant and then was gone.

The world was spinning metal and broken glass and sickening howling. Something grabbed Beth by the hood and yanked her back. A steel paw clanged off the cobbles where her head had been.

The Scaffwolf bayed. She saw it and heard it and felt it in her gut. A blunt muzzle formed by a skeleton of pipes emerged from an unformed body, a cloud of scaffolding whirling in constant, chaotic motion. Jaws creaked on hinges as they snapped, and clouds of blood-red rust sprayed from flaring nostrils. As Beth watched, rods spun and locked into place and a paw the size of her head lashed out, shattering the life from another lightbulb man.

"Victor!" Fil yelled over the screeching metal, "we have to fall back!"

The old man was dancing a strange jig, trying to dodge the rain of metal. "Da, you *think?*"

The Scaffwolf snapped at them with jagged teeth and sharpened screws and Fil hauled Beth backwards. Her entire body rang with the impact as the jaws slammed shut on empty air. She shoved herself upright and together they ran for a narrow lane. Gutterglass crawled and spilled and swarmed under her feet.

They wormed their way into the narrow gap in the bricks, Blankleits scrambling after them. Mannequins watched dully from a shop window and it took Beth a second to realize that the shop was set into a wall at the back of the lane. Panic rose in her throat.

The lane was a cul-de-sac.

Everything shuddered as the wolf pounced. Its toes gouged the cobbles at the mouth of the lane. It was huge, its shoulders wider than the alley. The Scaffwolf rammed against the buildings, baying and snapping. Brickdust flowed like snow from the scarred walls. Its head extended nine feet into the alley, but it could come no further. It snarled in frustration; the sound was like a braking truck.

Beth pushed out breath as hysterical relief washed through her. She looked at Fil for reassurance, but she found none. His knuckles were pale around his railing and his face taut with fear

Cogs whirred and nuts loosened. There was a *shinking* sound and oiled struts slid closer together as she watched. The muzzle at the mouth of the lane grew narrower, the neck and shoulders collapsing towards one another. The wolf shrank just enough to slide into the alley and sprang right at them.

Fil yelled, *"Victor!"* and the old tramp barked something in Russian. His light flashed and the Blankleits flared in response. Their light, springing back off the belly of the wolf, nearly blinded her. The Scaffwolf slowed down in midair. It sank sluggishly and landed just short of them, growling and shaking its head from side to side.

Beth's back was pressed to the glass shop front. Around her the Blankleits' hands were extended towards the beast: a forest of glass arms with incandescent veins. The fine hairs were standing up on Beth's skin. The Blankleits were pushing out some kind of force at the wolf.

Beth's head whirled. She felt giddy. *How?* She couldn't breathe. *How?*

The glass men had slowed the beast, but they hadn't stopped it. Slowly, inexorably, it placed one paw in front of the other, its metal neck bent against the invisible power they projected.

A glass man stood transfixed in its path: the round one, the first one to sign up. Beth wished suddenly that she knew his name. The wolf loomed over him, jaws hanging open, slavering rust. Other streetlamp men stepped forward. She could see every filament straining, but they couldn't stop it.

Every light flashed, but Beth's scream was the only sound as the wolf's jaws crunched shut.

It turned to face her, a tiny bit quicker now with one of its enemies dead. Its feet rang off the street as it loped towards her with casual malice. The whistling of its breath echoed all around, filling the alley. As she cast around for some sort of weapon she saw a Blankleit collapse, exhausted.

Something gray blurred past her. Faster than a hummingbird's wing, Fil launched himself at the beast.

His spear stopped before he did, torn from his grasp by the same magnetism that had slowed the wolf, and he caught the lower jaw and swung up like an acrobat, landing precariously on the beast's nose. The Scaffwolf lashed its head furiously but Fil windmilled his arms and some- how kept his balance.

Beth gasped and breathed again.

"*Filius*—" The voice was a wet hiss of air. Gutterglass sounded horrified. He tried to accrete towards his ward, the wrapping paper arm outstretched.

"Beth!" Fil snapped, his concentration fierce, "hold him there!"

Beth threw herself down hard, clawing at the rub- bish. Rats hissed wildly and bit her and the beetles scurried through her hair, but she clung onto the garbage body and Gutterglass could not escape her.

"Hold it!" he cried, crouched down like a surfer. His head was bent over as though he was listening for some- thing. A look of incredulous hope emerged onto his face. "Hold it, that's good, lads," he cried. "Hold it now!"

The Blankleits had gathered around the sides of the wolf. They stood now, palms out, hemming it in with their force. The animal was torn between smashing them and shaking loose the boy who hung from its neck, taunting it. The spear rotated slowly in the air in front of the Scaff- wolf, like bait. The animal's breath whistled through its pipes, echoing off the narrow alley walls.

Another whistle sounded as if in answer, higher- pitched, a sound that seemed to come from inside the bricks of the buildings themselves. A heavy, churning rhythm started shaking the ground. An electric fear para- lyzed Beth. *Don't wolves hunt in packs?*

"Hold it!" Fil was screaming now. "Hold it there!"

The whistling from the buildings grew louder, and the ground shuddered in a syncopated rhythm: *Thrum-clatter-clatter.*

Beth had heard that sound before. *Maybe it blames you for its mauling*, she thought suddenly. *Maybe what it wants is payback—*

"Hold it!" Fil was hanging by one hand from the wolf's shoulder and as it turned and snapped at him; its teeth sliced the air inches from his face. His fingers slipped on the metal. He was going to fall—

Beth couldn't watch; she turned her head away and gazed sightlessly into the shop window. The dead gaze of the mannequins met hers, and behind them . . .

Behind the glass, two tiny pinpricks of light were growing.

"Hold it! Hold it!"

Thrum-clatter-clatter-thrum-clatter-clatter-thrum-clatter-clatter—

The points of light in the window swelled into head-lamps and wind whipped Beth's hair against her forehead. The whistling climbed to a shriek.

"Hold it." Fil's voice was frantic but triumphant. "*Hold it!*"

The shop window exploded.

Beth curled into a ball as shattered glass rained down. Hot pain flared where it lacerated her. Dead-straight grooves like tracks ripped through the cobbles—but they swerved *around* her. Lights rushed past barely an inch from her head.

For an instant, she saw it—*her* Railwraith—but it

looked vague, weaker than she remembered. *It can't survive away from the tracks*; that's what Fil had said. It was already dying. But she looked in through its windows and saw its ghostly passengers: sewing and chattering and texting; every face was fiercely determined.

Fil leapt, snatching his spear from the air as the Rail-wraith rushed towards the wolf's empty eye sockets.

Metal screamed for a long second, then silence.

Beth touched her ear and felt something wet. She was shivering, she realized. She rose to her knees, and fell straight back. Twisted scaffolding filled the alley, glowing red-hot and seething with smoke. A steam-whistle cry ghosted from the air.

Beth twitched her toes. They responded, so she tried to stand again, and this time she made less of a hash of it.

Fil lay where he'd been cast against a wall. His skin was livid with cuts, but he was sitting up before Beth reached him. His eyes were glazed and his nose had been snapped hard to the right. His grin was crooked. Glas?" he asked.

Beth groped for the eggshells in her hoodie pocket. They were whole. She set them down and, after a second, rats and worms and beetles started writhing out of the brickwork, building their master around them.

Gutterglass could barely stand. Fil had to support him. "My my," he murmured. "What a mess."

His eggshell eyes fell on Beth and a little rill of shock went through her. "Nicely taken," he said, and pointed at his eyes. A grimace crossed his garbage face. "Filius," he murmured, "I need to talk to you alone." Leaning heavily on Fil, he lurched out of the lane.

The alley had been badly damaged: windows smashed, stone and brickwork clawed. At the mouth Beth could see Victor, semaphoring to the crowd of Blankleits with her torch. Their glow reached back into the cul-de-sac, and Beth could see that barely half of them had survived. The rest were dust and burn-marks on the ground.

Beth staggered in amongst the wreckage of the wolf. There was no sign of her train. Desperately, she tried to think: where were the nearest train tracks? The Underground ran close by, that nexus of lines at Oxford Circus. Could her Railwraith have reached them in time? *Please*, she prayed inside her head, *please have made it.*

There was an electric sense in the air, like the ghost of an emotion, a residue the wraith had left behind it. It was a feeling of *pride*, of making amends. The Railwraith *had* swerved around her, she thought, awestruck. She hadn't imagined it. She remembered how ashamed it had seemed when it fled from the freight train's attack. *You were a passenger*, Fil had said. It hadn't been stalking her, it had been *looking out* for her.

Anyone who's crazy enough to ride one Railwraith and shout at another needs all the help she can get.

Apparently, her Railwraith had felt the same.

She felt grateful, and sick, and like she didn't deserve it. *You think they can't feel, and think, and bloody love?* His words rang round her head. *There's more lives at stake here than the ones that look like you.*

A lump filled Beth's throat and she found herself starting to cry.

"Beth." Fil and Gutterglass had reappeared at the mouth of the alley. Ants still raced over Glas' cheek, filling in gaps with scraps of matchbox, but he looked steadier now.

Fil's scratched and burned face scrunched up. His voice was gruff, as though he'd been shouting. "Beth," he tried again.

Gruffness didn't suit his voice, Beth thought; he was just a teenager, like her.

He took a step forward, then looked back at Gutterglass as if for support. The rubbish man smiled grimly and motioned him forward.

"Beth," Fil said, "you need to leave. Now."

TWENTY-FOUR

Pen shivered in the tower as dawn crept into the nooks and crevices of the building site. She had been longing for sunrise, but it let her down: the daylight failed to banish her nightmare.

Below her, the machines worked on remorselessly. Immobilized as she was, only when the wind tugged the tarpaulin away could she see glimpses of a crane at the top of its arc, or a flash of yellow tape on the flank of a digger. The sources of the screams stayed mercifully out of sight.

Chatter floated up: tourists at the cathedral. To them, this carnage would sound like any other construction work. It did to her, too. Nothing about the *sounds* was special; it was her *hearing* that had changed. She heard the cries of pain from the foundations as they were shredded, and they chilled her.

When the red faded out of the sunrise, the wire decided it was time for her to sleep. *Rest*, it scratched with her finger in the dust. Then it bent her at the knee and the waist and laid her flat on her back. It was rigid around her, like a wire coffin.

Maybe it's nocturnal, she thought, *or maybe it thinks I am. After all, when it caught me I was stumbling around in the dark like a drunken girl.*

The wire had been forcing her into strange poses and stretches, reconfiguring her, like a child trying to learn the limits of a new toy. It ran a barb caressingly over her skin, and left her a few seconds to stare at the drab concrete ceiling before its tendrils reached for her eyelids and pulled them shut.

It was the first time in days it had let her close her eyes, but Pen couldn't sleep. Her heartbeat went through her skull like nightclub bass. When she was a kid she'd read stories about martyrs under torture who'd dislocated their minds from their bodies. They'd prayed to Allah and transcended their flesh. Inside their minds, they'd laughed as their tormentors labored fruitlessly on.

Pen had never believed those stories, but now, with the metal barbs holding her eyes shut, she started to pray.

Over the beat of her heart, she could hear Reach, speaking. He hadn't stopped repeating the same phrases since she'd arrived here:

"I am Reach."

"I am Reach."
"I will be."

Pen tried to pretend her body didn't matter. *Your soul is feather-light,* she whispered in her mind. *It will peel from your body like lantern-fruit skin.* But it was no good; she was panicking again, breathing faster—she couldn't make herself *believe* it.

What if the body was all there was? She couldn't stop herself wondering, what if there wasn't any *soul* at all? What if there wasn't *any* part of her that the wire hadn't gripped, torn—

—*stolen.* If that was so, then she was entirely its thing.

"I am Reach."
"I will be."

Reach forced his voice over those of the dying. Pen realized it wasn't English, or Urdu; it was the language of destruction itself. The words vibrated through the barbs in her scalp, as if the wire monster was dripping its consciousness through them and into her.

"I. Will. Be."

With mounting awe Pen realized she was witnessing a birth. Something was hauling itself into being, stamping itself out, and she shuddered at the will it took.

Reach was carving itself from the living bones of the city.

Eventually exhaustion washed over her, and the voice followed her into darkness.

———————

Pen woke as a breeze rippled over her. She started to reach for her duvet, only to find she couldn't move. For some reason she couldn't open her eyes. She jerked and kicked, or tried to, but her skin tore on things that felt like cold thorns and she remembered where she was.

There was a scratching flick at her eyelids. Instinctively they obeyed and fluttered open. It was night; the moon glimmered sullenly through dirty sepia clouds, far out-shone by the brash neon on the sides of the cranes.

The wire creaked her to her feet and bent her head down. A message was scrawled in the dust: *sustenance*. A rill of outrage ran through her. It had used her body in her sleep without her even knowing.

It's kidnapped you and skewered you and sleep-deprived you—and you lose your temper over THIS? But the anger remained. Another boundary had been so casually breached. Her body felt less her own than ever.

Sustenance.

She felt her arm rise of its own accord to point and an instant later her neck twisted the same way. The wire had brought her presents: a Flintstones-iced birthday cake; three halves of assorted sandwiches; a mound that smelled like cat food; a ragged heap of fur with the rotting stench of roadkill; a squat column of soft red clay; and a battery,

220

with live wires hissing and spitting from it. The smells twisted in her stomach; here was all manner of sustenance. The wire didn't know what she ate.

Her feet scratched the ground as she was walked towards the food.

All the while Reach's cacophonous monologue went on behind her:

"I will be."
"I will be."
"I am Reach."

Flies waltzed in the air over the roadkill, casting fat shadow blots on the wall. She fell to her knees beside it and the smell streaked up her nostrils, down her throat, and punched her in the gut. Suddenly the pressure eased in her right arm and she wiggled her fingers. Pins and needles raced down it, but she could flex her hand! She rolled her shoulder and the wire rolled with her, the barbs gently dimpling her skin. Excitement swelled at the bottom of her throat.

She tried her left arm. "Ow!" The barbs bit deep and blood spread immediately. So the cage around her left arm was staying.

But she'd been able to—

It was true: the wire around her jaw had loosened. "I can shout—bloody hell, I can *talk*!" Pen laughed, and it echoed back off the concrete, sounding scarily manic.

Her neck was jerked to the side, forcing her to look at

the food. Her laughter faded and she understood the reason for her newly granted movement. The wire wanted her to feed. It wanted her to *choose*.

Her stomach contracted and she felt sick. *Why?* Why did the wire-monster want to feed her? Why had it made her sleep? The questions rattled around her skull: what was this thing keeping her healthy for?

"*No*," she whispered and the slack around her head gave her just enough space to shake it, a tiny gesture of defiance.

The coils sighed as they slid over her, almost regretfully tightening up. Pen's last free breath was cut in half in a silly gulp.

Her eyes kept peeled wide, she watched her hand reach out towards the food. Every fiber of her wanted to turn away, but of course she couldn't. The rotting roadkill was half an inch from her hand. She knew the wire wouldn't hesitate to shove it down her throat.

"*Wait——*" She subvocalized the word, hoping the wire would understand even through the mangled consonants.

The wire froze, and then relaxed again, and this time Pen slumped forward. The bread of the sandwich felt clammy as her fingers closed around it. A trickle of warmth ran down her cheek: a tear. She couldn't brush it away. The food tasted of ash and mold. The wire flexed around her jaw, helping her to chew.

Afterwards she lay on the ground and stared out into the night, where the cranes cast their monstrous shadows in the arclights. She could feel herself slipping again. She wondered if she could vanish into herself, forget where she was.

She wondered if she could make herself go mad.

But that would be to totally cede her body to the thing that gripped it.

It needs you, she whispered to herself. *You're its host. It needs your body, and that's important. That's a weakness. That's a weapon. Bide your time, Pen. Bide your time.*

A neon lamp revolved and she stared fiercely into its glare. Below her Reach worked. She didn't even know if it knew she was there.

"I am Reach."
"I am Reach."
"I will be."

Pen sucked her lip in between her teeth and bit down, hard. It was all she could do with her fraction of an inch of freedom. And it felt good.

Yes, she told herself. *I will be.*

TWENTY-FIVE

"You know what?" Beth snapped. She folded her arms and glared at him. "Piss off!"

Gutterglass turned and inspected her reflection delicately in a windowpane.

Beth had only been slightly surprised when the old man made of rubbish had slowly rebuilt itself as a woman this time.

"What?" Fil asked.

"Piss off," she repeated.

"Well … that's pretty much what we *were* going to do."

"I know—piss off with your pissing off. You can't just piss off. You need me—"

"What for?" Gutterglass enquired mildly. "Your extensive vocabulary?"

Beth glared at her. "You want to hear my extensive vocabulary? You patronizing cu—"

"*Lizbet!*" Victor cut her off, sounding so scandalized that she actually blushed. "Not ladylike!" The Russian sat on the pavement beside his huddled, glass-skinned soldiers, who'd all promptly yawned and stretched and fallen asleep the moment the sun had come up. He swigged from his vodka bottle and looked mournfully from one to the other, muttering, "Not ladylike at all."

Fil took a step towards Beth. The edges of his eyes were red-raw, a shockingly human color on him. "Beth, I don't think you're listening to me."

"No? I reckon I heard you tell me to get lost loud and clear."

"Beth!"

"*Fil!*" she snapped. "I'm not going anywhere."

His jaw set, he sniffed hard and turned back towards Gutterglass. "Well, we are. Come nightfall you can have this place all to yourself."

Beth grabbed her backpack. "I'll follow you."

He whirled, his face taut and furious. "You couldn't keep up—that's the whole point: you need protecting all the time."

Beth shoved herself towards him, jutting her chin pugnaciously. "Why? Because I'm a *girl*?"

"No! Because you're slow and weak and bloody ... " He tailed off, grasping the air in frustration. "You're bloody *human*! And I've not got the eyes—and she's not got the eggshells—and neither of us have the spare arms to keep dragging your skinny arse out of trouble every time we meet one of them." He pointed to the twisted remnants of the Scaffwolf.

He breathed in deeply, then let it out slowly, regaining control of himself. "I'm sorry, Beth," he said. "I thought I could cover you, but I can't. You were *this close* to getting bitten in half. I won't have it."

Beth stood eye to eye with him. "Oh, you won't?" Her throat was tight and dry, and her voice came out in a growl. "You're the one gave me this, remember?" She tugged her sleeve up to show her skyscraper-crown scar. "'Give up home,' you said. 'Give up safety, forever.' *Forever*. Not 'until we get into a scrape and Beth gets a bit knocked about.' Well, I gave it up, willingly. You can't make me go back now."

He looked away, shamefaced, so she swept her mutinous gaze round to Gutterglass. "You put him up to this, didn't you?" she accused, her voice climbing shrilly. "He was fine with me getting my arse kicked bloody before you turned up. He'd've been perfectly happy to have my guts hanging from the nearest one of those!" She pointed at a crane arching over the Gherkin in the distance.

"Oh dear," Gutterglass murmured softly with a wince, as though Beth just had displayed a painful level of naïveté. "No, he most certainly would not—quite the opposite, in fact."

Beth gaped at the wretched-looking boy who was blushing almost black. Her thoughts flashed back to the day before, after they'd delivered their ultimatum to the

Mirrorstocracy, that moment their lips had hovered over each other. She felt a twinge in her chest, like someone had tapped her heart with a tiny hammer.

Gutterglass cleared her throat primly. "Indeed, the prince is so concerned for your wellbeing that in view of your fragility he is *reluctant* to enter combat for a second time while you are with him. Were you to come to harm, I expect he'd be beside himself, weeping, wailing, beating of breast, et cetera—"

The prince fixed his tutor with a glare.

Beth managed to stop herself from saying the first thing that came into her head. Unfortunately she blurted out the second thing instead: "That's not *my* fault! That's him being a pussy—!"

"Oh, for Thames' sake!" Fil's spear clanged off the cobbles as he threw it to the ground.

Beth rounded on him. "Oh, I'm *sorry*," she snapped. "Did the weak, slow, helpless little girl hurt your feelings?"

He slumped onto the ground beside Victor, dragged the bottle from his grasp, and swigged off a hefty measure.

"*Beth*," he said. Or at least he tried to say, but the booze had apparently scoured his throat and he only managed a lame rasp.

"Beth," he tried again. "I can't ask you to—you can't ask me to—look, you can't come, all right? I'll break both your legs before I let you follow me somewhere Reach could hurt you."

Beth could feel herself starting to tremble: a 9.9 on the *dear Christ please don't let me cry now* scale.

"I'll tell the world about you." She unslung her back-pack from her shoulder and shook it, rattling the paint cans. "I'll tell everyone. If you don't take me with you, I'll paint your face forty feet high on the side of every building east of Big Ben. You won't get any peace. Everyone who sees you will harass you. People will come looking for you, searching for the *freaks*."

The word was cruel, but she was ready for cruelty now; rejection was sharp in her chest. They couldn't chuck her out; she'd make it too damned painful for them. "Armies of 'em," she promised nastily. "Scientists and tourists and the sodding *zoo*—they'll hunt you down."

Gutterglass was looking at her gravely. Fil's lip twisted and he thrust his hands in his pockets. "They really won't, Beth," he said. He sighed. "Go to the asylum in Brixton Road; ask if anyone there's seen a walking lightbulb, or overheard a statue talking—I guarantee there'll be one, maybe even a few. Noggin-wranglers' notebooks all over London are stuffed with the kind of stories you could tell."

"Some of them even have illustrations," Gutterglass interjected. "There are already paintings of me, Miss Brad-ley, forty feet high and four inches high and everything between. And yet no matter how loudly a few benighted wretches scream and point at me, no one else takes a blind bit of notice."

Beth faltered. She looked from one to the other, sud-denly feeling as helpless as a child. "How?" she whispered.

Gutterglass spread the hands Beth had given her as though to plead ignorance. "It's none of our doing that no one listens to the few people who let themselves notice us. People believe *stories*, not facts, and we don't fit into theirs, so they don't tend to believe in us. We're easy enough to miss, after all."

"What did you think?" Fil asked sympathetically. "That we were some kind of secret? We live in your streets, Beth. You live in ours— you have done your whole life."

Beth felt a pinch in the hollow of her throat. *You live in our streets.* She remembered him, that night under the streetlights, arms outstretched as if to embrace the whole city's glow. *Home?* he'd said. *I could bed down in any square inch of London town. Welcome to my parlor.*

That's what she wanted: not safety, *home.* To be able to curl into the warmth of that word. To call the city home— to *be* home, with him, on these streets. She pulled herself up tall, held herself rigid against the tremor that threatened to run through her. "Fine," she said coldly. "Go your own way. But the first place I'm going when you do is St. Paul's. I'll take on Reach by myself, even if I have to headbutt the bloody cranes to death."

Fil snorted. "You don't mean that."

"YOU DON'T THINK SO?" Beth yelled at him.

He stepped back, alarmed, and fury boiled up in her throat like hot tar—rage at being left behind, at there being nothing she could do about it—and she realized she *did* mean it. She really *would* take on Reach alone, just to prove a point. She didn't know where it came from, this urge to spite the street urchin so strong that she would contemplate suicide-by-crane-god, but it was strong in her.

"You were going to run," she said, swallowing against the humiliating advance of tears. "Remember that? You were going to run and *I* made you stay. Maybe I can't run as fast as you or climb as high as you can, but fuck you, Filius Viae, I *helped*."

Her eyes were treacherously wet, but she wasn't about to blink; she wouldn't give him that satisfaction. He stared back at her for long, long seconds, then he turned and walked away...

...and then, just when it felt like her heart had fallen down a well and there was no way to get it back, he paused, as if he'd just thought of something. He muttered to himself.

"What was that, Filius?" Gutterglass asked.

"I said, she's right."

Beth blinked some of her tears back in. "What?" she said.

The rubbish-woman's tone was glacial. "A good question, Filius. *What?*"

"Thames, Glas, don't make me say it again." He sighed. "She's right: I *was* going to run. She was the only reason I didn't."

Gutterglass' face creased into a nervous smile. "But that was *then*; that was before—"

"*That* was five days ago—before what? Before *her*, Glas, that's the only 'before.' We owe her." The look he shot at Beth was guilty.

A thrill prickled her scalp. Whatever his protestations,

Fil wasn't doing this out of any sense of debt to her—in spite of himself, in spite of his fear, he *wanted* her there.

"But you said it yourself," Gutterglass protested. "She isn't strong enough—she isn't fast enough—"

"But we can make her faster, can't we?" he said. "We can make her stronger."

Gutterglass' eyes stretched open, their enamel white insides turning almost outwards as whatever had just occurred to her ward touched her mind as well.

"*Blood flowing Thames,*" she swore.

"Can you make me braver?" Fil asked quietly. "Because given the suicidal bloody nature of the enterprise I'm on, it looks like she can."

There was silence then, broken only by a pigeon making a nose-dive for the bit of bun that formed Gutterglass' left ear.

"Would the two of you *please stop talking about me like I'm not here!*" Beth yelled.

Gutterglass' eggshell eyes didn't stray from her prince's face. "You had better tell her, then," she said. "Tell her what you're asking her to do." She turned away and crouched over the Blankleits, muttering and petting them, checking that none of their hairline cracks had opened up.

Fil looked pale, elated, and scared all at once. "Come on then." He took Beth by the arm.

"Where are we going?"

"I'll explain on the way, but we need to get going now. I *really* don't want to meet them in the dark. Glas, Victor," he called back over his shoulder, "look after the Lampies for us while we're gone."

Victor grunted and swigged from his bottle, but Gutterglass answered acidly, "Oh, *absolutely*, your Highness! And should I wash your jeans for you too? Maybe you've got time for a foot rub before you go? What with having only your babysitting to do I can't think what I'll do with all my *spare time!*"

He glared at her, but though worms writhed through the eggshells, she didn't blink. The street prince caved first. "All right," he said at last. "What are you going to do, then?"

"What you should be doing instead of running off on a wild wraith-chase. I'm going to put together an army. I'll start with our Mistress' priesthood."

"Our first port of call," Fil said. "They wouldn't listen."

A beetle tugged a thin smile across Gutterglass' lips. An unmistakable new confidence infused her shape. "They will listen to me."

Beth dragged her arm from his grip. "Fil, please, tell me where we're going."

The smile, when it finally made it onto his face, was the very opposite of reassuring. "We're going to get you what you want."

―――――

Paul Bradley paced the streets of Hackney in a kind of aggravated daze. The light from the streetlamps made his hands look jaundiced. Early evening frost crunched under his feet. He spoke to himself in an angry mumble, which sometimes rose to a frightened shout. Tramps eyed him from their sleeping bags. He knew the couples hustling past him, huddled into each other, were assuming he was drunk, but though he'd been tempted, he hadn't had anything stronger than coffee. He knew he wasn't mad—madness would be to *stop* talking to himself, to stop urging himself on. Madness would be to succumb to the almost irresistible urge spreading from the pit of his stomach to curl up in a doorway and shut his eyes until the world went away.

"Think, Bradley, *think*," he hissed to himself, over and over. "*Think*. You *can* find her." *Walk, Bradley, walk,* echoed the unspoken instruction to his legs, and obediently he shoved one foot in front of the other.

When the glowing woman's last light had faded he'd stumbled away from the shattered place behind the railway, walking until his knees gave way. He sat on the pavement outside a closed Internet café on a ganja-scented high street, clutching the picture of the boy with the railing. He'd not smelled the sweet dough rising in the Caribbean bakery next door, or noticed the taunts of the kids strutting past in their hoodies and baseball jackets. The sound of passing police sirens did register, and he'd felt a pang— but what could he tell them? That his missing daughter's best friend had been kidnapped by a cloud of barbed wire? If he was banged up in a cell for wasting police time his chances of fixing this fell to zero.

When the café opened, he scanned Beth's sketch of the skinny boy and posted it on as many message boards as he could find. Then, seized by a horror of inaction, he ran back out into the street to walk London's endless, twisting pavements until he was as breathless as he was bewildered. But he had to keep walking, because the one time he'd stopped, just for a moment, just to ease his aching feet, he'd fallen asleep. In his dream a kindly faced woman in a headscarf had demanded, over and over again, in his own voice: "Where is my daughter?" He awoke soaked in sweat, and as cold as the morning frost that webbed the tarmac.

He knew exactly how Parva's parents would be feeling now: the way they'd be reassuring themselves, repeating, "I'm sure she's fine" over and over because although they weren't sure she was fine at all, they had no idea what to do if she wasn't. He knew the symptoms; he was a carrier. Having a lost child was a disease he was spreading.

But he wasn't looking for Parva, even though the guilt for that fact sat, toxic as bleach, in his belly. His only goal was to find Beth.

When he recognized a hardware shop on a street corner he realized his feet had automatically marched him close to home. "Think, Bradley, *think*; where would she go?" But he didn't know; his mind was a blank. He didn't know where she hung out, where she ate, where she shopped; apart from Parva, he didn't even know her friends.

Marianne would have known. *Oh, love, where are you? Where have you gone?* He hadn't spoken to his wife in the silence of his head like that in months. She had always known what to say. Whenever Beth had been sent home from school with a torn shirt and a bloody nose, it was always Marianne who made the long walk up to the little room in the attic and brought their daughter back to them. When he'd asked her what she'd said to Beth, she'd smiled and said, "I backed her up. It's what mothers do for their little girls."

He curled his fist around the photo of Beth's drawing of the boy, now bent and street-soiled. To his deep shame, this was all he knew of his daughter.

He almost stumbled over a pile of concrete scraps and stopped. Tires hissed over tarmac on the road behind him. He didn't sit down because he was afraid he wouldn't be able to get up again. But the darkness came over him like a suffocating blanket, and another step seemed impossible.

Walk Bradley, walk. But he didn't. A poisonous, paranoid voice in his mind said, *There's no point. She's already dead. You'll see her body. You'll see her dead body.*

The pile of broken lumps of concrete that had tripped him sat in the middle of the pavement. It looked like some kid had scribbled over it in black paint—

He froze. He tilted his head and slumped, trying to bring it into focus. Slowly, the sharp angles of concrete and paint materialized into a shape:

A rhino, horned and heavy-hoofed, was stampeding out at him.

He let out a tiny whimper. He recognized it instinctively, that sense of damage and violence that lurked in the everyday, waiting to ambush you. Slowly he let the picture of the street boy uncurl from between his fingers. He barely dared to breathe. He could see it there, in the whip-lines of ink: the rhino-in-concrete was by the same hand.

You know one more thing, he thought. *Wherever she is, she's painting.* She was leaving a trail of ink and paint like breadcrumbs.

Walk, Bradley. But he didn't walk. He ran.

TWENTY-SIX

"Gutterglass won't say so, but I'm fairly sure my mother was ashamed of me. Now, now, no need to choke up. I'm not looking for sympathy; I only want to explain, give you the context, so you'll understand why she did what she did.

"She must have been gutted when I was born, with these fingers with their bones so easy to break, these eyes that can see only seven colors. I was so small compared to her—she was this goddess, this city, and me? I was a tear-and-turd-squirting bundle constantly yammering to be fed.

"I once asked Glas if my father was human, and though she always said she didn't know, I think either my old man or one of his relatives must have been. The weaknesses bred true.

"I know, I know, brings a tear to your eye. But that's

how it was. Of course, I was still the son of a goddess, and that had its perks. If she'd just left me to grow naturally my arms would have been as strong as girders and I'd have out-run the trains. But for what she wanted me, that wouldn't have been enough.

"Mater Viae needed more: she needed me to shine like the Thames on a summer's day. She needed my bones to outlast the city foundations, and more than that, she needed me to be proof of her, to carry her name.

"She took me out east, out to the docks, though London's old port belonged to Reach then. She walked it wrapped in rags, with only Fleet, the bravest of her retinue of cats, beside her. As she passed, the street signs yearned to change, but she bid them hold.

"She kept to the brickways, the roads of fish and sew-age and opium and knotted rope, the old paths—as hard as Reach tried, he could never gentrify the docks. They were loyal to her spirit, even while he reared his towers up over them.

"She walked beside the canals and the wrecks of the old tea clippers raised themselves out of the depths, eager to relive their memories of bringing her tribute. She shushed them down again, gracious but urgent: she wasn't there to be noticed. Fleet wound her way, meowing, around her mistress' ankles, and my mother stroked her with slate-skinned fingers. They crept along, me in her arms, my mother cooing road-shanties to keep her infant child becalmed, her voice low enough that the vibrations in the air wouldn't disturb the crane struts—

"What? *What?* I'm building a picture up, all right? I'm 'setting the scene.' You want me to get on with it? *Fine.* It's night. It's dark. It's enemy territory. They're sneaking. It's risky. Get it? Good. Excuse me for trying to make it interesting.

"So anyway, there's this old abandoned dye factory, hunched over the river like a hungry old man scouring it for fish. The men that live there, the Chemical Synod, they exist beyond my mother's sway, but she'd done deals with them before—making deals is their reason to be.

"She'd given me all she could of her own power, but to challenge Reach's growing strength, to be her champion, I needed more.

"And they smiled their oil-black smiles and rubbed their frictionless palms together. They bowed deeply and in their quiet, courteous voices, they named the price.

"You see, this city is built on a lot of things: brick and stone and river clay, but under that, under everything, this city is built on bargains. Those're the true foundations of the city, those intricate contracts. Deals are sacred here.

"Behind the factory lies the chemical marsh, where the effluent of the docks has seeped into the city's flesh. These are the Synod's cauldrons, where they brew their experiments. They mix liquid chaos in carefully measured quantities, pouring it from rusted drums, peppering it with more exotic ingredients—splinters of skull from road accidents, or a vial of rainwater that flowed through London's gutters in Roman times.

"And then, at eventide, with the Thames at low ebb,

they sit in their fields inhaling the mist of the alkali fens and discuss in slick-tongued sibilants the markets they can make for that day's brew.

"These men showed my mother through one gate and then another, laughing as she slipped over the sodden ground and swayed giddily through the gas. Her hands went numb and I nearly slipped from them, and the Synod reached out, eager to catch me, to claim their most exotic ingredient yet. But she gripped me tighter and set her shoulders and walked on.

"They led her in circles, letting the poisons they farmed seep into her blood, until she was impossibly weak when they arrived at their destination: a ragged-shored pool slick with a rainbow sheen.

"My mother unwound the billboard scraps that she'd swaddled me in. Fleet flattened her ears and hissed, threatening the Synod, and they smiled their black smiles and spread their hands and stepped away,

"My mother held me by the ankle, her all-too-human child, and she stared her defiance at the cranes on the horizon as she lowered me into the pool.

"And then what, you ask? What do you think? Then I *changed*. I took on those aspects of the city the Synod had hoarded. My sweat became petrol to keep me warm on the coldest night. I could flow as silently and as quickly as shadows. My wounds would close as fast as oil over a stone.

"And their part of the deal given, the Chemical Synod demanded their payment.

"Gutterglass found me, the way she always has. Her pigeons spotted the baby lying in the marsh and bore her to me. Fleet was still hissing and yowling to keep the Synod at bay. Glas always says I wasn't crying, just staring up at the clouds, giggling, drunk on the fumes. I wasn't even aware my mother had gone.

"No one but the Synod knows what was demanded, but whatever the price was, Mater Viae didn't have it. That's why she went; had to be. She had to go hunting for it. That's why she disappeared.

"Not long after, Fleet vanished too, following her, and from that day to this, from Shepherd's Bush to Cripplegate, neither Mater Viae nor her Cats have been seen.

"And now she's coming back—who knows why? Perhaps she's completed the task the Synod gave her, retrieved whatever rare commodity they need for their next experiment in mortal chemistry.

"But still, she's been gone a long time. And sometimes I catch Glas' reflection in a windowpane, when she thinks I can't see, and her face... Well, I can't help but wonder if she thinks that I cost her a goddess, for all those years at least.

"So that's where we're going, Beth, if you're willing: out to the chemical marsh, to put petrol in your sweat and steel in your bones. We're going diving for a new you amidst the opium and tea and the old bloody brick. I asked you to give up home, give up safety, and you did, and I'm grateful. Now I need you to give up this one more thing. It's double or quits, Beth—I just hope it's not sudden death.

"Do you really want to be like me?"

TWENTY-SEVEN

Docklands: the eastest of the East End, where the dense tangle of office blocks and high-rise flats peters out, diminishing into miles of low concrete with a few desultory parks and stagnant ponds full of water.

The city's three tallest skyscrapers rise hundreds of feet above the squalor, with the lesser towers, each a glittering palace of law or finance, clustering around them on a small island in the docks. Canary Wharf is like a mask, a false-face, shouting that all in the East End is prosperous. But in the shadow of the towers the warehouses groan empty, and haggard-looking regulars have almost grown into their seats in the chilly pubs.

Do you really want to be like me?

The two of them stood on the riverbank, in front of the old dye factory. Beth's brain buzzed. She looked at Fil now and saw her future.

He avoided her gaze, and Beth's heart tightened in her chest.

Give up home.

Give up safety.

I need you to give up one more thing…

A sound made her look towards the factory. Six completely black figures slipped away from the rusting hulk and strode towards them across the marsh, seagulls wheeling around them. The midday sun shriveled pools of shadow to nothing.

The men's oil-slicked faces had a rainbow sheen. Their lips made faint sucking noises as they parted for breath. *Click click click* went the cigarette lighters—each of them had one, and they snapped them open and shut as they walked, open and shut, *open and shut*—

Their acrid stench cut through Beth's sinuses like sandpaper and tears stung her eyes. Fil had told her about their appearance, the smell, even the lighters. The one thing she hadn't expected was the *symmetry*.

They tilted their heads and smiled their black smiles identically. When one of them raised his right hand in greeting, another on the far side raised his left. They spread across the marsh like ripples on a pool of oil, graceful as dancers in their pitch-black tailoring.

Fil leaned on his spear and watched their display, his

attitude all show-off cocky, but Beth saw his jaw clench. Maybe he wasn't afraid, she told herself; maybe he was only fighting the smell.

The tallest of the Chemical Synod stepped forward from the center and the others stepped back and out in precise formation.

"Johnny Naptha." Fil's smile was tighter than a violin string.

"Filiuss Viae," the oil-soaked man acknowledged. His deep voice was smooth, pleasant. "The Sson of the Sstreetss. Pipssqueak of the Pavementss. Visseroy of the Viaductss. Sswame of the Ssidewalkss. Malingerer of the M25—"

Fil sighed and interrupted. "Could you possibly stop taking the piss, Johnny?"

"Sstunned that you would ssuggesst I would commit ssuch ssacrilege, Filiuss." Johnny turned to Beth and the Synod bowed to her in unison. Oil dripped from their foreheads to splash on the pebbles. "And who is this Kiss-met-kisssed courtessan who iss kind enough to accompany your Highnessss?"

"I am not," Beth said flatly, "a bleedin' *courtesan*."

Fil's brow wrinkled. "A what?"

"It's a nice word for 'hooker,'" said Beth, who'd learned it from Pen.

"Sso ssorry, a ssimple ssemantic sslip." Johnny inclined his head. "A conssort, then."

"Not one of them neither."

"Ah." Johnny Naptha's smile widened and a strange

thought occurred to Beth—that his smile was indestructible, that you could put Johnny Naptha through a car-crusher and his grin alone would come out whole on the other side.

"I'd certainly ssooner commit ssuicide than distress such a ssoul further," he said smoothly. He gestured back towards the dye factory. "So pleasse, come insside."

———————

The door of the dye factory led through to metal-walled cloisters covered in oceans of rust and continents of dead brown moss. The Chemical Synod formed up around Beth as they walked, wrapping her in dizzying fumes. The snap of the lighters filled her with a thrilling premonition of fire. She was beginning to feel lightheaded, and she snarled inwardly at herself to stay alert.

Johnny Naptha and Filius Viae loped side-by-side up ahead, apparently haggling over the price of her transformation. Johnny Naptha bent his head, listening closely while Fil described what he wanted.

Beth studied his sinewy back, noting the oily sweat that slicked it, the way his sharp shoulder blades protruded. Then his shoulders slumped and he gestured once, as though protesting, but his heart didn't seem to be in it.

Johnny Naptha produced a clear bottle from inside his jacket and Fil resentfully took a long swig—

Or that's what it looked like, but the level of the liquid in the bottle didn't go down; instead, it changed color, grew darker. Fil handed the bottle back to Johnny Naptha, who snatched it from his reluctant fingers and slipped it back into his coat.

Do you really want to be like me? he'd asked her. And there was only one answer: to be like him, to understand this place the way he did, to *belong* to the city the way he did. The idea stole away her breath and sealed it in a secret place under her heart.

———

"That's *disgusting*," said Beth. The famous pool was thick with oily filth and fringed with blackened grass. A chain-link fence surrounded it, and a rust-eaten sign warned interlopers:

BEWARE RUDER ARM

Some joker had graffitied in an arm in black, making the rudest sign they could think of. The Synod's members stood around the perimeter, snapping their lighters.

Fil faced Beth across the water. "What is?"

"*That*," she said, pointing at the pool. "It's *filthy*."

"It is?" He sounded surprised.

"Look how polluted it is—"

He looked incredulous. "Of course it's polluted! What—did you think you could pick up powers like I've got by swimming in *clean* water? You might as well go home and take a bloody bath!"

"The day I take bathing advice from you, petrol-sweat," she countered, "is the day I kill myself." Her reflection wavered dimly on the oily surface. She could make out the outline of her head, but the face set into it was a blank.

"So," she said. Her voice was steady, but her heart was hammering.

"So," he replied.

"Better get on with it, I guess."

"I guess."

"Just wasting time here."

"Yep."

"No going back now."

The Synod symmetrically shook their heads, and Beth felt a jolt in her chest. It was like hearing a heavy door slam behind you in a dark house.

She sat down on the bank of the pool, kicked off her trainers, and pulled off her socks. Oily black mud chilled the skin between her toes. Tentatively she stuck one foot into the filthy water—

"Ow!" she cried, and yanked it back. The skin had blistered red. She looked up at Fil.

"I did tell you it could hurt."

"*Right*," she muttered under her breath and stood up. She poised herself on the dead grass at the edge and bent like a diver, ready to get in. If she plunged in as fast as possible, she figured, she'd at least get the shock over with.

The blood thundered in her ears like trains, like traffic, like hollow pipes in the basements of tower blocks, like tides of the river itself.

Do you really want to be like me?

She tensed her muscles.

"Beth," Fil said. "I'm proud—"

She dived.

TWENTY-EIGHT

Beth involuntarily screwed up her eyes and clamped her mouth shut. She exhaled hard through her nose as the thick meniscus of the pool slid over her face. Then the water swallowed her.

Liquid rushed into her ears, roared in, drowning out her heartbeat. She felt her T-shirt billowing as the water covered her stomach, prickling it like insect feet. Blisters erupted on her neck, inside her ears, between her fingers, stinging her lips.

Don't breathe in, don't breathe in.

She pushed more breath out of her nostrils. She couldn't imagine the pain of having the toxins flood her sinuses, but the pressure built up steadily in her chest. She held her mouth shut.

Don't breathe. Don't breathe. Don't panic.

When you have to tell yourself that, a voice in her head countered dryly, *you're already screwed.*

The water savaged her skin. She could feel warm blood pouring out through her pores.

The pressure grew as the liquid squeezed her until every beat of her pulse felt fit to crack open her head. There was a vacuum in her chest like a black hole. The water seeped into the corners of her mouth, burning her gums, making her teeth fizz horribly in her mouth. It levered at her jaw, straining to be let in.

Don't breathe. Don't breathe. Don't panic.

The breath died from her nostrils. The bubbles rippling over her face ceased.

Breathe. Breathe. Don't panic.

I watch as she goes limp, spread out in the water like a black star. It would be a lie to say I'd thought this was without risk. We both knew this could kill her, and as good as she was at hiding it, Beth was horribly afraid of her death.

So was I.

I want to dive in after her, but instead I bite my lip and taste the petrol. This is a war, and that makes us soldiers—and what kind of soldier backs out because a friend of his might get hurt? It's a fifty-fifty shot, better than Reach would give her. "This is my fight now," she said, and I will myself to respect that.

ebbed away. The water was *healing* her flesh, smoothing her blisters to a finer grain the texture of concrete.

"*How in Thames'...?*" The thought tailed away. It didn't sound like her; it sounded like *him*.

An image struck her: rain pouring over the city, water flooding down sewers, through gutters, seeping through the earth, teasing up tiny particles of London and carrying them here.

Liquid chaos, and other more exotic ingredients.

Here, *into* her.

The heat of the fire forced droplets of sweat from her and she felt them clinging to her skin, insulating her from the heat. A petrol tang touched her lips.

She remembered Fil putting his hand on the streetlamp girl's arm. The heat should have been agonizing, but he'd shown no sign of pain.

She kicked towards the flames.

————

The Synod's grip on me slackens and I spring forward, my heels spurning the earth as I run towards the fire. One second of pain, that's all it'll take, and I can reach her, pull her clear. At least *they* won't get her body.

A shape bursts from the water as I reach the bank. The flames in its hair sputter out and it collapses in front of me, coughing up great lungfuls of rancid water.

I damn near fall over her as I drag her onto her back. Her chest is still under her sodden hoodie and I grab her arms and shake her idiotically, yelling her name two inches from her face: "Beth! *Beth!*"

There's no response, and a sickening certainty grips me: she *can't* respond. *Sudden death.*

Mad, frantic, I begin to push at her chest, but there's no sign of life. I slump over on her, my ear to her rib cage, and still I hear nothing. "Oh, Thames," I whisper, and at last, I feel a faint flicker through her hoodie. I flail about, almost smacking her in the side of the head in my haste to jam my fingers into her mouth and pull it open. I draw in chemical-heavy air, ready to breathe it into her.

"You about to snog me, *Phyllis?*" She wheezes the words, her lips an atom's breadth from mine, trembling, but slowly creasing into a smile.

I sit back, gazing at her. Her skin is gray, the silver-gray of the water she just climbed out of, the color of steel and concrete. The color of mine.

A thin shadow falls across my shoulder. "Filius."

"I don't understand." Confusion and leftover terror pound through me like a jackhammer. "You *burned* her."

Johnny Naptha bathes me in his eternal grin. "This is a *special* conflagration," he says, "purchassed at great expensse. It cleanssess and corusscatess, maimss and makess anew. That iss what you assked for, after all," he adds with a certain pride. "The Ssynod always does what is asked."

He and his oil-slick brothers turn and walk back towards the factory, their feet falling in perfect time. "Filiuss," Johnny says without turning, "inform your friendss:

the form of our agreement iss now fixed. Forgetting would not be forgiven."

My stomach plummets for a second. Symmetry: every deal has a cost as well as a benefit. The chemist's equations always balance.

"Exit by your own endeavorss," he says before they turn away.

Beth lies there, eyes shut, chest slowly rising and falling, now and then spluttering up a little more oily water. It's a joy just to watch her being alive. When the Synod have retreated back into their cloister, I collapse down beside her. Exhaustion drags my eyelids together. I press my arm along Beth's and we lie there, absorbing the sunlight.

TWENTY-NINE

Fire. Strands of black oil stretched between grinning lips. A lighter flame, neat and symmetrical as a dagger point. *It cleanses and coruscates*, a slick voice was saying. *It maims and makes anew.*

Beth opened her eyes slowly and then winced. The daylight hurt her eyes. The warmth of the sun made her want to sleep.

She could feel the ground under her, the city rubbing up against her skin. She could feel the charge that built up between them. *Urbosynthesis*, she thought. A smile split her face, so wide it made her mouth ache.

She sat up. Fil was lying beside her—he looked exhausted.

Maybe I should let him sleep. She considered the idea for a second, then shouted, "Oi, Phyllis, wake up!"

He popped one eyelid. "This is an uncivilized bleedin' hour," he grunted. "I'd kind've hoped that you'd see the merit of kipping in the daytime now."

"Kip? How can I kip when I've got this—when *we've* got this—" She flailed for the right words; she was buzzing. The energy of the city was in her and she could feel it charging her. It felt like Christmas when she was little, when Mum would stomp around, scowling good-temperedly down the stairs with bundles of newspaper-wrapped presents she'd bought with their meager...

Bought.

The thought brought Beth up short. "Fil?" she said, suddenly worried. "What did this cost? What did the Synod want for changing me like this?"

He sat up, groaning, and scratched himself with his spear. "Not a lot, given what we asked 'em for." He yawned like a giant contented cat. "I told 'em to make you as close to a child of Mater Viae as they could. All they wanted in exchange was some poxy ingredient their stores were missing that I happened to have. Long as I live, not something I'm goin' to use. But they were dead keen on it."

"Seriously?" Beth was dubious. "That sounds... cheap."

He shrugged. "There's no predicting the stuff the Synod are going to prize. Like Petris said, they'll make a commodity out of anything."

"Was that what was in that bottle? The one that he got you to drink from? Was *that* their price?"

Fil smiled thinly. "That was part of it."

By the time he clambered to his feet, Beth was jigging with pent-up nervous energy. He dusted himself off and picked up his railing. "All right, all right." He spoke with the knackered kind of good humor she'd overheard dads using with their toddlers in the park. "What do you want to do?"

There was only one answer to that. She shivered with pleasure as she said, "I want to run."

Beth led the way, her gait impossibly smooth, as Fil stumbled behind her, missing his footing, groggy in the daylight.

She ducked inside the back door of the factory and raced between its moldy walls, which echoed back their voices as they shouted with laughter.

The factory passed in an eye-blink and then they were back out into the sun. He was at her shoulder now, his face lined in concentration, his feet blurring as he ate up her lead. Exhilaration built in her chest as the urban scrub gave way to tarmac and they pounded along a main road. Horns screamed as traffic vanished in a smear behind them.

She caught a flash of his grinning face as he overtook her and she gritted her teeth and pushed herself harder. She understood now how he could run so fast: each footfall drew more power from the asphalt, each step charged the next. Their sprint was growing ever faster.

Beth crowed gleefully into the wind; Fil whooped in

answer. Her feet were *learning* the city: every time her bare soles hit the ground she knew she would never forget that piece of slate, that patch of tarmac, the texture. She could find every inch again with her eyes shut.

Gradually, Beth pulled level. On the first day she met him she'd collapsed, breathless, in his wake. Now, children of the city, they raced side by side through their home.

A small marina opened up before them, a couple of hundred yards off the river, anchored boats bobbing in the murky water, sails furled tight around their masts. Without pausing, Fil sprang onto a sailboat; his momentum bore him into the nearby rigging until he was swinging from yard-arm to yard-arm.

Beth stormed up to the marina's edge.

Go round, a nervous voice in her head urged, *go round*.

And a louder voice overrode it. *Screw that*, she thought, and leaped herself. Her stomach lurched as she swung from a crossbeam, but her grip held. She let her new instincts carry her through the forest of masts to the far side of the marina where Fil waited, his arm pointing upwards to Canary Wharf.

Her eyes followed his finger, and widened.

"Enjoy the climb? How about one of them, then?"

The three giant skyscrapers reared overhead, lights glowing in the oncoming evening gloom. They were only a few hundred yards away.

Beth swallowed hard. The middle one, Canada Tower, was the tallest in the city. The glass-and-steel edifice soared over the capital, the silver pyramid that capped it piercing the underbelly of the clouds.

He winked. "I'll race you."

The bricks smeared past. Beth's blood, her *new* blood, pounded in her veins. Was it still red, she wondered, or tar-black? The few people skating on the ice rink in Canada Square barely saw the gray-and-black pair blur past them.

He shinned rapidly up a steel pillar beside one of the skyscraper's revolving doors and hauled himself up to the first floor. He started scuttling crabwise up the side of the building, squeezing himself flat into the dark spaces between the brightly lit windows. Somehow his fingers and toes found invisible crevices in the smooth metal on the outside of the building.

Beth skidded to a halt, her feet felt suddenly heavy, lead instead of quicksilver. She found herself shaking her head. *He's scaling sheer steel.*

She couldn't—

She couldn't do that.

She began to pace back and forth, squinting critically at the sheer metal escarpment, embarrassed that she couldn't keep up with him.

A tendril of metal caught her eye: a cable running all the way up the side of the tower. It was supporting a window-washing platform. She grabbed it and found it a perfect fit for the rough new texture of her hand. She lifted her feet off the ground and dangled, relishing the feeling of so easily supporting her own weight.

With a wide grin, she set her shoulders and began to

haul herself up, hand over hand, gripping the cable with fingers and toes. Her reflection slithered over the metal as the wind whipped her hood into her face, billowed her clothes out like balloons. She looked down only once, and laughed at the toy-like city beneath her.

She could see his wiry silhouette on top of the tower, waiting for her.

"You took your time," he said as she pulled herself over the lip of the roof.

Beth lay back against the slope of the roof, the breath in her chest burning. "We can't all climb like bloody squirrels, y'know."

"Really? You think I'm like a squirrel?" He sounded proud.

"I wouldn't get too excited. Squirrels are just rats with a blow-dry."

"And what's wrong with rats?"

Beth didn't bother to answer. She rolled away from the edge. The silver pyramid rose steeply above them. A light flashed on and off, a warning to low-flying aircraft. Steam snaked from the air-conditioning vents, diffusing the beacon's light, and directly below it—

She felt her jaw slip open.

"Um, Fil?" she croaked.

"What?"

"Is that a *throne*?"

Cut into the western face of the pyramid was a seat with high sloping arms. It was *vast*—nothing could possibly be big enough to fill it. But even as the words left her mouth, Beth knew whose throne it was, because cut into the chair's high back was the Tower Block Crown.

Fil glanced upwards and snorted in amusement. "Nah," he said in a deadpan tone, "it's the Maharajah of Madras' diamond left buttock." He paused, then said, "Well identified, Beth: it is, in fact, a throne. Congrats. Your power to observe the bleedin' obvious is a credit to the human race." He looked out over the view and whistled appreciatively. "It is quite something, though, don't you reckon? I can never quite get over it when I come up here. You've gotta hand it to old Rubbleface—he can *build*."

"Rubbleface?" Beth looked at him in astonishment. "You mean Reach?"

He looked at her. "Okay," he said slowly, "so maybe your grasp of the obvious isn't quite as good as I thought. All skyscrapers are Reach's children, Beth. Think you can build one of these things without cranes? Canary Wharf was his biggest, baddest accomplishment. A mirror to his ruptured face that the whole city could see—and Mater Viae took it, and *sat on it*."

He chuckled. "You'd better believe that sent a message. No more petty heresies. Friar Archibald and his Apostates of Stone went *awful* quiet. No one said a bad word about the Old Girl for a good decade." The beacon flashed and lit his wicked grin. "Wanna try it out?"

Beth stood slowly, gazing up at this vast, empty chair on the roof of the city. "Are we—you know—*allowed*?"

The throne's seat swamped both of them. They sat side by side, Beth cross-legged, Fil sprawled back on his elbows.

Darkness rendered the city a mass of shifting squares of light, a puzzle waiting to be solved. It was a chaotic beauty, but no less pure for that. Beth gazed across it, her muscles knackered into relaxation. She was thrilled, and sad, and wistful, and ecstatic, and—she didn't have the words for the feeling, but she knew she'd never forget it.

"Beth, what is it?" Fil sounded alarmed.

"What's what?"

"You're crying."

Beth touched her cheek, a little shocked to find it wet. Her tears smelled of chalk. She wiped them away and smiled ruefully. "I was thinking of Pen."

"Pen?"

"My best friend." She looked at his narrow concrete-colored face with some astonishment. Had she really never told him about Pen? "Inseparable, they used to call us," she said, "like it was ordinary. Like it wasn't a bloody miracle to have someone who could tell you'd got a broken heart by the way you buttoned your coat." She exhaled hard into the cold night air. "I could never put how I feel right now into words, not if I had a hundred years. But with Pen, I wouldn't have to. She'd just know."

"How did you get so close?" he asked.

"Don't know—I guess if I could explain it, it wouldn't be a miracle."

He smiled, maybe a little sadly. "Sounds like you were in love with her."

Beth shut her eyes, remembering Pen's face. "She made me feel brave."

"What?" He sounded puzzled. "You're brave anyway, stupidly brave—*suicidally* brave, else there's no way you'd be here."

Beth was touched by his confusion. "Nah," she said, "I was never smart enough to be properly scared. So how could I be scared enough to be brave? Pen always said: 'Only the people you love can scare you witless enough for true courage.' I thought she was quoting someone, but knowing her she probably made it up. She was scared of everything, especially heights, but she'd still follow me onto any roof."

Beth waved a hand over the echoing night below them. "One night we were muraling this rooftop in Camberwell. It'd been raining, and the slates were all slick and shiny, y'know? You could see the moon in them, it was beautiful..." Beth felt the memory cinch her throat tight. "But it was slippery, and Pen fell." She rubbed her fingertips together; she could still feel the silk of Pen's hijab where her desperate fingers had snagged it as her best friend slipped away.

"*Thames!*" Fil swore. "She *died*?"

"Thank Christ and your mother, no. There was another rooftop about six feet down. She didn't even break an ankle." Beth snorted. "Happy endings all-round. But for one second, the longest second of my life, I thought I'd lost her. That was the most afraid I've ever been. There was enough loneliness in that one heartbeat for a lifetime. She was the thing I cared about most in the world, and I thought I'd lost her—and the worst of it was, she wouldn't have even been up on that sodding roof if it wasn't for me."

She felt a wiry arm around her shoulder pulling her in close. She felt the rough texture of him, the matted tangle of his hair against her cheek. "You can't begin to know what that's like," she said.

"Yes I can." He hesitated before he whispered back, "That's *exactly* how I felt when I saw you in the fire."

Beth kissed him—it happened before she let herself think about it. Her lips pressed against his, and for a moment she was acutely aware of every tingling inch of her skin. His rough fingers brushed her neck.

Neither of them melted into the kiss; instead they held it, electrically still, each terrified the other would pull away, but neither of them did.

Eventually, Beth broke contact. Fil's skin was hot as she laid her own face against it.

"Wow." He was actually stammering. "That was … that was … "

Weird? Fantastic? Scary? Hot? Beth licked her lips nervously. *Does he think it was rubbish? No, 'course not, he's probably never kissed a human being, got nothing to compare it to. But still, that Lampgirl, they looked tight, maybe they were even in love …*

The word leaped out at her: "love." *Oh Christ, Beth,* she thought in alarm, *what if that's—? What if this is—?*

How would she know?

Love. There was a hollowness to the way the thought rang in her head, like chiming glass.

Love...

The thought wasn't hers.

Beth's eyes snapped open. She twisted her head, hardly daring to ...

A tiny spider dangled from an air-conditioning vent by a filament wire. It was no larger than a common house-spider, but it glittered like fiberglass and hissed and buzzed with static.

Love...

"Fil!" she cried, and threw herself at the spider with the speed of a chemical reaction. Her hands clamped over it, trapping it against the slope of the roof.

"What? What?" He sprang to his feet, spear already in hand.

Beth's voice came out in an excited hiss. "It's one of *them*—one of the spiders! I can feel it crawling all over the inside of *my fingers*. Ow! It's like shuffling thistles—Fil, don't just stand there, bloody help me!"

He merely gestured with his spear. "Let it go, Beth."

"What? Are you mental?" Beth was scandalized. "It's one of *those* spiders. I'm not letting it go; it'll eat my face!"

He frowned. "Pylon Spiders don't eat faces, Beth."

"It'll make an exception for mine. I have a very pretty face."

"Um ... er ... yeah." He looked uncomfortable.

"How about a little more enthusiasm?'" she snapped. "You kissed it—"

"Seriously, Beth ... "

"It'll kill us," she said stubbornly.

"One that size? Against both of us?" He cocked his head. "Let it go."

Beth glared up at him. "Come and stand here," she ordered him.

"Why?"

"So if you're wrong, it's *your* face gets eaten," she grumbled.

"Let it go, Beth," he said again calmly.

Gradually, she lifted her palms half an inch off the metal and peeked under them.

Needle-pointed feet flickered. "*Love*," the glassy voice whispered gleefully in her head. "*Weird and fantastic and terrifying love—*"

"Shut it," she told it as she retracted her hands.

Fil squatted in front of the spider and cocked his head to one side as though listening. "Speak up," he said after a moment. "Let Beth hear."

"*Weird, fantastic…*" The tinny chorus broke off suddenly and another voice spoke: "You survived, then." The words carried an unmistakable note of disapproval. "Harder to shift than a takeaway-curry stain, the both of you." It was Gutterglass' voice, coming from the spider.

"Mostly they swallow voices." Fil didn't stop watching the creature while he murmured in Beth's ear. "But you can persuade 'em to spit one out every now and then, if you make it worth their while."

"The two of you have been gone for almost a whole day," Gutterglass' voice lamented, "so what in Thames' name have you been up to?"

They exchanged a look, and then both erupted into a simultaneous fit of embarrassed coughing.

"Nothing much," Fil managed.

Gutterglass emitted a skeptical snort. "*Fine*. Well, while you two were gallivanting around in the docks, I went on a bit of a recruitment drive. You'll be happy to know we have some proper soldiers on side now: some of the Pavement Priests—a minority, admittedly, but a significant one—have seen the light. They've come in under the nominal command of the angel-skinned one, Ezekiel. Did you know he can actually fly? Limestone wings and all. It's quite astonishing to watch. He says you can lead the stoneskin regiment with him if you like." The voice was positively smug. "How's that?"

Fil's face fell. "Ezekiel? What about Petris?"

"Alas, the old sinner broke out in a rash of democracy and decided to stay with the majority of the priesthood. Funny moment for a man like him to come over all gallant, I must say. He said, "I can't in good conscience lead my people back into bondage." Honestly! Ezekiel ought to be high priest, really; he's a much better advocate for Our Lady. A true zealot, a dying breed almost, but still there if you know who to talk to."

Fil folded his arms, hugging his spear to his chest. He looked slightly irritated that his old tutor had succeeded where he'd failed in recruiting his own mother's priests.

"Do come swiftly, Filius," Gutterglass was saying. "I've heard rumors; the pigeons and the gargoyles on the taller towers say there's been movement at St. Paul's. Reach's cranes are restless."

The young prince nodded, his face set. "We need to strike before he gets moving," he agreed. "If his wolfpack catches us in the open, they'll take us apart."

"My sentiments precisely. Oh, in the name of all that is clean and Holy..." The voice crackled away for a second and then returned. "That Russian of yours wants me— hurry, Filius! Ms. Bradley," Glas acknowledged formally, and then the spider dissolved into the air with a white-noise fizz.

Fil smiled at Beth. For a second, she wondered if he was going to kiss her again, and then his eyes fell on her crown-scar. "Come on," he said. "Like you said, it's your fight too now. Time to join it." He grabbed the cable attached to the window-washing platform. "This how you came up, was it? Nice. Economical. I approve."

Without another word, he swung back off the roof. She watched his narrow form plunge into the night and start abseiling down the tower.

Beth made to follow, but then paused. She reached into her backpack for one of the black Magic Markers she kept there. *After all,* she thought, *I can hardly come to London's highest rooftop and not tag it, can I?*

Crouching, she did a rough sketch of them both on the rooftop, side by side. Underneath she wrote an inscription: *Beth Bradley and the Street-Urchin Prince on the day they stood on the roof of the world.*

Sounds like a fairy tale, Beth. Here's hoping it ends like one. The taste of the kiss was still on her lips, as heady as petrol fumes. For a second she imagined Pen's face, drawn in beside hers, watching her. *What would you think of him, Pencil Khan? What would you say?*

Maybe one day soon she could ask her.

"Oi, Bradley!" His voice echoed up.

Beth seized the cable and, daring herself with a shout, leapt out across the city.

THIRTY

Pen dreamed of her parents. She was sitting at the kitchen table, and her father sat opposite her, sleeves rolled up over his teak-colored arms. He peered though his glasses and scribbled in an old-fashioned accounting ledger.

His forehead rucked up in concentration, he muttered, "This bloody thing simply will not add up."

Her mother fussed at the hob, skipping out of the way as the fat spat. Behind her, pakoras and samosas were piled high on the kitchen counter, the paper beneath them transparent and glistening with grease.

"Mum?" Pen said. It was hard to shape the words because of the scars on her lips. "What's all the food for?"

Her mother gave her a bemused look and squeezed her shoulder. "Why, it's for your wedding, dear one. Why else would I be putting myself to all this trouble?"

Pen stood up to help, but her mother waved her out of the way. She didn't protest. Of course she was getting married soon, although at that precise moment she couldn't remember to whom. "Well, Mama," she said, "it is only *slightly* more than you'd make for a light lunch for the three of us."

They all laughed heartily at this weak joke.

Her father threw his pen down on the table in frustration.

"Damn it, I cannot make this add up at all. We'll have to call it off. All of it."

Her mother looked disappointed and began to dump platefuls of hot food into the bin.

"Mum!" Pen was appalled. "Dad, what is it?"

"Your dowry—come, see if you can make this work out."

Pen stood up and came round the table. She looked over his shoulder. Instead of rows of numbers, a face had been drawn in Beth Bradley's distinctive style on the lined ledger pages, a face with swollen scars and twisted lips.

"He'll want an exorbitant sum to marry that," her father said, rubbing her hand fondly where it sat on his shoulder. "But I suppose we'll have to try to find it."

Pen put her hand to her face; she felt the scars and the bruises. Her fingers brushed air where one earlobe used to be. "We'll do the best we can with you, my daughter," her mother said kindly. "But it won't be easy with a face like that."

Pen looked past her and saw her own reflection in the kitchen tap.

Wake.

Wake Wake Wake Wake Wake Wake Wake Wake Wake Wake Wake.

Air ripped in through Pen's nostrils and she coughed and opened her eyes. This was the first time she'd dreamed of her parents since she'd been taken. She'd *imagined* them while she was awake: coming home, her mother scolding her with relieved tears in her eyes. But they'd never entered her sleep until now.

The wire gripped her and rolled her over.

Wake Wake Wake Wake Wake Wake Wake Wake.

The word was all around her, scratched in the concrete in massive, jagged letters. Fresh dust caked her finger. Her wire exoskeleton was vibrating over her skin. She felt its eagerness—or was it her eagerness? It was becoming difficult to know which of them any given emotion belonged to now.

What? she thought to it. *What is it?*

In answer, it lurched her to her feet and used her hand to pull the tarp aside. Pen squinted in the site's arclights for a moment. A sound of tearing metal echoed around the half-finished architecture. Pen watched in astonishment as clamps unlocked, scaffolding bars slid free, and the metal framework that had been bandaging the buildings fell away in an iron avalanche. But instead of crashing into a heap in the dust, struts swiveled around joints into new configurations, moving faster and faster, forming clouds of blurring metal. The wire's excitement flowed through Pen as she watched, and she found herself almost panting.

Then suddenly, the whirring metal reformed itself into more familiar shapes: massive metal animals like dogs, or wolves even, and skeletal men. The steel men reached down and patted the gleaming necks of the beasts, who put their heads back and emitted echoing iron howls. Wolves, then.

The scaffolding creatures loped from the building site.

We ride, the wire scratched on the wall with Pen's shaking finger, and adrenaline filled her. The wire felt no fear, so neither did she. Her legs bunched under her and she jumped. The air stung her cuts as she plummeted; the lights of cranes flashed past. Barbed tendrils flashed out from her feet and touched earth. Two spindly legs of wire contracted under her, bearing her slowly to earth, breaking her descent gently.

A wolf bent its neck in deference and Pen climbed on. The wire lashed her securely to its back and with another baying howl the beast turned and padded after its pack-mates.

The iron giants strode beside her. The clang of their footsteps on the shale of the building site was like war drums.

THIRTY-ONE

I remember the first stories Gutterglass ever told me about my mother. Glas was a woman at the time, and she had her rats stretch her lap out for me, and we lay back on the side of a mountain of tin cans, condoms, and mulch. Glas always found the grandeur of the landfill comforting; it was easier to talk about the good old days there, without the sour milk spilling from her shells.

That smell of decay still makes me think of home.

Glas rocked me to and fro, and although I pretended scandalized pride, I secretly loved every second.

"Your mother," she began, "is an incredible thing…"

I'd never been able to remember my mother; I'd barely even been aware I was missing one. But I knew this was important. I stopped feeding congealed special fried rice to her rats and listened, and I discovered that my mother was that most incredible thing: a goddess. I also learned that out of all the things she was, being "my mother" was by far the least important.

But even with that momentous revelation, I got bored and I wriggled out of Glas' lap and set to work building a castle out of old paint tins. I really didn't understand.

But later…

Our memories are like a city: we tear some structures down, and we use rubble of the old to raise up new ones. Some memories are bright glass, blindingly beautiful when they catch the sun, but then there are the darker days, when they reflect only the crumbling walls of their derelict neighbors. Some memories are buried under years of patient construction; their echoing halls may never again be seen or walked down, but still they are the foundations for everything that stands above them.

Glas told me once that that's what people *are*, mostly: memories, the memories in their own heads and the memories of them in other people's. And if memories are like a city, and we are our memories, then *we* are like cities too. I've always taken comfort from that.

A decade ago, a six-year-old boy raced a glowing-glass girl through the warm brick warrens of the Lots Road Power Station, and if you'd asked him then, he'd've said, "*'Course* I've met my mother."

If you could get him to stop showing off for the horrified lightbulb girl by swimming in the station's water tanks, if you could get him to tear his eyes away from the spectacle of her plugging herself into the mains and glowing as bright as a tiny sun, and if you could get the inarticulate little squirt to shape the words, he'd tell you *all about* his mother.

"Are you blind?" he'd say; "Are you daft? She's there. Right there—"

—with him and Electra as they dared each other to do ever more suicidally stupid things for the honor of their genders (never mind their species). He'd tell you how he and his mother had fought side by side against the cranes; how they'd lassoed the moon and dragged it into the sky, leaving it hanging there like an old tire on a rope. He'd remind you how when she sang it made the river still, and that once she'd baked him a tarmac cake *this* big (he'd extend his short arse six-year-old arms to maximum stretch) and he'd eaten all of it—of course he had, were you calling him a *girl*?

He'd tell you all of this, and it would be true, for him, because he *remembered* it. He'd built the glass buildings in his mind. And it was a long time before he could tell the difference between these fantasies and the older, deeper truths they reflected.

———

Once, when I was a lot older and I'd all but forgotten all those almost-memories I'd imagined, I thought I was finally about to meet Mater Viae for *real*.

I was in an alley in the Old Kent Road, and a dustbin fell over and a stray cat darted out and for no reason I can now fathom I thought, *It's Fleet*. I was *certain* that any minute now cats would spill from the shadows in a purring, hissing, flea-bitten flood. *And then I'll see her, and then I'll finally know…*

But the letters on the street sign stayed the same, no matter how hard I stared at them, and although I waited until long after the lone furball found some tiny, scrabbling morsel to chase, no other cats followed it. A fox did, and a drug dealer who didn't see me, and a couple of his customers who were too high to care who was watching while they screwed against the wall, but no more cats.

And you know what? More than anything else, I felt relieved—because all my fantasies, all those *almost*-memories, they were safe.

That's worth something.

THIRTY-TWO

"Do you think you could at least *admit* you have no idea what you're doing?" Ezekiel asks. He doesn't make the effort to change his overface's expression, but although the stone mouth is still singing a hosanna, I can see the disdainful curl of his lip beneath.

"I'm quite serious," he repeats. "Because if you persist in pretending you know how to lead an army while handing out idiotic instructions, I'm going to have to tell my boys their goddess' child is an imbecile. It'd be a blow to morale, but I'd take that over the risk of any of them actually *listening* to you."

We're on the Embankment, on the north side of Chelsea Bridge. Ezekiel's got himself a plinth on the corner outside the Royal Hospital Gardens. The graceless bulk of the old Victorian infirmary looms over us; it's under heavy repair and I watch the scaffolding surrounding its brick skin nervously, but nothing moves. It's probably normal, lifeless steel, but all scaff makes me nervous these days.

Calm down, Filius, I urge myself, trying to give Ezekiel my full attention. "What's so stupid about the idea?" I ask, in what I think is a very reasonable tone.

"That's a stupid question."

My remaining patience hisses out in one exasperated breath. "Look," I snap, "we have to find a way to maintain the element of surprise, and when you've got a hundred tons of ambulant bloody *rock* on the move, that's easier said than done. All I suggested was since we have to march at night because of the Lampfolk, you stoneskins should make like empty statues: you all shuffle up from one plinth to the next until we get where we're going and Reach'll be none the wiser."

I'm actually quite proud of the idea, but I can almost hear Ezekiel's eyebrows grazing the inside of his punishment skin as they climb his face.

The tone of his voice could wither lichen. "First of all, we are *Pavement Priests*. We are the honor guard of the street goddess; we do not skulk and we do not sneak and we most certainly do not *shuffle*.

"Second, do you have any notion of how hard it is to move a punishment skin? That's why they're *called* punishment skins, Highness. If you want us to have any energy left to fight with, we need to go by the most direct route possible, not 'shuffle' from plinth to plinth, zigzagging across the city until we can't even lift our own limbs.

"And thirdly, you did not just 'suggest' it, you said it in front of my men, who are both soldiers and clerics: they take a 'suggestion' like that from a deity—which, sadly for all of us, is what you are—as an *order*. An order which in effect means they are to kill themselves by the most exhausting and humiliating means possible—oh, and incidentally, to hand almost certain victory to the enemy.

"I had to tell them you were joking, so now they think the son of their goddess has a sick sense of humor, but that's better than them realizing that he's either a gibbering idiot or, very possibly, insane."

"Look, mate—" I start, but he cuts me off scornfully.

"I am not your mate. I am either your mother's obedient servant, and therefore bound, reluctantly, to serve you too, or else I am the man who will put his limestone gauntlet through your chops for being the annoying little maggot who's interfering in the running of my order. Either way, *mate* doesn't really cover it."

I'm this close to chinning him—if he thinks he can take me, I'm more than happy to educate him. "Fine," I hiss, "but why are you suddenly so hostile? Gutterglass said you agreed that I could lead 'em with you—"

Ezekiel freezes. Being a statue, he was pretty still anyway, and now he's even stiller. And that, take it from me, is pretty bloody scarily still.

"That's one way to put it." He spits the words out between clenched teeth.

"Oh? And what's another way?"

"Another way would be to say that Gutterglass raised

it. I laughed at it. Then I realized he was serious and I argued for two solid hours, at the end of which he threatened to give my body back to the Chemical Synod and to ensure that I spend my next incarnation inside an abstract sculpture with holes in all the most uncomfortable places. At which point, yes, I suppose you could say I 'agreed' you could lead them with me."

"Oh." I had been proud of that, too, imagining myself fierce at the head of a battalion of stone warriors. Now I can feel that pride swan-diving towards my bowels.

"Gutterglass wants you visible." Disgust sours the stone angel's voice. "He wants us reminded who we're fighting for. Frankly, I think a stuffed cat and a scarecrow would be a better symbol for Our Lady's terrible beauty than you, but sadly, you're what we have."

A creaking of stone drowns out any attempt at self-justification. His vast gray wings extend on either side of him, cloaking me in shadow. "If she wants to us to be inspired, then she should come and inspire us herself." I can hear the bitter complaint in his voice. "I need *real* advantages, not symbolic ones. I need Fleet's war party; I need the Great Fire, the only weapon our foe has ever really feared." He exhales wearily. "And I need a rest. We're going into battle against the *Crane King*, for Thames' sake—

"I need a god. And instead I have you " He shakes his heavy stone head and flaps laboriously away.

THIRTY-THREE

An army was gathering in Battersea Park. Streetlamps flickered beside the river and white light rippled along the road to Chelsea Bridge as bright spirits filled empty bulbs. The Blankleits flexed their fields and chattered in excited flashes. A few had fused together peaked caps from glass, semblances of military uniform, and now they threw each other badly executed salutes. The Russian in the ragged coat leaned against a lamppost and drank, shaking his head at their enthusiasm.

Gutterglass had been busy too. Foxes and feral dogs yipped and barked and play-fought on the grass. They'd bounded with canine obedience after the Pylon Spiders who'd come by their bins, interrupting their scavenging with stories of a hunt to be joined. Deep in the park's wooded thickets, far from the white lamps of the shore, glowing amber figures practiced their war-waltzes, building their charges with slow turns. Shockwaves uprooted trees and twisted the fallen leaves into whirling vortices. All one hundred and eleven Sodiumite families were called, and most came, but of Electra and her sisters there was no word. Rumor fluttered through the ranks that Filius Viae was biting his blackened nails at their absence.

Pavement Priests moved through the throng, giving benediction in the name of the Lady of the Streets. Their steps were painstakingly slow; they were hoarding their energy for the battles to come.

And, sitting on a park bench, facing the Thames, Beth was pouring the prince of this little war party a cup of good, strong tea.

———

"These"—he sprayed crumbs over the half-empty packet of HobNobs resting on his lap—"are amazing."

"You should try the chocolate ones." Beth said. "They'll blow you away."

"There are *chocolate* ones?" he said in an awestruck voice.

She laughed. "You have much to learn, Grasshopper."

"Grasshopper?"

"It's a kind of insect."

"I know what a grasshopper *is*, Beth, I just don't know why you'd call me one. I'm at least two legs short, for one thing, and I can't jump like they do. I mean, I *wish*, but—"

"Fil, it's just a—" Beth interrupted, but the odds against

him being familiar with *Kung Fu* were astronomical. She sighed. "Never mind."

Steam whistled from the kettle and she smiled her thanks to the Blankleit whose lap was heating it (she couldn't pronounce his name, so she'd nicknamed him 'Steve'). She poured water into the two chipped Mr. Men mugs she'd dug out of a skip. She counted to ninety in her head, fished out the tea bags, added milk, and handed one to Fil.

Who stared at it.

"What am I supposed to do with that?"

"You drink it."

He squinted at the liquid suspiciously, and then took a large gulp.

Beth smiled and sipped her tea while Fil doubled up coughing and spluttering. "*Ow*," he wheezed hoarsely.

"Hot?"

"It's *scalding*! People actually drink this? Voluntarily? That's *barbaric*."

"We usually let it cool down a bit first." She reached across and lifted a HobNob from the packet on his lap. "So what you're saying," she said, returning to their previous conversation, "is that we're totally boned." She made sure that her face was turned away from Steve so he couldn't read her lips.

"I didn't say that at all," he protested. "It's simple: all we have to do is get this little lot"—he jerked a thumb at the variegated horde in the park behind him—"across that bridge, east into the city to Blackfriars. Get 'em formed up

and then march on St. Paul's without ol' Rubbleface noticing it."

"Yeah." Beth dunked her HobNob. "But the Whities
and the Amberglows will be trying to rip each other's
throats out as soon as they get within a hundred yards of
each other. I can't imagine that will attract any attention.
And the Pavement Priests are determined to charge on
Reach with flags waving and a bloody fanfare. *And* I have
no idea how to control the dogs. Remind me what happens if Reach's forces catch us in the open?"

Fil raised his tea cautiously back to his mouth, darting
furtive glances at Beth to check that he was doing it right.

"They pull us apart like an overfull binbag," he replied.
"Probably."

"Oh, so we're only *probably* totally boned."

"Exactly."

There was a long silence.

Neither of them had mentioned the kiss. That moment
on Canary Wharf was stranded in time, like a lonely shout
that needs to be taken up before its echoes fade, or be forgotten.

Be careful of that kiss, Beth cautioned herself harshly.
They were at war. She thought of her dad, frozen in grief
at his kitchen table. How could you ever let yourself love
someone—yes, she let herself think the word "love"—
when they might not survive the night?

Fil was engrossed in a one-sided staring contest with
the last remaining HobNob.

"It all seemed such a good idea at the time," he said.

"Simple: meet a girl, round up a ragtag army, carry out an all-out assault on a skyscraper god." He gazed at the biscuit. "Discover HobNobs."

Meet a girl. Beth stared carefully ahead and said nothing.

"Fair point," he said into the silence. "Put like that it sounds like a really terrible idea. But it's at least half your fault. I was all for scarpering. I'd have been out of here faster than a sewer rat down a pipe. It was you got me to stay."

Beth's smile was tight-lipped. "That's me, the siren call to self-destruction."

He gazed out over the water for a while, and then, later enough that it was almost a non sequitur, he said, "I'm glad, though. Glad I did stay."

Beth looked at him. "Even if it was a terrible idea?"

"Even if.

Beth studied the paving between her feet as though following the cracks might show her the branching of her possible futures. She splashed the dregs of her tea onto them and stood up. "Fil," she said, "a word?"

She mouthed goodbye to the Blankleit and led Fil through the treeline, under the cover of the massive beeches. Fallen leaves crunched under her feet. Finally, she turned to face him. Her heart was clamping up hard in her chest, but she saw he already knew what she was going to say.

His expression was neither wounded nor indifferent, both of which she'd feared. Instead, his gray eyes were intent. "This is about last night?"

"Yeah."

"You think it was a mistake."

Beth swallowed a boulder of empty air. "Yeah."

"You think—what? It'll distract us? It's too risky?"

"Yeah."

"You think we should just be friends?"

"Yeah."

He stepped in close to her. The frost-cloud of his breath washed over her face. "You wanna do it again?"

"Yeah ... "

There was supposed to be a *but* somewhere on the end of that, but somehow Beth never got it out because his lips with their rough pavement grain were already against hers, and she was tasting the heat of his tongue. Their hands rose, and they held each other's heads as though the kiss were a promise they were holding each other to: a promise simply to be there, a promise to survive.

But they couldn't keep that promise, could they?

Beth wound her fingers into Fil's hair and pulled him back, hard, and he came away from her, gasping. She looked at him, really *looked* into his wide eyes, and saw him for the trap that he was. His voice sounded in her memory: *Reach is going to kill me.*

It was like standing above some unimaginable precipice, her toes curling over the edge. This was too much of a risk. An image flashed into her head: a floor littered with photographs. Now was the time to stop. Little detonations were filling her veins. The blood in her ears was artillery-loud. Now was the time to back away. Her head was ringing.

Now.

They fell in an awkward tangle of limbs into the chill leaves, their hands hovering uncertainly on one another's bodies. For a fraction of a second Beth thought she wouldn't have the nerve. Then she pushed her fingers inside his clothes and as her hoodie rode up she felt the shocking heat of his palms pressed up against her bare skin. Then he was tugging at her T-shirt and she was pushing it off over her head. And it was happening, it was happening so fast, and she was going to let it happen—

No, she thought, *no, she was going to make it happen.* She pushed into him and kissed him, determined to be bold, guiding his hands to her bra.

Unfortunately he struggled a bit with that, and she broke away after a few moments. "Christ's sake, Fil, it's a bra, not a Rubik's cube."

"A what?"

"A puzzle—"

"Puzzle? You mean like a test? I have to pass an *exam* for this?"

"It's not the worst idea I've ever heard." She laughed. "Here, let me." She unhooked it and then hesitated, suddenly aware of him looking at her in a way that made her shiver all over. She'd never simultaneously wanted and not wanted something, *anything*, so much as for him to look away . . .

Okay. In her head it sounded more like a prayer than a decision. *Okay.*

"Take your jeans off, then," she said as she wriggled out

of her own. Nerves made her voice haughty and she winced inwardly, but he didn't seem to mind.

He didn't look away, of course, and neither did Beth as he stripped. She studied the play of his muscles under the skin intently, and the sharp lines of his hips. It would have been rude not to.

They stepped towards each other tentatively, like new dance partners. Beth blushed as they each put cautious hands on the other's hips, and she saw his face color too. They broke into enormous, jaw-straining grins.

"Wow," he said.

A sound came through the trees: a commotion, blowing the silence apart. She could hear shouting, and the crackle of branches broken by running feet. From overhead came the thud of churning air, stirred by heavy stone wings.

Fil dropped to a crouch, pulling Beth down with him. For a moment, Beth was certain they'd been busted, and a burning tide of embarrassment went through her, halted abruptly by the chill realization that it was much more likely they were under attack. She cocked her head, probing with her newly sharpened senses, listening for the enemy.

And then she heard Ezekiel's voice over the beat of his wings, pealing out again and again with evangelical joy: "It's the Cats! Filius, come quickly, it's *Fleet*! The Cats are here!"

Fil stopped rooting through the undergrowth for his clothes long enough to turn to Beth with a sheepish little shrug, but she cut him off before he spoke.

"Later," she said, vibrating with a mix of relief and

aching disappointment and a kind of anticipation that made her knees feel like untied knots. "I know."

―――――――

Four lithe feline shapes threaded their way over the grass, following the indirect and mysterious paths that cats always do. Pavement Priests and Lampfolk all stood back in awe as the four-footed legends slid through their ranks, imperiously swishing their tails.

Names were whispered, passing through the ragtag army like a breeze through rushes, names from never-quite-forgotten stories:

Cranbourn, the Herald.

Wandle, the Dream-guide.

Tyburn, they whispered fearfully, *the Executioner.* A black cat bared its teeth as it passed.

Fleet...

Fleet!

Now and then one of the Cats would stop and stretch and rub itself along the inside of somebody's leg, and that fortunate soul would immediately collapse in a state of religious ecstasy.

Fil shoved his way through the milling crowds into the clearing where the Cats circled. Beth raced in a fraction of a second behind him, pulling her hoodie over her head, only to find she'd got it on the wrong way. She clawed the hood out of her eyes in time to see him fall to his knees.

The mangy tabby at the head of the group bounded into his scrawny arms.

"Fleet," he whispered. "*Fleet*—dear Thames, we've needed you." The tabby purred back at him, loud as a motorbike.

The other Cats—one black, one black and white, and a Persian gray with a chunk of its ear missing—rolled on the grass and chased the rippling light spilling from the Blankleit skins. The Persian sat down, put its hind leg behind its head, and licked itself clean with long strokes of its bright pink tongue.

"Um, Fil," Beth said, watching the infamous feline war party with growing unease, "aren't they just, you know...cats?"

He didn't answer, but an indignant voice from inside a bronze of a World War II fighter pilot shouted, "Blasphemy!"

Beth ignored him; she was following Fil's gaze. He was looking past Fleet, past the eager soldiers, straining to see into the dark. Beth knew what he was looking for: a shimmer of vast estuary-water skirts, a smile of church-spire teeth, hands that had cradled the fabled Great Fire. He was searching for some sign of the One these feline bodyguards ought to be *protecting*.

But as they stared together into the darkness of Battersea Park, only the darkness looked back.

THIRTY-FOUR

Paul Bradley stood on the dead tracks and gazed at the walls of the abandoned railway tunnel. His mouth was drier than the brickdust in the air. He'd run from picture to picture, street to street, scouring walls, phone boxes, billboards—anything that Beth might have used as her impromptu canvas. Once he had grown accustomed to her style, he could instantly spot when graffiti was hers.

He'd followed a running ostrich here, a flamenco dancer in a black hat there—there must have been hundreds of them, always half-hidden, coyly poking out from behind bushes or imprisoned behind drain-gratings. Their sheer number shocked him.

He was surprised at the jealous ache that suffused him at the time his daughter must have spent with the pictures.

Why? He mocked himself with the thought. *You were hardly clamoring for her attention at the time, were you?*

Exhausted and enervated, he'd entered a kind of fugue state, aware of the pattern of every manhole cover, the thin shadows cast by the naked branches of every tree. Beth's paintings had been hidden in the random jumble of Hackney's mass of graffiti-like code words in a cipher text, but now he knew how to decrypt her. There were places where the pictures were more numerous, places where he'd *felt* her presence more strongly, and he'd followed those feelings like a pilgrim.

Eventually, the trail dead-ended at the fenced-off abandoned railway. He had threaded his fingers through the wire loops and gazed blankly up the length of the tracks, to where they disappeared into the tunnel under the main road, when he'd spotted that one of the stones between the sleepers had been painted with a tiny, stylized black rabbit scurrying into its burrow.

Paul had smiled, wedged his toe into the fence, and started to climb.

Inside the tunnel he'd found a torch, still working. When he'd switched it on and seen the pictures, he'd swayed a little on his feet—so many fragments of Beth's mind—but none of it *meant* anything to him. In that moment of panic, an impossible distance seemed to stretch between them…

He remembered fretting when she'd been late learning to talk, laying awake, imagining his daughter grown but still emitting the same baby-gurgles, trying to work out how he'd cope if he couldn't *talk* to her. Marianne had laughed at him, but his fear had felt so real.

And now, here in this strange deserted tunnel, there was so much violence in the shapes on the walls, as though Beth had discharged all her anger into the bricks. Here was a black bull charging, there a snake coiled around a clarinet, and skeletons and stars and butterflies danced across mountain-ranges, and—

Marianne.

He exhaled hard, as though he'd been punched. Marianne, his wife, Beth's mother, appeared over and over again, smudged and pale as a ghost.

The other graffiti was a garden of bright neon dreams, and amongst it, the white chalk lines that brought Marianne to life were so unassuming that he'd almost missed her—he would never have believed that, but he'd *missed* her.

He looked again at the charging animals and flying planets and soldiers and monsters, and this time he saw the battles Beth had fought, the world she'd escaped into, and the memory, etched in chalk, that haunted it.

He reached into his jacket pocket and his fingers brushed paper. He pulled out a crumpled paperback from his inner pocket. Yes, he understood.

He exhaled hard into the tunnel's chill. "Beth," he began, "I'm so—" Then he stopped and bit the apology back. When he said sorry, he promised himself, he'd make sure she heard it. He looked up at one of the chalk sketches of Marianne and swallowed.

"I'll find her," he said. This time his voice didn't waver.

He knew he wasn't the first person to have spoken to that image of Beth's mother, and warmth spread through him. For the first time since his wife died he felt like he understood a little bit of the girl who had drawn her, over and over again, in this dark, safe place.

He turned off the torch and started for the mouth of the tunnel. His wife's chalk gaze watched him go. Despite the tiredness settling like silt in his limbs, he found he could manage a shambling run. He had a lot of ground to cover in his search for fresh paint.

THIRTY-FIVE

"Is this sign enough of her favor to satisfy you, Stone-wing?" Gutterglass' speech was oddly formal. "Our Lady of the Streets has sent her most trusted warriors to herald her arrival."

They were gathered inside a shuttered ice-cream stall in the middle of the park. Ezekiel had knelt in front of his prince as soon as he'd landed, leaving his stone robe riven with cracks. Beth guessed that the gesture of respect was as much for the threadbare tabby Fil was petting as for the street prince himself.

"It is. It surely is." Ezekiel couldn't stop staring at Fleet, and his voice was hoarse with awe. "And I do heartily repent of my impertinence to you, Highness. My lack of faith—it was a sin." He hesitated, then bowed his head again. "I will willingly—*willingly*—undertake any penance your Highness sees fit to—"

"His Highness" held up a hand to silence the Pavement Priest. He glanced sideways at the teetering form of Gutterglass, and then at Beth, who shrugged. He looked deeply uncomfortable. "Get up," he said at last.

Ezekiel creaked to his feet in a shower of stone chips.

"Get out," Fil said.

Ezekiel began to protest, but he was cut off.

"Get over it."

When the stone angel had clunked from the room, Gutterglass murmured, "Well, that was *abrupt*."

"It was embarrassing, is what it was," Fil snapped. "And I don't know what he thought he was apologizing for; he was right, I *was* being an idiot. Saying sorry for calling me on it is just bollocks."

Gutterglass' eggshell eyes squeezed shut: a silent prayer for patience. "Be that as it may," he said then, "it was not appropriate of him to show you disrespect. You are the object of his devotion … "

"*I* am not—my mother is."

Gutterglass gazed at him dispassionately. "You bear her name. You bear her blood. You bear her worshipers."

A frustrated breath streamed from Fil's nostrils. "Right."

Rats' tails poked out from under Gutterglass' shoulder blades as he leaned to peer out of the door after Ezekiel. "Are you sure you can't be persuaded to dole out at least some token punishment to Stonewing?" he asked. "After all, he is a zealot. Without chastisement he'll probably feel cheated."

Fil shook his head firmly and Gutterglass sighed and bowed. A dozen chittering bodies bore him from the room like a kind of furry conveyor belt.

"Thames' *sake!*" Fil slid to the floor and dropped his head into his hands. Fleet coiled into his lap and began to mewl comfortingly. Beth sat beside him and slid an arm around him. She still felt a little jumpy at the proximity of his skin.

"You okay?" she asked.

"I'm a god. Doesn't that mean I have to be?" His lips curled upwards, but it wasn't a smile.

"Do you want to talk about it?"

"Nothing to talk about," he said. "But—this—something's not right, whatever Glas says. 'Herald her arrival'? You never see the Cats without their mistress—it's never been heard of, not since Fleet disappeared after her decades ago. This is *not* how it's supposed to go, know what I mean?"

Beth looked at him. He wore an expression she recognized: he'd never admit it, but he was scared. He was struggling to thread together a story, to make some excuse for why he was facing this all alone without a parent to shield him.

Not for the first time, Beth felt a surge of anger towards the absent goddess. She took a deep breath and gave him the only answer that had ever made her feel better. "You don't need her," she said. "We'll do better without her."

He rubbed his eyes, and then looked around. "Thames and rotting riverfish and bugger it," he declared. As he stood up and squared his shoulders, Fleet bounded from his lap. "Let's get on with it, then."

"Get on with what?" she asked.

"Getting this damn circus on the move. If they want a god, I'll show 'em one, but I don't think they're goin' to like it much."

The Lampfolk hadn't even set foot on the bridge when the first fight broke out. A full-hipped Sodiumite girl moved towards the Thames. Rather than walk, she floated ostentatiously an inch off the ground on her fields, fiber-optic hair streaming, a show of strength to the Whities she thought so contemptible. Behind her, white and yellow lights stood in separate groups on the pavement. Her kindred jabbered, nervous of the river, but this girl had a spark of pride in her and she would not be cowed.

The incessant flashing bickering dimmed for a moment and there was a sense of held breath as Blankleits and Sodiumites alike watched her in silence. The bridge's vast suspension cables stretched in taut triangles before them like the outline of a ship's sails.

The Amberglow girl's courage lasted until she was a good ten feet out onto the bridge. But then she looked down at the rippling, lethal water below her, jumped three feet into the air, and came down, shrieking incandescently, accusing the nearest Whitey of shoving her.

Whether the accused Blankleit was guilty or not, he didn't expend voltage denying it. Instead he launched himself at her, and an instant later they were grappling together, an inch apart, over the concrete, their fields interlocked. The roar that went up from the crowd was like the muzzle-flashes of a cannon battery. The yellow girl took the upper hand, arching forward, her arms scissoring. The young whitey was almost doubled over backwards in mid-air, glass teeth gritted behind his transparent jaw. Tiny hairline cracks spread from the small of his back, and every wire in his body burned hot with pain.

Something darted between them, a smear of gray too fast to see, and the two glass figures flew apart. The white one cracked his head on a post.

The blur resolved itself into a gray-skinned boy balanced lightly on the balls of his feet, standing in the middle of the road, railing-spear held ready. Filius Viae's eyes were flat and hard.

Both Lampfolk turned as one and attacked, coming at him from opposite sides. His spear wavered as their fields tried to grip it, but he was too fast, too slippery. He uncoiled in a burst of savage motion, swept the knees from under the Amberglow girl with his spear-shaft, pirouetted on his heel in the follow-through, and slammed the butt into Whitey's chest, sending him sprawling.

He came to an instant stop, no motion wasted.

Beth watched him. The silence of the Lampfolk made

it seem dark, but she could see his chest swelling as he angrily sucked in breath. Then he was moving again. He coiled his fingers into the Sodiumite's glittering hair and dragged her, kicking and flashing, to the balustrade.

Beth gaped in horror as he flung the Amberglow girl over the side. The Lampgirl flared out a brilliant scream, and then went dark.

Beth felt her heart almost stop. Around her, the Lampfolk gazed on in frightened, angry shock. *He didn't just—?*

No, there she was, almost invisible in her mute terror, hanging limply in midair.

"The next light-person, white or yellow, to hit a fellow soldier takes a bath," Fil called out. He let an inch of fiber-optic hair slip through his knuckles. The only light Beth could see was the flash of Victor's torch as he spread the word.

"If you *really* want to fight somebody so bad you can't wait for the cranes, come and tap me on the shoulder," he continued. "I've got some aggression to work out."

"No kidding," Beth muttered. She tingled with fear as she watched the girl hanging from his fingers.

He held the Sodiumite over the river for a full silent minute, and then dumped her in a shuddering, barely flickering heap on the roadway. He picked up his railing and stalked across the river, a furious silhouette, leading the way north.

Beth shouldered her backpack and sprinted to catch him up. Their army, stunned by the sudden outburst of violence, began to shuffle dumbly after him. Beth saw a couple of rebellious flashes behind her, but before she could react, Victor had hauled the young Blankleit boy to his feet, flashed his light in his face, cuffed him, and pushed him back over to his parents.

Beth found Fil leaning on his spear. He must have heard her coming, but he didn't turn around.

"Jesus!" Beth shook her head. "Knocking heads and taking names? If that girl had slipped, you'd have had a full-blown mutiny on your hands."

His anger had evaporated and now his gray eyes were anxious. "Yeah," he murmured, "but if they'd mutinied *together* at least that'd be something."

Beth stared at him incredulously. "You were *waiting* for this?"

He smiled wryly. "If they think I'm biased, they'll blow up faster than the Walthamstow Fireworks Factory. But now the Blankleits have seen me beat up an Amberglow, and the Sodiumites have seen me take a Whitey to the dust."

"Your idea?"

"Glas. She said if I could get 'em pissed off at me it'd bring 'em together ... for a little while at least."

"And after a little while?" Beth asked.

His smile faded. "Hopefully by then we'll have my mother on hand," he said. "'Cause the word of their goddess is about the only thing that'll keep them from grinding each other back into the sand they're made of."

———

Electra pressed her back to the scum-caked wall of the sewer and tried not to breathe. The smallest glimmer could give her away.

The metal wolves were prowling not five feet from the mouth of the tiny access tunnel where she was hiding, padding through the filthy ankle-deep water. The only light was the vague glow of decomposing leaf mold, but Reach's scaffolding army was unaffected by darkness. The only guide they needed was the hissing scratch of wire on brick: the signal of their mistress.

Like all young Sodiumites, Electra knew the sewers like the wiring in the back of her hand. The tunnels were the only way to get around the city during the day without being blinded by the daylamp. Lec had groped her way to one Hackney manhole cover hundreds of times so she could sneak off to meet Filius while her grandmother was too sleepy to snap at her about it. When the wolves and their scaffolding handlers had descended into the roadworks gouged into Tinker's Gate, it had been a simple matter to follow them into London's guts.

Electra kept to the narrow maintenance tunnels running parallel to the main sewers, well clear of the deadly water. She peeked around the corner: the Wire Mistress was mounted in the center of the file of wolves. The darkskinned girl bound in its coils, looking as shriveled-up as the meat of an old nut, was the core of its strength.

Lec imagined lashing out and crushing the girl's windpipe with her fields; she imagined the Wire Mistress, furious but weakened, unspooling from its dead slave just as she hit with all the power she could dance up.

Fight it. Kill it. She craved it so badly her filaments ached, but instead she bowed her head and stifled the light from her thundering pulse as she let the thing walk past the end of the access tunnel.

She couldn't fight it, not down here—down here all the Mistress needed to do was scratch Electra's glass skin and expose a live wire, and the methane in the tunnels would do the rest.

Waiting felt like being torn slowly in half.

After too many hours the tunnels grew a fraction lighter. Lec could see the dirty shimmer of the nighttime city in an opening at the far end, and an unmistakable sound filled the air: the swishing rush of the river.

Lec shrank back up an accessway as the wolves pressed on past. She groped with her fields until she found a rusting metal ladder.

Fresh air hit her like hope and she scrambled from the manhole. A monolithic redbrick building reared up in front of her and she tried to get her bearings. There was the river, in all its churning deadliness, and spanning it, a bridge with fat suspension cables, and—

Lec went utterly dark in shock.

Spilling across the bridge, jostling each other like fireflies in an updraft, were hundreds of glowing figures. But it wasn't the figures themselves that shocked her; it was their *colors*—white and yellow, mingled together so closely that their individual lights were almost indistinguishable.

Together! Lec stared in disbelief. A skinny figure, a mere sliver of shadow amongst all that light, walked before them, waving them onwards with his railing.

And finally Lec realized she was looking at an army. That was why the Wire Mistress was here. Sodiumite and Blankleit weren't just walking together; they intended to *fight* together.

A few yards away, the first Scaffwolf bounded up onto the Embankment, landing lightly on its steel paws. Electra dropped back behind a parked car. For a moment she hesitated as a part of her saw the coming battle unfold through her grandmother's eyes, the wolves pouncing on the unprepared white figures and the ambers who'd sided with them, their fangs rending glass and wire—

For a second Lec imagined the massacre with satisfaction. Then the second wolf landed, shaking the tarmac, and she made her choice.

She turned and ran up the middle of the road, blazing out the semaphore with every vestige of voltage she could muster.

"Filius, you're under att—"

Her filaments shuddered as the steel wolves overtook her.

THIRTY-SIX

"I wish the priests would get a bloody move-on. I'd cut them out of that armor if—"

"Fil!"

He looked up. "What?"

"Does that mean anything to you?

His gaze followed Beth's pointing finger. "It's some yellow Lampie," he muttered. "I can't see who. What's she do...?" He paled and reversed his hold on his spear.

"Get ready," he whispered to Beth. Then he arched his back, sticking his ribs out, and bellowed in a voice louder than all the city's din, "WE'RE UNDER ATTACK!"

The Scaffwolves came first, baying and slavering, bounding past the empty steel skeletons of their handlers. The weight of their paws tore great rents in the road.

The Sodiumites linked fields, every vein blazing with

suppressed static. They stumbled as they danced, struggling to place their feet right as the ground shook. Beth felt her hackles rise at the electricity in the air.

The first shockwave sheared away the lead wolf's front legs and with a whimper of steel it crashed muzzle-first into the road—but others leaped over it, kicking the bones of their packmate into the river as they charged.

Two hundred yards. One-eighty. One-fifty. Beth gauged the distance. Time slowed and the pack's headlong rush became a series of freeze-frames. Each jagged tooth and ragged metal claw fixed in her mind. She saw the glass dancers, stepping in another war-waltz—*too slow, too slow.* Fifty yards.

Beth shut her eyes and tensed herself for the impact.

"Oi, Bradley!" a voice yelled out. "What the hell do you think I got you those powers *for?*"

Beth snapped her eyes open. Her view was filled, side to side, with snapping howling jaws.

In Mater Viae's name, screw it! she thought.

She hurled herself forwards and the mêlée took her.

———

Beth hears my shout and I'm running, a war cry bleeding from my lips and lost in the wind. My speed smears the streets, turns the river to quicksilver. I can taste the fight in my gullet. Sodiumites vanish behind me in scars of light. Only foes stand before me now; only flashing fangs. Only prey. My lip twists. I am the savage street.

I snarl.

I may be no kind of general, but I can *hunt*. I fall on the wolves, and they fall to my spear.

Beth's ears sang as metal teeth sheared past them. It was a tornado of steel and she was in the eye. She sprang from strut to strut, from muzzle to back. Her balance was instinctive. Her sweat slicked her path through the air. The Urchin Prince and his spear were everywhere, as pervasive as gray smoke. And by his side a huge beast, twice the height of a man, like a bear made out of swarming rats and pigeons and the city's rubbish, tore at the underbellies of the wolves.

Lithe feline shapes darted through the fray: Fleet's war party. The skinny moggies hissing and scratching at the steel skeletons were almost comical, though Reach's monsters seemed to take them seriously enough. They chased vainly after the Cats, grasping for them, twisting their legs up and dislocating joints. Their motions looked panicky.

They're scared of them, Beth thought. *They're scared of the Cats, and that's screwing them up.*

Beth's army cheered on their champions as metal giant after metal giant collapsed, their limbs confused by the infamous Cats.

But they weren't the only ones who fell. Glass figures were caught in steel jaws. Bright amber flares reflected off steel: the last shouts of the dying. Beth bunched her legs and fired herself from the hindquarters of one animal right at the face of another. It snapped, but she twisted out of the way. Cold metal struck her palm and she seized it, clinging grimly to the scruff of the wolf's neck. Terror and exhilaration ran through her. A familiar voice welled out of her memory: *I had arms that could crush steel girders.*

She reached forwards and seized the corner of her wolf's mouth. The beast bucked, mashing its jaws together, but the teeth were too widely spaced to puncture Beth's hands. Knuckles white, she felt the steel give under the pressure of her fingertips. Gritting her teeth, she gripped harder, and pulled.

The wolf screamed, a shocking animal howl of pain as she fish-hooked it.

The beast's jaw flapped sideways, connected only by a thin ribbon of scrap-iron tissue. The wolf whimpered and crumpled forwards onto the tarmac.

Beth lay for an instant, blinking stupidly amidst the steel bones.

I did it. I brought a Scaffwolf down.

Iron fangs met in her shoulder, and she screamed.

———

Beth goes down, and something lurches sickly inside me, but I can't help her. The space between us blurs with metal. The bear that is Gutterglass roars and crushes one wolf, and then morphs into a giant fist, which smashes another. Fangs tear his side, and he hemorrhages worms.

Under the railway bridge, a ring of Sodiumites is spinning wildly in a devil-dervish. Strange shadows coalesce and divide on the pavement. The air stinks of cordite. An avatar of pure light springs outward from the heart of their circle and grapples a scaffolding giant to the ground. A second later it gutters out, but its work is done. The molten slag that was once the giant is welded to the road, jutting curves of metal like frozen waves.

A claw falls towards me. I parry and strike back. I risk a glance back under the bridge. The five glass women who raised the avatar lie flat, drained of their light. They have no more such devils in them.

Beth's scream made the air around her vibrate. The wolf shook her, its teeth rending her shoulder, a horrendous, sawing to-and-fro pain. She could feel the consciousness begin to seep out of her. The hand held to her breast was smothered in viscous, oily, black-streaked blood that clotted under her fingernails.

Play dead, play dead. She didn't know what put the thought in her head. She went limp. *Play dead.*

In a few seconds, she wouldn't have to pretend.

The wolf dropped her, the impact jarring her body. It straddled her, metal-pipe muzzle stretched wide...

... and never shut it.

Beth blinked up in astonishment. The hinges at the corners of its makeshift jaw squealed with the effort, but the Scaffwolf couldn't close its mouth. Clouds of rust gusted from the animal's nostrils.

"Da, lads! Da! Very many good!"

Beth winced as she rolled onto her shoulder. Through the waves of sickening pain she saw Victor standing on the pavement a few yards away, greatcoat flapping wide, waving his torch as though conducting an orchestra. All around him eager Blankleits stood, bright as miniature stars.

There was a manic glint in the Russian's eye. "Now boys, my good boys, *more*," he demanded. "*More*."

And the glass boys adjusted their peaked caps and bent their backs, perspiring pure light from their brows.

The wolf's jaws opened wider and wider, the hinges screeching resistance. Beth watched in horrified fascination as the two halves of the animal's muzzle suddenly inverted, and with ear-splitting protestations Reach's monster was turned inside-out.

Woozily, Beth stood up. Gusts of vodka-tainted breath washed over her as Victor stooped to inspect her shoulder. She could already feel it healing, the cement in her blood scabbing the wound.

"What *are* you, Tsarina?" he muttered, almost hypnotized by the strangeness of her blood. "They no teach this goddess medicine in Spetsnaz."

Behind him she could see more wolves prowling, their jaws glinting in the light of their foes. She shoved Victor angrily away. "They're surrounding us!" she shouted in his face. "Come on." She ran for the orange glow of the Sodiumite ranks. Heat washed over her neck as the Lampmen jogged in her wake. Pain throbbed through her as her wounded arm swung.

Goddess, she thought. *Who's a bloody goddess?*

———

Reach's initial wave has faltered. His wolves whirl, gnashing the air, but they are far fewer than they were. Then again, so are we. I break into a run, shattered glass biting my feet. A trash-tiger bounds beside me and a ragged cheer goes up from our side—only two or three audible voices, but a chorus of silent ones, glowing back off the clouds. They think we're winning.

But now the handlers move, swaying metal skeletons, shambling unsteadily up the road, their footsteps pealing like bells. They crouch amongst the wreckage of the wolfpack, sorting the scrap with fingers too small and clever for their massive hands. Instead of fingernails they have wrenches and sledgehammers and shears, and quickly, cunningly, they reconnect the joints. Shoulders rise on haunches, supporting half-reconstructed skulls.

The fallen wolves shake themselves and drag themselves snarling from the tarmac while our dead remain as dust on the ground.

A rebuilt wolf rears in front of me, still groggily shaking its head. I spring off its shoulder and slash a handler through the kneecap. He falls, but his fellows are already rebuilding him. It's Metal Medicine, and we have no answer to it.

"ZEKE!" I manage to bellow, just before the animal I used as a springboard takes me in the stomach. "WHERE ARE YOU?"

———

The air moved against Beth's skin, stirred by heavy wings. All along the riverfront, hands clapped over the stone embankment, water droplets glimmering on their fingers. In all manner of shapes, dressed from a dozen centuries, stone figures pulled themselves jerkily into view.

They had trudged, slowly, to get here; the mud on the riverbed still clung to their feet. But now a regiment of statuary stood on the Embankment. Through the gaps eroded by time and the elements in their armor, Beth could see bared teeth and throats pulsing as they sucked down air.

The Pavement Priests were building up to something.

Beth looked in through the eyeholes of one. His eyes were stretched wide with effort.

Then, as one, the Pavement Priests vanished.

What—? Where—?

A screeching clang answered her. Across the road, a scaffolding giant had fallen to its knees, gripped by a nude bronze and a stone scholar. Their hands blurred, tearing metal like paper, and Beth found herself gaping as the slim bronze woman in front of her twisted her hips and ripped the metal skull from the giant's shoulders.

The pair of statues vanished again, and reappeared to scythe the knees from another handler.

A crazy hope filled Beth like warmth.

How come you never see statues move? she thought in wonder. *Is it because they move too slowly, or is it because they're much, much too fast?*

The riverbank was a battlefield. The Pavement Priests flickered, vanished, and rematerialized on top of their enemies, their sheer weight dragging the metal monsters down. The air was alive with panting, praying, and screaming.

The Priests took casualties. Real blood ran from their wounds, black and sticky with lack of water. She surveyed the battle, a terrified elation burning in her throat. She dared to hope the Pavement Priests might be turning the tide.

It isn't happening. The priests aren't turning the tide.

As I fight, I can only glimpse the carnage. The poor stoneskins are running out of steam, slowing down like toys with their clockwork spent, and all over the road the wolves are tearing them down. Statues litter the battlefield, close-fitting tombs.

Perhaps a quarter of the wolfpack remains, and a small huddle of their handlers. It will be enough: already those clever fingers are reworking the scaffolding joints.

Where's Beth? I can't see Beth anywhere.

My spear feels heavier than I remember, and it's only then I notice the flesh of my right arm is torn. Pain pours through my shoulder, almost as if it's been waiting for me to notice the wound so it can jump out and surprise me. The scaffolding giants shake the streets with their footsteps.

Already the wolves are circling. Raw fear swills around my stomach. There's only one thing left to do.

"Fall back," I shout. "Fall back to the river!"

For a second, Glas stares at me. Then he nods and reforms as a giant rubbish head, shrieking in the voice of a hundred rats, "FALL BACK! FALL BACK!"

My soldiers, glass and flesh and stone alike, waver, then they're all sprinting as fast as they can towards the water. Pavement Priests with severed limbs are dragged by Sodiumites, fields wrapped around them like fishing nets. I stand, urging them on until the last Lampie has passed me, and as I turn myself and hare off on its tail the Scaffwolves howl joyously and race in pursuit.

It's less than a hundred paces to the riverbank. The distance dissolves. I can feel the chill breath of the wolves on my back. As the first of my army reach the water's edge, they mill about in confusion. Some look back my way with perplexed, betrayed expressions. I know what they're thinking: if the wolfpack traps them against the river, they'll all be slaughtered.

I catch Gutterglass' eye. We've only got one chance at this.

"BREAK RIGHT!" I bawl as Glas shouts, "BREAK LEFT!" and I bound into my army's ranks and start almost throwing glass bodies westwards up the riverbank. Glas is more efficient, morphing into a giant hand that sweeps scores of Pavement Priests in the opposite direction.

Glass girls and boys are screaming, pale yellow light flashing haphazardly. A priest is crushed to bloody gravel under his fellows. But a gap opens up in the middle of our ranks. The wolves try to check their charge, but their momentum is too great and as they barrel past they twist to snap at our ankles. Their metal paws pulverize the concrete barrier and they splash into the glittering river beyond.

Ragged breath tears through me. I give Glas a smile.

The wolfpack stirs, swishing ankle-deep in the water, turning, making ready to pursue us. But then they stop.

One of the handlers looks down at the surface of the river, and I know what he sees: the reflections of Metal Men and Scaffwolves are surrounded by other reflections, hundreds of them, some besuited, others dungaree'd or wearing battered camouflage. They are reflections without originals, reflections that smile grimly as the welding torches they're wielding spit and flare into life.

I jump onto an empty pedestal on the Embankment just in time to see a Mirrorstocrat touch his torch to a wolf's reflection. As he does so, the real wolf shrieks horribly and its muzzle glows white-hot, then begins to melt.

My ears are still ringing when a heavy stone hand claps me on the shoulder. I look up into Ezekiel's face; he's congratulating me on the feint. I nod absently. Below me the wolves are trying to back out of the river, but their reflections have been chained and muzzled, and though they strain at them they might as well be trying to tear away from their own shadows.

Feeling a little sick at what I've got the Mirrorstocracy to do, I turn away—

—and what I see freezes me in shock.

In the dim light on the other side of the road, a Scaff-wolf stands alone. A girl mounted on the beast's back is watching me. Her hair is bound in a silk scarf. Her face is streaked with metal and dried blood. Somehow she projects pure *loathing*; implacable hatred emanates from her shape. Almost lazily, she extends an arm towards our ranks.

"No!" I mean to shout it, but I don't even know if I make any sound.

Tendrils of barbed wire, hundreds of snakelike strands, are unfurling at ferocious speed. A Sodiumite girl younger than me barely has time to flinch before wire crunches her neck apart.

Oh no. Oh Thames, no: the Wire Mistress—

More tendrils, more broken bodies, more death. Reach has sent his high priestess to see us wiped out.

I shove myself towards her, but my legs are reluctant. "You're the only one who can stop her!" I shout at myself, although frankly, that's optimism gone barking bloody mad. She's got a host, so she'll be at least as strong as me.

The Mistress's host springs from the back of her wolf and runs towards us. A buzzing cloud of gleaming metal surrounds her and I imagine those tendrils dipping into the river, stirring the water into foam and obliterating the Mirrorfolk and the wolves' reflections.

She could still undo everything.

You're the only one who can stop her. But I don't have to do it alone.

I scream, part war cry, mostly plain terror as I meet the steel-wrapped girl. Barbed strands fly around me and I manage to shout, just a few words, before they seal up my mouth.

———————

"*Beth, help me!*"

Beth looked down the Embankment. That voice, the voice of the streets, spurred her muscles, though dizziness washed over her and she stumbled.

"Fil!" she shouted. "*Fil!* Where are you?"

There was no answer, but now she didn't need one: she could see the seething mass of wire standing on the very edge of the river. Pavement Priests were trying to get close, but wires lashed out like whips, keeping them at bay. They all looked terrified of the thing.

A gray arm bleeding from a thousand little cuts thrust out of the coils, holding an iron railing, but the wire had looped around the wrist and he couldn't plunge the weapon home.

Beth ran at the tangled, jagged cloud of metal and started tearing at the strands. The wire coils hissed over each other, slashing at her face, making every inch of her skin burn with pain, but she didn't pull her hands back to protect herself.

Fil, she thought desperately. *Filius… hold on!*

She plunged into the heart of the monster.

Two figures waited for her: Fil, on his back, horribly contorted, his torso streaked with blood. His teeth were bared and his arm cocked, spear ready, but the wires held his limbs and he couldn't uncoil.

"Beth!" He forced his voice between the barbs in his lips. "Beth, take my spear. Kill the host."

But Beth barely heard him. She was staring at the wire thicket's other inhabitant. The other inhabitant stared right back at her.

Pen looked like one of those cartoons of electrocuted people, except instead of lightning bolts, there were wires holding her off the ground and splaying her limbs, forcing her into a X shape.

Some useless part of Beth's brain registered that she'd lent Pen the jeans she was wearing—they'd looked a bit tatty in the charity shop, but they looked far worse now, all slippery with gore. Pen's right nostril had been ripped away and her mouth was slit wider: a jagged grin towards her ear.

But the eyes were just as Beth remembered.

Those eyes *knew* Beth as well as she knew them.

"Beth! Help me!" The yell tore Fil's lips and his railing clattered onto the pavement at her feet. "*Kill. The. Host.*" The breath was being squeezed from him.

Beth wrenched herself forwards, sickened and horrified, and reached for the wires that held Pen's throat. Her nails gouged Pen's flesh as she tried desperately to pry the metal away and the barbs tore her own hands. Her palms were slicked with blood.

"Pen," she gabbled absurdly, "Pen, are you okay?" Pen didn't answer; her lips were stitched gruesomely with wire.

Beth saw Fil out of the corner of her eye as, just for an instant, disbelief etched his face like physical pain. Then the wire-thing's tendrils dragged him over the balustrade and plunged him into the river.

Wires flashed out and bound Beth's arms and legs. The barbs bit into her, but the pain seemed distant—everything was distant except her best friend's mutilated face.

"Oh G-god, Pen—" she managed to stammer.

She suddenly became aware of orange light: a naked, shining glass girl was forcing her way towards the tangle of wire. The glare seared Beth's eyes, but she didn't shut them. She could read the pain written on Pen's skin. The glass girl drew level with Beth, but she didn't look at her. Beth was vaguely aware that the glass girl looked familiar, then realized she was the first Sodiumite she'd ever seen.

Oh God, Pen, I'm so sorry.

The glass girl extended a hand towards Pen, burning bright with the effort. Fine cracks laced themselves up her arm; she raised the other arm and began to step in a formal circle, a tightly controlled dance.

The glass over her chest fractured and went cloudy. Fragments of her skin peeled off and spun, glittering, trapped in her own magnetism.

The wire slid backwards, inch by grudging inch. Agonizingly, the barbs slid free of Beth's arms, leaving red pucker marks. Without them to support her, she fell. The strand that was holding Fil under water was taut now, and looked almost fragile.

Beth, help me!

Beth's teeth were chattering with shock, but she groped around and found the railing-spear by her feet. With a snarl of effort she lifted it and slashed the wire tendril in two.

The wire monster recoiled in pain at the touch of the spear, and Pen's face blurred as the barbs contracted around her, as though it were clutching Pen to its heart. Then, like some vast insect, it rose up on hundreds of spindly legs, bore Pen up onto the bridge, and skittered away.

Pen...

"*Fil!*" Beth was bewildered, drained. She tried to follow, but she found she couldn't walk. She collapsed to her knees and crawled to the balustrade. There was no movement on the water. Warmth on her skin told her the glass girl was there.

"Filius," she gasped. "He's down there. He's—I have to—" She tried to push herself up, but she was too weak. The wire's barbs had leeched the strength from her.

A metal parasite, he had called it. *Oh my God, Pen—*

She slid backwards, cracking her jaw on the stone.

Electra shot Beth a pitying look and closed her eyes.

Beth saw fear through the transparent lids for only a second.

Then Electra drew herself up and threw her fractured body headfirst into the Thames.

For an instant Beth could see her glow, shining up from

the depths. Then the water began to seethe and boil, and stale-smelling gas wafted up and filled the air.

Beth watched, helpless, but she couldn't make out what was happening until two bodies broke the surface. Fil was screaming weakly, barely conscious. The skin where Electra was holding him bubbled red, then turned black. Electra's head was arched back, her bones flaring white and fizzing away. Her jaw was clenched tight, and her filaments had started to disappear like burning fuses, but she managed to drag the boy onto a sandbank.

The dirt clung to the weeping flesh of his burns and he coiled up, fetus-like, to protect himself. "Lec." It was only a whisper, but Beth heard it clearly from the Embankment above. "Lec." He groped behind him, grasping the glass girl's hand. His own skin smoked where he touched her.

Electra smiled. She glimmered something in her own language that Beth didn't understand.

With a grunt of pain, the Son of the Streets reached out to touch her cheek, but the reaction reached Electra's face and it burned away under his hand.

"Fil!" Beth slipped down the side of the Embankment onto the sandbar. She staggered to his side. "Fil! What can I do? What can I *do?*" she shouted at him desperately, idiotically. "*What can I do?*"

She fell to the ground beside him and cradled his head. Cuts covered his skin, and a burn on his wrist had all but obliterated his Tower Block Tattoo. River water bubbled out of his throat when he tried to answer.

"*What can I do?*" she whispered into his hair.

"You know what she said?" he gasped after hacking up a gallon of muddy water. There was a kind of wonder in his face. "She said, 'If you're going to bring the White bastards in, you'd better teach 'em to dance.'" His head fell back onto her lap, his eyes closed. But his chest was still rising and falling. He was unconscious, but alive.

Beth became aware of a fluttering sound, like pigeon wings.

"Come on, girl," a voice gusted on rubbish-scented breath. "There are more wolves on the way, and we're in no state to fight them. Give him to me."

Fat gray pigeons flocked all over Fil's body, and Beth felt dozens of pigeon claws seize her jeans, her hoodie, and her hair.

"Come," Gutterglass whispered, his voice hoarse with the strain.

As she was born into the air Beth could see glimmering bodies below her, and flashing lights: Ezekiel and Victor marshalling the retreat. A scaffolding muzzle slipped below the water. But Beth knew what she would remember most, the image that would haunt her quiet moments...

The fragments. The tiny, tiny pieces of the men and women and children that she'd led here. Ground glass, and gravel, and blood.

THIRTY-SEVEN

Moonlight bleached the statues where they stood amongst the gravestones. The deep shadows made the stone figures look tired. A sound carried on the breeze: slow regular breathing, the odd snore. Slumped inside their punishment skins, the Pavement Priests slept.

It was very early in the morning. They'd worked all of the preceding night.

The sound of stone wings had filled the cemetery, and one after another, they'd looked up. Ezekiel delivered the first body in silence: a boy, swaddled in the statue of a Victorian scientist. He'd dropped the boy at Petris' feet as if it was nothing at all. Petris nodded as he accepted the burden. He gazed at the clawmarks in Ezekiel's stone armor with a kind of jealousy.

Is that all I am now? he wondered. *An undertaker? Is this how quickly the sword passes to another fist?*

After that first body (*Lasulo*, Petris thought, careful to recall his name), others came. Their surviving battle-mates brought them, balanced stiffly on shoulders or pulled through the dew-wet grass on makeshift sleds. The priests of the graveyard moved to help. Nobody spoke. Brother faced brother; hard-eyed husbands salved their wives' battle wounds in silence. The last words they'd exchanged had been ugly ones, words like *slave* and *whore* and *heretic*, but this wasn't the time to rehash those arguments, not with dead to count and bury.

No one had to speak. Everyone knew what needed to be done.

They grunted and muttered curses as they lifted the dead onto the empty pedestals. They mixed mortar and melted bronze according to each of the fallen's materials and poured it around their feet to set them in place. A few paused to gape at the sheer *number* of the entombed. It was the largest mass funeral in decades.

And then, at four o'clock, the hour of stone, the *true* witching hour, the Pavement Priests began to sing. Petris led, and every other brother and sister joined in, even Ezekiel, wheeling overhead at a disdainful distance.

The hymn of the Pavement Priests rang out across London, as pure as bell chimes and as deep as a midwinter night, carrying over the growl of London engines, and everyone who heard it stopped and listened. Without knowing it, the people on the streets observed a moment's silence for the fallen.

The words of the song were simple enough: *Under the skin gifted by the quarry and washed away by the rain, a fragment of the human remains.* The song was a prayer that those fragments become whole again, that the most human of virtues be restored to their fallen siblings, the virtue that allowed them to die. They prayed that their statues would cease to be punishment skins and became simple graves.

The prayer's target, of course, was Mater Viae herself. Only she could consider her debt paid and buy the priests' deaths back from the oil-soaked traders she'd sold them to.

The irony of praying to a goddess they'd rejected even as they stood in the ruins of her temple almost made Petris smile. But this was a funeral, and she was the only goddess they had. Who else could they pray to? As Johnny Naptha had once lisped in that stupid way of his, *Weddingss and funeralss force the faithlesss to fake it.*

The song finished and Petris ended the ceremony with a scattering of brickdust at the feet of the dead. The soldiers took their scars back into the night. Ezekiel beat his way laboriously north. They had wounded to care for, and a war with Reach to gloriously lose.

But the majority remained. Like Petris, they'd turned their backs on the goddess who'd enslaved them. As he turned and walked away from the tombs, Petris hoped that none of them felt as much a coward as he did. Most of them had only managed a few steps before collapsing into an exhausted slumber inside their armor, but Petris couldn't sleep. He was kept awake by a pain in his chest, a sharp longing to be with the army, to fight, to feel the pores in his stone soak up blood. It was what he had been re*born* for, to be a soldier. It was so long since there had been a war to fight.

But to fight would be to fight for *her*, and the men and women he spoke for were too angry to accept that. He scratched at his thumbs, flaking away stone: a casual rebellion.

The Carven Doctrines taught that there was no pain in a death in Mater Viae's service: such a death paid their debt and bought release. Petris grieved not for the dead but for himself, though he'd never in a thousand years admit it. The deaths of his flock only made his own imprisonment lonelier.

So he did what all religious men do when they're lonely. Quietly, so as not to disturb the others, he began to pray.

THIRTY-EIGHT

"I have to go back!" she yelled, but the pigeons ignored her. The wind from their wings buffeted her face. London flashed past below. She writhed and kicked, but their claws only gripped her tighter.

"I have to go back!" She sounded deranged in her own ears. A single thought filled her to bursting and seized control of her voice. "That was Pen! *That was Pen!* I have to go back!"

A plastic clown mask dangled from a pigeon claw. It twisted to face her. "Shut up."

"She's my *friend*."

"She's *its* host." Worms contorted the mask's lips into a grimace. The empty eggshells stuck into its eye sockets looked past her to where a frail, skinny young man hung from the heart of a flock of pigeons, trailing flecks of blood into the empty air. "Do you really think she'd treat you any differently?"

They passed over a crosshatch of roof tiles washed yellow by the light of ordinary, dumb lamps. Tower block windows glimmered for a moment, then were gone. They skimmed in low over a landfill site: hillsides of broken TV sets and microwaves and scrap metal. Snared plastic billowed like foliage. Streams of industrial solvent and rainwater carved up the landscape.

The instant the pigeons set her down, Beth was running, slipping, and stumbling over the filth towards Fil, who was lying on the ground, curled away from her. The wire had flayed half his skin off and a flap of it was hanging open like a grotesque curtain.

She skidded down on her knees beside him. His face was slack, unconscious. She drew breath sharply, remembering the look of horror, of outright *betrayal* before the wire-creature had plunged him into the river.

Kill the host, he'd cried.

But she couldn't. It was *Pen.* She couldn't—

Could she?

Pigeons flocked around her, beating her backwards with wings and talons.

Glas!" she protested.

"Get away from him." She couldn't see a face, but the voice was flat and angry. Bugs were swarming, building legs from the surrounding rubbish.

"But I have to help ... "

Suddenly the clown-mask jutted through the storm of

pigeon wings. "If you distract me and he dies, I will tear the eyes out of your skull. Understand, little girl? The best thing you can do for him is get away, *now*."

Beth stiffened. She stared at Gutterglass with gritted teeth, then turned and stumbled back down the hill.

For what felt like a long time, she trudged in darkness through the shifting murk. *Pen!* The thought filled her head like a screaming siren. Panic fired her muscles and she sprinted up the side of a rubbish-dune towards the glowing city, towards *Pen*, arms pumping. All she could see was her best friend, bound and bloodied by barbed wire.

But then Beth's fingertips brushed over one another and she felt the texture of the thin rough scabs those barbs had left. She stumbled to a stop. She'd had her chance to help Pen, her chance to *free* her, and she'd failed. What if she failed again? What if all that happened was that Pen was forced to watch while the Wire Mistress used her own hands to crush Beth's throat?

Gutterglass' voice seeped into her mind. *Do you really think she'd treat you any differently?*

Beth looked back across the landfill to where Fil was lying, bleeding and shuddering and barely breathing, amidst the filth and junk. Where *she'd* led him.

"*Is that your plan? Run?*" Her scorn rang so hollow now; she wished she could suck those words back into her. She wished she'd let him save himself.

She'd bullied and mocked and lured him here, just as she had with Pen by leaving that smug riddle about "fractured harmony" on the bricks by her house.

That's me: a siren call to self-destruction.

A sensation filled her like warm, slow concrete in her stomach and limbs. She sank into the rubbish. She couldn't fix it. She'd broken everything and she couldn't fix it. She didn't even feel the tears running down her cheeks.

All she'd done—all she had the power to do—was to make everything worse.

God, Fil, please don't die.

The little scraps of paper and cardboard and egg cartons and beer-bottle labels littered the ground under her like photographs, old pictures of someone lost.

This is how you felt, Dad, she thought as she stared at them. *Like there was nothing you could do.*

The helplessness boiled up in her, hot and black and poisonous, like it must have in him. And she'd hated him for it.

There's nothing I can do.

She bent over and cried, hard. It was a wrench to get each tear out, like they were pulling her insides with them.

There's nothing I can do.

She cried until she was empty; then she just sat. But the image of her father in his chair with his book was fixed in her mind and she couldn't shake it. She couldn't settle into the strangling fingers of her despair. She couldn't just sit there like he had—because she'd seen him do it.

She rocked slowly back onto her feet and looked down at the dent she'd made, a little alcove in the muck. *If it wasn't for him, I probably never would have got up.* It was a gift, she thought suddenly, one he'd given without even meaning to. She thanked him quietly and wished he could hear her.

She started to walk back down into the landfill. There was nothing she could do, but she had to do something.

Gradually the sky changed from the velvet darkness of late night to the permeable gloom of very early morning. In dribs and drabs, a slow trickle of bodies, the remnants of her army, entered the landfill.

The Sodiumites carried their wounded on stretchers woven from yellow and black electrical tape: near-shattered bodies missing arms or legs, or desperately reaching into their own chests to pinch together the circuits that kept their hearts beating.

The Pavement Priests used gateposts as crutches, but there weren't enough to go around and some had to crawl. One stone-clad figure collapsed under the weight of his armor, gasping, "No further..." until a sleek tabby cat melted from the ranks and rubbed itself, purring, up against the fallen priest. From somewhere deep within, he found enough faith to keep going, just that bit further.

As the survivors reached the heart of the dump, rats and beetles and cockroaches emerged. With chitters of mandibles and jerkings of sleek brown heads, they directed the wounded to alcoves excavated from the mounds of rubbish. Those too hurt to do anything else collapsed gratefully down on discarded mattresses. The most able set to work, dressing wounds with torn clothes, patching up flickering Lampfolk with used lightbulbs and bits of cracked champagne flutes and beer glasses.

A priest inside a one-armed statue was organizing the field hospital. He read out a list of injuries to a horde of eager rats while blood dried slowly around a wound in his own marble stomach.

The priest looked up in surprise as Beth approached him. Her eyes were raw with tears. She rolled up the sleeves of her hoodie. "What can I do?" she asked.

He appraised her through the peepholes in his marble mask. "Hell of a mess to clean up," he said. His stone lips were set in a heroic smile. He twitched his marble stump at her. "Fancy lending us a hand?"

So Beth bandaged and stitched and soldered, and wiped blood and pus from sticky wounds. *Work,* she ordered herself as she pulled on the needle and drew the sides of a young soldier's gaping thigh together through the gap in his concrete robe. These were her soldiers; she'd called them and they'd followed her, same as Pen had, and she owed them just as much.

Just work.

"I'm telling you, blud, it was four," the young priest was saying in a nasal Mile-End accent.

The bronze-coated figure on the next mattress over snorted. "Four, *right*. Remind me, son, who taught you to count? There was one by the river, one on the bridge, and the other by that brick hospital. Your ass only killed three wolves, Timon; don' be frontin' like you can top my score."

Timon hissed in exasperation, coating concrete lips in spittle. "All that green rust on your face makin' you blind, Al. I took down that fat rusty bitch down on the beach, too. Snapped its neck, like this—" He made a sharp twisting gesture with his hands.

Al sneered. "Timon, that bitch bounced back faster than one of your mum's checks."

"Shut up about my mum! You don't know nothin' about her."

"I'll shut up about your mum when you shut up about my face. It's the copper—ain't my fault this stuff corrodes. Anyway, *you* don't know nothin' about your mum neither; you been a priest *way* to long, so don't be trying to pretend you remember her no more."

Timon fell into an uncomfortable silence. Beth looked up from her needle. Something in his plaintive pride stung her. She knotted the thread and bit it off, and popped the cap off her magic marker.

"Hey, what—?" Timon started to protest, and then fell silent when he saw what she was drawing. Four stylized wolfheads appeared on his concrete shoulder, angular and snarling: trophies, like kills painted on the side of a fighter jet.

"There you go, Timon," she said. "One for each of your prey."

Al's jealousy was forgotten as he admired his friend's new markings. "I want me summa them too," he said.

Timon sucked his teeth. "Well, you're not dead yet, Al," he said. "That's some pretty badass trophy right there."

"True that."

Beth snapped the cap back on her marker and frowned. "I thought Pavement Priests couldn't die," she said. "Petris said that you wanted your deaths *back*."

Both Timon and Al erupted into hoots of scornful laughter. "Yeah, Miss B, we can die," Al said. "We just get born again. You know what that's like?"

Beth shook her head.

Al's green eyes stared mercilessly out through the copper. "You's a little baby," he said quietly, "stuck in a stone crib. No food, no water, no light, *and no idea why not*. You don't get all your memories back right away, see?

"Some of us don't never remember," he added quietly. "What the Synod did: it's no precise art, y'know? You get memories coming back from your old lives all ragged, but stuff's missing, and other stuff contradicts. They say Johnny Naptha has a room somewhere full of memories, bottles of copies he made of us 'fore he took us the first time. Don't know if I believe that. But I *do* know I don't remember committin' no crime to get me damned."

There was silence. Beth could feel Timon's gaze on the back of her neck.

Al hawked and spat through the tiny crack between his bronze lips. "Can't whine too loud though. Least last time I got reborn, it was in the graveyard, with another priest close enough to hear me cryin'. A lot of us isn't that lucky. A lot are never found … there'll be new babies stranded in statues all over London tonight after that ruckus, *believe* that." His voice was a bitter sneer. "Their wounds're only the first o' their problems. Your goddess *seen* to that. That's why we want our deaths back."

Beth put the cap back on her marker and stood up. The hand that held the marker was trembling. All those bodies, crushed and dying... *your goddess.* "Yeah," she said, "I'm sorry, I... I need... I have to..." She turned and bolted from the alcove.

"Hey, Miss B!" Al lifted a bronze arm slightly. "What about me?"

When Ezekiel found Beth, she was crouched amidst old crisp packets and cardboard, hugging her knees; a nowhere place in this nowhere dump. The stone angel clucked his tongue disapprovingly. "Guilt weighing you down?" he said.

She said nothing, and he ignored her glare. "Come now, young lady," he said, "I've been a priest for almost eight hundred years. If I couldn't recognize a gangrenous conscience then I ought to abandon the calling altogether and open a florist's."

There was a flicker, and suddenly he stood beside her, massive with his limestone wings. "Talk." It wasn't a request. "You'll feel better."

Beth continued to stare. She had no idea where to start.

"Blood in the river," Ezekiel sighed. "How does your lot do this again?" He creaked down beside her. Cracks appeared and resealed instantly in his cassock. "I bless you, daughter, for you have sinned, it's been... well, forever in all probability, since your last confession, so you're due. Keep it to the important stuff please; I have neither the time nor the inclination to hear about shoplifting when you were ten. Anyway, confess away. I'm listening."

Beth opened her mouth, stalled, and then the words came out all in a tumble. "It's too much. People follow me. I ask them … and they follow. Like Fil, and—and Pen, and all these people in their stone and their glass. And I'm *trying*, really *trying* to *help*. But now Electra's dead, and Fil nearly is … and these priests are just kids, and Pen … oh Christ and Thames, *Pen* … Oh God—" She stopped, trying to recover her breath.

The angel's beautiful carved face watched her. "I misjudged you, Miss Bradley," he said softly. "Guilt is not your problem."

"No?" Beth sniffed back tears. "Then what is?"

"Rampaging egomania."

Beth jerked her head up, thinking the angel was taking the piss, but he sounded totally serious. "'People-*huh*-follow-*huh*-me!'" He mimicked her exactly, even with the little gasps for breath. "'These priests are just kids.' Patronize us to your heart's content, Miss Bradley; we're all several hundred years old, but we don't mind."

Then he snorted. "Honestly! As if we have not eyes to see and minds to think as well as feet and hands to march and fight." A stone hand took Beth's chin. She hadn't even seen it move. "Listen to me. This will be bad for your ego, but good for your heart. Reach is a monster. He and his creatures kill indiscriminately. You know this; so do we. We follow you only because you happen to be *right*. And if it had not been you, we would have followed someone else. Filius would have fought in the end, with or without you.

"It is the will of the goddess." His voice rasped with urgency bordering on fanaticism. "As the appearance of Fleet and his holy felines shows. You carry the Lady's aspect, and I respect that, but do not let that fool you into thinking you are more important than you are. We are *all* vessels for her will."

He released her chin and retreated from her in a few unclear flickers of motion. Beth rubbed the skin where his fingers had been. The bruises were healing already.

"Oh, and Miss Bradley? You are about the worst triage nurse I've ever seen. Gutterglass' weevils keep having to unpick your stitches and redo them. It's embarrassing, and a waste of time. For their sake, if not your own, find something to do that you're actually *good* at."

THIRTY-NINE

When Beth found Gutterglass, he was crouched over a Sodiumite girl so badly wounded that she could barely light his face. The trash-spirit's incarnation was tiny, no bigger than a toddler, and he stroked her fiber-optic hair with soda-straw fingers and whispered to her that Mater Viae loved her.

There was a hissing, cracking noise and half a dozen rats nosed their way from the rubbish-dune, dragging a live electrical cable burrowed from some part of the national grid. Gutterglass slid condoms over his fingers like surgical gloves and set to work.

Beth didn't disturb him 'til he was done. "The compact look suits you," she said. She eyed his avatar's oversized, collapsing-football head. "In a creepy, decomposing baby sort of way."

Gutterglass didn't look at her. "I have 5,063 distinct organisms under control at present," he said snippily, "scavenging, shoring up defenses, and, in some cases, conducting open-heart surgery. Frankly, I'd like to see you manage half as much and animate a paper bag, let alone a fully functional avatar." The little refuse-marionette rummaged around, tugged out a battered pack of cigarettes, and lit one between his split-seam lips.

"You smoke?" Beth was surprised.

"Who better to have a filthy habit?" Gutterglass countered.

Beth watched smoke billow back out through his balsawood ribs. "Does it … do anything for you?" she asked.

"It used to." Gutterglass shut his eggshell eyes. There was a wistfulness as he spoke. "A long time ago."

When the eggshells opened again, the look Gutterglass gave her was cold and tinged with hostility. "What do you want, Miss Bradley?"

Beth looked at him through the smoke. "What do you think I want?"

———

The Prince of London had no mattress. His back and shoulders were raised off the ground by crushed rubble and chunks of brick. As Beth watched, the color of the rubble faded and his pallid skin darkened a little, but only a very little.

She crouched and brushed the hair out of his face. His jaw was clenched and his eyes screwed up. "He looks better."

"Of course he does," Gutterglass said flatly. "*I'm* his doctor. Although, to give him his due, the-little-god-that-could here is very hard to kill."

Air escaped the football-head in a sigh. "However, I have no way of knowing when he'll wake up," he confessed. "In the meantime I suppose that leaves you and me in command." He spat out the words angrily. "I'll need you to—"

"I'm going, Glas," Beth interrupted. She stood up.

The eggshells blinked. "Going? Going where?"

"St. Paul's. Pen needs me."

Gutterglass waited a long time before he answered. "Do you know what?" he said at last. "I should *let* you." To Beth's surprise his voice was harsh with anger. "I should wish you the best of London Luck and just let you waltz straight into the Scaffwolves' jaws. After all, you deserve it. I introduced them, did you know that? Filius and Electra? She was brave and powerful and graceful; she was his best friend, and she made him happier than anyone I've ever seen."

He twisted his head and looked at Beth with frank disgust. "Anyone except you. So for the love he bore you, I'll say this once. *Don't go.* You think you can make it better? You can't. Reach will rip you asunder. Walk into the Demolition Fields looking for a happy ending, and an ending is all you'll find."

He fell silent. For a long time Beth held his eggshell gaze. "You're still going, then?" Gutterglass said eventually.

"What do you think?"

A cockroach in Gutterglass' mouth clicked in disapproval and something bumped against Beth's shin. She looked down. It was Fil's corroded railing-spear, born on a swarming tide of beetles.

"You might need this." Glas' little face looked exhausted, but in a strange way satisfied. "In the unlikely event you get close enough, drive it into the Crane King's throat."

Beth's fingers closed around the spear. The grooves and pits in the metal seemed to fit her hand precisely. She could almost feel the shape of Fil's handprint on it.

"It's not much," Gutterglass said, "but without Mater Viae's Great Fire, we must improvise."

Beth exhaled slowly. "I'll kill him, Glas," she swore, tasting every word. "For Fil, and Electra, and Pen. And for me."

Gutterglass' seam-smile said he didn't believe her, but he nodded. He disintegrated slowly. His eggshells watched her to the last.

When Gutterglass had gone, she bent down and kissed Fil's forehead. "You brought me home," she whispered into his ear. It physically hurt her, deep in her chest, to leave him like this, but he had Gutterglass, and Gutterglass had his army, while Pen—Pen who she loved more fully and deeply than anyone else, who she'd almost let herself forget—Pen had only her.

Fil had believed she could be like him, so she owed him that: to do more than just run. "I saved your life once, remember," she whispered as she turned to go. "Don't let it be wasted effort. I'll try to do the same."

It was only a hundred feet to the landfill's perimeter fence. The tarmac felt nourishing under her feet as she ran, and London blurred past, all lights and noise and grandeur and stink, the spear pointed due south before her.

Before long, cranes began to rear on the horizon, and she turned east. The bulk of St. Paul's emerged like a vast black beetle crouched against the sunrise. The Demolition Fields were drawing closer.

FORTY

"I can't make this add up at all."

Parva looked forlornly at her father across the table. She knew how this was going to end. She'd struggled into her green wedding sharara, which had hurt because it was over-ambitiously small and there were cuts under her arms.

Her dad wouldn't meet her gaze but remained hunched, scowling over his ledger. "Come here and help me, Parva."

Obediently she stood and went to his shoulder. Behind her a knife scraped over china as her mother dumped the food into the bin.

"See?" her father grumbled. He smelled of nuts and dry tobacco. "He'll want a fortune."

Parva gazed into her own mutilated face. Her father

held the pencil, but it was Beth's style that characterized the picture.

Her father slumped forwards and sighed, his breath stirring the white hairs on his brown arms. "I can't afford it. I can't. It will ruin me. I'll have to sell the practice."

A crash made them both look up. Parva's mother stood over the shrapnel of a broken plate. Her hand was trembling. "Why, Parva? Why couldn't you take better care of yourself? I *taught* you how." She sounded tearful, and she looked terribly old.

"I'm afraid it's worse than you think, Mrs. K," a familiar voice said. Beth ambled in from the front room, her hands thrust into the pockets of her hoodie. "Do you mind?" She lifted the pencil from Parva's dad's unresisting fingers and began to scribble over his picture, her tongue between her teeth as she worked, her face all concentration. Under her pencil, the true extent of Parva's injuries became clear. She twirled the pencil in her fingers and used the rubber end to erase one nostril and half an ear. She drew in a ragged scar at the corner of the mouth.

Pain flared through Parva's face. She put her hand to her cheek and felt blood. She probed with her fingers and felt the skin where her lips met split and separate as through dragged with an invisible wire.

When Beth had done, Parva slumped to the ground, her nose and mouth full of the tang of metal.

Beth dropped the pencil down on the paper. "Sorry, Mr. K," she said. "I don't think you'll find any takers. Not for any price." She extended a hand to Parva. "Come on, Pen," she said.

Pen reached out with the thumb and three remaining fingers of her right hand. She smeared Beth's palm red as she grasped it. She followed her best friend from the room.

Pen woke slowly, the crash of demolition like a call to prayer from mosques in some dawn in her childhood she barely remembered: tower blocks for minarets, wrecking balls for muezzins.

She opened her eyes cautiously, but it was only the matted web of sleep that held them shut. Her mouth felt parched; it tasted of resentment and old blood. She sighed, expanding her ribs as far as she could against their wire corset.

Kill the host… That's what the skinny boy had said as she squeezed him. Pen found herself furious with Beth for not obeying him. In the brief, feverish periods of sleep she managed to snatch, she dreamed of Beth: both rescuer and mutilator, cutter and cure. It was an addiction, tenacious as a weed. She had to stop. Neither blaming nor hoping for Beth was going to help her.

A long strand of wire uncoiled from her arm and reached up to a scaffolding strut and wound around, tautened, and pulled her to her feet.

Staying focused was all but impossible now. The things Pen wanted were as slippery as wet soap. Hours passed now when she didn't think of escape at all. She was horrified she'd catch herself lusting after the hunt, wanting nothing more than to swing out on wire cables across the city, to find the asphalt-skinned boy and kill him: to make the Crane King proud of her.

She knew she hadn't *originated* these desires—they came from the Wire Mistress—but she felt them, and her hands shook in their metal cage with the craving. The desires were in her skin. She didn't *want* to want to kill, but she wanted it all the same. Her borrowed bloodlust scared her.

Still, unlike the desire to be saved, it didn't make her feel like a victim.

The morning sun burst over her like a fireball, reflecting off the roof of St. Paul's as she swung out into the air. The wire mask around her face shone bright with glare. Below, the machines worked, digging to unearth Reach.

"*I am Reach. I am Reach. I will be. I will be.*"

That was *his* desire; she shivered with it, the most primal in the world. She understood him better now. He was constructing himself, *making* himself *be*. He'd burst through into the city over and over again down the centuries, and yet, in a way, he'd never even finished being born.

The barbed wire strand unspooled and she descended towards the rubble. There was a crack in the hoardings ringing the site, an entrance into the labyrinth of collapsed masonry that separated Reach from the rest of London. The Wire Mistress walked her towards it.

Just before she slipped into shadow, she saw something out of the corner of her eye: two massive pneumatic drills were hacking one corner of a mouth from the earth. She could see lips with cracks and capillaries. A creature with a mouth that size would dwarf the cathedral that rose above them.

She wanted to be scared of it, but she wasn't. A part of her, a big part, was excited.

She didn't *want* to want it, but Pen wanted to see Reach stand.

FORTY-ONE

"Wake up! Wake up! Christ, you snore like someone's shoved a hedgehog down your throat!" A horrendous ringing filled Petris' skull—one he couldn't put down to last night's pint of garbage gin. His eyes grazed open against the inside of his punishment skin and bright wintry light stabbed into his retinas.

"Wake up! Wake up!" The girl who was shouting at him wore a filthy hoodie. The reason for the ringing in his head became abundantly clear: she was repeatedly hitting it with an iron railing.

"Gerrroffofit," he snarled, sour alcohol-flavored bile bubbling in his throat. He swiped at the railing with a gauntlet, but the girl jerked out of the way easily.

"Who in the name of my sadistic goddess' tits are you?" he growled at her.

The girl ignored his question. She cocked an eyebrow as his breath washed over her face. "It's what's inside that counts, huh? Well then, I guess what counts for you is about ten pints of booze."

A face from Petris' memory battled through the alcoholic fug—but that face hadn't had the gray-tinted skin, the concrete-colored eyes. His gaze lighted on the railing. The tip on its spike tapered to vanishing point. "You're *Filius*' bit of fluff?" he burst out incredulously. She glared at him. He coughed and recovered himself. "Well," he said, "Beth, is it? You've ... changed."

Beth sniffed. "So have you. Last time I remember you having manners."

Petris waved a hand dismissively. "Oh, I'm *hungover*," he explained. "I always drink when I pray."

"Tough being religious, is it?" she asked.

Petris barked out a laugh. "It's like sleeping with another man's wife," he told her. "Nine parts guilt to one part ecstasy, and somehow you're always alone again in the morning."

Beth snorted. "Bitter, much?" she said. "Well, I'd love to have the time to care." She clapped her hands abruptly. "Get it together, stoneskin. Sober up, rally your troops. There's a war on, or haven't you heard?"

Petris shook his head. Even the tiny motion made the world blur alarmingly and his pulse slammed unpleasantly at the base of his skull. He was very much not in the mood for idiots, which was a shame, because the girl was talking like one. With extreme effort, he hefted his heavy legs under his stone habit and walked into the shade of a leafless oak tree, big enough to cast enough shadow to get him out of that bastard sun. Only then did he rasp, "Come again?"

"Rally. Your. Troops." Beth craned her neck over her shoulder, looking southwest.

With a sinking feeling, Petris realized he didn't need to ask what she was looking at. "That's what I thought you said." It had taken all of ninety seconds for him to regret waking up this morning.

"I'm storming the keep, Petris," she said. "I'm taking Reach's house. I need an army. Zeke's boys did their best, but they didn't cut it. I need more. I need the best. *'If there's one thing I'm better at than drinking it's fighting,'* huh?" She wrinkled her nose. "Well, little did I know just how big a boast that was. Time to make good on it."

Petris fixed her with a sullen stare. "I believe you were here when Filius asked the same," he said, "and I will give you the same answer: *No.* I cannot fight for Mater Viae's return."

Beth hopped onto the headstone for Stanley Philips. *End of an Error.* "Just as well," she said coldly, "because she's not coming back."

A shiver rippled up Petris' spine. He went quiet for a long time.

"Really?" he said finally, with forced levity. "That's interesting. Filius, Gutterglass, and Fleet's war party all say differently."

"Fleet's war party says meow and bugger all else," Beth countered. "But as for Fil and Glas, they're both wrong. I

356

don't know why yet, but I'm sure of it: Mater Viae is *not* coming back to London." Her voice was clear as she spoke. She didn't blink.

Petris swallowed down enough of the mingled hope and disappointment rising in his throat to growl, "How do I know I can trust your word?"

"You can't," she said bluntly, "so stop taking people's word for stuff. Work it out for yourself." She ticked off points on her fingers. "Her only son gets shredded by the Wire Mistress. Where was she? Nowhere. The first army to fight for her in fifteen years gets ground into dogmeat on the banks of the Thames, and where is she? Again, nowhere. And then of course there's the Cats."

"The Cats that are never seen without her, you mean?" Petris said, barely amused.

"*Exactly.*" Beth leaned forward. "Not once, not for one day. I asked around. Not in the whole of recorded history have Mater Viae and her whole retinue *ever* been seen apart. So why in Christ's name are they here without her now?"

Petris didn't answer.

"Unless," Beth continued, and paused.

She had one of those disturbingly intense gazes he could feel on the back of his own eye sockets.

"Unless she's somewhere else, somewhere the Cats can't follow."

Petris narrowed his eyes. "That's thin, girl."

"Thinner than a supermodel's cake budget, I know," Beth agreed. "But I'm sure it's right. It feels right, doesn't it?"

Petris breathed out and shut his eyes. *Yes, it feels right,* he admitted silently—but was that only because he wanted it to be true? Because he craved the simple joy of crushed scaffolding in his gauntlets far more than the intricate, addictive torture of secretly praying to a goddess who never spoke back?

"All right," he said at last, "I'll sing the Treaty Song. I'll put what you've said to the Stone Parliament. All I can promise is a vote, but it will take time."

Beth blanched at the word *time*, but she nodded in reluctant acceptance. This was as good as she was going to get. She stood and turned towards the gate.

"What?" Petris said. "You aren't going to wait for an answer?"

Beth shook her head. "Reach has got my best friend," she said. "Waiting's not getting her any more rescued."

"I've heard," Petris said soberly. He was pissed off and hungover and had no inclination to sugarcoat this. "The Mistress' host. I hope by 'rescue' you mean 'kill,' because that's the best thing you can do for her now. Her death's inevitable anyway."

Beth looked at him in a way that scared him. It was a fanatical look—a look that didn't accept that anything was inevitable, that *wouldn't* accept it. A look that despised him for being weak enough to believe that it was. She hefted Filius' spear.

"So you're going alone?" Petris was appalled. "Into battle, a ... *a god short.* That's ... " He floundered, and finally finished with, "That's rash."

A thin smile crossed Beth's lips, her face dappled red under the autumn trees.

"Paraphrasing a wiser friend of mine," she said, "rash is where I excel." Her smile fell away. "Gather your church," she said. "Get the right answer. Get it fast." And she ran off through the trees towards the hooting traffic.

FORTY-TWO

Beth raced through London. She felt the gaze of the gargoyles from Highgate's slated roofs, and haughty men stared down at her from tower block windows, reflections of people who weren't there. It felt like the whole of the city was urging her on.

Railwraiths clattered past her, dragging carriages of commuters for another day's work. The passengers were incurious; if they saw her at all through the trains' filthy windows, they didn't acknowledge it.

She leaped off the tracks near King's Cross, and as her spark-scorched feet hit the tarmac she wound her way past the Chinese takeaways and minicab offices on Pentonville Road, as quick and subtle as water in a gutter. The pavements were thick with pedestrians all bundled up in thick coats against a cold she barely felt, chattering into mobile phones, laughing, complaining about how little sleep they'd had: the lifeblood of the human city, sluggishly beginning to circulate after a cold night.

They were slowing Beth down.

She turned into the backstreets, whirling past graffiti-covered bins, homeless people huddled in sleeping bags, and winos sleeping in pools of piss near the back doors of strip clubs. Drum 'n' bass pulsed from an open window in a flat four stories above—a student, maybe, a rich one, given how high the rents were in this area. She'd tagged these streets years ago; she retrod them now, this time leaving only a scent of petrol and damp cement behind her.

As the buildings became older and grander and the streets more narrow, she slowed to a walk. The cranes reared over her; cruel hooks were connected to their jibs by umbilical cords of chain. A street sign on the wall above her read *Dean's Court, City of London EC2Y.* She grinned to herself. These pavements her feet were drawing sustenance from belonged to Reach.

She rounded a corner into a pedestrianized square where glass towers punctured the Old City's collapsing grandeur. Now people were *seeing* her; more than one of the well-heeled men and women who were walking into these buildings stopped to stare at this apparition of oil and grime, with her railing and her manic glare. On the front page of their newspapers she saw versions of the same headline:

Earthquake in London, Chelsea Bridge badly shaken.

"People believe the *story,*" Glas had said, "not the facts."

She grinned or grimaced or sneered—she didn't know how these smartly dressed movers and shakers would interpret it. She felt more affinity for the buildings around her than these people. The only thing they had in common with her was flesh.

St. Paul's loomed to her left, quite beautiful in the clear autumn sun, and she wove her way towards it. She felt a shiver as she passed through the cathedral's shadow, and she swore. She hadn't realized how much she'd come to dread it.

Now, if I were the King of the Cranes, where would I hide?

She looked up. The nearest cranes sprouted from behind the row of buildings straight ahead of her. She eyed them uncertainly, and ducked instinctively as one whirred around, afraid it might see her. She breathed in the dust of dry cement, listened to the clamor and clang of the construction machines, and started to walk towards them, but she found her joints reluctant to bend. The muscles in her legs were trembling.

All right, B, you're scared—no surprise. Don't make a big deal out of it. Walk. You can work out what to do when you get there.

She braced herself and walked briskly down the steps.

FORTY-THREE

I'm trapped in frigid water. The wires bind me, bite me. I struggle, but I'm held tight, inches away from precious air. I can feel myself ebbing as the blood flows from my wounds. The sacred river squeezes me like a fist.

And as I lie there bound and bleeding out, my last thoughts are of the girl on the riverbank, the girl who, like me, now has the city in her skin.

I wonder how she'll feel when the black-slicked figures come for me.

(I know they'll come; they always collect on their debts.)

She'll have to watch as they wade into the water and take the price I promised them. I try to imagine she'll forgive me, that she'll understand, but really, I know she never will.

Some poxy ingredient ... I wouldn't use it as long as I live.

I didn't lie with my words, but I lied with my tone and my manner, with my smile—I had to, otherwise the stubborn girl would have taken it onto her conscience, and there was no way I could let her do that.

Dying, I still feel like I betrayed her.

And then there's light, a shining human shape, diving towards the river, and my heart clamps up against my ribs. Panic swells my throat to bursting point. I thrash my head from side to side, choking on great gouts of the Thames as I struggle to shout NO!

As the shining girl enters the water, she starts to burn.

"Lec!"

———

"Lec—!" In my dream it was a shout. Now, in my ears, it's a feeble croak. "Lec..."

Rich garbage pours over my skin and I can feel the juices soaking into it, patching it up. I'm washed in old rainwater, in sticky Coca-Cola and congealing sweet-and-sour sauce. They *are* the city, as much as concrete and tar, these discarded treasures, and a nourishing broth to my almost-broken system.

After several attempts I manage to coax my waist into bending and I sit up. The blanket of rubbish tumbles away and my nice safe darkness is punctured by sunlight.

"Ugh." I spit out hours-old blood. I pat around myself, searching for my spear.

"My, my, what a mess. You're awake then."

"Glas?" My eyes adjust and he blurs into focus in front of me. After hearing his deep, rich voice, his body isn't what I expect. "A *baby*? Glas, promise me you'll never 'carn like that again."

"Why?" He sounds injured. Perched on a mound of milk cartons and old motors, he rests his chin on drinking straw fingers.

"Because it's creepy, that's why. You're almost as ancient as Father Thames, and kitting yourself out like a rotting fetus makes me feel *old*."

He snorts. "You sound like your girlfriend."

Light flares in my memory: sodium burning, fizzing away...

"Electra didn't speak aloud," I say.

Bugs bulge his cheeks in embarrassment. "I'm sorry. I meant—you know who I meant."

I scrub the grit from my eyes and look out across the landfill towards the city.

London's massed ranks stretch into the morning smog.

"Where is Beth, anyway? I think I dreamed she was here, she—" I dreamed she kissed me, but I hesitate to say that, not with the memory of Electra flashing in front of me.

Gutterglass shrinks a little. Beetles flee from his cuffs. "She's gone."

"What? She's gone home?"

His football-head deflates a little more. "She went to St. Paul's, Filius," he admits. "She's gone to try and kill Reach."

Something cold slithers inside my ribs. *To try and kill*

Reach. Such a roundabout way to describe suicide. I try to drag my thoughts together. "Is anyone else missing?" It sounds like the sensible question to ask, although at that moment I don't care about anyone else. *Beth's gone.*

"The Blankleits tell me that Russian you recruited hasn't been seen for a few hours. He'd taken a shine to the girl."

"Did he take any soldiers with him?"

"No, he went alone."

A poisonous taste is in my mouth. "Those two? Alone? The two humans—*Thames and Christ and city blood, Glas!*" I yell at him. "The only two who didn't grow up with the legends, who have *no idea* what they're up against—the Wire Mistress is there, Glas! Can you think of two people less suited to take her on? I have to go after her—"

I cast around, searching the ground. A sickening tightness seizes my gut. "Glas, where's my spear?"

"She took it to—" He breaks off.

I look straight into his eggshell eyes. "To drive into his throat, right?" I finish his sentence, my voice going flat. "Just like you taught me. I wonder what put that idea in her head." I glare at him. He told Beth how to kill Reach; he acted like she could actually achieve it. Thanks to him, she'll believe she has a chance.

I start to scramble over the heaps of rubbish, and pain flares around my joints, charting my injuries: an intricate topography of burns, bruises, and barely sealed cuts.

Gutterglass' eggshells track me. "Now that you mention it," he says, "yes, I can think of someone worse. How about a chemical-burns-and-drowning victim who's been half-flayed by barbed wire?"

I ignore him, doggedly trudging uphill in the refuse.

"Filius, you can't," he says, sounding serious now. "The girl's as good as dead; the same for the Russian. This is war. People *die*. It's too late for them. Surely they don't matter more than the lives you can still save? The rest of the city," he pleads. "Your kingdom. That's what matters now."

I don't answer.

"You have a responsibility," Glas presses on. "The army needs you. You're the son of the goddess. You have to be strong for *all of us*."

Finally I round on him, teetering on top of a smashed-in television. I feel furious, groggy, drunk on shock. "Yeah? Once you told her I'd collapse if she died. You were trying to get rid of her. 'Weeping, wailing, beating of breast'— remember that? I do."

He nods, reluctantly, but his resentful eggshells track me, and in my mind's eye I can see Electra's yellow eyes behind them too. Both are accusing me of getting too close to the human girl.

"You were right, Glas. If she dies, I'm wrecked." I stumble into a kind of half-run, Glas' baby-avatar skipping along beside me, born on a constantly renewing conveyor of insects. Painful pins and needles start to ripple through me as my muscles wake up.

"Filius—" His voice has climbed to a higher pitch; his infant face is stretched in despair.

"I'm sorry, Glas. I'm not proud of it, but she *does* matter more to me." I don't know if he heard me, because the wind is starting to roar in my ears as I run.

FORTY-FOUR

Particle-board hoardings were stretched across the end of a narrow lane off Ludgate Hill. Behind them, anonymous buildings had been torn down and a landslide of doors, window ledges, and unidentifiable hunks of concrete tumbled over the rim of the hoardings and sloped down into the alley: a natural ramp. Sweating despite the chill, Beth put her foot on the bottom—

—and hesitated.

A tangle of old scaffolding gleamed at the top.

And Beth stalled. She stared at the scaffolding, seeing it re-articulate into a snarling, snapping wolf in her mind's eye. If Fil had been there, he would have goaded her to do it—or else it would have been him that needed the goading, and she would have had to have been brave to see him through.

But he wasn't there. It was just her.

Beth shifted her weight, uneasily. *Maybe there's another way*, she thought. *Maybe the whole site isn't surrounded, maybe I can sneak in…*

Out of nowhere, the idea hit her like a steel wall. An idea so strange to her it made her gasp. *She could just walk away.*

Beth was appalled. She couldn't believe she'd thought that, even for a second.

But the voice inside her which suggested it lingered. *After all*, it whispered, vile and yet utterly convincing, *she'd already risked so much*. It wasn't fair; she'd pushed her luck to the edge of the precipice and she'd *found* the home she'd been searching for. She shouldn't have to risk it all again now.

She remembered Gutterglass' voice: *Reach will rip you asunder.*

Death. The realization came with cold clarity. That was the fear she had been fighting since she left the dump: *she was afraid to die*. She'd never been scared of it before, but dying had never felt as close and intimate as this before. She looked around at the streets that had become her home. Now she had something to lose, death terrified her.

She put her back to Reach's kingdom and took an experimental step, then another. As she started to walk out of the alley an odd relaxation trickled through her. Letting the fear win was kind of like pissing your pants: it came with shame and a mild horror at herself, but also a warm, numbing relief.

The railing-spear clanged onto the cobbles by her feet.

"Do more. Do more than just run." *Jesus Christ, what a pretentious, patronizing arse I must've sounded.*

As she reached the end of the alley, all the noise and color of the main road broke over her. She looked left and right, peering into the flow of morning pedestrians, preparing to throw herself back in. A slug of regret was lodged uncomfortably in her gut. *Whatever I do in this instant, I'll carry it the rest of my life.* She knew that was true.

She lifted her foot off the tarmac and made a decision.

Then again, that's likely to be about twenty minutes, so every cloud and all that—

She spun on her heel and started to run back up the alley.

You're an idiot, B, you know that? she told herself as she ran. *You ALWAYS had something to lose—someone—and you almost threw her away. She's waiting for you behind that damned hoarding.*

She picked up speed and scooped up the spear without breaking stride.

And now you've got someone else to lose. This is the only way to protect him.

She remembered jumping into the Chemical Synod's pool, the fear she'd felt then, and the spark of love for the boy who'd stood opposite her. She remembered the way she'd braced herself, tensing every muscle in her body until she almost vibrated, all so she could make him—

She thrust the iron railing-spear above her head. The

concrete ramp reared up ahead of her. The scaffolding gleamed.

Beth, he'd said, *I'm pr—*

A hand flashed out of a gap in the fallen bricks and snared her ankle.

FORTY-FIVE

For a horrifying moment Beth flew, feeling the absence of gravity sickeningly in her stomach. Then she smacked hard into the concrete, three feet short of the ramp.

"Argh!" Her nose and lips felt puffy and stung. She rolled and came to her feet crouched, spear ready, poised for attack.

"Sorry! Sorry!" a familiar voice said, "but Tsarina was about to self-kill. Was first thing could think of." Hunks of brick and concrete tumbled off a dusty tarp, revealing a figure in a threadbare greatcoat who wiped away the gray camo makeup from his face as he sat up. He pulled his beanie hat from his pocket, crammed it onto his erratic hair, and fixed Beth with a hopeful grin. "Sorry!" he said again, cheerfully.

"Victor?" It was one surprise too many. The last of Beth's cool tinkled into fragments on the floor.

"Da."

"Where did—? How did—? *How the hell did you get ahead of me?*"

"Well, back in Volgograd was—"

"Don't tell me you were on the Siberian Olympic sprint team; I won't believe it. I know you can't run as fast as I can, so *how?*"

Victor looked embarrassed. "I take—you know—I take underground train."

"You took the tube?" For some reason Beth found this deeply shocking.

"Da, why not? I am old man now. Just because Tsarina go on foot—"

"With what? You don't have any money."

He smiled. "Ticket collector, he from Old Country. He ask for ticket; I give him old Moscow greeting." He beamed.

Beth stared out at him skeptically over folded arms.

"An old Moscow greeting? Did this greeting involve wrist-locks, groin punches, chokeholds, or anything else you might have learned in the Soviet secret police?"

"Old Moscow greeting," Victor repeated. His smiling face shone with sincerity. "We understand each other very well."

Beth stared at him, fury and fright swelling in her. She shook her head firmly. "No way. *No way.* The Thames'll run with baboon sweat before I let this happen. Turn around, Victor, get out of here. This—it's not your fight."

Was this how Fil had felt, all those times he'd told her

to leave? This vertigo of affection and gratitude and the terrible knowledge that if this person you cared about got hurt, it would be your fault?

"I'm not owing another one like that," she muttered. "I *can't*. Go back, Victor."

The friendly grin retreated into Victor's beard and Beth jumped back in shock as he spat at her feet. "*Not* my *fight?*" he snarled. "Who are *you*, to say what is and not my fight? Kabul was my fight, and Tashkent, and Ossetia. You talk of *owing*? I *owe!*" He thumped his chest. "I lost boys, shining boys, shattered to little pieces by the monster you hunt. I owe them all." He looked at her, his eyes full of a gutting disappointment. "And you too, remember? I said, 'I make sure you no get too horribly killed.' Was no lie. I *never* lie."

Beth exhaled hard. "You don't understand. People who follow me, they get hurt—hurt bad. They die."

Victor nodded solemnly. "I know. They die because you are bad general." He ignored the look Beth gave him and went on, "Is not to be shamed of. I am pretty bad general too, but even I can tell you, charging headlong into face of superior enemy is stupider than poking adder with your own nose." He looked pointedly at the ramp Beth had been about to run up. "Frontal assault: very bad strategy. We try in Afghanistan, only Mujaheddin have land mines." He mimed an explosion with his hands. "Arms, legs, heads, kneecaps, blood everywhere, like whores on a *vor*."

He clapped an arm around Beth's shoulders, expelling a cloud of dust from his coat. His anger had evaporated. Now his voice had a fatherly tone. "If, on other hand, we make *reconnaissance*, like good little Spetsnaz, if we arrive early and do camouflage, then we might see interesting things."

He squatted a couple of feet from the hoardings and gripped a slab of concrete. With a stream of heavily accented invective he dragged it aside, revealing a jagged hole in the ground leading down into darkness. "Like private back door, where Wire *zmeya* drags bodies from; that kind of interesting." He sat and dangled his legs into the hole, kicking his feet like a small boy. The edges of his vast moustache twitched upwards as he regarded Beth fondly. "You are like granddaughter to me, so I tell you secret," he said. "I am scared of dark—no, really, do not laugh. Dark and small places, since little boy. Back then I think kobolds squat in the little places, to eat my little flesh."

His grin widened. "Who knows, maybe they still do." He gave himself a tiny push and dropped out of sight below the streets.

Beth kissed her teeth. "Only a bloody Russian could think their fairy tales were reassuring," she muttered, then seized the spear and dived into the darkness.

FORTY-SIX

"Pass the smokes, Timon."

Timon sighed. It was Al's turn to sort out cigarettes, but the bronze gangster was so busy making a pathetic fuss over the wound in his arm—*Blud, I think it's infected. Blud, I think the tendon's snapped. Blud, I think there's some fang left in it*—that it wasn't worth arguing. There was nothing else to do in this drain of a street but smoke. Gutterglass had sent them here, to Bethnal Green, for "recuperation," which just meant that there were more urgent claims on their mattresses in the landfill. Neither of them cared about that, but the inaction was embarrassing. They wanted back in the fight.

Timon checked up and down the narrow lane to make sure no one was coming, then groaned and twisted, shedding limestone powder as he bent down to retrieve the half-smoked cigarettes a couple of kids had stamped out earlier. He tore a couple of small squares out of a discarded newspaper and poured the leftover tobacco out of the dog-ends into them, then furled the paper up tight: nicotine necromancy.

Al dragged his bronze arm over Timon's forehead and sparks flew. The reanimated cigarettes guttered and smoldered.

"Cheers, blud."

As they smoked, Al regarded the wolfheads the *filia viae* had drawn on his friend's skin. "We need to get you some more of those, son," he said after a while.

Timon had turned away from the mouth of the alley when he'd bent down for the dog-ends, so the sweaty man who shoved his face right up to his limestone mask took him by surprise.

"I know you're in there!" the man cried. "Where's my daughter?"

Timon eyed Al; there was a flicker of bronze and the man flew at the wall. Air sighed out of his lungs as he crumpled to the ground.

"What's yer problem, boy?" Al demanded. "You lookin' to a couple of statues for a beatin'?"

The man croaked a couple of times before his voice came back, but when he spoke, he didn't sound cowed. "Those pictures on you—a girl drew them, didn't she? I need you to take me to her." His cheeks were hollow and gray bags hung under his wild eyes. "Please. She's my daughter."

It looked like someone had taken the contents of several statue gardens and dumped them in an industrial car park in Dalston. The air was vivid with London accents as the Pavement Priests chattered away their nerves.

Timon and Alloy had taken pity on Paul Bradley. To make sure he could keep pace they covered just a few yards at time in their here-now-suddenly-there stop-motion animation way of moving; they entertained themselves by striking poses with V-signs as they waited for him to catch up.

Their trajectory through the nest of city streets curved east in response to rumor, like electrons bending around a magnet. The *filia viae* was no longer at Gutterglass' landfill hospital, the gargoyles whispered. Stoneskins were massing, drainpipes gurgled, all of them, and some said that this was the surest sign yet that Mater Viae was returning. But there were other mutterings, from under manhole covers and around corners, that the Lady of the Streets' honor guard had abandoned their absent mistress and rallied to their own purposes.

"The stubborn little trollop's not here," the granite-hooded monk said when they led Paul over to him. His hands flickered between a basin of dark red clay and back to the deep cracks in his stone armor as he sealed them. A bronze statue of a seventeenth-century nobleman, complete with wig and doublet, hardened off the ceramic with a blowtorch.

"She asked me to sing the Treaty Song, then she buggered off—went to St. Paul's alone. Your daughter's dead by now, I expect."

Paul returned the monk's stare flatly. He wouldn't accept that. It was an article of his faith now that his daughter was still alive: his doctrine of salvation. There had to be *some* way for him to make amends.

Perhaps the old Pavement Priest recognized that in his eyes, because he snorted gently through stone nostrils. "I'm sorry, kid, I really am. I know where she went, and we're going there too, but this is an all-out attack, not a rescue mission."

He paused, then added, "If it helps, that's the way she wanted it." He blurred for an instant and then he was facing the other way, engaged in other business.

"Then I want to fight," Paul said to his mica-threaded back.

The monk released a startled laugh. "With what? You'll be butchered like a ten-week calf."

"Do you care?" Paul asked bluntly.

"You know what? *Now* I can hear the family resemblance." Petris sounded amused for a moment, then the humor dropped out of his gravel voice. "Who am I, of all men, to stand between a man and his suicide?" he muttered. He sounded deadly serious. "Obadiah!" he called.

Paul shuddered as the bronze nobleman slapped a handful of red clay onto his neck.

"No soldier of mine goes into battle without a uniform," the monk said. "We march in thirty minutes. Keep up."

He paused as a thought occurred to him. "One question, Mr. Soon-to-be-dead." Paul couldn't mistake the note of envy in the monk's voice. "*Why* are you so determined to fight?"

Paul reached into the basin of clay and slicked a double handful of the cool, heavy mud over his cheeks. *When this bakes*, he thought, *it will preserve my face forever.* He tried not to look as afraid as he felt. "Because this is Beth's fight, and that's what fathers do for their little girls," he said.

FORTY-SEVEN

Nothing to see but darkness, nothing to breathe but dust. Nothing to be but patient as the iron-eating rust.

Huh, I should remember that. It's the kind of thing Pen might like.

Stone grazed Beth's skin as she crawled through the tunnel. She kept colliding with the walls in the pitch darkness, even though she was groping ahead with her fingertips. She'd insisted on being in the lead. Victor had grumbled but eventually deferred with a muttered "Ladies first."

In some places the walls were tight on her—tighter than a coffin, tight as a birth canal—and she had to thrust her arms ahead of her, wedge her elbows and *undulate* forward. The spear was strapped to her back, the metal so cold against her neck it almost blistered.

Beth hated the close quarters, but more than that,

the sheer *deadness* of the place troubled her: there was no *energy*, no life flowing where her bare skin touched the masonry. This neighborhood had been broken, its vitality leeched out. Cold fingers of panic crept up Beth's throat, and she fought to keep calm. After being immersed so long in the living city, being trapped in here felt like suffocating.

In places the walls of the tunnel felt smooth, like glass, or—the idea came to her suddenly—burned skin.

Without the Great Fire, Gutterglass had said, *we must improvise.*

She was touching Reach's wounds from that first great immolation, ripped up and buried beneath later incarnations. These scars were more permanent than rock. She shivered at the intimacy.

The darkness made everything closer, louder and sharper. The engines clattered on the surface above and Beth jumped as gravel sifted from the ceiling. She swore at herself to keep calm.

Judging by the constant stream of inventive obscenity floating up the tunnel from behind her, though, she was doing better than Victor. "By Virgin's first missed period," he muttered, "is been seven years since I even sleep under *roof*. What in hell I am doing here?" He fell silent for a moment, and then said, "Tsarina not judge me too harshly, *niet?* I am not normally so cowardish."

Beth reached behind her and felt a worn, gnarly hand grasp hers. "I know, Victor. I know. If it makes you feel any better, I have a friend who hates little spaces too." Beth swallowed hard and looked ahead into the darkness. "And she's as brave as they come."

The minutes faded away. The only way Beth could mark the time was her heartbeat, and that was too quick to be much use. She felt an urgent desire to talk, to blabber. *What if we're lost?*

What if we miss a turning in the dark?

What if we're trapped down here?

She bit her lip so hard she tasted petrol and blood, determined not to give voice to her own fears. It would only make Victor's worse—

—but then she reached forward, and this time she couldn't stop herself crying out.

"Tsarina?" Victor said uncertainly.

"It's okay," she whispered. She'd felt something in the rubble, a warmth and a thrum, like a pulse. It was alive. Now as she wormed her way forward, she could feel the kiss of the living concrete on her arms and neck and her belly, charging her skin with the city again. She laughed, shockingly loud in the dark: the pulse coming through the ground was faint, but to her it was like fresh air after drowning. She laid her head on the ground. She heard something, and froze.

Was that *crying*?

It was very faint, the vibrations carried through the stone from deeper underground. She strained to listen.

There it was again: quiet crying, as though with pain, the kind of pain that you had endured for a long time but you still couldn't get used to. There was another sound, too, the creaking of rock under terrible strain. The sounds were synchronized, and each groan of the rock drew a gasp and a whimper from the voice, as though someone was drawing painful breath against stone.

Women in the Walls. Masonry Men.

Unbidden, the image of the mangled human shapes at the Woolwich Demolition Fields sprang into her mind and her stomach lurched. She suddenly knew where the life she was sensing was coming from.

She scrabbled at the unseen ground with her fingers, looking for a seam, slipping her nails into cracks until finally she found what she was looking for. She heaved, and a concrete slab jarred the tunnel as she cast it aside.

"Tsarina! Stop!" Victor shouted.

Beth ignored him. There was someone *alive* down there. She dug into the hole she'd made, until the smell of stale sweat and raw spirits enveloped her and thick, muscular arms seized her own.

"Tsarina, *stop*," Victor whispered in her ear.

She strained, but he wouldn't let go. "There's someone alive down there!" She braced herself, preparing to wrench herself free, even if it meant breaking his arms.

"Niet, no some*one*," Victor hissed, "some *many*."

Beth fell still, panting for breath. She felt a gentle pressure on the side of her head and let Victor push her to the wall.

"Listen," he said. "I begin to hear them a way back."

For a second Beth could hear nothing but the thud of her own pulse, then voices began to filter through the rock: women's voices, and men's; age-clotted voices, and shrill unbroken ones. They echoed backwards and forwards, sometimes answering each other with a few garbled words in bereft tones. But most of them just cried: weak but inconsolable.

"Wherever you dig," Victor said, "you will only bury others deeper."

After a moment, Beth understood what he was telling her. She'd only ever seen the *dead* before now; what she was listening to were the wounded, crushed under the weight of the Crane King's court.

"Come, Tsarina. Let's find your friend. There is nothing else to do."

But as Beth made to take her ear from the wall, a change infected the voices. The crying stopped, and in its place came a whisper: one word. It spread through the voices with the virulence of rumor: *Mistress*

Mistress Mistress Mistress Mistress Mistress—

Mistress Mistress Mistress Mistress Mistress Mistress Mistress Mistress

And then as one, the voices fell silent.

FORTY-EIGHT

"Victor," Beth hissed as a new sound filled the tunnel, a hissing scratch like steel coils sliding over stone. "She's coming."

Beth imagined the Wire Mistress' barbs hooking into the walls of the tunnel, dragging their human bundle along in their wake. The sound echoed around the stone walls; Beth couldn't tell what direction it was coming from.

She gripped the spear in the dark and imagined Pen's mutilated face.

As quick as a snake, something lashed through the air by her cheek.

Victor cried out, a cut-off gasp, and Beth whirled, the spear's iron point catching on the roof of the tunnel. Metal scraped over stone and a bright blue spark flared.

She saw Victor, in that instant's light, four feet behind

her. A thin skein of wire was wrapped tightly around his neck. The barbs were biting into his flesh. His eyes were popping out of his head and his tongue was bleeding where he'd bitten down on it.

Then darkness fell again and Beth was knocked against the wall as Victor's bulk was hauled past her and up the tunnel. "Victor!" she yelled. She pushed herself back onto her knees, still dazed, the spear gripped tightly in her right hand. The Mistress' hiss carried back down the tunnel and Beth followed, crawling on hands and knuckles and knees until the tunnel widened enough for her to lurch to her feet. Cramped muscles protesting, she broke into a shambling run.

She could see the next corner now. The clash and grind of Reach's machines was growing louder. She gripped her spear tighter as she swung around the bend, and then stopped cold.

Ahead, at the far end of the tunnel, she saw a chamber. Four walls had collapsed inwards and were taking each others' weight, forming a kind of pyramid. Pen stood in the center of the space, in a cat's cradle of light shafts. Dust motes spun around her and her wire skin gleamed.

"Move," Beth hissed to herself, willing her muscles on. "*Move*." She drove herself forwards.

Pen gazed out at her from her between the wires, her eyes wide with fear. Her lips were stitched shut with barbs.

When she was just inches from the opening to the tunnel, Beth saw why Pen looked so scared. A strand of wire, so fine as to be almost invisible, was stretched across the doorway at neck-height, ready to bite hard into Beth's throat. Arms flailing wildly, she tried desperately to check her charge, but she skidded on loose gravel and couldn't stop herself. She swallowed as the barbs tickled her neck.

Pale fingers lashed out and yanked the wire away just as Beth fell into the chamber. She rolled and came up fast, spear ready, eyes twitching for a target but unwilling to throw.

Victor staggered forward and then pulled back. The tendons in his neck stood out. One hand gripped the wire he'd torn from the door; the other was at his throat, where the coils of the Mistress bit deep. Beads of blood glimmered on his skin. He was white as death, but he smiled tightly.

"Not worry, Tsarina." His breath escaped in snatched wheezes. He leaned back and hauled on the wire. The muscles in his neck bulged. Veins emerged through his face like cracks in glass. "In Moscow was seven times Tug-of-War Champ—"

The wire around his throat stretched taut. There was an organic-sounding crack.

The Wire Mistress flexed her coils and slammed him into the wall with hideous force. He crumpled to the ground, his head a crush of bone, hair, and bloody wool.

Beth snarled in grief and fury. She looked at Pen and saw only the monster. She gripped the spear tighter, and charged.

The price of rage was grace, and the Mistress easily

sidestepped Beth's clumsy lunge. Needle-pointed wires lashed out and hot pain ran through Beth's cheek.

She turned fast, raising her spear high, but Pen, in the Mistress' grip, moved with demonic speed. A punch slammed into Beth's kidney. Pen's fist twisted as the barbs bit and ripped away the cloth and the flesh underneath.

Beth's scream echoed up the chamber and she reflexively swung the spear. It crunched meatily into Pen's ribs.

Unable to cry out, Pen fell in abject silence to one knee.

Blood oozed from Beth's side. Sickened with pain, she raised the spear over her head, ready to plunge it down into her best friend's chest. Wires uncoiled swiftly from Pen's shoulders, lashing and binding Beth's arms so she couldn't bring the spear down. Panic bubbled through her, and along with it, a tiny bit of relief.

Pen climbed to her feet, eyeing Beth warily. Skeins waved in the air like floating seaweed, twisting towards her. Time slowed down. The wire tendrils stroked curiously, almost gently, over Beth's face, as though learning it. They brushed the spearpoint, and then coiled back on themselves.

The spear, Beth thought. *The wire's scared of the spear.*

Drawing on all the inhuman strength in her muscles, Beth let the spear go and jumped sideways, dragging the slack out of the wire that bound her. She threw herself at the wall.

Pen's head snapped to track her, horribly fast.

Beth's shoulder slammed painfully into the stone, but she'd drawn the wire taut, and a fraction of second later the falling spear slashed through it.

The Mistress released Pen's lips, and she screamed.

The bindings fell away from Beth's shoulders and she snatched up the spear, but even as Pen screamed, the Mistress was propelling her fist into Beth's face.

Beth reeled. Her teeth were cracked, her lips hot and puffy.

The Wire Mistress pressed the assault, raining down punches, forcing incredible power through Pen's wounded body. Beth gave ground, warding with her spear where she could, taking other blows to her forehead, eyes, and face. A barb ripped a chunk of one ear away and Beth felt it fall down inside her collar.

Suddenly her right leg went from under her and, as she fell onto her back, the spear clattered away. Victor's glassy eyes stared at her. She'd caught her heel in his groin.

The Wire Mistress seethed above her, Pen trapped at its heart. Beth groped for the spear, but it was three or four inches from her hand: much, much too far. She felt the last of her courage bleed out of her. Pen drew a foot back, ready to stamp down on her face.

Beth shut her eyes. "This isn't you, Pen," she whispered to herself.

A heartbeat passed, then another, then another. Beth opened her eyes. She snatched up the spear and scrambled to her feet. Pen and the Wire Mistress were simply standing, a couple of feet away. Pen's left foot was still in the air, not moving.

For a long instant Beth stood there, staring, until she saw why she was still alive.

Pen was gripping the wall. Her fingers had found crevices in the stone and every joint was white with effort. She'd dug her right foot into a hollow in the ground. Through her torn shirt, Beth could see her muscles straining and her veins standing out blue, in stark contrast to the wires which roiled over her. The barbs goaded her, jerking back and forth horribly, opening ragged new wounds. Blood dripped off Pen like sweat, but *she would not move.* Her eyes were shut, her lips twitching in that way they did when she was praying. She would not obey. She was refusing to comply.

Suddenly Pen's eyes snapped open wide. She stared at the tip of the railing-spear, and then looked down, once, to her own chest.

With a jolt of horror, Beth understood. Pen was letting Beth kill her.

She drew back the spear.

Pen closed her eyes, her chest heaving.

Beth tensed her shoulder, whispering in her mind, *Pen, I'm sor—*

An idea struck her, then, with the force of a blow, and she almost fumbled the weapon in her haste. Instead of stabbing forward, she slid the spear flat across Pen's belly, between the wire and her sweat-sheened skin, and jerked it back.

The wire screamed, and Pen screamed. A tendril fell away in two.

Again and again, faster and faster, Beth wielded the

spear, dashing away the tears that blurred her eyes so she could aim, always cutting the wire, never the skin.

The Wire Mistress hissed and thrashed, but still it couldn't leave its host. Grim-faced with pain, Pen pinned it to the wall even as it tore at her. The last cord stretched out from Pen's belly button, an umbilical wire. Beth cut it, and Pen collapsed.

For a long time they slumped together on the floor of the chamber, leaning on each other, just breathing. Inch lengths of barbed wire twitched like blind worms around them in the dust.

Eventually Beth spoke. "Pen, Pen—I'm so sorry. I didn't mean for you to—I didn't want you to follow..." But she tailed, off because that was a lie. She *had* meant for Pen to follow her: *Look for me in broken light;* that's what she'd written.

Pen laughed, or gurgled, which seemed about as close as she could get. "That's what I do, B," she whispered bitterly. "I follow you."

Beth tried to hug her but Pen recoiled, hissing with pain, as Beth's arms closed around her. Beth sat up and properly took in the extent of her best friend's cuts. Her own wounds were already knitting, sealed up by that strange mix of oil and cement the Chemical Synod had put in her blood, but Pen...

Pen wasn't so lucky. Her slim frame and narrow face were covered in long gashes, not deep, but all of them savage and red. Her left nostril, earlobe, and bottom lip weren't there anymore; the skin where they ought to have been ended in short, jagged tears.

"We have to get you out of here," Beth began to mumble. "We have to get you to a hospital. Can you stand? I can carry you—shit, look at you, girl, you're a mess."

"And I always took such good care of my appearance." Pen coughed up a laugh. "I tell you what, B, we'll roll you in barbed wire and hit you with a railing and then see if *you* win any beauty pageants." She tried to smile with her one remaining lip. Then she swallowed and the half-smile fell away. "Listen to me, B: you have to stop Reach." Her eyes were wide, but whether with wonder or horror, Beth couldn't tell. "The Wire Mistress—its barbs were in my head; I knew its thoughts. We worshiped Reach, like a god."

We worshiped. *We*, not *it*. Her voice was thick with violation. "Reach is tearing the city up, building himself in its skin," she croaked. "He's *killing* it. He doesn't know it, but he's killing *everything*."

"I know," said Beth. "I don't care—it doesn't matter. None of it does. I have to get you better."

Again, Pen peeled that one-lipped smile off her teeth. "That's sweet, but it's bullshit."

Beth hissed in exasperation. "Fine, be like that. I'll sodding carry you." As tenderly as she could, she put her arms under Pen's torn skin and made to lift her.

"Ow! Ow! B!" Pen whispered. "If I was going to bleed to death I would have done it days ago. *Pakistani*, remember? I'm related to about four hundred doctors. I know what I'm talking about. Will you just *go*?"

Beth shook her head stubbornly. She braced herself to lift her friend again.

"Do you even know the way out of here?" Pen demanded. "You're in a maze, you know."

Beth froze as Pen pointed weakly to one of the exits from the chamber. "You're lucky. You're close. Reach is eighty yards that way. Straight line. You can't miss it."

"And the way out?" Beth asked. But she knew what was coming.

Bloody teeth showed through the gaps in Pen's lips when she closed them. She shook her head. It was the only way she could make Beth leave her here: *Not telling.* "Sorry."

Beth stood slowly and gathered up her spear. Pain flared out through her skin, but no bones were broken. She could still run. She could still fight. Frustration bubbled up in her and she punched the wall, hard. Her fist smashed half an inch into the wall, making dust trickle down from above.

Pen looked alarmed. "I get that you're pissed off, B; you don't have to bring the roof down on me."

As she fell silent, Beth became aware again of the noise that had always been there: the savage roar of Reach's machines, only eighty yards away.

"That picture you did of me," Pen said at last, like she had to offer *something*. "On the wall by my house. It was good. I liked it."

Beth smiled awkwardly. "I was hoping you might come up with a poem for it."

Pen's lip twisted. "All right:

"There once was a girl from Hackney,
who told me she always would back me.
She went off the rails, with me on her tail,
and this thing made of barbed wire attacked me."

She looked at Beth. "It's only a limerick, but I'm a bit rusty, you understand."

Beth's ears burned in shame. She didn't say anything.

"Sorry," Pen said after a moment. "I'm just—"

"—I know." Beth squared her shoulders and turned towards the exit Pen had pointed to. "Thanks, Pen."

Pen's breathing was shallow, like someone controlling panic. "You know I love you, B, but this isn't for you," she whispered. "This is for *me*. I *want* to want this."

Beth didn't understand what she meant. She crouched by Victor's body and closed his eyes. She felt a dangerous pinprick of sorrow for the old Russian, but she smothered it before it could grow.

Later, she promised herself. *Later.* She raised the spear to Pen and made for the passage.

The light was stronger there, and the pneumatic drills made the ground shake; the machines belonged to Reach, master of the Wire Mistress. The monsters had stolen her best friend, killed Victor, and destroyed so much of her city. She felt fury in her chest, as hot and black and viscous as boiling tar. Her feet were about to break into a run when Pen's voice rang up the tunnel.

"B!" She sounded fragile. "I'm scared."

Beth stopped. "Pen?" she called.

A long moment passed. When Pen answered, she sounded firmer, more in control. "No, I'm okay. Sorry, go on. I'm fine. It's just taking me a while to get a grip on myself again—go!"

Beth gritted her teeth, turned around, and for the first time in their friendship, she did what she was told.

———

Pen lay back on the shale, relishing the simple act of shutting her eyes. She took deep, painful breaths, ignoring her cracked ribs, expanding her diaphragm, *because she could.*

She regretted calling out, but even with the Mistress gone, her desires and fears kept flipping and reversing. She wondered if she'd ever again be able to *want* something for long enough to pursue it. She shifted, and winced. Every square inch of the fabric she wore was slippery with blood.

If I was going to bleed to death I would have done it days ago, she'd said. *I know what I'm talking about.*

It was the first proper lie she'd ever told Beth. Not bad for a friendship lasting three years, she told herself. Panic was swarming over her like tiny spiders, but there a rush too. A sense of pure freedom.

Her eyes snapped open as a new sound sneaked into her

ears under the all-too-familiar clatter of Reach's machines: hurrying footsteps.

Pen's heart lodged somewhere near her carotid artery. She opened her eyes and craned her neck to see.

FORTY-NINE

A rough rectangle of light, the door to Reach's court, stood open before Beth. Something intensely and inconveniently bright was shining directly through her exit, hitting her retinas like a battering ram.

Blood and stonepiss in the river, she swore silently. She was already deafened by the noise from beyond the doorway; even the panicked thud of her heartbeat had dissolved under the din. Apparently, she was going to have to go out there blind as well.

She hesitated. Outside, the King of Cranes, London's nemesis, was waiting: the beast in the city's skin.

He's killing everything.

She crouched there, wiped the oily sweat from her palm, and gripped the spear. Voices flitted in and out of her head.

You might need this. Drive it into the Crane King's throat.

Come on, B—

Do more than just run.

Reach will tear you asunder.

Come on, B—

An ending is all you'll find…

Do more than just—

She climbed to her feet and opened her ears to the full clamor of the building site.

—run.

She pelted out into the day.

At first she saw nothing but eye-scouring light as she ran headlong, clutching the spear, not daring to stop. His voice flew in from all around her, echoing in the churn and tear of steel and concrete: "*I am Reach I am Reach I will be I will be.*" And there were other sounds, too: the pounding of iron paws on rubble, the slaver and snap of Scaffwolves, horribly close.

Gradually her eyes began to cope: the light was the sun, bouncing off a pair of half-built skyscrapers. Reach had surrounded himself with mirrors. She shielded her eyes and looked from side to side. She sprang from one chunk of rubble to the next, sure-footed as a cat on the treacherous ground.

Cranes soared overhead, but they were just cranes, not fingers. They weren't linked to hand or arm or body. Where was he? *What* was he? Her fingers were painfully tight on the spear.

Drive it into the Crane King's throat.

I would, she thought desperately, *if I could find his throat!*

The edge of the building site reared up ahead, an impenetrable wreckage of concrete and broken wood and twisted metal piled up against the hoardings. A growl ripped through the air behind her. She skidded, kicked up dust, and turned.

Three Scaffwolves the size of horses prowled up over a mound of broken stone. Through the gaps in their steel skeletons Beth spied the far skyscraper, and reflected in its windows was her own terrified face.

The wolves advanced, heads slung low, ears back. Beth gave ground. She cast about helplessly, arm cocked back, ready to throw the railing-spear ready, but she had no target. She could see diggers, cranes, but no vast construction god. All her pent-up courage was fizzing inside her, but she had no way to release it.

Rough stone bumped into her back. She had nowhere left to run.

She eyed the wolves, wondering if she could move fast enough to take them all. Bravado bubbled in her throat, tasting like blood, and she snarled at them, defiant.

Yet more dormant scaffolding sheathed the half-built tower blocks. Beth knew that even if she could cut down the metal monsters advancing on her, others would immediately take their place.

The wolves stopped. They growled their hollow growls and began to patrol a perimeter, marking a semicircle around her. Beth growled back. She hawked and spat at them, and they grinned at her with their jagged teeth, begging her to commit to an attack.

And all around them, the storm of construction thundered on: the cranes cranked up their loads and the diggers hacked at the earth, though the cabs were all empty. There was no sign of the force which controlled them.

Beth's blood hammered through her.

What are you waiting for?

Something slammed into her right shoulder from behind. She staggered forward, and then felt herself being hauled bodily back. Pain burned up and down her right side; the bones were grinding together wrongly. Her spear-arm went limp.

———————

Beth looked down at her shoulder. Pain made her dizzy, made her sick, made everything slow.

A metal point was protruding from her hoodie. It was smeared with oily red, and if she looked closely, Beth thought she could see tiny white chips of bone caught in the blood. The rest of the hook emerged from the back of her shoulder. A chain was connected to it; linked to that was a cable, a three-inch-thick steel cord, which stretched from her punctured flesh into the sky.

A loud whirring filled her ears and the crane's winch kicked in.

Beth screamed. The wolves snapped at her heels and

she screamed again, short bursts of sound between panicked breaths. Waves of hot-and-cold shuddering pain rippled from her shoulder to the tips of her toes. Acid bubbled into her mouth. Her feet kicked empty air as the crane lifted her.

Her weight, dragging down on the punctured shoulder, was unbearable, and she found herself blabbering incoherently, on the verge of passing out. She could feel her shoulder blade clicking against the steel hook, tendons beginning to tear under the strain. Any moment now, she thought, the hook would rip itself clean out of her.

But it didn't. That alien substance in her blood was already clotting around the wound, setting like cement, sealing Reach's grip, and she rose, the wolves baying under her. Her voice gave out before the crane reached the top of its arc.

Some hundred and fifty feet above the building site, the crane whirred to a halt and Beth jerked on the hook like a fish.

The Scaffwolves prowled over the building site, pawing and sniffing at its craters; diggers rumbled past on their caterpillar tracks as they moved busily to and fro. One lowered its metal jaws to a ridge of stone that looked almost exactly like the bridge of a nose.

And suddenly, Beth *saw* Reach.

From up here, the contours in the earthworks made sense in a new way. *That* crevice was the hollow of a cheek; *this* crack in the concrete, a parting of lips. A pitted ball of stone was an eye.

It was rough, not yet even half-finished, but it was definite. The King of Cranes had a face. Beth had run all the way across his forehead.

"*I am Reach,*" his voice screeched in the gears of his machines. "*I will be.*"

She gaped, numb with awe, as two diggers beetled towards one of the massive stone eyes. They lowered their drills and together ground a pupil-like hole in it. Then they altered position and began to dig again. Great chunks of rock flew in all directions in a cloud of dust and noise. The change was subtle but clear: the eye was now staring directly at Beth.

Beth sagged from her trapped shoulder. A fuzzy blanket of shock muffled her pain.

"What *are* you?" she whispered.

"*I am Reach,*" Reach said, but Beth didn't think it was in answer to her question.

"Why—?"

"*I will be.*" There was no malice on the Crane God's hewn face, no hatred for her in its voice. Here was a girl wearing the aspect of his greatest enemy and carrying her son's weapon, and yet there was no mistaking the expression on Reach's face—

Curiosity.

Childlike curiosity: like a toddler who's found an interesting bug under the climbing frame. Even the way his features were only half-defined was reminiscent of baby fat.

"*I will be, I will be.*"

Christ and Thames. The idea came to Beth through a

fug of pain. *He's a* child. Beth didn't want to believe it, but the conviction settled in her gut and wouldn't shift. *He's a young child, too, not yet fully born.* The diggers and drills were still birthing him from the rock.

Fil had told her once, *this is war, there are children everywhere.* He hadn't known how right he was.

"*I will be.*"

What if that was all Reach wanted—all he was sophisticated enough *to* want? He wasn't a god. His wolves and their handlers weren't his worshipers; they didn't follow his *orders.* He wasn't able to give orders. All he could say was *I am Reach* and *I will be.*

The wolves must be part of him, Beth realized. Like antibodies, eliminating threats to him.

A breeze caught her and she began to creak back and forth like some absurd pendulum weight on her cable. As the world spun slowly beneath her feet she noticed things peeking out from under the rubble: a severed leg of a statue; a twisted bar of iron that might once have been a streetlamp, its shattered glass scattered over the ground. She thought she saw fragments of a reflected face, once haughty, now screaming. She saw the price of Reach's life.

"He doesn't know it," Pen had said, "but he's killing everything."

Reach was just a baby trying to get born; he wasn't capable of knowing or caring how many deaths that birth was causing.

A screech of steel broke Beth's reverie. The Scaff-wolves howled and wheeled around, bounding eagerly past. Frantically, she threw her weight from side to side, trying to see what they were chasing.

"Beth!" a familiar voice cried out, and her heart lurched.

"Fil?"

"What in the name of my mother's iron underwear are you doing up there?"

A wolf snapped and then whined, and Beth smiled. Even unarmed, the Son of the Streets was formidable.

"Beth! I'm comin' up under you. I need my spear—drop my spear."

Beth tried, but her fingers wouldn't respond. All the muscles in her right side had gone into spasm, and she was gripping the spear as though it were a vital organ.

She glared at her hand. *He's down there tangling with three pony-sized metal wolves and I can't even drop a railing? Unacceptably embarrassing. Let. Bloody. Go.* Fighting her own muscles, she peeled back one finger, then another, then another until the spear was pointing downwards, clenched between finger and thumb.

A gray blur shot over the rubble below and into her field of vision: a dark streak across the plain.

"Beth!"

Fil's jump overshot and came up hard against the boundary of the Demolition Field. He kicked off the wall, launching himself back towards her.

Her index finger straightened and the spear fell.

The wolves snarled, racing towards it. The pavement-skinned boy ran, his hand outstretched for the weapon, intense concentration on his face. The wolves bounded closer, the rusty smell of their breath washing up over Beth.

Fil jumped for it, and a wolf snapped its jaws shut on empty air as he closed his concrete-gray fingers around the spear's iron shaft.

FIFTY

I manage a half-arsed swipe at the closest wolf on my way down, but I don't know if I connect. The ground jolts through me as I push hard off the stone and I can feel fangs cleaving the air near my neck, but I don't dare risk stopping to fight.

Faster, faster, I will myself. If I could run even half as fast as my heart's drumming, they'd never catch me. The rubble of Reach's killing fields is dead; there's no help for me here, no power to lend speed to my feet. The lifeless stone makes my skin crawl.

My chest is tight with excitement: I am armed and ready, and inches away from my mother's foe.

I stumble over deeply grooved ground; the furrows make up Reach's ferociously ugly forehead. A ramp rises before me—the bridge of his nose. As I race along it I can hear steel ringing off stone behind me. I can taste the metal stink of the wolves.

I look down as I jump off the end of the ramp. A pair of massive lips, cracked like hot pavement, pass underneath me. I land awkwardly on the fat bastard's overly round chin, my feet slipping over the smooth surface. A sharp pain rips up through my ankle and I fall, smacking my face on a random lump of stone that protrudes from the earth apparently for the sole purpose of spreading my nose over my face.

"Bugger!" I yell, pain and frustration flooding through me. The wolves' bounds shake the ground. Sweat greases my palms as I try to push myself up, and I fall back. My wounds have reopened; I can see blood oozing down my arm.

Drive your spear into his throat.

I've just been on Reach's chin—which means that the lump of rock I headbutted is exactly where his Adam's apple would be.

The pain in my ankle changes, becomes deeper, bloodier. There's something sharp punching through the bone. I scream, shove myself up one arm, raise the iron spear in the other, and plunge it down into the rock.

Everything stops.

I know this because suddenly my scream is the only sound and it cuts through the air with shocking clarity. I hear no cranes, no diggers, no construction; even the wolves behind me have stopped growling (although for the one that's got its chops wrapped around my ankle that's not surprising; I am *quite* a mouthful).

My heart almost stops.

For an ecstatic, terrified moment I think, *I've done it. I've killed the Crane King.*

"FIL!"

Beth's shout rips my head around. Gears whir. A metal lanyard rotates. Suddenly all I can see is a hook on a cable, swinging in fast and low over the broken ground towards me. I try to get up, but the wolf has my ankle and anyway it's too late.

The hook slams into my gut.

FIFTY-ONE

Beth hung uselessly from the crane arm. Her warning curdled in the air, souring to a horrified, useless cry. Far below, Fil crumpled to his knees, then forward onto his elbows. The point of the hook emerged from the small of his back for an instant and then vanished again as Reach withdrew it. Blood welled at the base of his spine, gleaming wetly in the morning sun.

"Fil," she echoed herself softly. "*Filius.*"

As if answering her call, he began to pull himself arm over arm through the rubble, his legs dragging clumsily behind him like an anchor. His spine must be severed, Beth thought. Nausea and pity welled up in her. All his nimbleness and city-grace was gone. He looked as frail as a broken bird.

The Scaffwolves pawed at the masonry around him,

but they didn't attack. They snuffled at his spear for a few seconds and then loped away.

"*I am Reach...*"

With a screech of gears and a growl of engines, the machines in the site returned to work, spewing clods of earth and rock. The motors on the crane holding Beth kicked in and her stomach plunged as she shot towards the ground.

As she dropped, she saw that Reach's expression had changed. That childish curiosity was gone; now the Crane King looked bored with her.

Her bare feet touched earth and the hook ripped itself free from her shoulder. The pain *drenched* her, but she gritted her teeth against it and staggered over the broken world to Fil's side.

"It didn't work," he gasped as she knelt beside him. He sounded perplexed. His eyes lolled dangerously in his head.

"Glas said—his throat—but it didn't *work*." He pawed at his spear, still stuck into the ground like an empty flagpole, marking the spot where he'd failed.

"I know," Beth said. "I know. It's okay." It was nowhere close to okay, but she didn't know what else to say to him. She pulled the railing-spear free, wormed her good arm behind his shoulders, and hoisted him into an almost-standing position. She felt horribly exposed, just standing here in the heart of the site, and she didn't trust Reach's sudden indifference to them. The skinny boy was frighteningly light and his legs hung lifeless under him, like a doll's.

With his arms clasped around her neck, Beth dragged him back the way they'd come. His toes etched tracks over the dusty rubble.

The wolves prowled, their hollow eyes following the fragile boy and girl but uninterested in them.

"I am Reach."

The cacophony of the diggers battered Beth like storm winds. Her arm hung prickling and cold at her side. The sleeve of her hoodie was so saturated that it drizzled blood onto the ground.

Just inside the entrance to the labyrinth she stopped, dizzy and exhausted from blood loss. She could go no further. She propped Fil against the wall and gripped the spear in her good hand.

Why did you let us go?

She eyed the doorway mistrustfully. Almost the instant that Fil had driven the spear in, Reach had lost interest. She had seen the bored expression on that huge, infantile face, the way the wolves had snuffled at the spear shoved into their god's throat and just *left* it there—

—because it hadn't hurt, she realized suddenly; the spear had done nothing at all to Reach. All the Urchin Prince had done was to *prove* he wasn't a threat.

Beth found herself laughing out loud, caught somewhere on the wrong side of hysteria. Reach was a *baby*, with a baby's attention span. They had shown themselves to be neither novel nor dangerous, and so they weren't of any interest.

"Where is she?" Fil muttered, slumped over like an

empty glove puppet, his hands gripping his knees. "*Where is she?*" He drew down a shuddering breath. "Where is she, Beth?"

"Where's who, mate?" she asked. She forced lightness she didn't feel into her voice. She didn't know what she'd do if he gave in to despair now.

"Where's my mother?" His eyes flickered and he stared at the wall, but Beth knew he was really staring east, towards Docklands and the pits of the Chemical Synod where Mater Viae was last seen.

"She should have been here … by now … I thought … " He was rambling. "I was so stupid—I thought *I* could be *her.*" He tried to laugh, but it sputtered out after a few breaths. "Where is she?"

Where's my mum? The question caught in Beth's chest. She remembered all the desolate months she'd asked the same question. Now she smothered the question instantly whenever it arose in her mind. Awkwardly, she tried to embrace him. "I don't know—I'm sorry, I really am. I don't know."

He laid the hot weight of his head against her shoulder and she smelled the petrol tang of his blood.

"I wish—" he began.

The world shook and a haze of cement dust washed down from the roof. Beth felt him tense against her.

"*What in Thames' name was that?*" he whispered.

Beth gently released him and propped him against the wall before sidling to the doorway. Her stomach clenched. She was half-expecting to see some new beast of Reach's clattering towards her. Gripping the spear tight in her good hand, she ducked her head out of cover and looked—

—and gasped.

The whole back wall of the building site had collapsed, as though punched through with a vast fist, but that concrete barrier had been replaced by another made of stone: stone *bodies*. Rank upon rank of war heroes, scientists, suffragettes, leaders, even abstract geometrical shapes, hundreds of them: the Pavement Priests had come. More stoneskins than Beth had ever seen stretched back up the narrow brick alley and out of sight.

She breathed in sharply and a wild hope swelled her chest. "It's Petris," she whispered.

The granite monk was in the front rank. When he spoke, his voice was as merciless as winter homelessness. "*Delenda Reach.*" The command boomed over the shattered wasteland. The Pavement Priest battalion stirred. "*Sic Gloria Via. Delenda Reach.*"

"*Delenda Reach.*" They took up the chant, singing it like a hymn, their voices deep, liquid. "*Delenda Reach.*"

The warrior priests stepped forward as one, the thud of their feet the percussion to their chant. They were the guardians of the old faith, wearing skins in the shapes of London's heroes from other times. They sang their eulogy for their fallen city.

Metal wolves and Metal Men and other, stranger shapes clambered from the faces of the tower blocks and stalked over the rubble to meet them. Steel paws clanged on masonry as they picked up speed.

The first rank of Pavement Priests flickered and Beth shrank back, involuntarily, every muscle tensing as the armies of London charged.

Stone and steel crashed together. Beth felt their impact like concussion. The wolves screamed, their rusting fangs rending granite skin like paper, but the pavement hymn didn't waver. Though the song diminished when one of the priesthood fell, it never stopped.

"They're—" Beth began, and then a wide grin broke over her face as she understood. "They're *digging*."

One battalion of priests, screened by their fellows, had fallen to their knees and were tearing double handfuls of rock from the earth, great gouges, straight out of Reach's face.

"*I am Reach*," the diggers screamed in pain.

A wolf tore the head from Winston Churchill. Three other statues pulled the animal down, but then collapsed from exhaustion.

Under Petris' boomed orders, Mater Viae's priesthood knelt and prayed, "*Delenda Reach... Delenda Reach...*," worshiping through fighting, as their steady hands chewed through the bedrock and cement Reach had carved himself from.

One priest looked different from the others. He moved more slowly, and his punishment skin looked more like hardened clay than stone. As he gouged at Reach with a fragment of steel girder, Beth thought there was something familiar about him, although in that moment she didn't know what.

"That's good, lads," Petris shouted, knee-deep in the silt of Reach's throat. "Dig the bastard's heart out, a-bloody-men!" But around him stone-covered bodies were slumping from exhaustion. The Scaffwolves continued to harry and hamstring them until they were all oozing their slow, sticky blood. As they fell, they became indistinguishable from the murderous landscape around them.

"*Delenda Reach*," they called, but their song was waning.

Fil heard the weakness in it. "It's not working," he muttered feverishly. "We need Mater Viae. We need my *mother*. We need the Fire—we need the Great Fire, oh Thames…"

Beth tried to hold him, but he shook her off wildly. His face was crumpled and white as waste-paper. "I was such an *idiot*. It was impossible! It was always *impossible*—how could we ever cleanse the city without the Great Fire?" He sounded despairing.

Cleanse the city…

Beth went very still. Something in his words hooked a memory and dragged it to the surface of her mind. She tried to concentrate past the fury of the battle. She remembered the crackle of flames on a polluted pool, and a viscous, oily voice: "*This is a special conflagration, purchased at great expense. It cleanses and coruscates, maims and makes anew…*"

"Oh God," she whispered. "What if *that's* why she didn't come?"

Fil looked at her sharply. "What is?"

"The Fire." The idea was so simple, so horribly mundane,

that Beth hesitated to give voice to it. "The Great Fire. Your mum's greatest power," she whispered. "What if the reason she's not here fighting is she doesn't have it any more? What if, without it, she's *scared?*"

"What are you talking about?" Bewilderment and fear and outrage were plain on his face.

"You never knew what the Synod charged her, did you? What if the Great Fire was their price? *A special conflagration, gained at great expense.* What if she gave it up in payment?" Beth asked, leveling a finger to point at the crippled young god. "Payment for you."

He shut his eyes and the last of the color drained from his face. He looked more than scared. He looked *dead.* But when the ground shuddered again, his eyes opened, and now there was an air of tense, concentrated discipline about him. "Beth," he said quietly, "I need you to do something for me."

"Okay, sure. Anything. What?"

"Pick up my spear."

Beth bent and grasped the weapon. The black iron was tacky where she'd bled on it. "Okay," she said, uncertainly.

"I'm going to count to three," he said, and swallowed. His gray eyes looked directly into hers. "Then I need you to stab me in the heart."

Beth almost dropped the spear. "What!" she shouted. "Are you *mental*? Did your brains bleed out of your guts?"

But his gray eyes were as clear and sane and sad as she'd ever seen them. She knew he meant it. "*Why?*" she whispered.

His smile was frail. "'Cause making bad deals with the Chemical Synod runs in the family."

For a second Beth stared at him, wondering if the pain and disappointment and blood loss had finally driven him mad. "What are you talk—?"

Then understanding slammed into her like an avalanche. "You *lied*," she snarled at him. "I asked you straight up what you promised them: "*Some poxy ingredient; I won't use it long as I live*." That's what you told me."

"Technically that was true." Fil tried to shrug. "Since I promised them my death."

Beth gazed at him in horror, sickened by her complicity, by her willing *gullibility*. She looked at her pavement-gray skin. How could she possibly have believed that *some poxy little ingredient* had bought her that speed, that strength?

Fil spoke urgently. "We need Johnny Naptha's boys *here*, Beth, now; Thames knows we do. If they have the Fire—" He jerked his head towards the battlefield. "While that bedlam's still raging, there's a chance. They'll come for me, to collect their debt. Get 'em right in, right in the heart of it, understand? Reach won't tolerate 'em, just like he wouldn't tolerate me. Make them get *involved*."

"*If*," Beth snapped back, "*if* they come—*if* they even have the Fire. *If. If. If.* It's all bloody guesses. Christ, Fil, what if you're wrong? What if *I'm* wrong?" She prayed she was—she desperately wanted to be. She wanted to grab the treacherous words she'd spoken from the air and shove them back into her mouth.

The gray-skinned boy looked at her. "Then we're wrong," he said. "But that's our city, dying out there, and I'm all out of ideas."

Beth raised the spear. She tensed her shoulder and gritted her teeth, but she couldn't drive the weapon home. Tears blurred her sight as all her half-formed, desperate, unspoken love for this boy flooded through her. She turned away, unable to bear his gaze.

"I can't," she said. "It's too much."

His voice hardened. "It's not your call, Beth."

His eyes, the color of the city she was refusing to try and save, bore into her, but she couldn't do this. It was too high a price.

When he spoke again, his voice was a whisper. "Remember what Petris said: *the outlines, the very definition of a life?* This is my definition, Beth. I'm choosing it now—I'm choosing the chance that you're right. If you take that away from me, you're no better than my mother."

Beth swallowed hard, a choking mix of salty tears and air, and tried frantically to think of something else, some other explanation, something they had missed. *Think, Bradley, think,* she swore at herself, but nothing came.

In that moment, she hated Filius Viae more than she'd ever hated anyone. She wanted to throw away his vile spear and walk back down the tunnel, to leave him paralyzed in the darkness. She wanted to abandon him the way he was about to abandon her. But she couldn't, because she knew that years from now she'd still see Masonry Men and brick-born babies lying murdered. She couldn't, because however childlike Reach was, he wasn't *innocent*. Her people were dying on his claws.

And she couldn't, because although she hated him, she could never walk away from that skinny, wretched kid.

She set the spear between his ribs. He smiled encouragingly. The spear scratched a lopsided red-black star against his flesh as she shook.

"Christ, Fil—I—"

"It's okay, Beth." He held her gaze. "Do I scare you witless enough to make you brave?" he asked her.

"Yes," she whispered.

"One," he said. "Two…"

Beth rammed the spear forward.

He gasped and his eyes stretched. She felt a crunch as his ribs gave way. She gritted her teeth and twisted the shaft. His bare heels drummed the ground for an awful moment, and then stopped.

Five seconds. She counted them carefully. That was how long she looked into his vacant eyes. Then she snarled, "I'm not shutting your eyes for you, liar. You can watch what you made me do." She bent and picked him up. He sagged over her good shoulder, infinitely heavier in death. She ducked under the lintel and ran.

FIFTY-TWO

Noise exploded over her as Beth burst from the labyrinth. She weaved right and then left, ducking iron jaws and fallen bodies. A stone sword slipped from a Pavement Priest's hand and whistled past her, grazing her knee. She raced between the legs of a metal giant, deep into the very heart of the battle.

"*Delenda Reach*," a ragged choir croaked. The Pavement Priests were pitifully few now, but still they tore at the earth with their stone hands. Beth ignored their horrified stares as she dumped the limp body of their prince into their midst. There was no time—no time for grief; no time for fear; no time for anything resembling a human emotion, or else this would all to be for nothing.

"Here he is," she shouted into the din. "Here's your price!"

She cast around desperately, but all she could see were bodies and carnage. Despair scratched deep in her chest—

—and then a petrol smell stung her nostrils.

Six black figures walked unhurriedly through the chaos of battle. Their movements were perfectly synchronized; their oil-soaked suits were untouched by the flying muck.

"Over here!" Beth's scream tore her throat. "Over here! *Here's* what you're owed."

The Chemical Synod always collected on their debts. Deals were sacred.

As they strode over the rubble, two priests moved to confront them, but Petris' command boomed out: "Let them come."

Reach issued no such instruction. As these fresh, *powerful* interlopers stalked over his scarred face, towards his very throat, amid the noise and stink of the attack against him, Reach panicked. Beth could feel it. The whole of the building site seemed to tense around her.

"*I will be!*" Reach shrieked, and a crane-born hook shot through the air and impaled the rightmost black-slicked man.

The Synod's expressions became grim. They didn't break step, but the five remaining men spread out to repair their symmetry. As one, each produced a cigarette lighter, flipped the lid, and ran the spark-wheel up the leg of their trousers.

Heat punched into Beth's face as the Synod caught fire. She shielded her eyes. They kept on at the same calm pace, burning like Guy Fawkes effigies on Bonfire Night. Where their feet fell, the ground—Reach's body—bubbled, hissed, and melted.

"*I will be!*" Reach shrieked.

Two of the fiery men peeled off from either side and strolled over to the cranes. A Scaffwolf snapped at one, but he didn't even break stride. The corona of heat around him melted through the beast's jaw and hot slag ran into the contours of the rubble.

Johnny Naptha approached one crane and extended a burning hand towards its cab, almost as though in greeting. The metal glowed and warped and buckled as he touched it, and as she looked around she saw the other members of the Synod, stationed all around the building site, doing exactly the same thing, in precise time, with other cranes.

Beth expected Reach to cry out, but no cry came: the engines which produced his voice were silenced. The Child-King of the Cranes died not with a scream, but with a slow hiss of metal like an exhausted breath.

The Scaffwolves creaked on their hinges; the iron giants groaned. Jaws slid sideways over one another. Knees bent the wrong way and the monsters subsided into the dust.

Beth sat down hard in the rubble. She gazed vacantly at Fil's body. The wound in her shoulder had reopened, and her hoodie was clammy with fresh blood.

Johnny Naptha approached. His flames, the flames that had ignited the Great Fire of London, guttered out. His suit and skin were now the crisp gray-black of charcoal. "How pleasant of you to prepare him for us." He looked down at the gray body, lying sprawled across Reach's throat. A touch of sarcasm entered his voice. "And how precisely placed."

He crouched, picked up the body, and without ceremony slung it over his shoulder. Gracefully he rose to his feet, turned on his heel, and walked away. The rest of his coven converged on him. One of them had their fallen brother in a fireman's lift, dripping oil down his burnt back.

Beth sagged sideways. She felt voided, utterly empty. She'd forgotten how to feel, forgotten how to stand up. The boy ...

The boy with the city in his skin was dead.

Pavement Priests clustered around her. Their stone faces looked grim, accusing.

"I had to kill him," she croaked. "I had to bring the Chemical Synod."

"We know." The voice belonged to Petris. "We know better than most the prices of their services." His stone mask contorted painfully into a smile.

Beth stared up at him. That expression looked so out of place in this bloody tangle that she didn't trust it.

"Beth, there's someone here who wants to see you."

"Beth? Beth!" The clay-caked figure she'd seen in the battle shouldered his way between the statues. He was limping. Up close, she could see patches of pale skin showing where the crust of ceramic had been chipped away. Bright red blood—*human* blood—ran from a gash on the man's forehead, dripping down a face she knew.

"Beth." Her father dropped to his knees beside her. "Come on, Beth. We'll get you to a hospital. You'll be okay."

Beth gazed in wonder into his brown eyes, suddenly sharply aware that hers were no longer that color, but the mottled gray of London skies. "*Dad?*" She studied his cuts, stupefied by his presence. Her gaze fell on the girder he was still carrying.

"You *fought?*" she murmured incredulously. "Weak and slow and bloody human—and you fought—?"

He nodded, almost shyly. "Because it was your fight," he said quietly. "Because I thought you'd want me to."

She held out a hand to him, and he grasped it gratefully and pulled her to her feet. Her fingers stayed tight around his for a few moments.

"We're not done," she said. "There's someone we need to get."

———

Pen was lying where Beth had left her, staring at the ceiling of the pyramidal chamber. She showed no sign that she was alive until she heard Beth coming, then she blinked and a smile spread across her face. "I did it, B," she whispered.

"Yeah, you did it Pen," Beth agreed, not understanding what she was talking about.

"I did it—I beat it. It held me, but I held it back."

"Uh-huh," Beth said, crouching down beside her.

"I was afraid, but I held it down. I beat it. I *chose.*"

There was a glassy caste to Pen's brown eyes. She was rambling, delirious. "I'm not afraid any more," she whispered. "I *chose*."

Beth put her hands under Pen's shoulders and tensed her legs, ready to lift. She was afraid that Pen would cry out in pain, but there was just a whimper, quickly stifled.

"Come on," Beth muttered. "We have to get you better. There's a woman—or a man, or a—I don't know what it is. Its name's Gutterglass—if anyone will know how to fix you, it will."

"No!" Pen's cry was shockingly loud in the dark. Her face snapped around, almost scandalized.

Beth swallowed, quailing slightly at the ferocity in her friend's gaze. "No further down the rabbit hole, B," Pen said. "No more. If you want to take me somewhere, take me home." For a second she stared at her, her face mottled in fury and relief and blame; then, to Beth's shock and utter gratitude, Pen threw her arms around her neck. "God, I've missed you, B. I could never let you go."

Beth nodded. There was nothing more to say.

IV

VITAE VIAE

FIFTY-THREE

Beth's overriding impression of the hospital (it was only the second time she'd ever been in one) was that it was *squeaky*. The wards were filled with high-pitched noises: rubber wheels scraping over lino; children squealing for their parents; and machines bleeping all over the place, announcing vital signs at different stages of degradation. It was a little like listening to the birds at sunrise, except the electronic edge made everything threatening.

She paced up and down beside Pen's bed and then slumped into the vinyl chair and looked at her friend, who resembled a sixth-form art project: a collage of gauze, bandage, and plastic wrap. The harsh stink of antiseptic filled the room.

"They got through to your folks," Beth told her. "They're

on their way. Apparently your mum's bringing lamb samosas. I thought they knew you're a vegetarian?"

A gap in the bandages revealed the brown ovals of two closed eyes. Pen was awake, but she didn't want to talk.

Beth set her jaw. She wished she'd never left Pen's side, that they'd discovered the Railwraiths and the streetlamp dancers and the Crane King *together*: a secret they could have talked about in hushed tones whenever the rest of the world came battering too hard at their door.

Secrets like those were threads that could stitch a friendship back together.

Beth slumped a little lower in her chair, then yanked out a pencil and grabbed an empty sheet from the medical chart hanging beside the bed. Smoothing it out over the back of a dinner tray, she began to sketch.

She'd had no plans to draw anything in particular—she was just scratching an itch—so it was with a faint thrill of shock that she watched Fil's cocky face emerge from under her pencil. For a second she couldn't breathe, but she forced the pencil over the page. She felt compelled.

She drew the Son of the Streets exactly as he had been, no portrait-flattery. When it was done, she bit her lip in frustration. What a staggeringly inadequate way to bring him back.

"Beth?"

Beth looked up sharply. Pen didn't open her eyes. Her voice was dry but surprisingly strong. "Will you do me a favor?"

"Sure, Pen. What do you need?"

"My compact's in my jeans—in the back pocket. Can you bring it to me please?"

Beth pulled Pen's barb-shredded clothes from the bedside unit and dug around for the compact, a slim square of hinged plastic. She held it out to Pen.

"Open it." Her voice remained calm, sterile as the hospital floors. Still she didn't open her eyes.

Beth felt her heart begin to beat a little quicker. She swallowed hard. "Pen—don't you think you should wait—?"

"Open it," Pen said again, firmly. "I'm ready."

The compact opened with a tiny click, revealing a palette of foundation and a small round mirror.

"Hold it up for me to see."

Wordlessly, Beth lifted the mirror. Pen opened her eyes.

For a second, Beth thought, it was as though someone had slipped a knife in between her best friend's ribs. She could see the slight widening of the eyes, the tension that twisted her face. Pen hissed and gritted her teeth to keep from swearing.

For long seconds, Pen's gaze roved over the mirror. She lifted her chin, stroking the lines of the bandages, probing the raw wounds underneath with tentative fingers. You could see her tracing the lines of future scars. Her expression, frightened at first, took on a kind of calm. She looked like she was saying goodbye.

At last, she shut her eyes again. She leaned back onto the bed. "Okay," she said, a soft whisper. "Okay."

Beth snapped the compact shut with trembling fingers. Pen," she began. "I'm so, so sorr—"

Pen's voice was like a whipcrack. "Tell me you're sorry, Elizabeth Bradley, and I will kill you *dead*."

Beth blinked in confusion. "I never meant to—"

"I know you didn't, B, but these cuts are *mine*. Not yours, not ours; *mine*, understand?" Pen's eyes opened again, revealing a mix of pain and fierce survivor's pride. "I own them. The barbs bit *me*. You weren't there and you'll never understand what it was like, so don't try, okay?"

Beth pursed her lips and nodded, burning from the rebuke.

"They're my scars," Pen said, her tone softening a little. "I'll deal."

As Beth stood, a rich smell of curried lamb and spices drifted into her nostrils.

"*You.* Get away from my daughter." A short, angular man with teak-colored skin parted the curtains around Pen's bed. A tiny woman in a shawl and veil followed him, clutching a Tupperware box.

Beth drew sharply away from them. "Mr. and Mrs. Khan."

Pen's parent's actually collided in their haste to reach their daughter's bedside. Her mother almost collapsed in relief. Her father kissed her forehead and stroked her hair, murmuring something in Urdu that might have been a prayer.

"It's all right, child." Mr. Khan spoke in English now. His voice was tightly controlled, but every second he looked at Pen's injuries aged his lean face. "We can fix this."

Pen's mother said nothing as she held her daughter, just wept the tears Beth felt that Pen should be shedding.

Pen, who simply stared at the wall.

"I know plastic surgeons. There—there is money. We can get you back to—"

"Shhh." To Beth's astonishment, Pen shushed her father. She continued to stroke her mother's hijab with light strokes of her fingers, murmuring, "It's all right, Mum. I'm all right. I'm alive . . ." There was no missing the exultant shimmer in her brown eyes.

"And I'm *free*."

FIFTY-FOUR

Back in the Accident and Emergency waiting room, two burly male nurses were wrestling a drunkard into a wheelchair. An irascible old woman was barking incomprehensible hostilities at an unoffending triage nurse, and then repeatedly stealing her fobwatch and giggling as she dropped it on the floor.

Over the ranks of the sick, beer-soaked, and disturbed that occupied the orange plastic chairs, the bandaged head of her father reared like a snowcapped mountaintop. He looked up from the tatty paperback he was reading as Beth approached. The sight of Pen's facial injuries had shriven Paul. He'd looked on with a haunted gaze as they'd wheeled her into surgery, and accosted everyone in scrubs who emerged with questions and fervent thanks.

"How is she?" he asked.

Beth shrugged. "Her heart's in better nick than her face. I think she'll be okay."

"Thank God." He sagged with relief. "And you?"

Beth looked around a little conspiratorially, and then yanked the collar of her hoodie out past her bra strap. The fat, jagged wound in her shoulder was sealed over with new grayish skin. An ugly, rippling seam of tar ran through it like a scar.

Her father stared for a moment, swallowed hard, and then nodded.

Get used to it, Beth thought. *Daddy's little girl has the city in her skin.* She glanced at the book in her father's lap. *The Iron Condor Mystery.* She barked an abrupt laugh. "You brought *that* with you?"

He cradled it defensively. "It was your mother's favorite."

Beth sighed. "Yeah, I know it was, Dad."

He drew himself up, seeming to steel himself. Then he held the book out to Beth. "I'm done with it."

Beth looked at him, startled.

"You should read it some time," he said.

Beth turned the pages, feeling the paper flake, ready to disintegrate from years of constant reading. She didn't know what to say.

He held his arms out to her then, and she embraced him, pulling herself tight into his chest. Uncertain fingertips pattered over her neck for a moment, feeling the pavement-texture of her skin. Then his hug engulfed her.

"Beth, I know I haven't—I want to make it up to you—I mean, I know I owe you so much—"

He fell into a surprised silence as Beth reached back and put a hand over his mouth.

Deals are sacred. She thought of the symmetrical oil-soaked men. *Our equations always balance.* Fil's body, lying in the rubble, his own spear bleeding him dry.

You saved my life twice. By my reckoning that means I owe you.

She'd already lost too much to the brutal mathematical economy of debt. "It's not about owing, Dad. This can't be about *owing*." She pulled back to look him in the face. "Let's just try again."

The old drunk in the corner started to make high-pitched yipping noises and they let each other go. Beth sniffed back what felt like a gallon of mucus and looked at the book her father had given her. A sheet of crisply folded white paper was set inside the back cover.

"What's this?"

He looked embarrassed. "I thought you might want to know a bit more about him."

"About who?"

He frowned as though it were obvious. "The boy you were following around."

A shiver, like a pricking of insect feet, ran down Beth's back. With numb fingers, she unfolded the sheet. It was a printout of a page from *The Evening Standard*'s online archive. The photo showed a haggard-looking woman and man appealing to the camera with their eyes. The headline read, *Hunt For Williams Baby Called Off.*

Beth started to read the text to herself.

Two hundred and eighty-one days after eight-month-old Michael Williams disappeared from the home of his parents, police have admitted the active search has been wound down.

Detective Inspector Ian North, leading the case, said, "We are not closing the book on the search for baby Michael, but there has been no new evidence in nine months. Our hotline of course remains open...

Beth stopped reading and her eyes returned to the photograph. The caption read, *Genevieve and Stephen Williams, in public appeal for news of missing son.*

"I recognized him when you carried his body out," her dad was saying. "It's weird—I only printed this out because you went missing."

A cold weight had settled in Beth's gut. She rummaged frantically in her pocket for the sketch of Fil, unfolded it, and held it next to the printout: the portrait of the prince beside the photo of the distraught parents.

Beth's dad's face crinkled in sympathy. "The poor kid looks just like his dad—Beth, what's wrong?"

Beth had sat down hard, missing the orange plastic chair and bruising her coccyx on the concrete floor. She wanted to protest; he was *wrong*—her *own eyes* were wrong. Filius Viae couldn't be these people's son. It was a mistake—he was the Son of the Streets, the son of Mater Viae. He had *powers*. He could outrun a Railwraith, tear scaffolding in two, scale the side of a skyscraper...

All things you can do too, since your dip in the Synod's pool, a quiet voice inside reminded her.

Questions and doubts bloomed in her mind, but withered again as logic provided the obvious answers. Questions like, *Why did Reach try to kill Fil with a Railwraith anyway?* Three quick steps carried her to the broom cupboard in the far wall. She reached in and jerked the railing-spear free from where she'd hidden it amongst the pile of plastic sheets. She crashed through the door to the fire-escape and whirled up the stairs, her dad huffing despairingly behind her.

"Where are you going? Please, don't go, Beth, not again. I've made up your room—I—"

Beth burst onto a fourth-floor corridor. Bleak fury sat in the pit of her stomach like an ember. She'd been lied to—and what was worse, so had Fil, lied to about *everything*. A rain-spattered windowpane revealed what she was looking for: a slim black telephone wire stretching out from the hospital's outer wall. The window was one of those that only pivot open about six inches, but Beth had been remade; she undulated, and slid her way out with ease onto the sill, her own oily sweat smoothing her passage.

Her dad stood inside, hands pressed to the glass, eyes wide. She could see him mouthing, "*Come home.*"

Beth hesitated, then called back, "I will, I promise, but there's something I have to do first." She sidled crabwise and settled easily as a pigeon on the insulated phone wire. After the rain, the moon was bright. A sharp wind cut the air, but Beth wasn't cold.

"Beth!" Through the glass, her father sounded desperate.

"I'll see you soon, Dad," she promised, and then raced away, along the cable, into the night.

FIFTY-FIVE

Gutterglass swept the pathways between the rubbish dunes
with her stiff-bristle broom, whistling as she went. Her
mopstring hair was tied back and her binbag skirts blew
in the breeze. She considered it a criminal waste of time to
leave spring cleaning until spring.

The dump was beautiful on clear mornings like this.
Its scrap-metal peaks shone in the still-rising sun and
chunks of broken glass twinkled like embedded jewels.
The fragrance of rotblossom and forget-me-all-too-soon
lingered headily in her nostrils. Somewhere in the distance,
garbage trucks groaned as they spilled further trash trib-
utes, adding to the foundations of Gutterglass' city.

A silhouette high on a ridge caught her eye, a scrawny
figure with an iron railing over one shoulder. The pose was

so familiar that Glas faltered, the tangled worms of her heart missing a beat.

Then she smiled. "I was hoping you'd come," she called.

The figure didn't answer, but it drew back its free hand and threw. A dark speck drifted through the air. Glas stretched out her hand and the thing came to rest, docile as a pigeon, in her palm: an airplane, folded carefully from a photocopied sheet of newspaper.

As the skinny figure stalked down the hill towards her, Gutterglass unfolded the page and began to read.

———

"The boy who thought his name was Filius Viae," Beth said quietly, "was no child of a goddess." She was approaching Gutterglass carefully, a hunter's walk.

The rubbish-sculpted woman gave no sign that she'd heard.

"When you know that, you have to ask: who in all London would want to convince him that he *was*?" She advanced until the spear was a moth-wing's thickness from Gutterglass' cardboard throat. Her voice was a dead monotone. "Maybe the same person who'd want to plant a rumor that that goddess was coming back? Maybe someone who'd been on the scrapheap ever since her mistress toddled off, but who now was getting listened to again? Someone who was back in charge? Tell me, Glas, is it nice to be *grand* again?"

Gutterglass studied the article. Eventually the broken

eggshells looked up. "Michael was his name, was it?" she said. "Hmm. I never knew that." She knocked the spear aside with a deft flick of her broom handle. "Enough of the drama, Miss Bradley," she said briskly. She extended a hand in invitation. "Walk with me?"

Beth didn't take her hand, but Gutterglass turned anyway and began to hike up the side of the nearby hill. A miniature landslide of broken doorknobs, busted cassettes, and rotting banana skins skidded under her feet. "There's something I want you to see."

For a moment Beth felt an almost overwhelming urge to run up behind her and plunge the spear in between her milk-carton shoulder blades—but that wasn't what she was there for. *Killing the liar won't kill the lie.* Swearing softly, aware that she'd lost the initiative, she followed. She'd have to wait for her chance.

The landfill hospital had yet to discharge its last few patients. Lampie heartbeats glimmered from caves in the rubbish. Rats scurried to and fro with hypodermic needles in their mouths. In front of a full-length mirror, a cloud of flying beetles moved a scalpel with extreme precision. On the other side of the glass a tough-looking girl watched an incision climb up her abdomen.

"Let me tell you something about Mater Viae," Gutterglass said. "She didn't deserve a priesthood like the stoneskins, or a servant like me, or a son like Filius. She was a *coward*." Her words were steeped in hurt, hurt that had fermented into rage. She knelt beside a shivering Pavement Priest, bashed a hole in his punishment skin with a chisel, and poured in some analgesic fluid. "Rest softly," she murmured, her throat humming with the buzz of flies. "Rest well. And may the Lady soon grant you your death."

The young priest calmed visibly at Glas' words, and as they moved on, Beth thought she could hear him start to snore.

"His *death*?" Beth hissed furiously. "How can you keep promising them that? Mater Viae has their deaths, and no one knows when she's coming back!"

Gutterglass raised a pipe-cleaner eyebrow. "*I* know when," she said, "and so should you—come, Miss Bradley, did you never ask yourself the obvious question? All those deaths of all those Pavement Priests; all those fragile, precious mortalities paid to the Synod: they were a *commodity*. Did you never ask yourself what Mater Viae bought with them?"

Beth's eyes narrowed. She shook her head.

"She bought her *own*."

Beth blinked. It took a moment for the meaning to sink in. "Suicide?" she whispered. "Why?"

"You know why," Gutterglass said soberly. "You saw what Reach was."

The pudgy, baby face looking curiously out of the rubble swam into Beth's mind, and with it she heard Fil's voice: *Generation after generation ... my mother always took care of Reach.*

"She killed him," Beth murmured. "Again and again— for hundreds of years—burning the same innocent, the same *child*." Beth was staggered, appalled.

"*Her* child," Gutterglass snorted. "He was born of the city, after all."

"Thames—God—I can't imagine—No wonder she couldn't take it—"

Gutterglass' retort was as harsh as a slap. "She was a *goddess*. It was her duty to take it!" Anger shook her control, and liberated insects swarmed madly over her paper face. "She didn't die straight away. It took the Synod more than three-quarters of a millennium to brew the draft, to blend the petty perishings of mortals into a death strong enough to claim a goddess. And all that time she lied, blithely." Gutterglass spat. "When the first generation were reborn into stone, she called it *punishment*. She said *they* owed *her*."

Gutterglass tilted up her chin, and her voice took on a proud calm. "And then, one clear autumn morning like this one, she was gone. And when Demolition Fields started erupting in the city again, growing like tumors, it fell to me to give London something to believe in."

"Fil," Beth said.

"He was the first child young enough my rats could find. They carried him on their backs through a carelessly open window. But it was when I drew him out of the Synod's pool that Filius Viae was *truly* born." She smiled at the memory.

"Mater Viae's substance was still in there, the Synod's fee for their intervention. It was enough to give a child a shimmer of her aspect." The eggshells took in Beth's granite-gray skin. "Enough to give it to more than one, it appears," she said, and her smile grew wider.

Beth went to speak, but Gutterglass put a ballpoint-finger to her lips. "Hush now. This is what I wanted you to see." They were approaching a low alcove, rusting railway sleepers supporting a corrugated tin roof. Beth ducked her head and peered inside.

Two glass bodies lay tangled in the sleepy embrace of post-coital lovers. One glowed a sooty orange, the other a pure white. Their light mixed and washed over the crushed cans and old springs in the wall. Beth thought she recognized the Sodiumite whose life Gutterglass had saved.

"See what a little faith can do?" Gutterglass whispered. "They've been taught from birth to hate one another on sight, and yet here they are. They fought side by side for their goddess, and now they lie side by side for themselves. Who knows—we might even have a glitter-litter of tiny bulbs soon." A broad smile conquered her features; all the anger seemed forgotten. She motioned to Beth to come away.

Together they crested the top of another ridge and stood on a discarded sofa. London lay below them, an ocean of rooftops glowing in the sunrise.

Beth stared out over the city, suspecting and dreading what Gutterglass was about to ask.

"They'll need someone to believe in when they wake, someone who can finish what Filius began," Gutterglass said. "They'll need a story to understand and accept. So will the Priests and the Masonry Men, even the Mirror-folk." Her voice cracked a little. "Even me," she said.

She turned and looked at Beth. "Be that something, Beth. You bear the aspect; you carry the spear. It was you who brought the Great Fire down on the Crane King. *Please*—" There was a keening hunger in the rubbish-spirit's face. "Give us a goddess we deserve."

Beth held the eggshell gaze. She saw Glas' sincerity, heard the hope, weak but still audible, in her voice, like a lost child who never stops believing that her mother will come get her.

Beth gritted her teeth. Sympathy flared hot as a match and died just as fast in her chest. "You're wrong," she said. "It wasn't the Lady of the Streets they fought for, it was the streets themselves. These people don't *want* a god no more."

Gutterglass began to protest, stuttering and spitting rubbish juice, but Beth raised a hand to silence her. "You know, something's been bugging me. Why, after fifteen years of ignoring him, would Reach suddenly attack Fil—and why use a Railwraith to do it? After all, he had a whole wolfpack at the tip of his cranes."

She gazed at Gutterglass with utter loathing. "Then I realized: it was all *you*. It was your rats that got into the grid's cables. You couldn't control a Scaffwolf, so you used a wraith and laid the blame oh-so-carefully at the front door of St. Paul's. Reach wouldn't take any interest in Fil, not unless he was a threat, so you *made* him one."

Beth's lip curled. She thought of what he had told her the first night they met: *Something that big and angry comes*

at you, your first instinct's to stick it with something sharp.
Gutterglass had known her ward well.

"You manipulated everyone I ever cared about. That lie your goddess told? You told it *again*, and again, and you kept telling it, letting the hurt sink in." The words tasted bitter in her mouth. "The lie's over, Glas. People need to hear the truth."

She turned and began to stump down the landfill towards the city. A hand made of ballpoint pens clamped onto her shoulder.

"You really think they'll believe you?" Gutterglass hissed. "You spread this *pathetic* excuse for a myth and I'll bury you. I'll make you a changeling: the girl who killed their god. The very streets you walk on will hunt you."

Beth seized Gutterglass' wrist and ripped the hand off her shoulder. She squeezed, and felt the bugs flee in panic under her fingers. She bent it back slowly, turning around. She stared into those shells, and saw the hope was gone. Only blank white hatred remained

"I'm not going to tell 'em," Beth said. "You are." She pulled her hoodie to one side to reveal the tiny spider, glittering like fiberglass, in the hollow of her throat. "In fact, you already did."

Gutterglass uttered a strangled cry and swiped at the tiny creature, but in a flicker of light and static it was gone, its message replicating and copying at the speed of radio waves. Gutterglass' voice—the voice that had for so long spoken falsely for London's goddess—would utter its confession on every street corner. Beth felt a tiny surge of triumph. Her city would know the truth tonight.

"Come back!" Gutterglass called after it. "Come back, *please*! I'll pay!" But it was pointless. Beth and the spider already had a deal.

For a long moment Gutterglass just stood there, her paper face smooth with shock; then she exhaled. She began to pat herself, searching for something. She popped a cigarette between her lips, but couldn't find any matches. She looked utterly lost.

Moved by a strange pity, Beth picked a half-empty plastic lighter from amidst the rubbish and lit Gutterglass' Lucky Strike. She turned to go, but then paused. "What was their price for you, Glas?" she asked quietly. "When you made Fil what he was? What did the Synod make you pay?"

She looked over her shoulder at the decaying woman.

"What did you use to be?"

Through the smoke that twisted between them, Beth saw the sour-milk tears stain the paper face. And below them a smile that remembered happier times.

"Beautiful," Gutterglass said.

FIFTY-SIX

Beth Bradley and the Street-Urchin Prince, on the day they stood together on the roof of the world.

Beth's sketches of her and Fil grinned out from the metal. Above Beth's image, a signature had been scrawled. The space over his face was empty.

Beth leaned back to scrutinize her handiwork. It was still rough, but it was definitely coming along. A vast three-dimensional map now covered the back of the throne: streets, squares, parks, plazas. St. Paul's, Big Ben, the Wheel: London as she could see it from the top of its highest sky-scraper. The Tower Block Crown sprouted from the middle of the financial district, camouflaged as just another set of anonymous offices.

Beth's spray can clanked as she dropped it back into her backpack and rummaged around for the silver. Before she was done, every Lampfolk encampment, Demolition Field, and god-possessed crane would be marked on here. She shaded her eyes from the sun and got her bearings, and then began to spray in a crop of tiny streetlamps. She'd already painted in the Motherweb, the radio tower to the south.

Monument; memorial; mural; it was an invitation to anyone who came up here to tread in her footsteps and see what she'd seen. It was risky, but somebody crazy enough to climb this tower in the first place, somebody able to trust the map enough to follow it—well, it might be worth it.

A tickle in the back of her throat was her only warning. A second later a hacking cough burst out of her. She bent double, bracing her hands on her knees, until eventually she was able to straighten up.

"Testing," she said tentatively, still feeling a little giddy. Her voice came out as a dry whisper. "Testing, one-two-three."

She sighed. Bloody typical: her voice had decided to return when she was a seven-hundred-foot straight drop away from any possible conversation. She glanced at the metal railing that ran around the pyramidal roof and—just for a wild moment—she considered vaulting it and scrambling harum-scarum down fifty stories. After three weeks of silence, the prospect of a chat made it almost worthwhile.

But there was no time. Instead, she squatted down on Mater Viae's oversized throne. She *definitely* didn't want the Pylon Spiders to think she was reneging—deals were sacred, after all. "Might as well talk to yourself then, B," she said huskily, letting her voice swim around her in the air.

The thought that she might have forgot what she sounded like scared her.

"Salamander. Loop-de-loop. Bling. Cocker spaniel. Supercalifragilisticexpiali-bloody-docious." She smiled. "Fuck, shit, bollocks, piss, and crap." She exhaled hard. "Love."

She looked at the picture she'd drawn.

"I really did love you, you filthy little bastard," she said. It felt important to speak it aloud when she could.

A static crackle carried through the air and she sighed. Time was up.

She felt needle-pointed feet pricking between the fine bones in her foot, and then they scrambled up her leg. She only saw the spider for a second, when it crested her shoulder, then it vanished under her chin and prickled in the hollow at the base of her throat.

"*Ready?*" The spider's voice had been borrowed from some sports radio broadcast.

"Yes," Beth replied, and she felt two pricks where the spider's mandibles split the skin of her neck.

"*Set. Go!*"

It didn't hurt, but her vocal cords went taut and she felt the sound bleed out through the puncture wounds, drop by drop, syllable by syllable. She was gripped by an irresistible urge to swallow, to steal a few decibels back, keep a whisper for herself—but she knew it didn't work like that. The deal had been for everything: her entire voice. The Motherweb had a long history with Gutterglass, and their price for helping Beth to expose her had been very high. The "volunteers" the spiders kept lashed to their radio mast never lasted long; they were exposed to the elements, and without food or water their voices soon dried up and died, leaving the spiders to range out over the city again, tapping the wires for the forgotten and vulnerable.

Beth had offered her own voice, strong and sustained—they could have whatever sustenance it gave them, for the rest of her natural life. The only condition was that they had to collect it from her in the wild. She'd let the Pylon Spiders farm her, but at least she'd be free range. And if she gave them everything they needed, then they didn't need anyone else.

Last night Beth had watched as the red-haired girl had stumbled free of the spiders' tower. She, at least, had embraced the chance to face the world again.

After the spider had finished feeding and gone, Beth sat for a while on the roof. She took a deep breath and opened her mouth, but nothing came out, not even a hiss. She looked up at the mural, her story, etched in paint and pigment on the city itself, and her lips twisted into a wry smile. It was worth it.

———

Pen waited for her at the bottom of the tower. It was a Sunday, so there weren't many people walking the steel-and-glass-lined streets of Canary Wharf. Those who did stared at Pen's scars, making Beth wince, but Pen stared fiercely back, which made Beth prouder than anything.

"All right, B. How's the picture going?" she asked.

Beth nodded and shrugged at the same time, universal sign language for *Okay, I guess.*

Pen's face softened. "The spider come?" She stroked the side of Beth's face with her fingertips. "You okay?"

Another shrug-and-nod combo.

Pen hugged her tight. "That's backbone, Beth Bradley," she whispered into Beth's ear. "Proud of you."

They walked slowly around Westferry Circus and into Limehouse. The skyscrapers gave way to brick terraces and concrete blocks of flats. Whenever they found a quiet spot, Beth would crouch and ink in a quick marker picture—a turtle, or a crane. Pen occasionally jotted a line down in the pad she carried, but she didn't tag. Graffiti had always been more Beth's thing, and Pen didn't feel the need to copy her anymore.

"Back to school tomorrow."

Beth nodded.

"I wonder what the other girls will make of this." Pen traced her fingers over her face. She started to say something else, then changed her mind. Instead she asked, "What about you? Are you coming back tomorrow? I asked at Citizens Advice and they said Gorecastle was well out of line for booting you out for what we did. We can get your exclusion lifted." They paused at a junction. "How about it, B? That hole of a school won't be the same without you."

Beth bit her lip. She'd moved back in with her dad, at least nominally, and it was going okay. She felt safe there now, but she still spent most of the time out in the streets. And there were times, especially after rain, when dusk fell and she looked up at the monolithic gray tower blocks, at the sodium light washing against clouds, and felt a pull.

If you do this, a voice in her memory said, *you give up home, give up safety forever.*

Beth didn't know if a single bed in a two-up, two-down would really be home again.

"Let me know what you decide," Pen said; then, "You coming?"

Beth shook her head and pointed at the street ahead. She wanted to stay out in her element a little longer. She smiled at Pen and jogged off up the road.

Pen waved goodbye and watched her go. She'd come so close to telling Beth about Dr. Salt—the words had been halfway out of her mouth—but then she'd hesitated, because she knew how Beth would react. She'd be stunned and furious, and she'd blame herself.

Pen wondered at what point in their relationship she'd become the one who protected *Beth*. As for Salt... Pen still had the clothes she'd been wearing the day he'd... forced his hands on her. They were screwed up and tucked under her bed—she'd been too terrified of her mum finding them to put them in the wash. She was grateful for that now. She fished in her pocket for her mobile. She'd found and saved the number for the police station that morning. A tight anxiety balled in her chest. Would they believe her? Even if they did, would they do anything? She hit dial. She had to try.

And if they didn't believe her—well, she had a friend who was handy with an iron spear, and that was always comforting to know.

FIFTY-SEVEN

Dusk crept in. Beth decided to cut through the park. Wet grass squelched between her toes. The shadows under the trees and by the swings grew longer, wilder. The clouds above the tower blocks darkened until the sky was almost exactly the same hue as the concrete walls and the edges blurred into the sky.

Beth flexed her fingers. The iron railing-spear was under her bed, and every night, as darkness fell, she wondered if tonight would be the night she would pick it up, scramble through her window, and race out over the streets.

I could bed down in any square inch of London town. Welcome to my parlor.

The piercing wail of a crying baby snapped her out of her reverie as she approached the park's west gate. She looked around, but there was no one else there. The sound was coming from the bushes next to the railings that separated the park from the street. A crazy thought flashed into Beth's head, and she started to run.

Down in the weeds by the railings, an old limestone statue lay on its side in the long grass. It was roughly hewn, its features eroded by hundreds of years of weather, and initials and tags had been scratched into it. The baby's cry was bleeding from the pores in the stone.

Hardly daring to breath, Beth picked up a pebble and struck the statue, not too hard, just a tap, and the stone cracked like eggshell. Beth's fingers trembled a little as she smoothed away the fragments.

Inside, the baby lay curled in its womb in the heart of the stone. It opened its screwed-up eyes and pushed an arm out of the hole Beth had made in the stone. Reaching past her, it wrapped its pudgy fingers around one of the park railings and instantly ceased crying. The child's skin was the color of concrete, and marked in black on the inside of its wrist was a tiny crown made of tower blocks. It looked seriously at Beth, perfectly calm as the stone began to reform around its outstretched arm.

Beth stared at it for long seconds until the baby jolted her by shrieking again. He sounded hungry. She jumped to her feet and staggered around in circles, trying to remember where the nearest corner shop was. As soon as she'd fed him, she decided, she would go to the graveyard in Stoke Newington. Petris and Ezekiel, they'd know what to do.

She couldn't be certain, of course—all Pavement Priests wore the Tower Block Crown. If you were a soldier in the army, you had to wear the mark. But there was something about the skin color, and the way he was holding that railing…

What was it Timon had told her? It's years before we get our memories back…

But he'd said it: *we get out memories back.*

Beth could wait. Her stomach did the kind of backflip she thought she'd never feel again and she broke into a run as the child's cry followed her out of the park. The way the wind cooled her sweat made her shiver. She felt her chest tighten and she released a silent, joyous shout into the city.

Above her head, in their cages of glass, the Sodiumites woke and began to dance.

THE END